I0526213

The True North Series: Truth Hurts

Book 3

MARILYN GREGOIRE

Copyright © 2018 Marilyn Gregoire

All rights reserved.

ISBN: 978-0-9989603-5-7

DEDICATION

To Bea Berg

Dangling participles, be damned! You have been a true friend throughout these first two trilogies! And I know that, like before, grammar in the last three books of this, *The Sisters in Silence Collection*, will be the least of my worries! Whether one whole book at a time, or chapter-by-chapter via email, your patience and passion for sentence structure has been my blessing, time and time again!

Having sat beside you, both to brainstorm plot twists and to correct my tense, or use of commas, I've appreciated both your passion for God, Father, Son and Holy Spirit, and your intelligence. Hearing you say, "I like the way your brain works," was the highest praise I've heard! Thank you for your encouragement, your friendship, and your 'teacher-voice.' Though others may hear it differently, it is music to my ears! You are truly appreciated!

(To those of you who haven't met Bea, she's one of my dear friends up in the St. Jude's choir loft in Thompson, North Dakota. She was the organist who taught me to trust myself enough to cantor in church, but also to know that my message of hope for the abused would get out there, with thoughts and twisted sentences untangled.)

This book has been a monstrous re-write, but with your help, the outcome is so much stronger than my first attempt. Together we've slashed the original and moved vast amounts of story and drama to and fro. But you've stuck with me.

Bea, your love for God, your family, for your own little state park, and your friends has never gone unnoticed. How could it? You have worn it in your friendly smile, your sense of humor, and your open arms.

May God bless you deeply!

CONTENTS

ACKNOWLEDGMENTS

Bea Berg (see Dedication)

David Hillman for Alcoholics Anonymous background. I'm an adult child of an alcoholic, but you've lived it, empowering others. I value your insights!

Ernie & Joan Olson: Photo credit for book cover

And for general support & encouragement:
Jon Gregoire, Nina Platt, Doug Berg, Brad Reissig, and Carl Iseminger

NOTE TO READERS

Yes, it's true, there are MANY characters in these books—this time even a Halee and a Hailey, both different as day and night. Please stick with me. 'It takes a village to grow a child.'

1 SOMETHING'S WRONG

It's a confusing thing, when others make plans for you. Although she had been fighting the decision deep within her heart, Laura had to take the next step, to dare to take her stand.

While sitting in her car, staring at the Lutheran church door, Laura coached herself. *This reckoning with Jack, it will be worth it in the end. He has to know the truth, and I'm sorry, but sometimes, truth hurts,* she lamented.

His untreated alcoholism was exacerbating his own narcissistic, self-focused mind. Success with AA involves humility. Jack didn't own a stitch of humility, nothing. Earlier in their relationship, Laura wanted so much to help him heal, but now she just wanted out. She'd fallen out of love. He was just a child to look after with his egocentric mind. By being Jack, his personality had put out the flame of Laura's personality. Many had claimed that her only hope was Al-Anon, but Jack was sure that, *no matter what those snoopy churchy people have to say, you don't need to go to Al-Anon.*

Well, that's where you're wrong! She laughed aloud and proclaimed to the steering wheel, "No! I insist!" claiming her own independence. "No! We are SO done," she ended quietly, mourning the loss. Then as quickly as he had put out her flame, she reignited her certainty, "No! I don't love you anymore, no matter what you say. No!" She hugged the steering wheel briefly, then checked the rear view mirror.

Determined eyes stared back, "Yup, we're gonna do this, right now!" She wiped the tears that gathered and grabbed her purse and keys. "When you lost your identity and apartment in New York City, it wasn't the end of the world, and neither is this." The Al-Anon meeting was about to start inside that Lutheran church in Cavalier, North Dakota, and she wasn't going to miss it.

The barn owl's flight over the backyards and alleys of that small town was innocent enough. His wings were silent, but his intended prey was aware, breathless. A bird on the hunt, but he wasn't alone. In any small town there is very little that can remain anonymous. This was also true of Cavalier, North Dakota. *I've got laundry to do,* Laura had said, and she had looked tired, so when she left for home making claims of going to bed early, all was justified. But Jack was suspicious.

Since being hired on at Providence Farms, Jack had gone through two drivers, and he was on his third. Dave Walters had been hired by Alan to drive Jack wherever he wanted to go, 24/7. Jack felt Alan had forced Dave upon him. Dave swore up and down that he had never divulged his position as Jack's AA sponsor, but Jack had been suspicious of a conspiracy and that doubt remained.

For a reasonable recovering alcoholic the thought of relying on your sponsor for transportation everywhere you went would bolster one's progress in his recovery. Dave was intuitive and identified the dry drunk that Jack was experiencing, thus Jack tried to avoid Dave as much as possible. So instead of going to Cavalier to check on Laura, Jack called one of his other helpers. "Todd, I need you to help me. I need to talk to Laura, but she's not answering her cell. Can you go to her apartment?"

"Ya, sure," Todd agreed, and within minutes he called back. "She's not here."

"No?" Jack's suspicions were verified.

"No. She has the red Escort with Vermont plates, right?"

"Yes, she does," he calmly said as his mind raced.

"I'll keep lookin'," Todd promised. He soon called again, "I checked the laundromat, but no. I'll just go around the block. Oh, hey, here she is. Her car is here in front of the Lutheran Church."

Jack sounded friendly and casual. "Oh, well, don't bother her there, but, Todd, can you come and give me a ride to Cavalier? I want to surprise her."

"Yeah! Romance!" he chuckled. "Women love surprises. I'll be right there."

Days were lengthening in mid-June and Laura's blonde hair still sparkled in the late day sunshine as she stood on the church steps. "I cannot tell you ladies how much I appreciate you! Al-Anon is exactly what I need!" Joyce and Eva had made a special bond with Laura that evening. Others were moving to their cars, but Joyce, Eva, and Laura lingered.

Joyce reassured, "God is watching over you, Laura. You are never alone."

Eva added, "And now you can call us, too!"

"Yes, I have your numbers. Please excuse me if it's late. I really don't know what to expect. I've been saying this felt like I've been living in a warzone and now it feels like I've found a fort to take shelter in." Laura said with heart, "Thank you so much for your help. You really do understand."

"Just keep coming back to the meetings and call us as often as you want."

"Nothing could stop me from coming and you'll soon tire of all my phone calls, thank you!" Laura expressed in tears. "Good night!" The trio hugged and were soon on their separate ways.

Laura, Anna, and Erin had shared an apartment the winter before. Now both Anna and Erin were married to their sweethearts, both were expecting babies, and the one bedroom apartment that Laura had moved to was across the hall from Erin and Brandon's new place. Jack sat waiting on Laura's sofa.

As Laura opened the apartment door, his glare stole the grin from her cheeks. "Jack."

"You don't look so tired now, and the laundry," his tone was dripping with sarcasm, "that sure was fast. Where's your laundry basket?"

"Jack, I can explain."

"No, no more explanations." He quietly moved to her bedroom and carried out the suitcase he had packed. "You lied to me. Clearly you can't be trusted. So, you're moving in with me tonight." He set the bag next to the door.

She stood by the sink pouring a glass of water and staring at him. "I don't want to move out," she quietly declared.

He grinned and quickly drew a long knife from the block and pressed it to her neck whispering, "Yes, you do. You said you want me to be happy, Laura, or was that a lie, too?" His tone was sinister and very serious.

"I do want you to be happy, Jack." Tears of fear quickly flooded her eyes.

He slowly set the knife back into its spot and opened the door. "Then let's go."

In the apartment hall, Laura saw her old roommate. "Erin!" she shouted.

Jack quietly warned, "Don't draw attention."

Laura reasoned as she wiped the tears from her eyes, "Well, I have to say good-bye." Erin waddled towards Laura's door as Jack came from around the door with a pleasant grin. Laura explained, "Hey, I'm going to stay at Jack's for a while."

"Oh!"

"Yeah, we've been talking about it for a while so we're takin' the plunge," Laura said with a happy grin. "I'll keep renting here and I still plan to babysit. OK?"

Erin's confusion showed but she said, "OK, sure. Call me later, OK?" Erin's apartment door was open.

Laura stopped and turned back, heading into Erin's kitchen. "Oh, hang on, Jack. I need my lucky mug." Erin stared at the mug in Laura's hand as she picked up her purse and headed out the door. Laura disliked the mug, but hadn't discarded it since her grandma Adelle had given it to her. Her roommates knew that the mug was never used unless all others were dirty. Now she called it her 'lucky' mug.

Erin recalled the time when, as roommates, they both had cleaned the kitchen. Laura had laughed, "Only if my life was threatened would I use that ugly mug!" Erin's eyes shifted as she recalled and prayed. Finally Erin called Anna. "Something is wrong."

Panic filled Anna's voice, "Your baby? What's wrong?!"

"Not the baby. It's Laura," she reported, "she's using her ugly mug."

"What?"

"And last weekend she talked to me about breaking up with Jack and now she's moving in with him. It doesn't make sense. Why would she take that ugly mug?" Erin tried to figure.

"The brown one?" Anna was just as confused.

"Yes. Tonight she called it her lucky mug." It didn't make sense.

"Yes." Anna agreed, "Something's wrong."

~*~*~*~

Will greeted Halee at her car. Will Sturlaugson was on paternity leave, caring for a child he had known nothing about until the boy was dropped off at his doorstep. Halee could have been more affectionate to Will, since they were dating, having met a couple weeks before. Young love would have expected it. But she had questions since getting a mysterious letter. She made the trip from Williston, North Dakota, to Will's parents' farm in the extreme northwestern corner of the state to spend a couple days. Once inside she greeted the baby, young Chris, with cuddles, coos, and sincere affection.

Since getting Trish's letter, Halee wondered about the relationships she had so quickly formed. Will was dashing beyond her dreams and young Chris, the newborn baby, filled her need to mother. The doctors had told Halee she wouldn't be able to carry a baby. This was a secret she hadn't yet shared with Will, but when she met young Chris, she fell in love, thoroughly smitten. The wedding plans were rolling quickly along and Halee's head was spinning from the flurry.

It would be a small wedding. Both their parents would meet them in Las Vegas. Then they would say good-bye and honeymoon in Peru. Halee had no idea of what to expect, but she was in love with both these charming Sturlaugson men. She fed the babe while Will made lists of the items he'd need from his house in Cavalier.

Rose Sturlaugson, Will's mom, poured a cup of coffee and sat down next to Halee as she burped young Chris. "Rose, I have a question for you," Halee started. "Tell me about Will's grandparents."

The steam on Rose's coffee encircled her short salt and pepper hair, "Oh, well, there was Pat and Victoria from the ranch outside of Wolf Point."

"Yes, and Pat's in a nursing home?" Halee recalled.

"Yes, that's right. Victoria died about ten years ago." She shook her head, "He misses her."

"And your parents?"

"The brood from Oxfordshire? Yes, Nelly and Joseph Jacobs." Her eyes brightened at the thought, "Oh, there's a grand pair. They'll talk your ears right off! Ah, yes, Nelly, me mum, she was so relieved when Will went to see her a couple years back."

"Relieved?"

Rose continued, "Yes, Grandma Victoria had died never telling him who his real grandfather was."

"What? You said Pat."

"He's a step-grandpa. No," she told the tale, "Victoria had the elder Chris out of wedlock and no one, except her good friend, my mother Nelly, ever knew the whole story. Mum held that secret deep inside until Will went to visit. Then Will went looking for his grandfather and finally found him in Peru."

"Peru?" Halee asked, surprised.

"Sure. From England to Ireland to Peru. That's how he got so far in debt. Damn credit cards," Rose muttered. "Yes, that's who you're going to help, but you knew that, right?"

"The missionary?"

"Yes," Rose nodded.

"He's a grandfather to Will?"

"Yes."

Halee tried to fit all the puzzle pieces together. "What's his name?"

"Christopher. Father Christopher O'Donnell."

"Father," her eyes narrowed, "you mean he's a priest?"

"Yes, he is." At Rose's confirmation Halee nodded, patting young Chris' back, stroking his tiny back and bottom as she tried to let it all sink in.

After the babe was laid to sleep, she went to Will. He was finished making his list and her distraction was welcome since his next step was to call Alan Zimmermann and give notice of his intention to officially quit and to leave the country. He pulled her into his arms and cuddled her close.

Quietly, Halee asked, "Will? Would you tell me what you know about Father O'Donnell? Father Christopher O'Donnell?"

"The missionary?" A confident grin covered his face. "Yes, oh, he's a good man."

"Good. Is he or is he not your real grandfather? Your mom told me," she announced. "It's no secret."

"Oh, you know, he's a priest and he doesn't want anyone to know he's got a child so, though technically he's related, I just don't think of him in those terms," Will ended, wondering if she was buying his lame excuse.

"What would he know that would interest me?"

"Oh, you're back to that." He recalled their prior conversation about Trish, when Halee had first been alerted to this mystery. His charms had worked before, but keeping the lies straight was wearing on him, "You see, Halee, Trish is just jealous. She had some grandiose scheme about changing my mind about who I was taking to Peru, and I paid her no attention. Well, why would I?" he shrugged. "She was my vet tech."

Halee tried to follow his tangled web. "Wait. So, you were taking Calli to Peru?"

"Yeah."

She shook her head in confusion, "I thought she had Alaska on her mind."

"Well, I offered her the chance," he backed up.

"No, which is it? Were you taking Calli or not?"

"Yeah, that was the plan, but then she decided to take the job in Barrow."

"That's different from what you said before." Halee steamed, "You see, that's the problem with lies. It's hard to keep the story straight." Halee headed for the guest room and repacked her suitcase as Will considered his options.

She picked up her suitcase and grabbed her purse as Will stood in the bedroom door frame. "OK, I'm sorry. It was wrong to leave out the fact that Father O'Donnell is related."

"What would he know about you that would interest me? Or maybe I should send a letter to Calli in Barrow," she suggested. "There can't be too many Doctor Callis in their hospital."

Will fought his urge to overreact and calmly said, "Do what you want. Verify whatever you need to verify." He stood behind Halee and cranked up the charm on high. "One thing won't change. I'm still head over heels in love with you. And young Chris, well, he can't talk yet, but if he could, I'm sure he would second that notion." His hands pulled her into his arms as he worked to convince her heart.

In the short time she had known Will one thing was sure: his charms always sent her heart swooning, but in her mind Halee fought back, "There's a lie in here somewhere."

"About Fr. O'Donnell? I already explained that." He was losing his patience.

She pushed him off. "No, the bit about Calli and who you were taking to Peru. It's confusing. All I know is I'm starting to feel like a second or third choice and I want to talk to your real grandfather."

Will paused and finally sighed and said, "No, you don't."

"Why not? What?" she cried.

Will breezed over the truth, "He wants me to take up the family business," he said quickly and then dramatically winked and pointed to himself, "but I have a better idea."

"Family business. The mafia?" Halee asked. Will didn't correct her.

He shifted gears and poured on the charm, "Naw, my idea is to keep healing animals, and you and me together, we can help so many good people there on the road to Machu Pichu. It's good work. We'll be entertaining angels as God works through us to save lives and improve the natives' health, lower infant mortality. You know, we'll have our own family and teach them as we go. It'll be an adventure of a lifetime." As he pulled her into his arms, Halee vowed to herself to contact Father O'Donnell as soon as possible, even if it meant praying to God for help.

~*~*~*~*

Half of Laura's crew were busy cutting and packaging marble jack. Laura watched as another full rack of cheddar was loaded into one of the many aging chambers. The grand opening would have to happen without her favorite aged tomato basil cheddar. She set the fresh tank of milk to heat and dialed her phone. "Joyce, this is Laura. I can't talk long, but I'm wondering what you do for a living."

Joyce was one of Laura's new Al-Anon friends. "Me? Well, I'm currently under-employed," Joyce chuckled. "I clean at the hospital and I keep asking them to give me more hours, but…"

"Do you want a job here at Providence?"

"Me? Uh, yes! Doing what?"

"Cleaning, and you'll learn to be a cheese maker, technically, a fromagere." Laura looked around. "Can you come here and we'll talk in person?" She turned, watching as she spoke. "Something has happened," her voice fell off as she saw Jack walking her way, so she shifted gears, listing, "and three cases of mesophilic culture."

"What?" Joyce was confused.

"Yes, that's right, three cases. I'm running low."

Joyce caught on, "Oh, is he there?"

"Yes."

"And you want me to come," she confirmed, reaching for her jacket.

Laura smiled into the phone, "Yes, thank you so much. Bye."

At the sight of Jack, Laura instantly recalled the way she had cried herself to sleep the night before. She determined he was in strong denial and at least a little psychotic to have pulled a knife on her. Still he seemed justified and even righteous about his plans. Laura reminded, "Hey, you need gloves, a hairnet, and an apron if you're going to stay."

He batted at her hands, "You know I don't like that stuff."

"No, but it's mandatory." She pointed to the door, "I run a clean shop here, nothing changes that."

He backed up to what he knew as the safe zone, the door frame, where he could talk to her but would not have to endure hairnets. "I just want to use your computer."

"You're done with the windmill?"

"Yes."

"What's next?" Laura asked. In reality she couldn't have cared any less. She was done caring any more.

"That's just it. I need to find a different job, so I need to use your computer."

Colleen, one of Laura's workers, interrupted, "What's the next ice cream flavor?"

Laura checked a list, "White Chocolate Macadamia. Here's the recipe." An alarm toned and Laura moved back to the milk tank. "Colleen, if you need help, just let me know," she said, stirring the culture into the milk.

Jack watched her from the doorway, "What's that gonna be?"

"Gouda."

Jack was only mildly intrigued by her business. "Are you smoking it?"

"Yes." The thought of her friends at the butcher shop spawned a memory. "Hey, that reminds me. Rusty is going to need a place to live for a while until his house is ready. We have extra bedrooms upstairs. Do you think he could stay with us? Like a boarder?"

"Where is he living now?"

"At his farm, but they're about to torch the house," she explained. "He's in the middle, in limbo, until his house is ready."

"Yeah? I know the feeling. I don't care what he does." Jack warned, "But we're not stickin' around. I'm gonna use your computer."

"Go ahead," she said, watching the milk. In her mind she ranted, *Yes! GO! Go without me! I am not going to be twisted in the wind by your denial or your psychosis.* She set the controls to the next temperature and followed Jack to her desk.

"I'll check for positions at Kraft," Jack promised with an encouraging tone.

"Kraft? The Evil Empire?!" Laura reeled. "I don't think I want to work for *them*."

"Please," he begged, trying his charm. "If I find a position, will you at least consider it, for me?"

Laura promised, "I'll consider it. I have to go. The Gouda needs me."

"Damn cheese," he muttered. "It's always calling you," Jack quietly whined.

Laura pondered as she prepared the rennet. Jack hadn't gotten too far with his explorations into the world of cheese or any other dairy products. Early on Laura had been frustrated with his insistence that mozzarella and 2% milk were the full extent of the dairy products he would stomach. He even avoided ice cream which seemed unnatural and morally wrong. She could make all she wanted but he wouldn't budge. Laura recalled the reoccurring dreams where a handsome man came to warn her about a warzone. She wondered about him as the culture finished its work. Finally it was time to cut the curd. She double checked the temperature, then she stirred in the rennet. *Fine, Jack,* she thought as the whey separated from the curd, *I'm not making this for you anyway.*

~*~*~*~

Spencer Hillman, Anna's elder brother, was fit to be tied. But really, what could he do? The bill to scrub the raw eggs and eggshells off his lake cabin the few weeks before now sat before him on his desk. As a realtor specializing in lake homes, he'd always prided himself on having a fine home on a dynamite fishing lake. But three weeks before, he had come to his beloved retreat to find two women egging his garage, windows, and quaint little porch. This was the public side of his secret haven. The private side had been feathered with multiple pillows having been ripped and scattered. The swirls of wind seemed to help the women's effort to aggravate him even more. Now the memory pulled at his anxiety in having to pay to avoid the embarrassment. "NO!" he had exclaimed. "What are you doing?! Please stop!" he'd begged, dumbfounded.

The first woman had been defiant, "The man who lives here is a total loser! He, well, he took advantage of me, and so I'm assaulting him!" She continued lobbing eggs at his front door with fury.

"What? I live here! I've never met you! Please, what have I done?" He carefully watched and caught the last egg she had in the carton.

"You? No, it wasn't you." She eyed her egg in his hand. "What's your name?"

"Spencer Hillman, I'm a realtor, and generally a nice guy. What's yours?" He made his living on connecting with people, but this woman had him frazzled.

The other woman coached her, "Her name isn't important. Where is Jason Hillman? Doesn't he live here?"

"No, he's my kid brother! No! He doesn't live here! What did he do to you?! That little peon!"

"We were on a date. He suggested we come over here and he said he lost his key, but he knew where the extra one was." Spencer grumbled as she went on, "I suppose that he assumed that since he'd bought me a good supper, and he had this great house to go to, that I was going to let him, you know."

The other woman nodded and said, "Conjugal rights."

Spencer was shocked, "Con--," he stuttered. The acid in his stomach churned. He had tried to put the memories he'd had of his younger brother's sexual exploits deep, deep into the back of his mind. Now he was having to face those same memories, but the ladies before him gave him no time to ponder.

The first woman continued, "I said no and he said OK. Then he kept making me stronger and stronger drinks and when I came to, I was naked and obviously assaulted! He's not answering my calls or texts. I want YOU to get ahold of him and have him come here. I'm callin' the cops. He can face the law. I'm done with Minnesota nice!"

Spencer looked again at the bill for cleaning his house and back yard where the occasional feather still fluttered in bushes and dangled from trees. He had phoned his brother for the mysterious ladies, but *the little peon never showed.* Spencer sighed and paid the bill, wondering instead if he should tell their mom. That was a thought he'd wrestled with before, since high school. *Oh, she'd be livid!* he imagined, still haunted by having witnessed Jason's sins, but always hiding the truth from the light of day. Instead he just wrote the check and again, as always, asked God for forgiveness. The payee line, the amount, both digits and written, then his signature. It wasn't until he wrote the date, eyeing the calendar, that his next scheme was hatched. *Jason ALWAYS comes home for the Deuce!*

Alan and Elijah were grease from head to toe, rethreading the baler with fresh twine. The conversation during their work would have surprised many. Alan repeated his earlier question, "How can we help them? Your sisters, my wife, and the multitudes who have been abused, assaulted, and harassed over the years. How?"

Elijah's sisters were still stressed and confused because of the low-life, Mike, who had twisted young Deborah's mind and slandered Angelica's reputation. As their brother, Elijah wanted so much to protect them from the chaos that Mike spread about. He held his head, "But hopes and wishes don't do diddly."

Grady Baxter, who stood, arms folded, quietly leaning on the machine shed door, both announced his presence and shared his thought. "There needs to be a culture shift. We as people, male and female, need to stop agreeing to keeping these issues secret. Did you know that Andrea, my sweet, sweet, creative soul of a woman, that she had multiple issues with date rape and a stalker who tried to rape her?"

Alan noted, "Well, the second one was more public since the police were involved."

"Yes. I was shocked when she started talking about it," Grady admitted.

Alan agreed, "Same here, with Anna."

Brandon rounded the corner into the shed. "Anna? She just left for town. Want me to wave her down?"

"No, thanks, though. No, we're discussing the long history of how women and families in general seem to keep these private situations, like when Andrea was being stalked, secret," he motioned to Grady, "and how unless the law is involved, that the secrets stay secret. Grady suggested that our world needs a culture shift to make all people know that sexual abuse in all its forms is not acceptable. That's something that we men have to take a stand on. To band together and cull out the rotten ones."

"Good men need to do something. You're right," Elijah agreed. "But these are their secrets. We can't take their private nightmares and spread them out in the open unless it's their idea."

Brandon's head nodded as he stared deep into the ground, remembering the horror stories Erin had shared with him. "If it's the women's ideas, to bring it all out, then there's no stopping them. Then we just need to be there to support and love. Like we are now."

Alan agreed. "And support each other as we wait for them to make their move. When it happens, gentlemen, it will shake the world awake."

2 THE HOOK SHOT

It was a warm late-June day. Nick and Trish finished the watering system and sat on the porch swing. Lemonade waited as they cuddled. Nick's lips nibbled on her ear as she wrapped her arms around him. She turned toward him and kissed him tenderly. "You get extra points for being a good kisser." The sound of her cell phone spoiled the mood. "Hello?"

"Hey, Trish, you got company," Jim reported.

"I'm in some fine company right now." Trish wasn't willing to move.

"Yeah, I know. It's Jake, Jake Hastings."

"What?" she asked, dropping away from Nick. "What does he want?"

"He wants to see you," she heard Jim say.

Trish's heart pounded. "Are you sure?"

"Yes, that's what he said. Get yer tail home."

She clutched the cell phone as Nick's eyes smiled at her, obviously curious. She nodded, "Ha, yeah, I have company." She stood. "I need to go."

"Who is it?"

"Oh, it's just Jake Hastings," she said, waving her hand to brush off any concern. "I went to school with him. He was president of our senior class and, well, when prom came along he needed a date." She was nonchalant adding, "It was a real mercy date. Yeah."

"You are generous," Nick praised.

"Yeah, well. He was president of the chess club and the French club," she described, "and if they had had a club for computer geeks, he'd have been president of that, too. I think they said he went into dentistry."

"I get the picture," he sighed. "And he's at your house?" he chuckled, "Weird."

"Really, huh. Well, I'll go and see what he wants. He probably wants me to buy a timeshare so he can get a better deal," she casually suggested, though butterflies were tickling her innards.

As Trish disappeared into her car and quickly left Nick's yard, Laura drove in. He picked up the lemonade and met her in the kitchen. "The end of another day at the cheese factory? How did it go?"

"The Gouda behaved, putty in my hands, really," she lightly boasted. "Oh, and we divined a new Vanilla Juneberry Swirl sherbet. Yum. Where's Jack?"

"Working," he said sarcastically. "His driver, Dave, stopped to talk to Alan today when I was there. Since I'm a roommate they asked me into their conversation," Nick said with a knowing air.

"Yes," she agreed with his sarcasm. "Jack came to use my computer today."

"Dave's report wasn't complimentary. Alan's got Jack on a short leash."

"What did Dave say?" Laura asked, curious.

"Lately Jack's a lazy SOB, but he's still sober," Nick repeated, pouring fresh lemonade.

"That's true. He's looking for different jobs for him and me," she said adding, "he wants to move."

"Laura!" Nick said in surprise.

"I'm not going anywhere." Laura was very sure. "And I don't know that you've noticed but I'm moved in here. Last night."

He leaned against the kitchen counter, "Hadn't noticed."

"What else did Dave say?"

"Just that he wouldn't ever want Jack to date his sister."

Laura rolled her eyes. "Yes, and that would be wise. I want him to find a different job and just move away. Just go."

"No love there?"

"I don't know that there ever was," she admitted. "Just lust and blindness on my end. Yes, I moved in, pretty much against my will. But even so I'm getting my head straightened out."

Nick tried to follow her meaning, "How do you do that?"

"Al-Anon. It's a covert operation. Rusty is also moving in," she announced. "I invited him today. I hope that's OK. It's for my safety. We'll both pay rent. His house will be ready in October."

"Oh, sure, yes." Nick offered, "Do you want me to move upstairs, too?"

"No, that'll bug Jack. He doesn't like you."

"I don't like him. It's mutual dislike."

"Hey, where was Trish going?"

"She just went home. I guess some old classmate has come to visit Jim. Jake somebody. Starts with an 'H'."

"Jake. Jake Hoover, Jake Hanson, Jake Hastings."

"Right, that's the one. I guess they went to prom her senior year, a mercy date."

"We were talking about proms earlier in May, and as I recall, Jake Hastings was the guy she had a huge crush on. When his first, second and third choices fell through, he picked Trish to go to Prom. Mercy date? Yeah, but not the way you're thinkin'."

Jack and Dave drove into the farmyard as Nick scrambled to his truck and prayed. Acid burned in Laura's stomach, more nervous for what Jack might do than nervous or concerned about Trish or Nick. She had her own kettle of fish.

By the time Nick arrived, Trish had the grill started in the backyard. Nick could see the grill wasn't the only thing heating up. "Here are the hobo potatoes, Trish. You forgot them. Remember? We planned this picnic together. Hi," he greeted Jake, "I'm Nick, Trish's friend."

As in high school, Trish's eyes had seemed drawn into Jake's spell. She smiled at Jake, ignoring Nick, and led Jake to the shaded garden. Nick placed his pan of potatoes on the grill. As Nick stood by the grill he asked Jim, "Why is she so pie-eyed?" Nick and Jim looked her over.

Trish seemed oblivious to the competitive scent in the air. The courtyard of flowers, vines, and romantic vignettes of chairs and benches was their basketball court and Trish was the prize. Jim refereed from the side and said, "Jake, I understand you're a dentist," effectively handing Jake the ball. Nick was behind on the board since Jake had been making easy shots in Nick's absence. Now Jake could see he would have to make his play.

"Yes, I'm practicing in Grand Forks. I'm a dental surgeon."

"Practicing. Huh. It seems like the medical world is the only place where people get by with practicing on people and getting paid big money for it," said Nick

"What's your profession?"

"I'm an agronomist."

"Ah, plants. Can you name these?"

"Of course, these are," Nick reached up to the neighboring tree, studying its leaves, "acer saccharum or sugar maple, gypsophila or baby's breath, Hydrangea or Snowball, Echinacea or purple cone flower, and well, there's no challenge here. These are fairly common plants. Should we talk shrubs or grass?"

Jake was not having it, "You made your point."

"I practiced this stuff in college, yeah, so what brings you to the Red River Valley?"

"My mother is from just east of here in Minnesota."

"What town?"

"Karlstad."

"Oh, I lived on a farm outside of Greenbush for a while. What's her maiden name?"

"Tess Cerkoniak."

"Hmm, don't know her."

"Well, Trish does," he noted, smiling at Trish, then added, "She wanted to come live in the area after my father died."

Nick graciously offered, "I'm sorry for your loss."

Jake nodded, "Yes, and my mother is ill." Nick wanted to call foul in their imaginary game.

Trish's voice showed her concern, "Tess? What's wrong?"

"She broke her foot and has had troubles ever since. I can't be there 24/7 so she's in an assisted living home in Grand Forks."

She smiled, "Tell her I hope she feels better."

He leisurely dribbled the ball under his own basket. "I will, thank you. I have a nice home there in Grand Forks. Plenty of room for animals, Trish."

Nick countered, "But no room for your mother? Ouch. Do you have a barn?" Nick had stolen the ball and headed for a layup.

"No, I live on the outskirts of the city. They don't allow such things."

"Huh. I have a nice house and barn on a quarter of land with plans for two or more horses, right, Trish?"

"Yes, that's right."

Nick added, "And maybe a couple steers."

"Really?" Trish grinned, ear to ear. "That sounds great."

"Oh, sure, chickens and ducks, too. Do you want swans? There's a spring that feeds that creek. We could dam it to make a pond for swans and ducks."

"Wow, Nick, that sounds pretty but swans are sorta mean. I think ducks would be enough."

Jake sneered at Nick, then Trish caught sight of Jake's sour face. He quickly recovered. "Yes," he smiled, "that does sound serene."

Trish called a time-out. "I'd better get the chicken going." She left to go inside and both teams went to their benches.

Jim consoled Nick, "He doesn't stand a chance, man, you're doin' good, just be yourself." Jim patted Nick's shoulder and went to Jake and discussed old neighbors and friends. Nick turned to the back door. He did have home court advantage. He was quick to hold the door and assisted Trish at the grill.

It was a recipe he'd come up with and she just wasn't sure. He lit the gas fire to the side of the grill and settled the kettle of water. Trish reported, "OK, there's salt in the water and the chicken is cut up."

"Yes, just parboil the chicken and the excess fat melts off and it spends less time on the grill—the meat is cooked and spends less time above the flames which means it's less likely to get torched to black char this way." This was his game plan.

"OK," Trish shrugged, "we'll try it."

He checked the potatoes, "These look good, and the salads are ready?"

"We just have to toss the lettuce salad. Your fruit salad is wonderful—I took a taste. I never would have thought to add lemon pudding."

"One of Mom's tricks. I talked to her this morning, she sends her love," he said, reminding Trish of Nancy. Trish seemed to admire Nancy's spunk and relished a chance to visit. "OK, where should I set the table?"

Trish grinned. "Out here on this picnic table. It's such a nice night."

As Nick was inside planning his next layup, Jake settled Trish next to him in the wicker love seat. Jim hovered nearby continuing to discuss mutual neighbors and their woes. This conversation seemed to bore Trish and she excused herself to freshen their glasses with more ice and lemonade. She was surprised when she saw the table spread with a cheery blue checkered table cloth, the one she'd commented was her favorite picnic cloth. Nick went all out bringing out white china plates, salad bowls, linen napkins, cutlery and wine glasses, even setting lit citronella candles on the nearby tables to dissuade mosquitoes from her plate.

She met him in the doorway with her hands full of their lemonade glasses. "Let me help you," he said, backing her up into the kitchen. He unloaded the glasses from her hands onto a new cookie sheet, on which he'd tossed a summer placemat. Trish started toward the tray of lemonade but was quickly gathered up into Nick's arms for a quiet taste of passion. "Hmmmm, I love you so much, Trish. Hmm, you're the only woman for me."

"Ha, ah," she took a breath. "Nick you're very important to me, but I don't know if I'm ready for those three little words just yet."

23

Nick felt sure and wanted her to understand. "I don't see the big deal." She glanced at him like he'd stepped on her heart. "No, not those really special words, like, 'yes, we're engaged.' I'm talking about the l-o-v-e word." Again she gave him a look, but he continued. "What? I didn't say it out loud. But do you feel something?"

"Yes, something that makes me want to explore, to get to know you better."

"Ok, OK, keep that comin', OK. Just don't let this dentist spin you in circles, alright? Can I ask that much? I mean, I don't think you even mentioned this guy before."

"Jake? Oh, you know back, when I was younger, you know back before we met..."

Jim, the referee, came in from the back yard and blew the whistle. "Are you two OK? I'm runnin' outta chitchat." The game was back on.

Jim and Jake took their seats at the table as Trish served drinks and Nick manned the barbeque grill—a man's job. From his masculine perch Nick watched Jake sipping lemonade and tried not to growl.

As planned, the chicken was parboiled and slowly grilled with barbeque sauce being added in the last five minutes. As it cooked, Trish tossed the salad. When she emerged with the fruit salad and French bread, she noticed a small bouquet of daisies. She recognized them from the side garden next door. Trish had admired them from afar. She looked next door at her neighbor's flower bed. Would she notice there were five blossoms missing? They were placed in a vase right next to Trish's plate. Nick hugged her tenderly and seated her for her meal. Her eyes twinkled as they both shared their little secret. Nick plated the chicken and potatoes. He was pleased—everything looked wonderful.

Jake ignored Nick, the food, and the table, and turned to Trish, "You see, Trish, the reason I wanted to come to see you was that since I'm invited to a gala dinner, I wanted you to be my date."

"When?"

"The 20th of June."

"Oh, we will be gone on our trip."

"We?"

"Yes, Nick and I are secret shoppers. I'm shopping for two veterinarians." Next door the neighbor was arriving home. Trish kept a nervous eye towards the next yard.

"That's highly unusual."

Nick rose and walked around the picnic table studying the angle of the daisies in relation to the neighbor's back door, nonchalantly replying, "We go to three unnamed states. It seems that Trish enjoys making me curious. I can't wait," he grinned at Trish, then moved the vase, "we'll have so much fun."

"What does a secret shopper do?"

Trish grinned at Nick who beamed back a loving gaze. "We'll be pretending that we're married. I think that sounds fun."

Nick casually added, "Not much of a stretch for me."

She continued, "And we'll buy animals that need vet care, and then as Nick asks the stupid questions, I'll watch and listen to the vet and see if he's got the people skills and the animal know-how to be considered for a face-to-face interview."

"So, you're in charge of stupid questions. You'll do well at that."

Trish defended, "Oh heavens, Jake, you should hear Nick! He's very knowledgeable about all green and blooming things and he rides horses and he's a good around animals. He'll do great. What I'm excited about is wondering what sorts of animals we'll find at auctions and in humane shelters. He's looking for pets, so we might find some to bring home."

Nick casually noted, "For starters the colt you saw in that framed print at my house is for sale, Trish. My uncle said he'd meet us if we're anywhere near Colorado."

"Does he need a vet?"

"Yes, I think so. Something about his lungs. Otherwise he's sound. Trish, honey, you should talk to my uncle."

Jake judged, "A horse without decent lungs should just be put down. You're crazy to consider the shipping costs alone, much less paying for such a problem."

"Nick is right," Trish declared. "This horse has been a part of Nick's family for ten years. Nick and his parents watched him being born. There's no need to give up on him. At thirty-years-old, do you think someone should put you down just because you contracted the flu? No, Jake, you're out of line."

In Nick's mind, Trish had just made a three-pointer from center court and the crowd was going wild. He was very proud of her. He quietly winked his approval as he suggested, "Shall we say grace?"

They prayed the traditional table grace and the plates and bowls were passed. The food was enjoyed and after more cuddles and kisses between Trish and Nick over the kitchen sink, the evening continued with Trish cuddled into Nick's side. As she'd clearly made her choice between the sparring ball players, the imaginary ball bounced away, untended, and conversations turned to weather, the Providence Foods master plan, classmates and James' return from war. At the end of the evening Trish waved from Nick's elbow. "Bye, Jake, say hi to your mom."

"Thank you all for the fine meal. Jim, I'm glad to see you're feeling better. Nick, take good care of her, she's a treasure," Jake said, then kissed Trish's cheek. "You're the one that got away."

"You could've tried harder on prom night."

Jake nodded and thoughtfully replied, "I didn't get a kiss that night either, did I?"

Trish shook her head and waved her fingers, "Good night." The game clock ticked down to zero and the game was over. Nick put both arms around his trophy and squeezed, kissing her cheek as Jim turned to head inside. As Jake's car was driving away, she turned in Nick's arms and kissed him back. It was confirmed in his mind, *Yes! She still loves me!* Aloud, he praised, "You are so amazing!" He kissed her knuckles, "A gift, you really are a true gift to me!"

Halee had worked the three to eleven shift and checked her voicemail. She had been waiting for a call from the Bismarck Diocese. Gratefully her call came through. "Halee, hi, I'm Mary Cooper from the Bismarck Diocese. I have news on the mission church you're researching. Please call me during business hours." Halee's eyes looked skyward as she acknowledged the answered prayer. He was listening. With a sigh she set her alarm and tried to sleep.

3 OPTIONS

From Jack's bedroom Laura checked her safety net. She knew Nick was picnicking. *That's all Trish could talk about. That girl gets annoying sometimes,* she declared, hugging her arms. Rusty, with Ila's help, was settling in the next room. Laura and Jack were pouring over his resume on Laura's laptop. She was opposed to the work they were doing, but glad that Ila quietly grinned from the hall. Her knowing glances weren't lost on Laura, but Jack seemed so focused on his task he only heard and saw Laura.

"This sounds great. The resume is much better with your suggestions, Laura. You're very good. OK, to sign off on the application letter what do you think? Sincerely or yours truly?"

"Hmm, neither. Best regards."

"You're right! OK," he said typing. "Now let's do yours."

"Yeah, Jack, I looked at those jobs but neither one is suitable for my skills."

"Oh, come on, you have to try." Jack was still focused on his own documents, his own self.

Laura looked at the job description, "I'm a manager of a small creamery. This job is for a secretary. I can't do that stuff."

Jack re-read his own letter and saved it again on the computer. "OK, I'm ready to submit it electronically."

Laura encouraged, "Yes, good. It's on this tab," she pointed.

He went through the process and once all his attachments were added he closed his eyes and clicked submit. "Oh, that felt good! Now, which tab is for Kraft?"

"It's not on the computer. Here, I printed them out."

Jack read aloud, "Logistics coordinator. This position is responsible for day to day clerical duties." He scanned and read excerpts. "Able to handle multiple phone lines…processing weekly payroll, daily orders, accounts payable."

"No, Jack, come on. I don't have a clerical bone in my body. I make cheese. That's what I know."

"You could try it."

"No. With my luck I'd probably get the job only to screw up real people's pay checks. No, absolutely not."

"OK, the other one."

"Tell me again—why do I want to work for Kraft?"

Jack scanned the second job description. "See here? Comprehensive training with great advancement opportunities and top benefits."

"Jack, this job is for selling frozen pizza to grocery stores."

"Yeah, that's true."

"It's a glorified truck driver, Jack, see? I need to be able to pass a CDL test. Oh, and here's my favorite: desire to work on a winning team with the best product line of its kinds. Jack. All my entire life I've been making cheese to compete with Kraft. Now I have to drink their corporate Koolaid and sell Tombstone and DiGiorno Pizzas? I'll never be able to show my face in Vermont. Never."

"Yeah? Well, we won't be going there anyway."

The muscles in Laura's face twitched as she looked at him. "No Vermont visits?"

"No, I met your folks at Anna's wedding and I don't think they liked me." Laura's eyes blinked uncontrollably as he continued. "Yeah, your dad went on and on about good manners and how to raise your kids with values."

"What's wrong with that?"

"I don't plan on havin' kids. Your folks just add pressure and I don't need it."

Laura prayed, *Please God, help me to not blow up.* She started to clean her teeth with a nervous tongue and took a deep breath. This was his point of no return, she internally acknowledged. This was the end of her love for him. Smiling she nodded and caved to his wishes, typing her application letter, saying, "Whatever you want, dear." Jack stood and massaged her tense shoulders as she typed, "Kraft Foods has long been a dream employer for me. Please consider me an eager and qualified applicant for the position Pizza Route Sales Representative (Job ID CS934140-Minneap)."

"Shouldn't you spell out Minneapolis?"

"I'm doing this. On the sheet it says Minneap. Do you want me to apply for this job?"

"Yes."

"OK, then let me do it. Hmmm," she continued typing. "Pizza, the perfect collection of all food groups, has long been a favorite. For me to have the chance to sell Kraft Foods' 'Tombstone' and 'DiGiorno' pizzas would be a dream come true." Her eyes rolled as she pursed her lips to think, wondering *How long, God, how long can I keep up this charade?*

Jack looked at his watch and yawned. "Oh, it's getting late. I'm suddenly very tired," he said, yawning and stretching his arms to the ceiling. "You can get this submitted tonight and I'll read your letter and resume on the computer tomorrow, OK?"

"I'm not submitting anything on the internet," she said as she typed more lies.

"Why not? It's faster."

"No, I've been a victim of identity theft because of the internet. No, I'll mail the whole works tomorrow."

He yawned again. "OK, well, I'll read it in the morning. Make sure you sign your letter."

"I will. You go to sleep." Laura was surprised at this sudden turn. He had been wide awake just moments before.

~*~*~*~

At the sound of her alarm, Halee jumped up and in one fell swoop she dialed Mary Cooper's number. Still blinking sleep away, Halee hoped as the phone rang.

"Mary Cooper, can I help you?"

"Hi, this is Halee Rockford. You called me about the mission in Peru."

"Peru, yes. With most remote missions like this one we are only able to contact by mail, but since there is tourism nearby, there is a person who would take the call and relay it to Father O'Donnell, then O'Donnell will call you back, briefly."

"Briefly."

"He has no budget for international phone calls. He'll call you and hang up and you'll redial this number I'm going to give you. Make sense?"

Halee agreed, called, left a message and waited. The waiting was the worst.

After a long day of strategizing brands, labels, and marketing plans, Anna had invited Dara Marcoux home for supper that night. The two ladies were surprised when they opened the backdoor to see that Alan was there cooking in the kitchen, and he also had a guest.

Alan introduced, "Dara Marcoux, this is my cousin, Rene LaRoque."

Rene switched to French, "Dara, that's a lovely name. Marcoux, I have some Marcoux relative…"

Dara stopped him. "French isn't a language I excel at, sorry. For me it's pretty much just a salad dressing."

He smiled, "Did you understand any of…"

"You said my name, I think. Hi, I'm from Nebraska, new in town."

Anna joined in, "Yes, we've been developing marketing plans. Alan, you'll love her ideas. So, Rene, you're new in town, too. Forgive me, but I have pregnant brain lately. You're from Montreal, Quebec, right?" Rene nodded and Anna asked, "What is your profession?"

"Oui, now I am an electrician apprentice, but next summer I should be licensed and I'll open my own business."

They chatted as Alan and Rene cooked, but soon Anna had another visitor. She introduced her great-aunt and let her into the family room, "This is Christine Gislison, my favorite great-aunt," Anna added with a wink.

Christine smirked until she realized there were still other great-aunts on both sides of Anna's family. "Oh, dear, I won't tell!" she said with a girlish giggle.

Dara shook Christine's hand, "Hi, I'm Dara Marcoux. I just started a new job with Anna and Alan, Marketing. Good to meet you."

Christine's eyes quickly shifted to Rene as he bent to kiss her hand. "Mademoiselle, I am Rene LaRoque." He gently dropped her hand, and winked over a quiet grin.

Alan laughed aloud, "Yes, as with Anna's family, I have more than a few crazy cousins, and Rene is one of them." Alan stood six inches higher than Rene, but beyond Alan's long legs, there was a family resemblance that they agreed was from the French side of their heritage, though Alan credited his Grandpa Frank, and Rene graciously thanked Grandma Genny. Regardless of the science, both Christine and Dara were struck by Rene's gentle eyes and his thought-filled grin.

After dessert, Anna pulled Christine aside. "Aunty, you came here for something. Are you OK?"

"Yes," the elder announced, holding her water glass up, toasting, "I wanted to personally thank you two, Anna and Alan, for your help in getting that old Victorian house ready for us. My granddaughters and grand-nieces are clearing out of apartments and small houses here and there, making room for young families, for the good of the order. I miss my little house and the privacy that came with it, but I very much appreciate the time I can spend with these ladies."

Alan asked, "Are the rumors true? This house full of single ladies, are you bent on marrying them all off?"

She shrugged, "If that's what makes them happy?"

~*~*~*~

Laura stood at the post office counter. "I need to mail this. How many stamps?" she asked.

The postmaster was a new friend, Teri Olson. "OK, it's going to be sixty cents. Kraft? What, did they ask for your recipe?"

Laura smiled and winked, "Not yet, but they will! Let's see." Her pen circled the region of the envelope reserved for the return address. "What was my address in New York City?" she wondered aloud, then wrote her best guess. Above it she wrote, "Teri" and asked, "What's a good last name?"

Phonetically Teri replied, "Fee-a-cow-ski."

"Spell it."

"C-h-w-i-a-l-k-o-w-s-k-i."

Laura blew the hair above her eyes, "Mind bending. OK, now I need random numbers."

"11967, my birthday."

"OK, and a street name? I got it, Honorary Drive."

"What city?" she asked, trying the address in her computer.

"Memphis, Tennessee," Laura wrote, feeling giddy.

"Are you making all this up?"

"Yes, it's fun."

"Well, it'll get lost for sure."

"Zip code 0 7 9 5 2. Check it in your system."

"That's invalid."

"Really?" Laura seem surprised, then opened the big zip code book and randomly pointed and read, "0 4 5 4 7. Friendship, Maine. Oh, doesn't that sound nice." Laura scratched through her original numbers and wrote the new ones.

Teri stared suspiciously at the envelope. "Are you going to change the Memphis to Friendship?"

"No."

"This IS going to get lost."

"Good, I never want Kraft to receive it, but if Jack asks you, I did mail it. No one needs to know it was a fictitious address and you as a professional postmaster certainly wouldn't be prying into others' motives."

"OK, I'll cover for ya, but eventually you need to tell me the whole story—not because of my job or yours, but because we're friends."

"Yes, we are and I thank you very much. Hey, how's your mom?"

"They verified, the biopsy, positive. It's cancer."

"Oh, Teri, I'm so sorry. Hmm, hey, if she can handle dairy products I've got a nice sampler of ice creams we just put together. Anna's having fun with marketing all my creations. I'll bring it over tonight."

"What ice cream are you making today?"

"Oh, I don't know. I have a list. I'm a little scattered lately," Laura confessed, pointing to the letter, "and my memory is in the toilet."

"Well, feel better."

"I'll come visit tonight, but tell your mom I'm praying for her."

"You're sweet," Teri cooed, then looked at the envelope again, rolling her eyes, causing Laura to laugh.

As she walked out of the Post Office, Laura was still in awe of how God had made Jack so instantly drowsy the night before. Once the letter was done Laura had had a good night's sleep and with her resume bound for Friendship, Maine, she was even more relieved. Over breakfast Laura spoke in whispers to both Rusty and Nick telling them the truth about Jack's threatening nature. Rusty had offered to be her escort to and from work under the guise of car-pooling to save the planet. Rusty waited in the car and dutifully filled her need for a bodyguard. Once delivered to work, she focused on her job and for the first day in several, Laura was fun-loving and happy. The recipes worked right, the coworkers were happy, and necessary supply shipments arrived before they were needed. She even got to meet the new baker, Malla. It was a good day.

As she cut the curds on a batch of white cheddar, Laura prayed, *Please God, let Jack get the job he applied for. Please help him to move on, away from Mountain and away from me!* Her meditation was interrupted by a knocking on the window and Trish's voice, "Hey Laura, guess what?!"

She finished her job, reset the controls, and went out to see Trish. "You're getting a new puppy?"

"No, this is better! James is officially discharged from the army as of TODAY! He emailed me but he also wants to see me face to face, so I need to borrow your computer. You still have the camera, right?"

"Right. I use it to talk to my family in Vermont."

"I've got all the connection info. He'll be there at two o'clock, our time. Can I do this?"

"Well, yes, girlfriend!"

Trish hugged Laura tightly and swayed her from side to side. In tears Trish exclaimed, "He's coming home!!"

"When was the last time he was home?"

Trish wiped her cheeks, "He came to visit Grandma and me three years ago in Fargo. He ran away when he was seventeen and he came back a man. I almost didn't recognize him."

"Why haven't you gotten your own camera before now? You could have."

"No, he's been undercover on some missions. If he got an email out, that was amazing. No. It was for his own safety that he stayed out of contact."

"OK, I've seen movies about police in New York that go undercover, but how does a green-eyed guy named O'Malley do that in the Middle East?"

"No, my eyes are green like Dad's and Marty's, but James has deep brown eyes like Mom and Austin. She was Creole from Louisiana."

"Does he speak…"

"Arabic? Yes, we learned French in school. Mom made sure of that and he learned Arabic in the army. He's an Irish Catholic Christian undercover as an Arab Muslim. Two o'clock?"

"Yes, fine."

"I'll set up the connection now so it's ready."

"See you later!" Laura threw a cheesy grin over her shoulder and silenced her sarcasm by not adding, *Oh, bless your little heart!*

The mystery of those deep brown eyes kept Laura curious throughout the morning. During lunch Trish called with a problem. "Oh, Laura, help! I have to assist Dr. Tappan with a surgery now at one. It's a straight forward procedure but I can't leave like I planned."

"Who's the patient?"

"One of Alan's favorite cows, Lucy. She's got female trouble. But you should see, Laura, the surgery rooms in our new clinic? State of the art! Right now they're installing the hydropool for therapy sessions. It's such an amazing workplace. I'm so lucky! State of the art!"

Laura's patience for all Trish's detail was stretching again. She wasn't able to be as thrilled. *No one could*, she told herself, then nodded at Trish. "OK, I'll talk to him until you get here."

"Thank you!"

"Don't worry, you just take care of Lucy." The two friends were close in person, though Laura was privately getting less patient with her friend's giddy mood. *Is it jealousy? Am I that shallow?* she wondered. Truth was that Laura was faced daily with an overwhelming stress because of Jack. Laura's teeth gritted together at the mere thought of Jack's mind games. She kept pushing it off, not wanting to deal with it, but anyone could see that Laura's overall mental and emotional health was being strained.

The white cheddar curds were ready for cheddaring. The white mass of curd was resting on the bottom of her tank. With push of a button the curds were raised up and out of the whey, then sliced into slabs, three inches by seven inches. These were moved to trays where the curd was kept at one hundred degrees and turned every fifteen minutes. This cheddaring step usually kept three people busy for the two hours required. Laura pulled Joyce in. "It's called cheddaring. It's a warm job, you'll think you were in a sauna when you're done, but you can do this. Matt and Britney will show you how. I need to do something for a friend. Are you OK with this?"

Joyce was game, "Yes, it looks fun."

Joyce and Laura had bonded between Joyce's good advice and Laura's teaching of a new trade. Laura settled at her desk and double checked her inventory of ingredients against the list of the various products she'd be making in the couple weeks. The grand opening of Providence Foods had been the week before, and her cheese and other dairy products were well accepted. Now Laura poured over a full list of her finest recipes, concentrating and strategizing to make a master plan.

The crew's break room was nearby so as they took a break, Laura found herself rising to close her door so she could focus. Sitting again, she focused intently. She heard a quiet 'hi' so looked up at the door. No one was there.

"Hey, I'm over here." She looked around. "On the computer." Laura turned and found herself staring into Trish's brother's deep brown eyes. "Hi, I'm James." Chocolate brown eyes and a warm, brown sugar complexion caught Laura's mind by surprise. She grinned and gave a sigh. He tried again, "What's your name?"

"Uh, Laura, Laura Zimmermann. Yes, I'm Laura, Trish is going to be here shortly. She's assisting with an emergency surgery."

"Ah, saving the world one little animal at a time?"

"Well, this one is a big animal. A cow named Lucy. She's a good cow."

"Oh, are there bad ones?"

"Well, if they get hard to deal with, they become, um, hamburger."

James noted, "It's good they don't do that with people." Laura paused and smiled nervously. James asked, "Are you from around there?"

"North Dakota? No, I'm from Vermont."

"Vermont. Green Mountains, Montpellier is your capitol. And, let's see, you are not on one of the Great Lakes."

"Yes, that's all true."

"It's surprising what ya remember from high school. What's the weather like right now?"

"It's been rainy and cool."

Suddenly a man's voice asked, "What are you doin'?! James watched helplessly as Laura was pulled from her chair. "Can't I trust you at all?" The man accused her, "Sneakin' around, talkin' to strangers on the internet?!?" She was in trouble, but out of view. He couldn't see Laura, but he heard the slap and the man's rough whispers were followed by what James knew to be a female whimper.

"Hey," James shouted, "She did nothing wrong! I'm waiting to talk to my sister, Trish O'Malley." There was no response. He saw moving shadows. Had they left the room? James' fingers threaded together as he began to pray. God had gotten him out of tough scrapes before. Now he hoped to relay his luck with answered prayers on to the pretty blonde who had flitted into and then was yanked out of his life.

Soon Trish came running and slid to a stop next to Laura's desk. With a wide grin she sat and said, "There you are!"

"You're a sight for my sore eyes. How's the cow?"

"Resting, I can't stay long."

"Hey, tell me the name of the woman who was there."

"Oh, she was here? Good. That was Laura Zimmermann. I don't know where she went." Trish stretched to see out the window and reported, "Oh, she's out in the parking lot talking to her boyfriend."

"Trish, he just yanked her out of that chair and accused her of flirting, which she wasn't. I mean we were talking about Vermont and the weather. Trish, I heard two things that concern me. I heard what sounded like a slap, and I think she was crying."

Trish looked again out the window. "Yes, I see that."

"What's happening?"

"He's talking and she's crying."

"Can you describe for me what the hell his problem is?"

"He's my boyfriend's roommate. Oh, James, you have to meet Nick."

"That's your boyfriend, Nick?"

"Yes, oh, he is such a honey!"

"Good, good. OK, and the roommate?"

"He's a recovering alcoholic and I understand he's on a dry drunk, but I don't know what that means. He's been unpredictable and mean. She said he's been under a lot of stress."

"She's making excuses? Hey, I've been here for six years. I know stress on intimate terms. Even under stress a man doesn't treat his woman like that. Trish, you need to do something. I would but I can't. I'm a million miles away."

"Well, I've been wondering, what can I do? I don't know."

"Do you know where he works?"

"Yes, he works with me, sort of."

"Go to your boss and your boyfriend. They need to confront this guy. His name?"

"Jack."

"I'll be home in two weeks for Dad's birthday. Tell Laura Zimmermann that I'm pulling for her, OK?"

"OK. There's an extra bedroom in my house. I'll get it ready for you."

"Good, and I'll have to find a job."

"Dad figures you'll be running cattle with him."

"At Belle Fourche?" He didn't sound convinced. "We'll see."

"No, he's selling half the herd to my boss, next spring, I think that's the deal. You'd be living here with Dad and me."

"That could work but don't promise Dad anything. I want to check out my options. I know you like animals but I don't know that I want to fight with bullshit the rest of my life." He quoted their grandfather, "Bullshit or cowshit," they finished in unison, "the smell is the same."

Trish grinned, "You've got options. Just get home safe."

"Yeah, first I need to decompress."

"Post-Traumatic Stress Disorder?"

"Well, right now if I feel anger, depression, or anxiety, it's from what your friend's roommate and guys like him seem to get by with."

Finally, Halee connected with Father Christopher O'Donnell. As she dialed the tour guide's number she quickly prayed, "God, I don't know what he has to say, but please be with me and help me to understand." Prayer was starting to make more sense in her life.

The tour guide answered. Halee asked, "Father O'Donnell, please?"

"Hallo," he introduced himself in Spanish.

"Father," she said in poised English, "Do you speak English?"

"No, but I speak Irish. Is that close enough?"

"Yes, thank you. I'm an American. My name is Halee Rockford. I'm engaged to Will Sturlaugson."

"Will, you're engaged? He's gettin' married?"

"Yes, before we come to Peru to help you."

"Oh, is that it?"

"Yes, he's got a little baby."

"A wee babe?"

"Yes, and I'm a nurse."

"A happy family."

"Yes, we'll be married next week."

"Jesus, Mary, Joseph. Ma'am? Halee?"

"Yes, Halee."

"Halee, dear. Will, he can't be gettin' married."

"Why not?"

"It's been nigh on a year or so since he was here—it was last spring—your fall. When he was here he finally took Jesus Christ into his heart and embraced Christianity with all his heart."

"Yes, he told me that."

"Did he tell you he was called?"

"Called what? A nickname?"

"No, Halee, dear. He's called to be a priest."

"A Catholic priest?"

"Aye, lassie. He accepted the call when he was here and promised he'd go get ordained and come back to help me."

"Oh."

"Halee? I'm tellin' ya the God's honest truth. I'd never lie to ya, darlin'."

"OK."

"He has a wee babe? Are you the child's mother?"

"No, whoever the mother is, she abandoned the baby on his doorstep. He's a month old now."

"Jesus, Mary, Joseph."

"Father O'Donnell. I'm a Christian but I don't go to church much. The Catholic priests, they, uh…"

"We live a celibate, unmarried life. We marry the Church. She's our Bride."

"He accepted the call?"

"That's what he told me. I haven't heard from him but I guessed he was busy at some seminary. I've been prayin' for him. A Rosary every night. God only knows what he's thinkin'."

"Well, he baffles me."

"Aye. Where's he livin'?"

"At the ranch east of Westby, Montana in…"

"Aye, in northwestern North Dakota. I almost went there once. And the babe?"

"Young Chris?"

"He named him Chris?

"Yes, after his dad. They all live together. Sir, I'm calling off the wedding."

"Is that right?"

"It sounds like you've been a mentor to Will before. I'm thinking he'll be needing a mentor again."

After a long morning, Laura got another visit from Trish, relating the intelligence of Nick's new cat, Boris, a Siberian cat, like Alan's. Trish had been to the house where Nick, Jack, and Trish lived, and let Bobby Jo, Nick's new Golden Retriever, outside. Trish began, "This dog has obviously had some excellent training. Remember? Remember how Nick was able to balance a piece of bread on Bobby Jo's nose and verbally hold the dog still until he gave the 'OK'. I'm so proud of those critters! Ha!"

Laura doodled around her psychologist Roberta Simpson's phone number. No doubt Roberta had other clients to attend to, but Laura promised herself that she would call and leave a message. Her message had been thus, "I'm embarrassed to ask, but how do I tell Polly-Anna-Trish to leave me alone and go be a happy, chatty-Kathy somewhere else??"

The baking bread attracted one curious soul. Malla directed her new workers on the proper use of the steam oven that duplicated the special ovens she had used in Iceland. Neil loitered in the doorway hoping for a taste. "Always double check the controls and never be surprised when hungry store managers show up wanting handouts. They're like crows hovering over road-kill."

This comparison surprised him. His indignant stare soon melted into a broad smile. "You need someone to test that, don't you?" he asked, pointing to the fresh cracked wheat bread.

She waved him off, "Go, it's too hot and we're busy. I'll bring you a sample later." She continued in her instruction as Neil quietly backed out the door.

He took a stroll through the store checking the progress of installations. Four aisles were ready to be stocked. Shipments were starting to be delivered and his own band of new workers would soon need training. He stopped once at the butcher's block and twice in the cashier area to ask questions. By the time he made his full circle back to his desk, he had a visitor. Malla held a small plate with the fresh bread, a smear of Laura's butter, and a taste of Anna's homemade apricot jam, and handed him the butter knife. "Oh, now this looks promising. Thank you."

"This is the nicest-looking bite of the bunch. I took the opportunity to show them how cutting the bread when it's too warm is a mistake. The rest looks like an utter failure, but the training was successful, so thank you."

Neil's smile was setting off fireworks in Malla's head. "Did you say pleasing me was a mistake, but it makes you happy?"

She could see the flirtatious glint in his eye. Thoughts of romance had her stomach doing joyful flips as she considered her reply. "Maybe it just means the bread was too hot."

"Can I buy you dinner tonight? There's a nice steak house in Grafton. I'd like to get to know you, Malla."

"Dinner? Yes. Just dinner."

"Yes. Seven?"

She shrugged, "Seven, yes."

4 GONE HUNTING

After Jack's hostile behavior, witnessed by Trish's brother, both Anna and Alan had a 'come to Jesus meeting' with Jack. They had both been stern, and Jack seemed repentant for his rash behavior. The topic was dropped, the Zimmermanns opened their new grocery store, and begrudgingly, Jack behaved.

The country and townsfolk all agreed that the store was exactly what everyone in that corner of the world needed. It employed many more workers with amazing benefits, and Mountain was starting to bustle with activity.

But as exciting as the new store and the Fourth of July holiday was that year, early-July meant preparations for the annual ethnic party, August the Deuce. So distracted was everyone, that as Laura's life was feeling more and more crazed, her safety net around her was oblivious to her gradual drop, further and further into depression.

Jack came home one night and found her in tears. He'd had a truly stressful day having learned that the house being built for him was being delayed due to his poor credit. Now tears. He lost it and beat Laura. The next morning, Nick was the first to find her, bleeding and in shock.

Word spread quickly. Alan drove the car down the hill towards Nick's farm. Anna shook her head. "Cousin or not, he's out of line."

Alan agreed, "He needs some tough love."

Brandon, Laura, and Alan were all Zimmermann cousins. Brandon held Erin's hand. She was spitting mad and ready to tear into Jack. "Just stay calm, dear," Brandon cooed. "I know you're full term and you could go into labor any day, but do you really want to?"

Constantly reminded of the abuse she had endured, Erin's course tongue was on grand display, and understandably so. Erin's anger at her ex-husband, her baby's father, compounded her already hormonally rich emotional state. "She's not safe! We need to get her out of there!" This night brought back too many emotions resulting from her time in captivity, emotions that cut deep to her core. "She belongs in her own apartment, Brandon, right across from us." He held his arm around her shoulders. "I agree. My little cousin is not staying there another night, but you need to keep as calm as you can to avoid complications for yourself and the baby. Do you want to lose this baby?"

Brandon was right and she knew it. Erin's blood pressure had concerned her doctor in recent visits and she'd been told to avoid stress. Now she and her fun-loving roommate were in the middle of a stew of stressful emotion.

Trish and Nick were setting the table when their carload of company arrived. Trish smiled. "Come on in, everyone. Erin, honey, how are you? Is your blood pressure going down?"

"It was until this today," Erin quietly confided, rolling her eyes.

Brandon whispered to Trish. "We will only stay as long as she's safe."

Trish quietly nodded, "I understand. You protect her and that little one." She raised her voice. "Well, the lasagna's ready, Laura and Jack." She called up the stairway, "Supper's ready."

Jack appeared first. "Lasagna, that's one of my favorites." He sauntered into the dining room, unaware of the confrontational thoughts that surrounded him. Nick carried the delicious looking entrée to the table. Jack eyed his cousin, "Hey, Anna, my little pool shark cousin. I heard

you're pregnant. Ya finally made a man outta that virgin over there?"
Jack snickered. Alan's eyes glinted with steel as he smiled and waved
off the comment. Not getting a suitable reaction from Alan, he became
impatient with Laura. "Laura!" he called, "you're being rude. I wanna
eat." He looked again at the glass dish. "What are the rest of you gonna
have?"

Laura appeared from the stairway. She looked nervous and the women
all noted the extra layer of makeup that was painfully apparent to them.
Trish thought, *Is she hiding a bruise?* A flash of her conversations that
afternoon filled her mind. Now this was the fruit of those discussions. A
meal meant to surround and confront. Another car pulled into the yard.
Trish nodded quietly, "Now it begins."

Dave was accustomed to coming in the back door. Jack's appetite waned
when he saw his AA sponsor. "I don't need a ride tonight, Dave. You
don't need to be here."

Nick patted Dave's shoulder, "Sure he does. I invited him."

Finally aware of the ninth place set, Jack took a chair farthest away from
Dave, but was internally reeling when both Brandon and Alan sat on
either side. Dave shifted and took the spot right across from Jack. Dave
said, "Let's begin in prayer. God, grant me the serenity to accept the
things I cannot change, the courage to change the things I can, and the
wisdom to know the difference. Our Father, who art in heaven…"

The others continued in their prayer as Jack felt lured, snared, and
trapped. They said amen and Jack sneered, "What is this? Is this a meal
or is that lasagna just bait?"

Dave spoke directly, "Some people claim that you're on a dry drunk, but
that makes no sense. You're a mean drunk, and lately, though sober,
you're magnifying your anger with Alan or with me, or with God, I don't
know. But few people around this table would've known that when you
drink, you're a nasty, mean drunk."

"I'm sober," Jack defended.

"Yes and no. The bottle is taunting you in your mind. Your body wants the booze so much that your mind has convinced you that the alcohol is there, even without a drop, and your body reacts by getting mean and nasty. Now, Laura here. She's innocent. She has never known you when you were drinkin'. I'd guess the only one here at this table who might know anything about it is Anna."

Anna's blue-hazel eyes had turned black. "Yes, Jack, I've seen you this way when you've been drinking. Everyone always knew to clear a path for you and stay out of your way. You're a mean drunk. But my friend Laura comes along and loves you from the very start and you reward her unconditional love with violence."

Laura shook her head, "I didn't tell her, I swear, Jack."

Nick spoke up. "She didn't need to. I found her, bleeding, trying to hide from you, hoping you wouldn't come back. This isn't the only time that you've been rough with Laura. I talked to the butcher, Theo. Then there was Trish's brother who witnessed you yank Laura away from her own desk. Back then, a month ago or so, you promised that you'd be good, and you have been. Laura isn't sleeping upstairs with you anymore. She's going back to her own apartment. Brandon will be there on the couch and Rusty will be on the cot. Trish's brother James started this about a month ago, Jack. Laura had nothing to do with it. If you want to pick a fight, James'll be here in a couple weeks and he's Army Ranger Special Forces. His hands are lethal weapons and he'd love to rip you apart."

Alan nodded, "Laura, go pack your things. Anna and Trish, help her. Erin, go out into the car. Brandon and Nick? You take the ladies home. Dave and Jack and I have a few things to talk about. Trish, thanks for the lasagna, this looks good."

"Thanks, I have another pan to bake at Laura's apartment."

Jack shook his head, "A premeditated lynching."

Dave served himself some salad, "OK, Alan, you asked so now I'll tell you. A dry drunk can end in one of two ways." He reached for the

French bread, never taking his eyes off Jack. "Either an alcoholic can succumb to the craving for the alcohol, and then he's not a recovering alcoholic anymore, he's just an alcoholic."

Alan added, "An unemployed alcoholic."

Jack watched as Laura left, Trish and Nick carrying her bags. "Unemployed?" he asked.

"That's your call."

"Or," Dave continued, "he decides to absolutely change his mind and heart, avoid alcohol, returns to regular AA meetings for support, accepts the help of his higher power and his sponsor to handle life, one day at a time."

Alan repeated to clarify, "So a recovered alcoholic…"

"No, wait," Dave interrupted, "Recovering. We use the term recovering. There's no such thing as a recovered alcoholic. The only recovered alcoholic is a dead one."

Jack stared deep into his empty plate. Alan started again, "Jack, it sounds like Rambo is comin' after you in two weeks unless you change your ways. We just prayed for the courage to change, Jack. Dave and I are here to help you muster that courage."

While confrontation was the lot for some, Malla and Neil were looking at life through rosier lenses. True to his promise, Neil arrived at her home at seven o'clock. Dressed in a favorite colorful top, capris, and stylish sandals, Malla made a fashion statement, upgrading from her cotton white uniform. Neil, too, had made a shift from the humdrum, but allowed her color to outshine his subdued look. His white linen shirt had been pressed, its long sleeves rolled up. He reminded her of photos she'd seen of a handsome couple on winter vacation in Italy. "Are you ready?" he quietly asked.

Malla's mind replied, *take me anywhere!* She said aloud, "Yes. It's a nice evening."

They moved to his car and drove out of Cavalier while Brandon was bringing the others home; the carload was either in tears or angry over Laura's predicament. As a contrast Neil had soft guitar music playing in his car, gentile conversation. Indeed the evening was a glowing success in Neil's mind. The meal was delicious, the service superb. As they were finishing their meal, the conversation rolled around to children. Neil confessed. "Yes, I have one daughter, she just graduated from high school and is going to college in Grand Forks this fall. She's studying to be an actress."

"Is that right?" Malla responded. Reality was rearing. "Just one?"

"Yes."

"And she's grown."

"Empty nest. Yes, she just graduated, but I can already see there's more time to focus on my own interests, like you. I wanted to have more children but Alicia, my ex, she chose not to."

"What is with some women? They who can, won't. They who cannot, weep." Her voice trailed off.

Neil asked, "I'm sorry, what did you say?"

"Neil, you are very nice, but this won't work," she pointed from herself to him and back. "I cannot have my own children and I need to experience raising a family. For my soul I need that."

"Malla, I'm trying to understand."

"You're already done raising your child. I can't have children. I want children, even if they are some other woman's."

"You want to adopt?"

She excused herself to the ladies room. He waited in the lobby and they exited the restaurant quietly. As they settled in his car, the quiet instrumental music continued while she explained, "It is a nice evening. Neil, you are a very nice man. I'm glad to be working with you. Wasn't that a delicious meal?"

"Yes, it was. A good memory. Malla, I won't bother you anymore."

"You're no bother. I like you, you're a good person. I just don't see us going any further. OK?"

"I would've had more children if I could have. I have loved being a father. With my wife the way she was, my daughter has been my only consolation. It's a strong emotion that so many take for granted, parenthood. A rich blessing."

"Yes, it is, so you understand my need to wait for the right family."

"What if that family doesn't come along?"

"God already has a plan in the works. I met a man in Iceland. He's a widower and he's moving here with his family. He asked me to remember him as I was meeting new people. I got curious about you, Neil. Curious to know all the options. Now I know. I'm sure, very certain that this other man and I can have a future." Malla found herself exuding more faith and confidence in God than she would have believed, had she not already seen Drew with her own eyes. Indeed, God had a plan for her, an answer to her unspoken prayers, and her evening with Neil confirmed her dedication to waiting for them, Drew's children.

They visited on the long drive back to Cavalier, and then she stayed up pouring over Drew's emails and the photos of himself and all four children on his Facebook page. BJ cleaned up very well, the twins Tori and Nessa were identical and absolutely beautiful, and little Michael had his own innocent charms. The advantage of Drew was that the mother of his children wasn't an ex, she had died delivering his youngest, Michael.

A sad turn for Drew and his family for certain, but Malla quietly rejoiced how as she wouldn't have awkward moments on special days, or visitation schedules, and if she could convince them to call her Mother, in whichever the language, she wouldn't be competing with a second mother, confusing their hearts and hers. She typed an email to Drew asking, *Please call me at noon, your time, to wake me. I need to talk to you, I want to talk to you. I miss you.*

She fell asleep pondering their faces and was awoken at six o'clock to Drew's charming voice. "Good morning, Malla," he spoke in Icelandic. "I miss you, too."

"I want you all here, now. How much longer do I have to wait?"

"School is out this week. We're packing. Every night we're making some progress."

"Have you found a house?"

"No. I guess there's a housing shortage there right now."

"I have four extra bedrooms. If the twins share then…"

"That's a big commitment, Malla. Are you sure?"

"Yes, please, wrap me in your arms and never let me go."

"Oh, yes, darling Malla, I will, but you do understand, I have four LOUD children. BJ is a fair example of how wild they can get."

"My soul needs to be their mother and my heart needs a good man, like you. I see their faces, but I want to know their voices, too."

"We're coming. I long to rest my head on your pillow, Malla. Can you meet us at the airport in Minneapolis? This Saturday, two thirty in the afternoon, your time?"

"Yes, yes, I'll be there and we'll travel on home together."

"Home, that sounds so good."

~*~*~*~

Memories from her secret shopper trip with Nick, to find a new veterinarian, were gradually getting worked into several embellished scrapbooked pages. Trish worked at it every night after kissing her sweetheart good night, though her mornings and days were filled with setting up the new vet clinic. The trip from North Dakota to Colorado to Georgia to Vermont and home again had been exhausting but exhilarating, ending with having brought two veterinarians, Dr. Keith Spencer and Dr. Bill Tappan, both back to visit with Alan and Anna. As Trish had expected, both were hired.

Another serious outcome of their travels was that Nick agreed to completely drop the deadline for her telling the truth. That is, the truth about how, under Jim's roof, his son Austin, Trish's brother, had molested Trish at the age of 18. *No deadline, no pressure*, she recalled him to say.

Relieved of that burden, Trish's days were full with all the details of setting up her new clinic, but any extra time away from work was spent with Nick and the new animals they had brought back from their journey. The pair were inseparable since she had finally returned his quiet 'I love you' whispers with the humble, but sincere, "I love you, too, Nick," on their flight back to North Dakota.

That morning Jim was eyeing his lawn. It needed trimming again but he maintained, grumbling to himself, "I can mow my own lawn. I ain't payin' to have it done anymore!"

Nick arrived at Trish's house and saw Jim in the backyard. "Good morning, Chief. How goes it?"

Jim laughed at himself, "I must be nuts. I actually want to mow my lawn. Sure sign of healing, right? And you?"

"I think I might be rested up, finally, from that road trip with Trish." He stood quietly, staring into the petals of a rose, "She had me going in circles. Mr. O'Malley, you have one very lovely daughter."

"Her mom gets all the credit. Suppose I gave her some chromosomes."

The younger gentleman offered, "Wanna go juneberry pickin'?

The pair headed out to one of the well-guarded spots that Anna had alerted Nick to. As they drove, Jim noted, "Trish told me about the confrontation with Jack."

"Yes, I'm not even two months from major surgery and I can't really defend myself yet. I can't sleep wondering if he's gonna try to rearrange the organs I have left. It's like waiting for Frank Miller and his boys in *High Noon*.

"*High Noon*, Gary Cooper?"

"A classic."

"I remember it, but you're not surrounded by cowards, Nick. It'll be OK."

"He's just so unpredictable, Jim. I'm worried."

"Stay here, the couch is open downstairs. Trish has the spare bedroom upstairs torn apart to get ready for James."

"Good, James. I can't wait to meet him. What's he like?"

"I don't rightly know. I haven't seen him since he was seventeen."

"He didn't visit on leave?"

"He went to Fargo to see Trish, but we were calving and the weather was against us. We couldn't just up and leave. Then when we were caught up, he was gone again. Trish took some pictures. He's all grown up."

"What sort of work is he going to want to do?"

"I want him to help me run cattle, but Trish warned me to not hold my breath."

The pick-up stopped at a specific GPS coordinate. Nick studied his notes and the bushes around him, "OK, we walk in from here."

Jim surprised him. "Rules are rules. I grew up picking berries with my Grandpa. His rule was when you are out in nature, you shut up."

Nick brushed the dust from his ball cap and chuckled, "Agreed." It was a peaceful morning. But when they returned home and checked the mail at the post office, they learned from Magnus Gudmundson of Jack's latest trick.

Anna gave them the report. Dave Walters has a serious head injury and both Jack and Laura were gone. They disappeared. All the aging chambers and milk tanks had been checked before Nick and Trish and Jim arrived to help. Anna trembled, "This is déjà vu for when Erin disappeared, except now we have two good witnesses. They saw both Jack and Laura here on this farm, and then they saw Jack leaving, alone. She's here somewhere." All heads turned to hear a shrill scream. Nick arrived first as they all sprinted into the barn. Katlyn, Candy and Buddy's foster-daughter, had found Laura in one of the horse stalls.

Nick called 9-1-1 while Trish checked her out. "She's still breathing."

"Praise God!" Anna declared.

Katlyn came running with a first aid kit and a drink of water. Laura's face was bleeding, but otherwise, she was sound. Anna called Alan to report, "Laura's here. She's OK, now find Jack before anyone else gets hurt."

The ambulance, including their new volunteer, Rene LaRoque, was leaving with Laura, as Nick was offering Alan his help. He was told, "It's too dangerous for you. Hey, I've got an army of men able to help. 'Course, we have to milk late tonight, but we'll find him. Your latest check-up, what did the doc say?"

"I'm able to ride bikes and lawn mowers, but no plowed fields yet and no horses."

"Horses. That's what we should do. Brandon, head up a cavalry and scour the escarpment and ravines. Take all the horses, even the Icelanders. I'm taking a posse of pickups through the back roads." He turned to Nick. "Go, I know you've wanted to try out your new mower."

"Alright, I'll stay out of your way."

Alan directed a warning gaze at Dustin, Katlyn's older and wilder brother, "Dustin, you stay here."

"But I can help!" he protested. Dustin disappeared with a huff and Alan turned his attention to the growing group of men who awaited instruction.

Katlyn's wispy blonde hair flew in the breeze as she watched her brother sneak away with his bicycle. He had been scolded before for taking his life in his hands while biking down the steep gravel road that dropped four hundred feet at a six percent grade. There were no curves to break its steepness, only a straight shot up or down. Dustin thrilled in the downhill ride. Dangerous, but he loved to be daring. *But just like with hunting, it's all about timing.*

Internally Katlyn prayed and cheered for her brother. *He has every right to look for Jack,* she thought, *after all, I had found Laura,* she reasoned. She was thirteen, Dustin was a gutsy fourteen-year-old.

He had reached the gravel T-shaped intersection that would lead him to Schroeder's Hill. Dustin stayed off the road, his bike hidden beneath the lone spiraling evergreen. Dustin was surrounded by burr oaks. He looked below his feet to see deer droppings. Before him was the road that led to home.

Both Dustin's foster-dad, Buddy Hanneson, and Alan were working with Dustin to teach him hunting skills. Dustin stayed still as Alan's posse of pickups split into two groups before him, to the left and right. Now he had a choice: to follow the pickups or head out on his own. He looked at the sky. In the year and a half since moving next door into Candy and Buddy's home, they had been encouraged at every turn to bring their problems to God. Dustin never admitted it, but when he was allowed out to hunt rabbits he was prone to give the hunt to God and let Him lead the way. After all, He knew where the extra rabbits were, of this Dustin was sure.

Now he used the same childlike faith and nodded, smiling at the steep gravel road, "Let's do it!" he whispered. A doe and her fawn watched Dustin mount his bike, careful to keep his feet away from the pedals as he started to coast downhill. The wheels spun as fast as Dustin's adrenaline rushed. Once he got to the bottom he still had plenty of inertia to keep him rolling another half mile. That's when he saw a flash of white in the trees to the north. Dustin hopped off his bike and dug his binoculars out of his back pack.

Focusing, he could see it was Jack watching the pickups leaving. Dustin crouched to stay low on Jack's horizon. By habit he checked the wind by dropping sand onto the ground, then remembered Jack's nose wasn't anything like that of a deer or rabbit. But he had also seen Jack using binoculars. Again, Dustin looked to the sky.

He climbed back onto his bike and started to head directly for Jack down the section road. Dustin started to whistle and sing a song he had been forced to learn in school. Then, less than a quarter mile short of Jack's location, Dustin pulled off the road and pulled a retractable fishing rod from his back pack. He stood by the culvert that flowed with summer rain run-off and cast out his line.

Jack smiled as he peered through his eyeglass. "Goofy kid, there's no fish in there." He shrugged him off and continued on his journey. He was very familiar with the area having grown up playing in the woods below his great-grandparents' house. Jack had left Providence Farm in Laura's red Escort then hid that and doubled back to the office. As everyone hovered over Laura, Jack was stealing check blanks out of Ila's desk. He still had signatory power from Alan and Anna's honeymoon, and snidely reasoned that he'd be needing a few things. Now he had climbed down off the escarpment and was in the trees, brush, and creeks that flowed through Nick's farm.

Nick had the mower out and was checking the fluids and tires. The maiden run of any vehicle is an exciting thing. Nick felt useless in not being able to help in the man hunt. The mower was his consolation.

The small engine started, but after being tested, the throttle stuck open. He tinkered as the noise overwhelmed his sense of hearing, focused on the task at hand.

Jack's original idea was to start Nick's barn and house on fire, but a distracted foe with no hearing was an extra bonus. He found boards next to the compost bin. Alan had built it and he loathed Alan and all the goodness he stood for, so it was poetic justice that one of Alan's boards should be used to render his snoopy roommate unconscious, as Jack burned the buildings. Jack walked up behind Nick and took careful aim. The plan: first a shot to Nick's tender side and lone kidney, then a strong blow to the head.

The small engine roared as Jack took his stand. A sharp bite to his shoulder stopped him. He looked behind. Nothing but woods. Again, Jack turned to take aim. Now a sharp bite to his leg. Jack looked to see blood flowing. The deafening noise of the small engine blared, but it covered Dustin's voice into his walkie-talkie. Now he knew Alan and the posse were on their way. Dustin again took aim and squeezed the trigger of his pellet gun. He only wanted to wing him, so Dustin kept out of sight and squeezed off one good shot after another.

Both Jack's arms, both legs, and a shot in each of his butt-cheeks kept Jack as distracted as Nick. In Dustin's mind he compared him to a wounded bear and hid behind the trees between shots. Suddenly, Nick stopped the engine and went to the shop for tools. That was when Jack scrambled to hide in the compost bin. From within the fenced box where Jack hid, he could hear the nearby songbirds' calls quickly replaced by the roar of several pickups coming and the faint sound of a walkie-talkie's squelch.

Alan and the county sheriff drove straight to the compost bin and the officers quickly secured Jack, causing him to wince. Rusty asked, "Why are you bleeding?"

"I don't know! Who is it??" Jack hollered towards the woods. "Who's out there!?!"

Nick was finally aware of his surroundings. He watched as Dustin stepped out of the woods holding his pellet gun. "Hey, Alan, I decided to go hunting rabbits, Jack rabbits," he joked.

"Dustin Keifer?" the sheriff peered over the barrel of his own gun.

Alan winced, "Yes, that's him."

The deputies cuffed Jack as their sheriff warned, "Keifer, you'd better stick to rabbits from now on. Alan? Buddy? This is serious. Dustin? You could be charged and be behind bars in a heartbeat. Do you understand? Rabbits only, do I have your word?"

"Yes, sir."

"Don't disappoint me, boy. Your folks already made enough mistakes, don't follow down their path."

"Yes, sir."

Nick was in a daze as he watched the drama move around him. Suddenly realizing how vulnerable he had been, his hands shook uncontrollably.

Jack could have been charged with two counts of attempted murder, but neither Laura nor Dave would press charges, hoping to jump start Jack's recovery. They were treated and released and doctors worked to get the pellets out of Goliath's thighs, shoulders, and derriere before they admitted him to a nearby treatment center. Jack's eyes hid any hint to the truth. He felt no remorse but played the game he'd come to know from his string of treatment centers. Instead he contemplated revenge and the location of the items he'd stashed. Alan's blank checks would come in handy. Revenge would be sweet. He could taste it.

5 AMID THE CHAOS

With Jack safely contained and getting the psychological help he needed, Nick and Trish relaxed and sorted photos of their travel cross-country. Malla was making plans to travel to Minneapolis to meet Drew's family, and bring them to her home. But down the street at the apartment building, Laura was a whole other matter.

Erin tried to console, "Hey, of all people, Laura, I understand the chaos, the turmoil and how you feel like you need to protect him. Somehow. But believe me, it's not worth it."

"But I do love him, don't I?" Laura sobbed.

Joyce replied, "No matter how often you tell yourself that you love him, he is so far over that line of what's rational that you'll only drive yourself over that line, too. It's like he wants to drag you down, too. Misery loves company."

"Oh, Joyce and Erin, I need a vacation!" Laura moaned.

Anna overheard as she walked into the apartment. "Vacation? Good idea. Where do you want to go?"

Laura laughed, "Oh, the Bahamas, Montego Bay, maybe the Virgin Islands." She thought she was joking, but was shocked when Anna picked up the phone.

She said, "Ila, please arrange a vacation for Laura. The Carribean for a week, no, ten days so she can leave tomorrow." Away from the phone Anna asked, "Do you want to take anyone with you?"

Joyce raised her hand and smiled wide. Laura looked at Erin at seven months pregnant. Erin shook her head. "Joyce, call Eva. The three of us will go. And, Anna? I want to go to Vermont for a long weekend. Be realistic. I'll be back in time to get the last minute work done before the Grand Opening," Laura promised. She turned to Erin. "I know it sounds like I'm escaping reality, but I'm taking my Al-Anon friends along and if Jack asks about me tell him I'm getting my head on straight and he might get a second chance but he needs to listen to the doctors or there's no way. OK? If he does his part and tries to get better, maybe I'll find some real love. Tough love, but love none the less."

Anna hugged her, knowing in her heart that Jack needed a strong woman like Laura, but terribly unsure of her pool shark cousin.

Malla waited nervously near the airport door. Were they having trouble with customs? She mulled it over. He was a Canadian citizen with Canadian children, arriving from Iceland, all planning to live and work in the States. Malla tried to remember the various VISA restrictions, wondering how much had changed since she moved from Iceland. Deep in thought she stared over the heads of people passing by until a tall blonde surrounded by four blonde children all mounted the escalator above. BJ was in the lead but turned to walk up the escalator, playing with his sisters. Together they all three jumped onto the stable floor at the same time. Drew held Michael's hand and waved at Malla. BJ and the girls skirted around Drew and tried to climb the machine again.

Drew smiled at Malla. "BJ has been looking forward to seeing you," he said, then pushed the boy forward.

BJ laughed and turned to Malla, "Hi, we meet again."

Drew reached his arm around Malla for a half hug and introduced in English, "Malla, this is BJ, Nessa, Tori and Michael."

"Nessa's in blue. OK, hello. Very good to meet you all." Michael protested, squirming to Drew's side. "What's wrong?" Malla innocently asked.

"His English isn't very good. BJ's Icelandic is terrible. The girls? They have their own language."

Malla bent down to Michael, both girls listening intently. In Icelandic she explained, "Michael, there's no need to fuss. See? I know Icelandic, too." She looked at Nessa and Tori adding, "And Spanish and Norwegian and Danish and German and some Swahili. You let me know if you want to learn any of those, OK? Maybe you can teach me your language, too."

Michael peered at her, "Danish with frosting?"

"Yes, I'm a baker and I make Danish with frosting, too."

Tori was direct. "Daddy said you can cook and you're his girlfriend. Is that right?"

"Yes, I can and I am."

Tori retreated to Nessa's side where they shared their own language. "Drabia caf solle." Malla heard and studied the girls.

Drew broke in, "Malla? Oh, it's good to see you." He kissed her cheek. "We should get going." An airport attendant stood with a large rack of luggage at Drew's side.

"Yes, I got the rental trailer we discussed. Actually, I got a different car, too. The Fiat I had would never be big enough." She instinctively reached for the hand of the child closest to her, Nessa, and started off. Nessa held back until she had Tori's hand and the three led the way. Tori stumbled on a curb and fell. Malla swooped in and picked her up, brushing her blonde wispy hair from her face. "Drabia caf solle?" The girls giggled. "What did I say?"

Nessa grinned, "We can't say."

"Because it's silly?" The girls shrugged as they walked. "Because it's not nice?" Nessa nodded.

"Girls," Drew's voice boomed, "what are you saying?"

"Drabia caf solle," Malla repeated and the girls snickered. They had reached her new car, a van with seating for seven, and the rental trailer.

The men unloaded their luggage while the children explored the van. BJ started to sing a melody Malla couldn't make out, but gradually, finally she recognized his letters. "R-O-C-K in the U-S-A. "R-O-C-K in the U-S-A," he repeated over and over.

Drew tipped the airport worker and listened to his children, finally alone with Malla outside the car. "Where did he get that song?" Malla asked.

Drew listened and laughed, "It's been a long trip." He reached for her hands and pulled her to himself. "Thank you so much for being willing to take us in, under your wing." He kissed her on her soft lips.

For Drew the moment stood still until BJ commented, "Dad, that's gross."

Drew countered, "Get used to it," and turned back to Malla with more tender affection. Michael wasn't annoyed by watching Malla with his dad. He looked at them and smiled as BJ and the girls squirmed.

When Malla finally mounted the driver's seat and put her new key into the ignition, she heard a surprising question. Drew was checking seatbelts and Nessa asked, "Is this going to be like when Inge stayed with us?"

BJ added, "You were always tired and sleeping a lot."

Tori chimed in, "She was dumb and she smelled."

Drew backed up from the back seat toward Malla. He crouched before Michael and BJ and the twins looked on from the back seat. He twisted to face Malla saying, "Inge was a mistake," then back to his children, "and no, Malla will have her own room." Quietly he said to Malla, "We need to teach them morals."

"Yes, that's right. I have my own room," she announced. "And I bought new beds and bedding for all of you. Your father's room is farthest away from me. Your rooms are in between so we can both hear you at night. If you think I'm dumb, I'd like you to tell me to my face, so I can defend myself. If I think you're wrong about something, I will do the same. Once the grocery store opens, I will work early in the mornings and your dad will be handling breakfast and getting you ready for school, but I get off at noon and I have the afternoons to cook a tasty meal for us all, and time to attend your games and programs and help with homework, and I love to read bedtime stories."

BJ smiled at Drew, "She's got Inge beat."

Malla concluded, "And what your father and I do after you go to sleep is none of your business. Michael, is that OK?" He nodded, smiling. "Nessa?" She looked at Tori and shrugged. "Tori?" She nodded. "BJ?"

His voice was boisterous, "Let's do it!" as Drew moved to his seat and closed the door.

Malla confessed, "I'm not promising I'll be perfect, but I want you to give me a chance, Drew."

"Let's do it," he echoed, then reached over to kiss her again. BJ groaned and Drew repeated, "Get used to it." Malla hesitated to put the car into gear. "What's wrong?" Drew asked, looking around.

"Seat belt," she simply said, pointing at Drew. She glanced at Michael who grinned all the more.

The van and trailer pulled out of the airport onto the freeway. "Malla?" Drew began, "Will you let me pay you a boarding fee? The beds and bedding and extra food…"

"Yes," she nodded, "plus that will keep the gossip mongers at bay. I am not just any Inge."

"No, that's true. You decide on an amount."

"Besides the luggage do you have things being shipped?"

"Yes, part of the luggage is their favorite blankets and summer clothes and favorite toys. Winter gear is being shipped along with a few pieces of furniture including my desk. I'll be working from home until the hotel is built."

"Any kitchen gear?"

"No. What I had was pretty primitive. I left it for charity."

BJ piped up. "How cold does it get?"

Malla replied, "I don't know. I just moved from Milwaukee."

Drew offered, "It'll be weather like Manitoba." BJ nodded then shivered. He was the only one of the children who remembered Canada.

Malla watched him in her rear view mirror adding, "But not as dark as Iceland."

He confessed, "I hated the dark."

"Around Christmas the sun goes down at about 4 PM and up again at eight in the morning. But the weather is colder than in Iceland."

BJ stared at the businesses along the freeway. He still wondered about making friends, about bullies, and about what his teacher would be like.

Malla broke into his musings peering into the rear view mirror, "There are lots of kids in the neighborhood. You'll be able to make friends before school starts." BJ looked at the back of her head. Could she read his mind?

After a long drive and two bathroom breaks Malla pulled the van and trailer to a stop in front of a two-story home with a gambrel roof and cedar shakes.

Michael asked Malla as she unhooked his seatbelt, "Do you have a dog?"

"No, not yet. Should we get one?"

"Dad, can we?" the twins asked at once.

Drew replied from the back of the trailer, "It's up to Malla, it's her house."

"Yes, children need pets, lots of pets. OK, let's go pick out your room. Drew, I've got burgers ready for a picnic," she called as Drew unhooked the trailer door.

BJ peered down the street eyeing a boy on a skateboard. "Go," Malla encouraged, "introduce yourself."

"Malla! We need keys," Nessa and Tori called from the door.

Malla and Michael raced from the car to the front door. Michael won. The children giggled under her and Michael hugged her legs. Malla sighed and unlocked the door. "Go, explore!"

Nessa asked, "Malla, which room is ours?"

Malla was confident, "You'll know it when you see it, I'm sure." The children ran through the living room and dining room, through the kitchen and half bathroom and through what Malla knew would be Drew's office, racing to open one door after another. They all looked perplexed. Malla stood at the bottom of the stairs as Drew entered with a load of luggage.

Tori whined, "Where are the bedrooms?"

With a simple point of her finger, they bounded up the flight of stairs to open more doors. Malla took a suitcase in each hand and led Drew up. Both girls squealed, "Daddy!! It's beautiful! It's purple!!" they bounced.

"Yes, I saw your pictures. I could tell you like purple!" She had also lined each window sill with new dolls and toys.

Michael was quieter in his awe. Drew saw him in the hall and sensed his quiet joy. Drew pushed the door open and saw Michael kneeling next to the train set that encircled his bed and went under a desk and around a dresser. Drew pushed the button on the train to start the bells and whistles. The bed was covered in a quilt that was covered with cars and trucks of every sort. Next to the closet was a large red barn surrounded by a wooden corral. Inside it were several horses, cows, pigs and sheep. And a large rug on the floor was colored with streets and roads for his little boy amusement.

Drew quietly asked, "Do you like your room?" Michael nodded, his smile beaming. Drew encouraged, "Then go tell Malla you like it." His little legs scurried and caught Malla unaware as he wrapped his arms around her legs for a stronger than expected bear hug. She was in the twins' room next to the small table spread with tea cups and a purple ruffled tablecloth.

Drew followed him and set down a heavy black suitcase and Nessa quickly pulled the zipper. It was their toy box. As Malla stood locked in Michael's love-grip, she cooed to him in Icelandic as she ruffled his hair and watched the girls pull tutus and jeweled crowns from the case. They each donned their netted ruffles and royal tiaras and each grabbed a doll from the window sill, scampering off down the hall to open more doors, leaving Malla, Michael, and Drew looking on.

"Tell her what you told me," Drew encouraged.

"I like my room." Bashfully he added, "I like you!"

Malla melted and bending on one knee to his height she hugged his little shoulders, "I love you, too, Michael. Did you find the story books? Go, look. I'll help your daddy. Oh, wait. Come by the bathroom door," she directed. She led them to the door and Malla showed Drew the extra piece of trim. "This board is for measurements." She demonstrated with Michael next to the wooden trim and made a notch with the label 'M 6-09'. Drew caught the girls as they ran by.

"Daddy, we found your room!" Nessa exclaimed.

Tori pointed, "Ya, you're down there and Malla's over there," her finger twisting to the opposite direction, "just like she said."

"How do you know it's mine? Maybe it's Malla's room."

"No, silly, hers has pretty shoes in her closet."

"Girls, you stay out of Malla's things."

Malla smiled, "Not today, but one day soon, we'll play dress up with those shoes and I have a box of my grandma's old dresses and hats and long strings of pearls. Alright?"

Both girls giggled and squirmed. "Here, let's measure you," Drew grinned.

Malla did the labeling honors. Once done she asked, "Where's BJ?"

He came bounding up the stairs. "Where's my room?"

"Here, measure first," Drew directed, marking the spot.

BJ explained, "Carter, my friend down the street? He said I have new roller blades!" Drew released him and Malla opened the nearby door to his room.

BJ turned on the switch. Cued by Drew's comment about BJ's interest in space travel, the walls were painted dark blue and white Christmas lights were strung on the walls and across the ceiling. Where the central ceiling light would hang there was a model of the sun and the solar system rotating around it. Even the moons around the planets were included. Malla opened the shades and the extra light shone on two of his other interests: a guitar and a piano keyboard. On the floor next to the night stand was the pair of rollerblades.

Malla noted, "If they're not the right size, we can exchange them. Your dad said you have pads." BJ scrambled to try them on. Once his foot slipped into the skate, his face confirmed Malla's hopes. "Good, OK, and girls? Carter has a little sister who's seven. Her name is Nora. BJ? Show your dad and the girls where Carter lives. I'm starting supper. Picnic in the backyard in half an hour. Come when you hear the dinner bell. Oh, and bedtime is early tonight. You've had a very long day."

"Yes," Drew sighed, "we were up very early."

"Go, meet the neighbors. I'll start supper."

BJ asked, "What's for supper?"

"Cheeseburgers, potato chips and cookie salad. Scoot."

Malla found herself alone in her kitchen. Had the last four days been real? They were a blur for certain. The shopping and painting. The long nights unpacking her own boxes. Cleaning and fussing with the last minute flurry to set up toys and bedding. Preparing burgers. It had been too much. Malla was ready for an early bedtime, too. Before long she heard little feet running in the door. They stopped at the kitchen. "Malla! This is Nora."

"Hello, again, Nora."

"She wants to see our room."

Nora's father, Don, peeked around the corner. "Hi, Malla, you sure have a houseful now!"

"That's true," she agreed as she uncovered her hamburger patties and Don helped Drew with luggage. The men soon finished their chore and came in search of refreshments.

Drew squinted, looking at the lemonade on the picnic table. "Do you have adult beverages?"

Malla pointed with her wooden spoon, "Beer in the fridge and brandy and cognac above the stove."

The men agreed on beer, but Drew studied the bottles above the stove as he and Don discussed the neighborhood and the town of Cavalier. As Don spoke, Drew kept watching Malla working to set the picnic table. Every fluid movement had him intrigued. "Burgers are ready," she simply announced.

Drew asked over his beer, "Where's the dinner bell?"

Malla reached for the clanger and stretched above the potted flower by the patio door. The old metal triangle made a loud racket. "OK," Don nodded, "That's my cue to collect my varmints and skedaddle."

Malla explained, "Don has helped me with a few projects. I'd like to invite you and your family for a picnic, but not tonight. They've had such a long day."

"And you've had some long nights."

Drew looked from the fatigue in Malla's eyes to the house around him. Everything had been perfect until he and his motley crew had descended upon her. BJ arrived out of breath responding to the bell. Malla passed him in the kitchen. "Take off rollerblades in the house." A simple request, but bit by bit Drew could see that Malla was laying the law down with a tender hand.

As appetites were satisfied, Malla looked around the table. Her deep seated need to mother was satisfied as the four young faces around the table chatted with her. She glanced at the quieter than usual Drew and soon saw him dozing, leaning on his elbows. BJ confirmed, "He didn't get a nap on the plane when we did. And, he was up doing laundry and packing. Siggi and some others were over and stayed until late last night. I heard him tell Siggi that he hadn't been sleeping at night lately 'cause he was thinking about you."

"Me?" Malla was surprised. That sounded silly to Malla. Her fatigue was due to long nights of working to set up house for her young charges, but she hadn't given their father even a second thought. She watched him, his head minutely rising and falling with every slow breath.

BJ added, "He used to sleep all night like this."

"At the table?"

"Yeah, he'd put us to bed and then sit at the table. He said he didn't like his bed, but I knew he was missing Mamma." Malla looked at the half-eaten plate in front of Drew, emotions slowly pulling at her heart. BJ finished the last bite of his second burger and added, "That's when he met Inge."

"Was Inge nice to you?"

Tori repeated, "She was dumb."

BJ countered, "She wasn't used to kids. I don't think she liked us."

"How long did Inge stay with you?"

"A couple months. Dad was sad again after that."

"How long ago was this?"

"A couple years ago, we were five," Nessa said licking her spoon. "Michael was still in diapers," she giggled.

Malla looked at Michael who also started to doze. She pulled the sleepy boy into her lap and with eyes closed he cuddled into her bosom. She kissed the top of his head and quietly suggested, "I'll put him on the couch and we'll get the food put away. Can you three help me load the dishwasher? Then a quick bath and a short story tonight. With a full tummy and a hot bath you'll all sleep well, alright?" Her eyes studied them. They accepted this and every one of her suggestions. Yes, she was no Inge. She looked again at Drew. "Will he be OK?"

BJ smirked, "He'll sleep there all night."

Malla frowned, "Well, that won't do. The dew will fall, he'll get cold, and mosquitoes will carry him away." She looked again at Michael and the rest of her brood. One thing at a time, she handled the bedtime chores and with BJ's help, she managed to get Drew up the stairs and into his bed but was surprised by the next challenge.

"He has contacts," BJ announced. "I'll find his case."

As BJ dug through the black suitcase on Drew's bedroom floor, Malla pulled off his shoes and loosened his leather belt. The khaki cotton slacks he wore would have to suffice for pajamas for the night. BJ came to her side with the contact case and a small bottle of cleanser. She poked at Drew's arm, "Drew, wake up, you need to pull your contacts out." Her efforts were fruitless so one by one she pulled his eyelids open and slowly, carefully, she retrieved the left, then the right. Malla whispered, "Where are his glasses?"

"Here in his shaving kit."

"Hey, little man," Drew said drowsily, "thanks for taking care of me. I see you've got a pretty helper. I think that's what I see."

"Yeah, she is. OK, I'm goin' to bed."

Malla stood as Drew sat up. "OK, you can't blind me and then not know where my glasses are."

"Here, right here," she said handing them off. He held her hand with one hand and managed his glasses with the other. His charm, sleepy as it was, was making her nervous. "You need more sleep."

"Yes, that's true, but I need to brush my teeth first." He pulled himself up and off the bed and standing tall, stretched. A quick dig into his suitcase was rewarded with his PJ bottoms and a clean white t-shirt. Drew stood unbuttoning his shirt, looking Malla over. As his bare chest was revealed, he explained, "If you want to stay here tonight that sounds great, then this is the way this works: first I take off something and then you take off something. Pants or shirt, first or last, it's up to you."

Again he saw the eyes of a wild filly staring back at him in nervous disbelief. Malla was behind her own bedroom door within seconds. She soon heard him in the bathroom, then there came a knock on her door. His voice was gentle. "Malla, I'm not going to force you to do anything you don't want to do. I don't even want to come in, I'm too tired tonight anyway. I just want to talk to you. Will you open the door?"

Slowly the door opened. Drew watched it until he finally saw Malla. She purposely forced herself to hold herself in open body language. Her eyes seemed resolved about something. "Come in if you want."

He studied her face. Quietly, calmly, he began, "Where I come from this is unusual. It would be normal for us to meet socially, to date, to take our time and decide if we are right for each other. Would you agree?"

Malla nodded, "This is weird."

"Yes, so rushing myself on you would be wrong. But, Malla, you are very attractive to me. I'm very impressed both physically and your connection with the children, they love you already. I've been falling in love since the first little spice bottle hit the floor, even before I knew you worked here or that you had room in your house for us all. Does that make sense?"

"Don't be thinking that I'm going to tuck you in tonight, because I'm not. But maybe you want a bedtime story? Tori told me something interesting while I washed her hair. She said once she had to get up to pee one night and you were giving Inge a shower. She figured you were washing her hair. Yes, maybe they're in bed now but they hear and see when you don't expect it. Drew, I will not be another Inge in their eyes or ears. No, and I'm not a mail-order bride either. There have been no promises, no vows, no ceremony. We have a vague agreement about a boarding fee." As she spoke her hands trembled. "Physically? Nothing is making sense."

Drew reminded, "You told me I should come and wrap my arms around you and never let you go. I'm here."

"And you said we need to teach them morals. How can you have both? Be attracted if you want, but I don't know you."

He gathered her into his arms and quietly proclaimed, "I will never let you go. If I keep trying to woo you, it's not that I haven't learned how to be a good father. Together we will teach them good things. Yes, I'm attracted to you," he slowly began to kiss her neck, "as a woman," his breath was warm on her neck, "as a friend," her spine tingled from his touch, "as a bed partner, and lastly," he kissed her soft lips, "as a mother." Drew stepped away and whispered, "Good night." He turned and walked down the hall to his room, stopping to watch her as she peeked around the corner. A quiet wave and he was gone.

Malla's head spun as she hit the pillow. The reality of her situation was finally hitting hard. She had ignored him, but could no longer. She struggled with her choices throughout the night, finally she drifted off to sleep and awoke resolved, "Just let him. It's just kisses," she told herself. "What would it hurt?" Malla rose and brushed her hair wondering, "It's Sunday. What will the children be needing today?"

She headed down the stairs to her cozy kitchen with its sunny windows. Drew met her there. "I thought you would sleep in," Malla said.

"I did, considering my internal clock is still in Reykjavik. I've been up since five."

Malla looked him over, wondering when to spring her decision upon him. He would be surprised. "Are you hungry?"

"Not yet. It's Sunday?"

"Yes. I've been going to church with Anna and Alan."

Drew started slowly, "We could go with you." He shrugged and sipped his coffee, "What time?"

"Nine o'clock."

"Micky used to make sure we got to church. I guess I haven't pushed it."

Malla thought about the way Micky was brought up every so often. Inge was someone she could compete with. Micky was a bigger challenge. Her surprise would have to wait. She asked, "Which church did she go to?"

"Catholic. She had me convert after we got married. I guess I haven't been back since Michael's baptism."

Malla smirked at yet one more thing they had in common. She explained, "When I lived in Reykjavik my family was one of the few Icelandic families who actually attended the Catholic Cathedral."

"Christ the King? My house was a block away."

"Yes, my mother is Spanish. They met in Barcelona when he was on holiday."

"Does she speak…"

"Icelandic? Oh, yes. She is a languages professor at the University. Dr. Justina Cortez."

"What does your dad do?"

"Deep sea fisherman, Hilbert Sigurdsson. They are deeply in love. It's nice to see them together."

"What do they think about your bakery here in North Dakota?"

"I'm a disappointment. Mamma wanted me to get a college degree and make something of myself like my brother and sister. No, I'm the black sheep. Pabbi didn't want me to marry TEK. He didn't want me to move to Milwaukee either."

Drew recognized her Icelandic terms for mom and dad but hadn't ever heard of the name she mentioned. "Teek?"

"His initials. Terrance Edward Kensington. That wasn't tough enough. He went by TEK."

"Mrs. Kensington?"

"No. Hilbertsdoittur. I kept my father's name, an Icelandic tradition that's important to him, but he doesn't know that because he hasn't talked to me since before I left Iceland."

"What sort of work does TEK do?"

"Nothing. His parents are wealthy. I met him at the Blue Lagoon."

"So you moved to Milwaukee and married the tough guy with wealthy parents."

"And got a job at a bakery. I didn't want their money."

"Just the green card?"

"That's low. No, I married him for love."

"It was thoughtless, I'm sorry."

"You're not the first one to have those thoughts. No, for the first three years we were in love, but I wanted a baby and it just wasn't happening. I asked him to go to the doctor with me. His ego blew that idea."

"Then the mistress?"

"Church at nine?" She looked at the clock. It was seven thirty. "I've just lately started to go to church again," she confessed. "Almost as long of a gap as you. For me it's since high school."

"Did you go to confession?"

"No, I'm on surveillance mode first."

"Since converting I'm OK with being Catholic except for the whole confession thing."

"Have the kids been to catechism?"

"I've been thinking about that since you asked on Facebook. I didn't really answer you, did I? BJ was. But, no, I was angry with God after that."

"I started to go to church again since I think if I dare to be a fit mother, I'll need God's help to stand the test. Are you still angry?"

"No, I think no. God has become bored with me. It's a stand-off."

"My mother would be in your face right now, challenging you to…"

"To what?"

Malla channeled her mother saying, "To not let selfish pride step in front of His love for you, for them." Nessa and Tori scampered through the kitchen and Malla heard BJ stretching, yawning loudly in the stairway. Malla added, "She'd tell you to get ready for church."

"The Mass is ended, let us go forth to love and serve one another."
Surveillance mode was working for Drew, also. No serious
commitment. He heard the prayers, the sermon, sang some songs and
made no promises about letting the full impact take hold of anyone's
soul. The kids watched, too, in their own version of reconnaissance.
Introductions were made after Mass. Drew finally met Alan, the kids
met others their ages, and Sunday brunch at the local café was tasty.

Once home Drew set up his laptop for another Sunday tradition. When
his children saw the computer being assembled, they all came to the
kitchen table and waved, "Hi Nanna! Hi Papa!"

Drew grinned, "We made it in one piece. No injuries, no lost bags.
There was one stewardess who needs a new uniform."

"Nanna, that's not true!" Tori giggled, "He's just teasing. We were
good, like you said."

"Oh, that is so good to hear. What time is it there?"

"Almost noon. We're just one hour off now. Are you still planning to
come?"

"Yes, next week. Where's your sweetheart, Drew? I want to meet her."

"Kids, you talk to Nanna and Papa, I'll go find her." Malla was loading
the washing machine when Drew looked in the basement. Her mind was
far away. "Malla, there you are."

"And so are you." She abandoned her pile of warm towels and moved
into his comfort zone, brushing her bosom against him. Malla stared
deep into his eyes and quietly explained, "I was wrong last night to push
you away. Hmmmm, you have a musky scent."

"Uh, it's just deodorant."

"I'm ready."

"For, for what?"

"You're like a puppy who chases a cat then doesn't know what to do when he finally catches it. I'm ready for you to woo me."

BJ called from above, "Dad, Malla, come on!"

"Uh, I will, I sincerely will, but it will have to wait for later. My parents. They want to meet you and maybe I didn't mention this but they're coming next week. They're talking to the kids up in the kitchen on my laptop."

"Oh, no, I can't," she said rearing.

"Ah, there's that same wild horse."

"Horse? You think I look..."

"Like a pretty wild horse, a bashful wild horse."

"They have long noses."

"And your nose is small and beautiful. Everything about you is beautiful. Malla, you are SO sexy. But you can be bashful and that's OK because I'm not shy so we make a good pair. Just come upstairs," he pleaded.

"I can't."

"You weren't shy about meeting the children."

"No? I'd been looking at pictures and I almost died before you all got there," she explained with panic in her voice.

Drew pulled out his wallet. "Here. Here's a picture of my folks. How do you handle customers at work?"

"I pretend they're naked."

"OK. Do the same with my parents."

"But these are your parents. Do I look OK? This shirt, I don't like this shirt," she muttered, heading back to the laundry room.

"Do you promise you'll come up?"

"I promise. Find my purse upstairs. I need some lipstick."

Holding Malla's bag, Drew watched his children from the kitchen sink. They were telling stories about their farewell parties, their travels and their new home. When Malla finally appeared in the basement doorway, Drew reached out his hand and pulled her to himself. He whispered, "You are so sexy. Hey, do you ever pretend that I'm naked?"

"No," she looked toward the children, "hush!"

"You wouldn't have to pretend."

"Shhh!"

The sultry look had returned to his eyes. "Kiss me," he quietly demanded.

"In front of..."

"Yes!"

In the distance Malla heard Nessa boasting, "And Malla braided our hair this morning. Isn't it pretty?" Meanwhile, Malla raised one hand to Drew's chest and quickly felt both his arms envelop her. His lips were sure and thorough. Malla was distracted by the passion he was invoking as giggles pealed from the kitchen table.

Nessa exposed their secret, "Nanna, Daddy is kissing her!"

Drew turned Malla by the shoulders and whispered, "You don't need lipstick. You've got plenty of color now."

Blush had rushed to her cheeks and her eyes were bright and joyful. The twins pulled her forward and they and Michael all vied for a spot on her lap. So covered by squirming children, none could see the pretty blue in her blouse and how it brought out her cobalt blue eyes. But this wasn't lost on Drew. He was enamored by her beauty through and through. Drew knelt at her side with one hand behind her back. "This is Malla

Hilbertsdoittur, Ken and Amy Bjornson."

"Ken and Amy, hello. Oh, children, someone's going to fall." Her voice was firm, but had a friendly fun loving tone. "A girl on both sides and a little boy on my lap: that's the way it's going to be."

Drew directed, "BJ, take a chair on the other side and cuddle in. Here's a new family picture. Nanna, is everyone smiling?"

"Ah, BJ? Look this way. Look into the camera everyone—it looks good."

Drew clicked the mouse and the split second was caught for Malla's heart to ponder. "Did you save it?" she whispered, then suddenly she sensed that the hooks on her bra had been undone.

With his other hand Drew handled the computer's mouse and though Malla couldn't see Amy, she heard her ask, "Malla, the kids love you so, I understand you don't have children of your own?"

"No, I don't," she heard herself sadly confirm.

Ken jumped in, "I hear you're a baker."

This was a better topic. Through the chaos Malla smiled, her mind grateful to have Michael on her lap covering her wayward chest. "Yes, we've been making vinetarta all week, several flavors. Apple, strawberry, juneberry, and the traditional prune."

Ken smacked his lips. "I go for the traditional. Yum. I can't wait to come meet you in person." Their live picture reappeared on the screen and Malla watched as Amy left the picture.

"Oh," Ken stretched to see, then described, "We've got company. The Mitchells are here for coffee. Malla, we'll have to visit next week in person."

Thank God! Malla cried to herself and calmly agreed, "I look forward to that."

"Send us a copy of that picture, Drew."

"OK, Dad, will do." The screen went blank and Malla sat quietly snuggled by the other five. Michael turned on her lap and asked, "Can I have a story?"

Drew quietly suggested, "Nap time, everyone? It is Sunday." Yawns surrounded Malla. He cropped the photo and saved it again as Michael went to get his book and the girls followed suit.

BJ noted, "You need another frame, Dad. Can we print it out?"

"I will. It's a good picture. I have the paper and printer coming in our shipment." BJ yawned and headed for the couch.

Malla offered, "You can use my printer." She studied the faces on the screen before her. BJ's hand rested on her shoulder, each twin girl reached her hands to grasp both Malla's arms and Michael claimed his throne with a happy glow, his hands resting in Malla's.

The hooks and loops on her bra still gaped open. BJ had finally left the room leaving Malla a chance to collect herself, scolding Drew as he stared into the laptop. "Don't be unhooking my bra. What are you? A sex maniac?"

He turned to smile at her and admitted, "Well, it's been a long time, but hey, that was meant to distract you. I was just trying to help," he shrugged.

"It gave me more to be nervous about!" He seemed to ignore her plight, sending the picture to his parents. She stared into the photo, "I want to send this to my mom. She'll be surprised."

"Do they have a web cam? I wouldn't mind meeting them."

"Them? No, I was just talking about Mom."

"You've got to get him involved somehow," Drew shrugged. Finally realizing they were alone, he turned his attention to Malla. Standing, he reached for her hand. He leaned against the kitchen counter, his sexy gaze casting a heavy cloak upon her, rendering her speechless, motionless, but her eyes returned his lust. Again he drew her into his arms where they stood locked in the moment until squabbles erupted upstairs. Four tired children needed a nap. Drew left to handle them, turning to wink as he walked away. The wink was something new. Malla was surprised to be affected by his charms. That was never her intent. As this new reality was hitting her, she also finally noticed her bra was unhooked again, her skirt's zipper gaped open, and two button holes stood empty on her blouse proving clear evidence of his nimble fingers.

The Friday night before the annual Deuce of August parade was always unpredictable. The northeastern North Dakota locals were already receiving guests, a Friday night fish fry was planned, and a street dance with live music rocked there on Main Street next to the infamous Byron's Bar. There was every reason for Spencer Hillman to expect to see his kid brother, Jason. There were no plans made with their mom, Candy, but Jason wasn't the plan-ahead type.

Spencer stowed his backpack in the living room, planning to stretch out on the sofa for overnights. He chatted with Buddy Hannesson, their step-dad, then kissed his mother's cheek. "See you two at the street dance!"

His car found adequate parking a block down from Byron's Bar. There still weren't any replies from his text to Jason. Radio silence. As Spencer walked, he looked up from his phone in time to see Jason's two hands leaning on the back wall of the rock band's stage, leaning over a young lady who giggled at his jokes.

The closer he got, the more it made sense. Spencer held up his phone and snapped photos of the pair. "Bro," Jason introduced, "this is my brother. What are ya doin'?"

He snapped another pic. "What are YOU doing?" he asked, then turned to the young woman. "What's your name?"

"Layne. What's yours?"

"I'm Spencer." The conversation seemed light and airy until Spencer added, leaning into Jason's face, "I'm the big brother who is going to rain on your sexually active parade, Jason. Remember Jess?" he asked, holding up a photo on his phone. "She showed up at my lake house with her older sister and they both proceeded to throw eggs and feathers all over my expensive lake house, thinking that you lived there. Layne, do you want to know why these ladies would do that?" He held up a picture of both sisters. "Jess says that Jason raped her and she has medical proof." Layne took one more look at Jason and backed away, then turned and ran around the corner. Glaring into Jason's angry eyes, Spencer called after her, "You're a smart woman, Layne, good for you."

Many had gathered at the fish fry, but most conversations were riddled with laughter and old stories about old friends or family. Candy and Buddy innocently looked about, waving at neighbors, and settled with their plates next to Spencer and Jason. The two sons weren't talking, certainly not about the fist fight that had erupted earlier. It was a Sons of Johnny Hillman tradition, and as usual, a fight that ended in a draw.

Silence echoed as Candy looked at them, sensing her boys' rough and tumble relationship. Eating their supper was safe amongst this crowd of family, neighbors, and friends. Then suddenly Jason said, "You owe me money, old man." The five children of Candy Hillman-Hanneson had given their mom a china hutch for Mother's Day. Jason was the banker, a title he could be rarely associated with.

Buddy looked at Spencer as he settled at the picnic table. "Who are you talking to, Jason? I don't owe you a penny."

Spencer waved his fork, then spoke around his fish, "I purposely didn't pay you because now you also owe me money."

With this new confusion, Jason didn't have time to figure out why, since Jess and her sister approached, followed closely by a deputy sheriff. Candy and Buddy were only slightly more shocked with the confrontation than Jason was. The neighboring friends and family took it all in. The accusation, the proof of non-consensual sex, along with a blood alcohol level of .19. He'd gotten her drunk and taken advantage of her inebriation. When she'd come to, she had had the good sense to call her sister, Danielle Morrison, who was also her attorney.

Once it was clear that he was outgunned, Jason's eyes never rose from the ground. His mother, step-dad, and the friends and family who innocently listened on were flabbergasted. But not Spencer.

He had found Danielle's business card among the feathers in his back yard. He had contacted her and spoke of the possible opportunity to find and confront Jason. Then Jess and Danielle had paid Layne, their cousin, to find Jason and lure him into a snare, keeping him until Spencer showed up. After he and Jason had squared off with punches and jabs, the brothers agreed upon a truce, and Spencer bought them both a fish supper.

Spencer stood back and let it all happen to his brother, no longer willing to guard him or his secrets.

Erin had been up since four. At five she had finished her salad to bring to the Vikur Salad Luncheon to be served to Deuce of August goers after the annual parade. As she chopped the vegetables and cooked the pasta, Erin recalled the relatively short time that she'd been in the northeastern corner of North Dakota, and how much the people of Cavalier and Mountain had welcomed her. *Me, the victim of long-term spousal abuse, and soon the mother of that bastard's child.* She caressed her full-term baby bump, and the child inside pushed softly against Erin's hand. The image of her ex-husband's lifeless body flashed before her and was quickly pushed away, out of her mind. Someone else, a man whose mother had died at the hand of spousal abuse, had snuffed out Paul's life, leaving Erin the opportunity to run like mad, north, to find Anna. And run she did.

That was when Erin met Brandon. She knew she was pregnant with Paul's child and fully intended to abort it at the first possible moment. *No one, well, few would blame me. This little gal is the product of rape.* As opportunities came and went, Erin found she didn't have the stomach for more hard decisions. *That would have taken more guile than I have. I just want to live in peace. This may be Paul's child, but she came from my egg, she's my child. My little Glory Bea,* named for Brandon's kid sister and Erin's favorite aunt.

Brandon had accepted Erin, hook, line and sinker, pregnant, abused and battered. His had proven to be a tender, reassuring love that calmed Erin when she had flashbacks or fitful nights. The thought of their wedding, an elopement to Las Vegas, had Erin wiping her hands dry and pulling out the photo album and video DVD. She pushed play and stood back, remembering. Emotions were thick that morning.

Tearful eyes watched her hands combine pasta, vegetables, sunflower nuts, sauce, cheese, and meat. She felt an urgency to finish her task, the dishes, the sweeping, and finish everything else, too.

The bowl of salad was delivered, but Erin couldn't move too far from the long line of porta-potties towards the center of the parade path. She walked in circles, Brandon at her side. He was hoping she'd settle with a spot to watch the parade, so he could set down the chairs, cooler, and umbrella he'd brought.

She lingered nowhere, but kept moving. He chatted with people he knew and met a few new faces. The parade started when she was deep in the shade, stretching her back, legs, and arms on the east side of the Main Street. The porta-potties were on the west side. The parade innocently rolled along, cutting her off. "A problem, Brando, yes, a big problem. I have no bladder, none," she moaned.

He looked about to faces around them, hoping to find someone who had authority to pause the parade. She wasn't waiting, but set out between the weaving KEM Temple crazy mini-cars. Brandon watched on in terror.

The next in line was a nice convertible with the dignitaries from Iceland. Brandon waved back at them, then eyed the next float pulled by an Oliver tractor. The driver, a familiar farmer, saw Brandon's 'time out' signal, and allowed him to gather his gear and scoot across the parade's path.

Once she finally exited the porta-potty, there was panic in her doe-like eyes. "My water just broke."

A familiar face was watching the people from his perch on the set of bleachers, the newest member of the volunteer ambulance crew, Rene LaRoque. Before Erin knew what to think, she was in an ambulance and pulling into the Cavalier hospital. Four or five pushes later, she was an exhausted but exuberant mother, cooing over her slippery daughter.

Brandon watched it all in awe. Once Erin had drifted off to sleep, he picked up Glory, swaddled and wrinkled, but beautiful in his eyes. "Hey," he whispered, "I'm your daddy. Maybe not by nature, but I'll be your daddy anyway. Every little girl needs a daddy." He stood cradling the tiny bundle, swaying and gazing into her face, praying and glorifying God for the little life that almost wasn't.

Anna was tired, soon done with her first trimester of pregnancy. She pushed Alan to go and socialize, and she didn't have to tell him twice. He had a fun game of pool going with Rene at Byron's Bar on that Saturday night of the Deuce. Mountain, North Dakota's annual bash was hopping both inside the bar and out at the street dance. Alan paused to get another round, and Rene was busy racking the balls when the 22-year-old Brooke Hillman bounced in, discovering Rene for the first time.

"Ooooh! Hi, Love," she flirted with a wink. With a toss of her long, blonde hair, she asked, "How is it possible a handsome man like yourself is alone?" To his quiet shrug she added, "Hi, my name is Brooke."

"I am Rene."

Alan returned and handed Rene another bottle of beer. Brooke had been surveying the crowd, draped over the end of the pool table like a male bird on display. She caught one glance of Alan and moaned, "Ewww. You're with Alan? Ewww."

Alan pointed, "He's my cousin," then turned to wave at other friends in the crowd, leaving the two alone.

Brooke's sultry stare was only meant for Rene. She slowly approached him. "Rene."

He took a sip and looked at her with a dullness in his voice. "Brooke," Rene returned.

"Ooh, we're on a first name basis. See if you can shake that turkey cousin of yours and let's meet up, and," she added as she tugged at his shirt. Her remarks were for his ears only. He watched her walk off, turning to wink and smile.

Rene rolled his eyes and took another sip of beer. "What did Brooke need?" Alan asked.

He lifted the rack away from the balls and reached for his pool cue. "More self-discipline than she has," he declared.

Alan watched her with concern and quipped, "Yeah? My money can't buy that."

The crowd was growing with noise and new personalities. Rene watched people around him, especially one older woman. She was patiently visiting with family, but as the time was passing that night, Rene noticed a change in her skin color—more gray and ashen than before.

Later, as Eunice Johanneson collapsed into her daughter's arms, unconscious, Rene was there, performing CPR.

Eunice's daughter, Rita Carter, called 9-1-1 and Rene disappeared with the ambulance crew.

Brooke and JoJo, Eunice's granddaughter, arrived and Alan passed on Eunice's story. "Yes, JoJo, your mom followed the ambulance to Grand Forks with Rene doing CPR."

Brooke shook her head, "CP…and mouth-to-mouth resuscitation, too?"

"Yes," Alan nodded, "the whole deal. I got a text from your mom. Your grandma came to after they used the AED. Rene will ride back with the ambulance. That's two ambulance rides for him in one day!"

Brooke huffed, "Never mind that! Wow, JoJo, French kissed by a real Frenchman!"

JoJo was sensible. "What? Mouth-to-mouth resuscitation is not a French kiss. Not even."

Alan added, "Yes, and he's French Canadian. He told me that he's had to use that skill at a restaurant he worked at in Montreal. And last week at a job site, too. It was a roofer. The guy got half way down the ladder and collapsed."

JoJo was checking her phone for texts from her mom, news of any sort, and connecting with others from the Johanneson family.

It was like a wet blanket was cast onto Brooke's hot nighttime plans. "Pooh! Well, Alan, tell Rene for me that he might still have a chance tomorrow, after the tractor pull. We'll see." She shifted her gaze onto a man who had just walked in, who headed directly for the beer garden. "Hmm, an old friend. See you guys later."

The noise was picking up even more. Alan said, but no one heard, "We should all learn sign language."

6 GOING HOME

Psychologist Roberta Simpson's practice at Cavalier was Laura Zimmermann's least favorite place to be. Roberta was certainly helping Laura through her confusions, primarily her relationship with Jack Kasprowicz, but the process was draining.

Roberta was taking notes, "Let's get this straight, you were on your way home from your trip to Vermont and you called Alan?"

"Yes, that's when he said that the treatment center, where Jack had been, that they released him the day before."

Roberta looked at the calendar, "June 16th."

"Yes, I don't know what they're thinking but Jack was gone and no one could find him. This was when Trish and Nick were gone on their trip, because Alan was doing all Trish's chores and it seemed to be cutting into his time for searching, dividing his attention." Laura was honest as she vented. "He could've passed that on to someone, but, I don't know, that's one of the layers of resentment. Trish is so happy with Nick, that's another layer. Or maybe it's just plain jealousy."

Roberta kept writing and nodded to Laura, who continued. "They kept talking about some new vet, Dr. Tappan, and how very impressive he was. He was one of the two they ended up hiring."

"And Jack was nowhere to be found," Roberta summarized.

"No, and this was just before the opening of the new store. I had already left my family early to get back and work on the fresh cheeses and the massive commercial coolers full of yogurt, fresh milk and cream, cultured sour cream and buttermilk. Augh!! I didn't have time for his drama or the anticipation of his drama, real or otherwise!"

"Now that the store is opened and time has passed, what do you see when you look back at that time?"

"Honestly?"

"Yes, in these walls, we talk honestly. Fabrication can't help you like honesty can."

"There was another distraction. Trish's brother. The guy I talked to on her computer at Trish's office before Jack found me and smacked me around." She looked at Roberta looking back through notes, remembering aloud, "People think he's a nice guy."

"Yes, we covered that last time. The brother's name?"

"James O'Malley," Laura said slowly, the memory clear in her mind. It was at the Minneapolis airport. Laura had set down her bag and taken a seat in the waiting area. Her Al-Anon friends, Joyce and Eva, had been her companions in Vermont. They had coached her, to a degree, as far as their experiences went, but Jack was proving to be atypical compared to most alcoholics.

Another traveler, who sat with his back to Laura, Joyce, and Eva, stood to stretch and get a drink at the water cooler. As he swallowed and sipped some more, he studied the women, wiping his chin with the back of his hand. He stretched again and approached them. "Laura Zimmermann?" he asked.

She looked up and tipped her head, squinting, "You look familiar."

"Maybe if my head had a computer screen around it," he smiled, using his hands to frame his face.

"Trish's brother, uh, James!"

"Yes, I just overheard you say you've been to Vermont."

Joyce muttered, "It was a fast trip. The boss lady here couldn't relax, so we cut it short."

Laura felt justified, "We make a long list of dairy products and our stockpile from before we left was very popular when the store opened. We're behind schedule if we ever go low. No, even the long weekend that we took, it just doesn't pay."

"Maybe I can help ya. I'm looking for a job."

Laura studied him. "What's your favorite cheese?" This had proven to be a good question to separate the serious contenders, those she would trust with recipes, from the muscle she'd direct to the shipping and store rooms.

James nodded, "I like a good Emmentaler on rye with ham or smoked turkey. Yum."

"Yes," Laura smiled, "that's one of my favorite colbys."

"But Emmentaler is a Swiss."

"Ah, yes, you're right. Define it."

"It's nutty and it's sweeter than a regular Swiss since they use additional bacteria in Emmentaler. I think it's helveticus."

"Lactobacillus helveticus, yes, that's right."

"And, uh, I don't understand this, but I hear you can take the whey off the Swiss cheese curds and use it for Ricotta. I don't know if that's a myth or something."

"Yes, this is possible. Yes, we could use an extra hand." Laura recalled the exchange and how she'd laughed, "You'll be the bottom of the totem pole, so you'll be cleaning at first."

"He said," Laura reported to Roberta, 'That's OK. After six years in Iraq and Afghanistan I can appreciate a job that's mundane and quiet.' That stayed, wedged in my mind," Laura admitted as Roberta took notes. "There was mystery in such an image. Mundane and quiet. Who could vaguely imagine the reality of living in a warzone for so long, and coming out alive?"

"What happened next?"

Laura's memory was clear. "We were all on the same flight. My seat was behind James by three rows. It was a short flight to Grand Forks, just an hour or so. I had time to sort out some thoughts. Both Joyce and Eva had dozed off, leaving me to stare out the window. The magazine I kept in my lap, well, I looked casual enough. I saw the back of James' head from where I sat. I decided he was far nicer and more handsome in person than I'd recalled from our brief computer visit. He was tall and his arms and neck were highly toned." Laura paused. There was no need to tell Roberta about how, in the quiet drone of the airplane, how she had wondered about the rest of Mr. O'Malley. That had led Laura down a sultry path. Instead, she mentioned her other more practical questions. "Where would he live? Does he have a car? Is someone picking him up? Does he already have a girlfriend? What if she was at the airport? What did he do in the army?" Laura remembered brainstorming, while mindlessly turning the pages of the magazine.

"But what also comes to mind is that this mysterious man, James, he's the one who initiated Jack's confrontation. So I love him and I loathe him in the same heartbeat."

Roberta warned. "The female heart is healthier if she heals from one heartbreak before opening up that same heart to another."

"Emotionally," Laura whispered to Roberta, "I'm over Jack. Jack and I are done," she claimed, now more firmly. "He needs to get treatment and go bother somebody else. I just want to make cheese." Internally she scanned her supply shelves checking for the supplies for Emmentaler and quietly sighed.

The psychologist continued, "What happened next?"

"Anna took over, as usual. She more or less hired James as a bodyguard for me, since Jack was somewhere on the loose. Both Eva and Joyce kept reminding me to take it one day at a time or even one hour at a time. That's solid advice."

"A bodyguard? Seriously?"

"You know Anna. Drama, drama! Everyone was sworn to secrecy and I was agreeing to stay at their house, with the handsome bodyguard two doors down. She kept saying, 'No one needs to know Laura is home.'" Laura let out a nervous laugh, adding, "Joyce and Eva and I were supposed to continue our vacation at Anna's house. I call it house arrest, but the other touching part of all this was that Jim, Trish's dad, hadn't seen his son in a long time, and Anna set up a supper meal at her house for James and Jim to meet face to face."

Laura's heart drifted back into the memory. Anna had a pretty table set and, verbally, it was the aromas from Anna's kitchen that had James' attention. But Laura could sense that nerves over Jim's arrival, his reaction to James' surprise return, also had him tense.

Anna chopped vegetables for a salad and asked, "How long since you've seen your dad, James?"

"Eight years, I was seventeen and I ran away from home."

"Oh!" Anna coughed.

"Yeah, I expected we'd do this reunion in private, but a pretty lady needs my help, so," he paused, "I'll be here for her." He glanced at Laura who was listening from the door. Laura recalled feeling shy. Anna and James discussed logistics, the supper menu, which room would be best for his reunion.

Laura's mind rambled until Anna's voice brought her back, "I ran away once. My family had no idea where I was."

James' voice was pensive, "Did they forgive you?"

"Every one. They were just glad I came home in one piece."

Joyce was the sentinel, Eva at her side. "There's a car here now."

Laura glanced, "Yes, that's Trish's car. That'll be Jim."

Alan was coming in from the barn, and they met on the sidewalk. The men enjoyed each other's sense of humor, so Alan joked as they made their way in. "Where's Toni?" Alan grinned.

"When Anna called, the invitation was just for me."

"Well, that's odd, Anna, why not invite Toni?" he asked. Both men walked towards the kitchen and watched as Anna's hand pointed into the sunken family room.

"Hi, Dad." James tried a brave smile. Jim walked closer, down the two steps, and walked into his taller, broader son's arms. "I'm sorry for running off, Dad," James whispered.

Jim backed up and held James' chin in his palms, lightly tapping his cheek. James grinned all the more as Jim's smile brightened, "You're home! By God, man, you're alive!!" He felt James' arms, shoulders and hands in his, "And you're not wounded. Are those your legs?"

"Yes."

Jim pulled his son to him and hugged him tight. Weathered eyes glistened as he quietly proclaimed, "This would be a happy day for your mom."

"Yeah, I miss her, too."

"Alan?" Jim called, "It's time to slaughter that fattened calf!"

Anna smiled, "Will seafood Alfredo do? It's ready."

They laughed and headed to the table. Alan led them in prayer, "Lord, we thank You so much for James' safe return back into the arms of his father. Help them to catch up on whatever matters most. Help us to find

Jack and keep Laura safe. We bless this food that You've provided. Help us to live by Your hand and for Your glory, Amen."

James looked up from his folded hands, "Amen."

Laura dabbed tears with her napkin and let out a nervous laugh. Anna teased, "Thanks, Alan, thanks for making us all cry," she said with a laugh, wiping her own eyes. The salad and garlic toast was passed and Anna served the tasty dish. "It's ironic," she started, "but there was salad and garlic toast when I came home after having run away." She shared the experience in brief, giving God the credit for her safety.

"Yes," James nodded, "He's been there with me, too. Now I just want to live a simple life with family nearby and reconnect those family ties."

"Good," Jim added, "You can start by helpin' me get my ranch in order." Chewing garlic toast, James studied him as Jim added, "I'm sellin' Alan half my herd later next spring."

James swallowed and took a deep breath as his tongue nervously cleaned his teeth. Finally the silence was broken, "No, Dad, I can't do that."

"No?"

"Laura offered me a job."

"Making cheese. Ya, Trish warned me that this could happen. Laura, you're gonna have to watch him to keep him workin'."

"Dad, I was seventeen the last time you caught me reading magazines instead o' fencin'." His western drawl was peeking through, "I've grown up since then."

"Yes, I see that."

Laura nodded, agreeing with Jim, "I'll keep an eye on him." Laura saw relief in James' face.

~*~*~*~

"Enough memories! I'm done with the past." Laura looked back, into Roberta's face and reported, "The rest of the conversation was light and congenial, compared."

Roberta asked, "Are you still having patience problems with Trish?"

The laugh that burst forth surprised Laura, "Uh, yeah, yes, definitely. But that's Trish, James' sister, so I have to buckle down on having patience with my lack of patience." Roberta agreed and continued to warn Laura about keeping her heart guarded until Jack was safely back in treatment. But Laura's heart wasn't ever capable of such control.

Elijah drove north on highway 32, south of Edinburg. Alan and Anna's new store was open, but certain shop supplies hadn't come in yet, so he had to make a trip. He was deep in thought, mentally working through his list of things to do. Suddenly, he focused ahead on someone pulling a moving trailer. It was on the northbound side of the road and, naturally, he slowed down. In the first split second when passing the trailer he saw the mid-sized car with its hood open and steam billowing up from the engine, so he pulled over to help. A young woman was trying to find shade for her son. "Overheating?" he quickly diagnosed, walking closer with his tool box.

The hot August sun was beaming bright. "Yes," she agreed, "everything, everyone, all overheating." The six-year-old boy tried to play with the umbrella in her hand.

Elijah handled the hot radiator and was glad to have a supply of fresh water in his truck. "The hose, there's a hole. I can fashion a patch but it's short term. You need to stop in a shop and get a new hose." His chore was soon done and the car was started again. He backed away and motioned her towards the driver's seat.

She sensed the coolness of the air conditioner. The woman stood and admitted, "We're very grateful for your help, but I have no money to pay you."

Humble as ever, Elijah waved her off, "No need, ma'am, I'm happy to be of use." She loaded her son and was quickly back in gear. He was putting away his tools as she drove off and he suddenly wondered, *What's your name?* He looked at the shop supplies he'd picked up in Grafton, especially the jugs of distilled water. *Well,* he thought, *whoever she is, Lord, I'm glad you reminded me about the distilled water.*

Laura's patience was running short, not just for her chatty friend, but also with the security-heavy computer system that Alan had insisted upon since being a victim of fraud. "Another password?! Augh!!" She hated remembering the many obscure passwords in her life. When the opportunity to define the moment had arrived, she drummed her fingers, creativity was null. She yawned as Dara and Anna dropped by, bringing more label designs. "Ladies? What do you do about passwords? They are the bane of my existence! I need to get these orders done, for cryin' out loud!"

Dara coached, "Use passphrases, not just words."

Laura's fingers had been in motion. "Well, they don't let me repeat C0ffeeplz again. Hmm, away with the FluffEbunny7vudoo." With a certain morose tone, Laura declared, "The fluffy bunny dies," then added, "That was always hard to type, anyway."

Anna laughed, but Dara suggested through her smirk, "Find one word that defines your life, and make a phrase. Good luck!"

The pair moved on, but Laura realized that she was starting to appreciate Dara more and more. She was gentle in her manner, but authentic and sincere. Laura rose and found bottled water in the breakroom fridge. *A word, I need a word.* The memory of one of her sessions with Roberta came to mind. *She said I'm experiencing anguish, with the loss of freedom to be myself, but that it won't last forever.* The bottle of water soon consumed, Laura went back to her office. *"MyLife0fANGUISH,* she typed. *Well,* she paused to toss the plastic bottle, *if that isn't depressing.*

7 THE UNEXPECTED

Holly Christianson was back on familiar ground, sort of. In grade school she had been Akra's best little baton twirler, then in senior high school, her family moved to the Upper Peninsula of Michigan. When it was time for Holly to leave the nest, she happily hustled off to Milwaukee where she landed a job, found an apartment and fell in love, all within two weeks. Her baby came along quickly, and before her parents knew she was expecting, they were grandparents. They came to visit when she was in the hospital. But as soon as her dad had Holly's address, he disappeared, going to find the father of his new grandson.

Both Holly and her mom wondered what was happening, but soon saw Dad on the local evening news. He'd reported the young man as a missing person. Truth be told, he'd run Holly's sweetheart out of town.

Now, Holly studied her childhood home, Akra, North Dakota, with adult eyes. A single mom and newly hired to help manage the dozens of grocery store staff, Holly started to settle into Grandmother Bernie's old house. A daunting task for one person against all those boxes. The stacks stared back at her, adding to the already overwhelming day.

The neighbors in that little burg were curious to see who had moved into their neighborhood and arrived with a pan of coffee cake and a thermos of coffee. Seeing Grandma Bernie's old friends brought back memories of when Bernie was sick and Holly was a sophomore in high school. The pair would work on yarn projects, knitting and crocheting the hours away, wishing and praying away Bernie's aches and pains. It was such a precious memory, but suddenly emotional, too.

The closest neighbor, Karen, seemed to sense Holly's mood and reached over with a quiet hug. "We miss her, too. Now, can we help you unload any boxes?"

"Yes, thank you. We'll start with the kitchen. Do you know Bea Berglund? She works in the office at the grocery store. She's getting a couple of our store workers to come over to help assemble new furniture."

Karen pointed out into the yard at the pickup load of men who approached the house carrying tool bags. "A couple? I see four."

The older ladies all seemed to approve when Grady Baxter knocked on the door. "Hi, did Bea tell you that we were recruited to help assemble furniture? I'm Grady, this is Rene, Brandon, and Elijah."

None of their names meant anything to Holly. Her six-year-old son, Cole, peeked from her side as she shrugged, "She said a couple high school boys were coming. I recognize you," she said, nodding at Elijah. "You fixed my car today."

Elijah's smile widened as he announced, "I patched it, but now I have the right parts to fix it for good."

But mid-sentence her phone rang to squelch his news. Bea was calling to explain that, though her new hires, Kyle and Brody, were asked to come help, that they had to decline. Holly's eyes rolled as she looked at the four men who had dropped everything and replaced the two teens with a shrug and non-verbal instruction. They seemed to understand their tasks and all disappeared. Holly took a breath and looked into the kitchen. It seemed that the ladies had their world under control. *I'll rearrange later.*

What had seemed like overwhelming stress was now being handled by many hands from some people she knew and some new faces. The emotion from earlier was returning as she looked about, recalling Grandma Bernie's loving eyes. With a sudden knock at the door, there was no time to linger. What Holly wasn't expecting was her neighbor Magnus Gudmundson's face at the kitchen door with his hands full. He handed off the kettle of soup and explained, "I heard you had a crew over here." He pointed into his grocery bag of buns and grinned with pride as he pulled out a plastic tub, "Funeral spread, it's the best!"

Alan shook Malla's hand. "This was a wonderful meal, but if we keep this up, I'll be gaining weight. Last night Anna's lasagna, today your delicious samples and tonight your prime rib! I'm gonna bust!" Anna and Alan left from Malla's driveway.

The picnic they had been invited to was a grand splash to introduce them to Drew's children and his parents. Everyone else was still in the backyard playing catch and lawn bowling. This quiet moment was Malla's single moment of peace since his parents had arrived, aside from the hours training new staff on a million and one recipes. Her standards were being considered at work, but home was another matter.

"Malla," Drew called, "there you are! This sure has been a fun picnic."

Contrary to the reply Drew expected, Malla burst into tears. "This is hopeless! It's all a lie," she mourned.

Drew scrambled to reassure her, "You've done an excellent job. The food, uh, what do you mean, a lie?"

She pointed from herself back to Drew, "This. I don't love you, why do I let you kiss me? Oh, what sort of harlot am I?"

"Uh, well, I can see you've been overwhelmed, but…"

"Overwhelmed?! I've been overwhelmed since the first day we met!"

"Let's take a drive. You haven't been in my new car yet, have you?"

"What?"

"My car. Let's take a drive. I'll ask Mom to watch the kids. Can you meet me in the garage? Is this OK?"

Within short order Drew had his mother in charge of his brood and he was opening the overhead garage door. Malla was in the passenger seat. Drew opened his door. The new car smell hit him as her sobs hit his ear. Glancing he saw her hugging a box of tissues.

They drove away and quietly he began, "Uh, yeah, you're overwhelmed, and I'm feeling humbled. You're right. I've been single-minded and childish to not see you for the beautiful person you are." He looked away from the street and saw Malla looking out her side window. "Do you still want to be inspired?" he asked with a hopeful heart.

"Only if we can make this work. Otherwise you can just buy the house from me. I'll find a place." With this option verbalized new tears rolled.

Drew pulled the car out onto the highway and headed west. Once past the state park, he pulled off the paved road and onto gravel. He pulled the car over and parked with a new plan. "I'd like to start over. Hi, I'm Drew. I think your eyes are spectacular, I understand you're a very good cook and I have four children who need a mother."

"Stick with the eyes if you want the rest," she quietly advised.

"I want to be the one who inspires you."

"How are you going to do that?"

"First I have to ask you the absolute truth. When you first saw me, what did you think?"

"I thought you were handsome."

"So that's why you were interested?"

"No, you made me nervous at first, your stare. Then I decided to ignore you. But then I heard you talking to BJ's teacher."

"So the fact that I have children…"

"When you know you will never bear children, then that's all you think about. Yes, it's true."

After a long pause Drew finally asked, "When I kissed you good bye in Iceland and the kisses at the airport, all those since then, what was that to you?" He wasn't prepared for her reply.

"One of my ancestors, an aunt, my great-grandfather's sister, was a mail order bride. Auntie Helga. I tried to imagine what it was like for her."

"I'm very sorry for having been so shallow, so careless with your heart. But you see, don't you? I hurt you by not focusing on the person inside and I'm sure you didn't mean to, but you've done the same by putting my children first, before me." After a heavy sigh Drew pulled the car back into motion and drove south. They drove on in silence turning west, then north. That was when Drew finally said, as though he were in mid conversation, "I figured I'd start where you started."

"What?"

"With my mom and dad here it was a natural flow. That's how I figured I'd inspire you."

"I'm sorry, Drew to have hurt you. I forgive you, can you forgive me?"

"Yes, I want to inspire you."

"What does that mean to you?"

"I found your mother's name on Facebook, so I sent her a note. She sent one back and we're now friends." He glanced at Malla's face, but was dismayed to see her blank stare. He encouraged, "I want to inspire you to connect with your father."

"What if I don't want that?"

"Sure you do, every father wants the most for his daughter. I can share very private dreams I have for my little girls. He's a tough guy, a deep sea fisherman, which is very dangerous, but inside he's a marshmallow wanting to see you again, wanting to know you're alright. He loves you—it's an intimate level of love that's hard to explain." Drew pulled the car over again. He saw emotion in her eyes, then panic.

Malla was unglued, "Wait she can see your picture, your profile. That new family picture!"

"Yeah, I suppose."

"You suppose! Drew! When? When did she confirm you as a friend?"

"This morning."

With a heavy sigh Malla sat back, resigned to the fact, "I need to send her a letter. She's wondering who you are…"

"I told her who I am."

"Who are you?"

"Your new boyfriend and the father of four."

"She'll think I'm being unfaithful. She doesn't know about the divorce."

"Oh, I suppose."

"I have to write her a letter."

"Are you inspired?" He studied her but only saw that the blank stare had returned to her face. Drew shook his head asking, "Why haven't you been talking to your dad? What's the last thing he said to you?"

"Don't move away."

"What did you say?" Drew quietly asked.

"You can't stop me."

"By now your pictures are all over your mother's computer screen and so is your name, your father's name. He will see you and your name and he will be inspired."

~*~*~*~

"Holly, you're all grown up. Last time I saw you, you were wishing you could go to prom." Magnus teased. "Ralph and Bernie, yeah. I miss them, too. I know he had a couple boys. One of 'em is your dad, he moved off somewhere. Where'd you go?"

She listened and chatted with Magnus about Michigan, but a quiet yawn caught her off guard. There had been too many late nights with packing. The flash of an idea that had spawned on a late night in the quiet, the image of her opening a door to greet Troy, her sweetheart and the father of her little boy, to answer her invitation to come live with her in North Dakota. *It would be like him to just show up*, she quietly hoped. Surrounded by volunteers to both welcome her and work on boxes, Holly finally got a word in edgewise with Magnus. "OK, thank you for the soup," though that summer night was too hot for soup, "and sandwiches," her son Cole, certainly wouldn't touch either. *How to sound grateful?* she wondered. "It's been many moons since I had funeral spread!"

"Ham salad, but I like to make mine with bulk bologna."

"Hmmm, good to know. OK, I'm back to work on boxes." Ever the supervisor, she suggested, "Maybe you can help the ladies break down empty boxes?"

"Nope, just head cook for the night. I'll be back tomorrow for the kettle. Good night!"

And work was accomplished. All had headed home and Holly finally surveyed the quiet house with a stretch and a yawn. Later that night, as she rested her tired back, Holly's list of 'to do's' sat on the arm of the sofa. The packing, the surprise farewell party, all before a tear filled goodbye, these were the Michigan memories that lingered. But it wasn't all positive. There were those girlfriends' voices that kept rolling through Holly's mind. One quipped, "North Dakota has a bad reputation for cold. Troy always complained about the cold." The other girlfriend voiced one of Holly's fundamental fears, simply saying, "He wouldn't want to live there."

Holly doubted, But if I'm totally honest with myself, then, *No, he wouldn't want to live here.* She didn't need those girl friends to provide additional nagging doubts about Troy, she had plenty of her own. But somehow a splinter of hope still hung in her heart. *Will he show up? That would be nice."* Then countered her own wishes, *"He didn't want to have kids.* She recalled how he'd shown up at Cole's 4th birthday party two years before. Though it was held in a bowling alley, Troy looked and sounded more like a feral cat, stuck in a box. *Why would he give up bachelorhood to move even further north?*

Another more recent memory also stirred Holly. That evening there had been a whir of cordless drills and casual chatter from the men who came to volunteer their time. But when that constant background noise finally went quiet, all tools were repacked, and the quartet stood by the door. She thanked them all but no one would accept her cash, only her thanks. Both Brandon and Grady talked about getting back to their sweethearts. Talk switched to the newborn baby in Erin and Brandon's apartment, "Erin has adjusted to parenthood like a champ. I'm still getting used to it." Then from that to the house Brandon and Erin would soon be moving to.

Rene and Elijah just smiled quietly as they left. Now, as she remembered the men, both Rene's and Elijah's silence echoed in her mind. Even though Troy was on her wish list, she knew he was a loose cannon who couldn't be counted on. She had to wonder, *Rene? Eli? Are either of you the family man type?*

With a roll of her eyes, she quickly dismissed the thought with an independent burst of energy. Up and out of her chair, Holly pulled at the remaining boxes that still needed opening. She rearranged the stack, avoiding the photo albums and old high school memories until she found the one that would soothe her heart. It was labeled 'Yarn and Tools, Relaxation in a Box.'

A skein of yarn and two knitting needles were quickly accessed as she thought, *This far north? Yes, a new hat and scarf for Cole.*

~*~*~*~

Jack's footing was unstable around his unfinished house. He staggered, splashing gas onto the wood and wiring that lay vulnerable in the night. With a wicked laugh Jack took another drink of his rum and then stuffed a rag into the bottle, and staggering away from the house, he chuckled and lit a match, touching it to the rag, then hurled it into the framework.

Amused, he stood in front of the car he'd stolen and pulled out another bottle as the blazing rum ignited the gas. Once the flames grew to a height that satisfied him, he drew in a huge mouthful of rum and got into his new ride. Spraying rocks on the graveled street, he spun his tires and within a mile, Jack passed out at the wheel and hit the ditch, deploying the air bags.

The volunteer fire department's flashing lights strobed red onto Alan's face as he got the report. Only Jack's house was damaged. It looked like arson and the county deputies were down the road checking the crash scene. When Alan got there, the officers were finishing their measurements. "He was going 80 when he hit this culvert. It's a miracle he isn't dead. Airbags saved him," the deputy reckoned.

"Where did the ambulance go?" asked Alan.

"Grand Forks," the officer replied. "His injuries were not substantial, but his blood alcohol was off the chart. He'll dry out up there and then we'll arrest him."

"How can one person be so angry with the world?"

"Some folks drink cuz they're angry with God. Some are angry with themselves. My experience? That's the most common reason."

Alan walked back into the quiet of his own house. Morning hues were soon on cue in the east. James sat at the kitchen table. "James, you're up early."

"I heard you leave. I'm glad you're back."

"Jack, he's in the hospital. He burned down his house and put a stolen car into the ditch going 80."

"Is he hurt?"

Alan yawned, "Couple scratches."

"Is he a threat?"

"He's drinking again, so yes. He's like a wounded mama bear, and James, you are in charge of keeping that cub named Laura upstairs in one piece. She's my favorite cousin."

"Yes, sir."

"Do you need sleep or are you hungry?"

"Neither. I've had guard duty before. It doesn't pay to get hungry or tired."

"Joyce told me you're interested in working at the creamery."

"Creamery or cheese factory, same thing?"

"Yup."

"Yup, I'm interested. I've made wine before and I understand they are similar."

Alan nodded. "Similar. What kind of wine?"

"It was a winery in Missouri, and again in Pennsylvania." The two men bonded as Alan and James toured Alan's fermenting room and Splinter Alley, his wood shop. By the time Laura was awake, Alan was cracking eggs. "Laura, I like this guy, so give him a job, OK?"

"I was going to."

"You can relax about Jack. He's in the hospital."

Laura looked disgusted and shook her head, "What did he do now?"

"Grand larceny, arson, driving with no license, DUI, must I go on?"

"Do you think he has hit bottom yet? I mean the therapies don't work until they hit bottom, but they take down everybody else with them."

"Praise God, no was hurt but him and his house."

"Well, and whoever owned the car he totaled. See? It's a downward spiral," she whined.

James broke in, "How do you make Emmentaler? What did you say the extra bacteria is?"

"Lactobacillus Helveticus."

"Do you have some?"

"Yes, I think I do."

"Let's go make some. I want a tour."

Alan served the eggs, "Hey, the toast is ready. Have a bite. I'm heading for the shower, then I'll decide if I'm going to visit Jack or not. I hope you don't mind, Laura, but I'm pressing charges. He had me co-sign on that house and then he burned it."

~*~*~*~

Malla sat at her computer. His laptop sat at her desk, his Facebook account open for her to study. She turned back to her email account. What could be said? She studied again his first message to her mother.

"Justina Cortez, Please let me introduce. I'm Drew Bjornson, a friend of your daughter Malla. We live together here in North Dakota, USA. She is my sweetheart and helps me with my four children. If possible I'd like to be added to your friends list on Facebook so I can share recent photos." Signed, "Drew Bjornson, Cavalier, ND, USA."

Malla stared into the screen. "Please help me, God" she prayed, "I need Your strength. I need Your words. I need Your help!"

8 NEW BEGINNINGS

After his usual stint—three days at sea—Hilbert Hallgrimursson returned home for peace, warmth, a good meal, and hours of quiet to work on his hobby: studying family history.

"Hilbert!!" Justina screamed at the top of her lungs. "Hilbert! Come!!"

"What's wrong?? Woman, are you dying?!"

With passion common to her own Spanish heritage, she pleaded, "Hilbert, you must listen. Oh, God above, help me! Hilbert, my love. Please. First I got this message. See? It's a note from Malla's friend. Malla!! My beautiful Maria Haldora!"

Hilbert studied the note, focusing on Drew's signature block. "Cavalier?"

"Yes, do you know that place?"

"Yes."

"What is the ND?"

"North," he started, then recalled, "Dakota."

"Good, then I got this letter emailed from Malla." She saw him turning away, walking towards his desk where the family trees he researched for

others all called loudly for him to perfect his own family tree—to reach
out to his own branches. "Hilbert, you must," Justina begged. "Leave
all these old names and places and listen."

"People depend on me to find their ancestors."

"To the chagrin of your own offspring. This is more important. Listen."
She pulled the letter from her bosom and read, "Dear Mamma, I love
you and miss you, your voice, your touch, your good cooking. Much has
happened here in my life. Where do I begin?"

"She only wrote it to you?"

"It'll make sense later, just listen. 'Where do I begin? Number one:
TEK was unfaithful. He has a child with another woman. We are
divorced'."

"Good, I never liked that boy."

"Since he's obviously not the infertile one, I'm mourning the loss of
potential motherhood. My prayers go unanswered." Justina's face
showed the pain this reality caused her. Hilbert's eyes, too, flitted about
the floor as though he shared her quiet despair. After a brief pause and
deep breath, she continued, "I was alone in Milwaukee about a year until,
Number two: My friend Anna Hillman, now Anna Zimmermann, asked
me to help her run a special bakery. Their grocery store will have
American food, but also Icelandic. We opened on July first. It's in
Mountain, North Dakota, a small town that boasts its Icelandic heritage."
Justina looked up, "Wasn't that the town Halfdan was talking about?"

"Yes, it was."

"We have a brochure somewhere here for that town. We must find it."

"Is that all she said?"

"No, listen."

"Then read, woman."

"Oh, where was I? Milwaukee, bakery, July first. OK, here. 'As I arrived in North Dakota, Anna met me at the airport with tickets to Reykyavik to shop for spices and supplies for the bakery. Number Three: I'm so sorry for not calling you when I was home. I know I should have. Please forgive me'."

Hilbert grunted his dismay.

"Number Four," Justina continued, "while in Reykjavik, I met Drew."

Hilbert interrupted, "What kind of name is Drew?"

"It's short for Andrew, a good Christian name, now listen. As you can see from his photos on Facebook," she turned to her computer, "he is handsome. See, Hilbert, here's a picture of them together. Aren't they a beautiful couple?" Reading she continued, "He is also kind and funny and smart. He is starting a new job working for Anna and her husband, Alan, managing a new hotel. He is Canadian with Icelandic heritage and comes from a small town in Alberta, Canada, an Icelandic community called Markerville. Perhaps in Dad's genealogy studies he may have heard about Markerville." She looked at him, "Have you?"

"Yes, I have, now keep reading or give me the letter."

"If Dad wants to research Drew's family in Iceland, Drew is very willing to share his ancestors' names and when and where they emigrated from Iceland. Is this still an interest of Dad's? How is Dad? My prayer is that he's not still upset with me." Justina's voice began to soften. "I always kept the name he gave me, even though no one here can pronounce it. Please share this letter with him." Justina's throat began to tighten as she read, exposing her emotion. "Please hug him and give him my love. I miss him very much. Maybe I should be writing this addressed to him, too, but I don't know if he wants to hear from me." Self-control abandoned, she wept in Hilbert's arms.

He stood holding her, his own heart weakening. "Is there more?" he quietly asked. To her nod he offered, "Let me finish reading, alright?"

"Out loud, please, my love."

Hilbert took the paper and reread Malla's call from her heart to his. Quietly he continued, "There's a lot I don't know. I don't know if God is listening. I don't know if my boyfriend and I will make forever promises. I don't know if I'll have the guts to manage my new bakery to please everyone. I don't know.

"But I do know one thing is true. Dad was right about TEK. I just didn't know it at the time. I'd value his opinion about the above 'ifs'. Mom, yours, too. If Drew and I do get married someday, it will be a real wedding in a church since I'm having the elopement annulled. If and when that day comes, it's my prayer that Dad will walk me down the aisle. Drew's children are wonderful and Drew inspires me. I will confess, reconnecting with you was his idea.

"I'm sorry for complicating our relationship for all these years. Like with fishing, I'm casting out a line with a hope and a prayer, love, Malla."

"Hilbert, darling, look at her face. She hasn't changed a bit."

"Hmmmm, sounds like she's wiser. What do we know about Drew?" He went to his computer.

"Just what Malla said. But isn't it nice that since she can't have children that he has so many."

"How many?"

"Four, see, here they all are." She pulled up the family picture.

Hilbert stared into Malla's hazel eyes, then all those around her. As his own computer powered up, he recalled the Bjornson name in Markerville. It was a big family and Hilbert already had connected with a fellow genealogist who lived in Edmundton, Alberta. He reread the letter. Justina dug through a stack of mail as Hilbert commented, "She wants my advice on love, baking, and religion? It's the blind leading the blind."

Justina cried out, "Here it is! The brochure, Mountain. See? Their party is in August," she said seeing the date. "We've missed this years' party. But still, we have to go!"

"Now? August, no, you know I can't." A knock on their door disrupted their conversation.

The woman at the door described, "I'm Runa Gisslisdoittur from Nordic Realty. I've just sold the home of a friend of your family and I was instructed to bring you the proceeds for you and the charities of your choice."

"Who? Whose home?" Hilbert gently demanded.

"Drew Bjornson," she read, then handed Hilbert the envelope and turned to leave.

Hilbert opened the envelope and read the amount on the check. Justina thanked the woman and came back from the door, curious.

He muttered, "This makes no sense. Pack your things, Justina, and a few things for me, we leave on the next flight."

Justina scrambled to reach for luggage as Hilbert dug into his genealogy software. He typed 'Andrew Bjornson' and 'Markerville' and his data displayed before him. *Yes, four children. He had married Michelle Olafson and she had died.* He glanced from her death date and routinely compared it to the youngest child's, Michael's birth date. *The same day. The last known employer was the Hotel Esja in Reykyavik.* Hilbert turned to Justina's computer scanning each of Drew's pictures. Nodding, Hilbert pulled the realtor's check from his pocket and studied it. None of it made sense. Again he looked at the family history data. Drew had lived just two blocks away and now he was hoping to make Hilbert a grandfather. A quick climb up both Drew's and Michelle's family trees proved fruitful.

"Darling, I'm ready," Justina said, reaching her arms around his neck. "You load the luggage, Hilbert, I'll close these down." With a wink and a playful pat on his wife's backside, Hilbert hustled to his chore.

~*~*~*~

As the end of the last bedtime story was read, a hush fell over Malla's house. As she pulled the twins' door to nearly closed, Malla saw Drew coming from Michael's room. There was a gulf of awkward tension in the air, an elephant in the hall created by their prior frank and honest conversation confirming the old adage, 'Truth Hurts'.

Drawing from a children's story, Drew imagined he pulled a long sword, slicing through that tension, and asked, "Malla, can we talk?"

She returned his question with a question, "Aren't your parents expecting us?"

"No, they're playing cards." He motioned her toward the stairs. "A walk?"

"What if the kids get up?"

"Mom is going to check on them. I told Mom we need some alone time. Please?"

The pair walked quietly along the path that followed the lazy Tongue River in its summer-time trickle. Malla discussed the children's latest antics, their funny questions, their menu requests. "Michael is craving rice pudding. It was a comfort food of mine when I was young."

"You don't have to do this."

"The rice? I'm craving it too."

"No, I mean. What do I mean? Malla, when I agreed to come move here and live with you, I was under the impression you were attracted to me. To me, the man, not the father of four."

"How can you separate yourself like that? I can't do that."

"We can't go back to the way it was. The genie is out of the bottle. But I did enjoy believing you like me for me. But it wasn't true and now the truth shows such a different image."

"Do your parents know we…"

"Aren't a real couple? No."

"So, then," Malla looked up into the sky, "we are the only ones who need convincing."

Drew's eyes showed his surprise. "You're willing? Wait. No, you are not a mail order bride. There's no sense in you having to pretend."

"No, I am me. You and your children are guests in my home. You did inspire me, Drew. I don't know the outcome of my letter yet, but I consider you a friend who has my best interest at heart."

"Good. That's good."

"Set all the physical history aside, the truth, the move, my great-great-aunt, the confusing mixed signals, all of it. Put it in a box and lock that box shut. Let me know when you're done." Malla knew enough about men that compartmentalizing made sense to them.

"OK."

"Now, open a different box. It's the 'my new friend' box."

"You have the most beautiful eyes," he sincerely complimented.

She returned the volley. "In my letter I told them you are handsome, but also kind and funny and smart."

"What did you say about the children?"

"I didn't talk about them at all. As I wrote that letter I found myself more and more sure that you are someone special to me."

"Me?"

"Yes, you. I even went on to describe how if things work out for you and me, that I want a real church wedding and I want my dad to walk me down the aisle."

"Your first wedding was…"

"We eloped to Vegas. I didn't have a dress. Nothing." As they walked, Drew and Malla went through the gated fence and down towards the river. They soon found their path led them to a park. Malla settled on one of the swings and Drew took another. The pair sat and swung, finally moving to a picnic table and then a park bench. They talked for what seemed like hours. The sunset had long since faded to dark and the moon and stars came out to shine a path for their walk home. Once finally back, they paused at the gate. The dim garden lights faintly illuminated their images.

Voices whispered inside. Nessa complained to BJ, "Daddy's not here."

Tori came from the other direction, "Where's Malla?"

BJ listened at his window explaining, "They're outside. They were out there when I fell asleep and there they are still. Go to sleep."

"But I had a dream," Nessa reported.

"Was it scary?"

"No, it was funny."

"Then go back to sleep and watch it some more."

Tori commented, "I like Malla, she's nice. Daddy's kissing her!"

Drew held Malla's cheeks cradled in his hands. The children watched until BJ brushed them both towards the door, "Go to sleep." As the girls whispered down the hall, BJ's lonely father and his would-be mother cuddled within each other's arms. BJ dove for his bed as soon as he saw them heading towards the house.

Their conversation continued in the kitchen over a snack of ham and pickles and cognac. Sharing each other's history and multiple funny and heart touching stories, they spent the night within the relaxing pool of intriguing conversation. As dawn shone into the kitchen window Drew suggested, "Sunrise? Oh, the time! Hey, let's take a drive and watch the sunrise!"

The drive was one of the most romantic times Malla had ever spent. His eyes were constantly gazing upon her, explaining that she was his sun and he would watch her as the sun rose in her face, her eyes, her cheeks, her neck. The early morning encounter quickly turned sensual and Malla found herself having to decide. "Drew, the mixed signals I've been giving you have been since I'm drawn to you physically, emotionally, in an intimate beautiful way, but I hesitate to give into my desire for you."

"Hesitate? Why?"

"Did you know we are surrounded by people who are waiting for their wedding?'

"What?"

"My best worker at the bakery, Stacia, her fiancé and her, they're waiting for their wedding night to make love, have sex, whatever you call it. They're waiting and they're not alone. Our bosses, Anna and Alan, they waited too, and others."

"Very traditional."

"I'm a traditional person. Can you bear the thought of waiting?"

"Did you just propose?"

Malla blushed and bashfully asked, "Marry me?"

He stared deep into her eyes, finally uttering a quiet "Yes," then whispered into her hair, "You're worth waiting for!" At that moment the sun rose over the horizon, its brilliance beaming, streaming towards Earth, onto their tender kiss.

~*~*~*~

Iceland Air flight 677 touched down without any troubles in the Minneapolis International airport. Justina wrung her hands as they taxied, "Oh, Hilbert darling, the wait is torture!"

He patted her fingers on her lap, "I am eager, too. It's like the story from the Bible of the Prodigal Son, but instead of running to my child, I'm flying!"

"Oh, Hilbert. You cranky old fisherman, it's not like you to quote anything from the Bible."

"No, you don't see that side of me. When I have my crew out to sea, I read Bible stories in my bunk at night."

Justina's eyes showed her surprise, "When did you start that?"

"After I turned fifty, after Stoni died. We all have to face our maker someday, and when he died, I started studying for the final exam."

Her eyes glistened as she studied him, "God be praised! Prayers are answered, you salty old seaman!"

"We're in Minnesota?" he asked, looking out the portal.

"Yes."

"That's way too far from any ocean. What in God's name are we doing here?"

"You're helping to answer another prayer for me. Good, we finally parked."

Drew parents, Ken and Amy, were still visiting. Their plan was to head back to Calgary the next day. A picnic meal was spread out on the table and Amy cooked her special barbequed ribs. A tired, but blissful couple, Malla and Drew had been napping throughout the afternoon. Now, they spent the evening with their family. Malla stood near the four foot fence that surrounded the backyard. That was where she was standing when he saw her.

Alan and Anna introduced Hilbert and Justina on the deck to Ken and Amy, but Malla and Drew were far off in the yard distracted by the beaver who was working in the river beyond. Hilbert watched as Drew gently touched her shoulder with one hand and pointed into the distance with the other. He stood behind her and she soon pulled his hand to her waist. Interested children climbed the fence to see. From Hilbert's angle he could see her smile as she talked to the children. Her eyes were full of love as she looked up to be kissed by Drew.

Quietly he called in Icelandic from the middle of the backyard, "Little girl, Maria Halldora."

Time seemed to slow down. She brushed her hair away from her eyes and turned toward the voice.

He walked toward her, arms open wide, and stopped five feet away, whispering, "Little girl."

Malla's joy could not be defined or contained. She squealed like the little girl he remembered and flew to his waiting arms, "Pabbi!" Justina's smile studied her as Malla finally opened her eyes in the arms of her father. "And Mamma," her voice sounded as relieved as Justina's heart was at seeing her daughter and her husband in their collective embrace. "Pabbi, I'm so sorry for being foolish!"

"Na, na, na, you weren't the only one." The trio hugged again, Drew and his parents looking on.

"Daddy! The beaver, I saw it!" Michael proclaimed.

His voice pulled at Malla's heart, "Drew, come, these are my parents, Hilbert and Justina. This is Drew Bjornson," she laughed, her heart happy to announce, "my fiancé!"

Hilbert shook Drew's hand and looked back at Malla, "I've come as far from any ocean as I can be to bring you advice on love, baking, and God, but no, you don't need my advice."

"Yes, Pabbi, I do. How are those sea legs?"

"Air travel goes fast, but it makes me tired. Drew, it's good to meet you. Your children are as beautiful as Justina boasted."

"Hello and welcome. I'm hoping they behave. Justina, hello, so good to meet you. Have you met my parents?"

Justina bubbled, "My friend. Yes, at the door."

BJ pointed, "There's a beaver!"

Justina's face was animated, "Show me!" Malla watched as her parents and Drew's were all pulled into the children's fascination.

Hilbert turned from their gaze over the river and whispered to Malla, "As for baking, use eggs, but whip them first and use three cups of flour, not four."

"Which recipe is this?"

With a boyish grin he shrugged, "All of them!" Malla laughed at his silliness, her heart reveling in hearing him tease. "Which leads to advice on God." They smiled into each other's eyes, he finally admitting, "He usually has me stumped, but day after day He IS there and He does hear you. He even hears this salty old seaman." Malla hugged him all the more as Hilbert kissed her forehead, silently thanking God.

Malla fussed, "You've been a time traveler, you both must be weary. You two take my bed tonight and I'll have the couch."

One eye closed, Hilbert grinned, trying to figure. To Drew he shrugged, "That leaves you out in the cold."

"No, I have my own bedroom, where Michael usually ends up by morning."

Hilbert looked confused and Malla blushed, "No, Pabbi, we are waiting for our wedding."

"Waiting?"

"No sex," she whispered, "we don't share a bed." Slowly her reasoning sunk in.

He and Drew exchanged shrugs as Hilbert nodded slowly and watched Drew as he fixed Michael's toy airplane. Hilbert fought his fatigue and once the children were nestled in their beds, he took the chance to finally talk to Drew, alone in the kitchen. "Drew, I'm delivering this check."

"My check?" he looked at the piece of paper Hilbert had pulled from his pocket, "What's this?"

"The realtor, she sold your house and delivered the payment."

"I already received payment."

"What?"

"Yes, I sold it to Anna. I paid the mortgage and gave her a set of keys, then we started packing. That's not mine. I got paid and had enough left to get my belongings shipped and made a good down payment on my new car."

"This check isn't yours?"

"No, it's written out to you."

"It makes no sense. Maybe I'm just tired. Does this make sense?"

Drew repeated, "I sold my house to Anna. Maybe this would make sense to her."

"Who is Anna?"

"The woman who showed you where we live."

"Oh, I am tired. No, I do remember her."

"Your body thinks it's four in the morning." At Hilbert's yawn Drew patted his shoulder, "Sleep first, we'll contact her tomorrow."

The summer days were busy, but calm as long as Laura had her list of priorities set up and a calendar that made sense. Since Jack was again under lock and key, Laura forced her mind to focus on all things dairy, curds, and whey. Since arriving in North Dakota, James was catching the ins and outs of Laura's system, even sensing an occasional hint at humor from this woman whose life was in such disarray.

The day was done, but as Laura drove down Schroeder Hill, she had a strong urge to make a stop. She pulled up to Trish's house and went to the kitchen door.

The pungent aroma hit her first. James answered the door, "Hi."

"Hi, so what did you think?"

"About what? Working for you?" To her nod he replied, "It's OK."

"We haven't scared you off?"

"I can dismantle and reassemble an AK47 in the dark. A few cheese vats aren't going to scare me. But the mops and buckets? That could be a different story."

"What are you cooking?"

"Sauerkraut and onions in this pan with butter and fried summer sausage in this one." He added, "It's Aunty Betty's sauerkraut, yum."

"Sauerkraut?"

"And onions. I was so pumped when I saw the jar in the cupboard. I used to have two of these every day when I'd get home from football practice."

Her attention rested solely on the stove, "Onions and what?"

"A very mild sauerkraut. Do you want a taste?"

"OK, a little." She expected she'd taste a small forkful of the bubbling mass but instead, he buttered the toast, added the fried summer sausage, and used a set of tongs to pile on the onions and kraut on top, finishing with the second piece of toast.

Laura objected, "No, that's way too much for me."

He quartered the sandwich and placed a small square on a small plate. James assembled others while she took a timid bite. He watched her chewing as he worked.

After the first bite she nodded, "That's not as offensive as I expected."

"There's a compliment in there somewhere," he chuckled.

"The onions are sweet and the kraut isn't strong at all."

"No, it's Aunty Betty's recipe. It's just cabbage and salt."

Nodding, Laura dared another bite and studied the flavors. "Can you imagine if you had a sliver of Swiss in there to melt?"

"Grilled in a Panini? You read my mind. I've tried Swiss, but Emmentaler is best."

"Can you get her recipe? I'm sure Anna can replicate this for you," Laura added, pointing to the pint jar. "She cans everything and anything," she declared, reaching for a second quarter.

"Really?

"Well, maybe not right away, I think she's feeling better now. No more morning sickness."

"That's good, because Trish was gonna be ticked that I used her last jar. Do you want the other half, and a chair? I guess we're watchin' baseball."

"Ah, no. You two need your time to catch up."

"Yeah, no, you know what? Tony is actually T-o-n-i. Yeah, I didn't see that one comin'."

"Isn't she here?"

"Not yet, but we do expect her later."

"She's his nurse. So, you have a good night." She glanced back as she pulled the door closed, seeing that he had two plates loaded with sandwiches and pickles and was headed for the living room.

After lunch Drew and Hilbert came knocking on Anna's back door. As she cleaned the kitchen she poured coffee for the men. She easily switched to Icelandic and pulled out a plate of Halfmoon cookies from Malla's bakery. "These are samples." Between the flavors and the ease that Anna had with the Icelandic language Hilbert felt at home.

"Anna," Drew asked, "when I sold you my house you paid me in full, right?"

"Yes, yes I did."

"Then what happened?"

"You packed, I came home and here we are."

"Right, so why did a realtor bring Hilbert this check?"

"A realtor?" Anna made several quizzical faces while she wondered. "Before I left Reykjavik I handed the keys to a priest at the Cathedral with the idea that if someone needed a home that the priest would set it up for someone. That's what I did.

Hilbert inquired, "Who was the priest?"

"Father Paul, I think."

"Father Paulsson?"

"Yes."

"How did he know Drew's name?"

"I visited for a bit, talked about hiring Icelanders, Drew, Malla. We had a nice visit," she ended innocently.

"You did, ah," Hilbert nodded.

Anna smiled, "You know him?"

"Yes." Hilbert's mind was racing.

Anna's spun just as fast, "So, he sold the house I gave him?"

Drew acknowledged, "Yes, it seems that way."

She looked at Hilbert, "And gave the money to you?"

"Yes, it seems he did."

"Why?"

Hilbert's eyes studied the braided rug below. "That's something he and I will need to discuss." He and Drew left Anna's home feeling just as perplexed.

Drew asked, "What are you going to do with it?"

"I don't know yet, I just don't know."

~*~*~*~

Jack was going through DTs and hating all life had to offer. Out in the country, yellow caution tape still fluttered in the breeze around the burned shell of a house and insurance forms were being processed. The car that he'd stolen and wrecked was in the county impound lot in Cavalier. James surveyed the vehicular damage Jack had done from the fence and sidewalk. He got his supplies in Cavalier and headed back towards Highway 32.

On his way towards Schroeder's Hill, James drove past the quiet farmyard where Jack and Laura used to live. The memory was clear. He'd met Rusty in the driveway when he'd first arrived, saying, "Hi, I'm James O'Malley. I'm pretty sure, but is this where my sister's boyfriend lives?"

"Nick, yes. He's gone right now. I'm Rusty Johnson. I'm living here, too, until my house is ready."

"Oh, OK. Laura lived here, too?"

"For a while. It was against her will. She's been through a lot lately." They'd both agreed on that.

For almost three months James had been going to his dairy job. That morning, when he walked in the door, Laura was giving directions to his co-workers. He studied her strawberry blond hair and her fair complexion that quickly blushed to pink when she noticed him. Other than making her occasionally blush, James had no reason to assume she was interested. Still, that was enough to keep him working hard in her employ.

Marbled Colby had just been removed from the milk tank before him and since he was an old hat at the mechanical processes and was starting to get more than curious about the recipes, he dove in to prep the vat for the next recipe. As he worked, he talked to Joyce who gravitated to James' buckets and mops, preferring that to handling curds. Joyce asked, "What do you mean?"

"Raw wine, after it's done fermenting, it's just as critical to keep it free of bacteria as those curds are."

Laura had been listening, "Wine? You make wine?"

"Yes, I did years ago, why is it that wine and cheese taste so good together?"

"They do," Joyce agreed, "but my husband, Kenny, he put me off any alcohol. I just can't enjoy it. The effects of the alcohol far outweigh the taste."

"Only if you abuse it in excess," James defended. "No, the flavors, when taken in moderation, can enhance a good meal. Good wine is like a good woman, she should be savored, appreciated, and lingered over."

This made Laura blush again and she disappeared into her office. Mindlessly studying her lists and calendars, Laura's cheeks proved her quiet interest.

Holly knocked on the door. Soon an older woman answered. "Hello, I'm Holly Christianson. Anna Zimmermann said that she'd set up daycare for me here with you. Are you Gwenny?"

Dr. Will Sturlaugson slipped quietly into town after Labor Day in an unceremonious return to Cavalier. His paternity leave that had been extended was at an end, but Anna had reassured him that she had found daytime daycare for the child. He unlocked his house and moved his sleeping baby into his bedroom, then spent the next couple hours setting up the crib and nursery gear in the next room.

Young Chris was ruling Will's new roost. His young whimpers and burps, and the condition of his bottom, were all Will had in mind as the elder attempted to make a suitable home for the younger.

Will's schemes to lure and snatch a beautiful nurse to take to Peru had been foiled by a mysterious letter. One he was sure had come from Trish's hands. Now as young Chris drifted back to sleep, Will contemplated her challenging words, *Will you do the right thing?*

These words had echoed in his mind in the two months since he had seen them in one of her emails. She had been gone, looking for a new vet, and he had just been dumped by Halee. Trish could have meant providing a good home for young Chris, and he was doing that. But in his heart this would-be priest knew the true meaning of her challenge.

The power of the pen had long since mystified Will. He was surrounded by books he had collected. Books he had on bookshelves since coming to Cavalier. Books he now poured over during and between feedings. Though these pages took time to consume, he was fed by their meaning, consoled by their power, and gradually inspired to serve mankind, to serve God.

He picked up a devotional given to him by his mother called, "Come Away My Beloved" by Francis J. Roberts. The original work had been renewed and updated to an understandable dialect. The piece that had Will in its grip was simply titled, "Return Unto Me." The Bible passage it focused upon was Romans 12:2, "Do not be conformed to this world but be transformed by the renewing of your mind, that you may prove what is that good and acceptable and perfect will of God."

The devotional message described Will so clearly. It was like God was calling him out. God had called him to be a priest at his altar, *and I just turned my back and ran,* he thought, strong emotion taking hold.

Tears streamed down his cheeks, wetting the baby's fine hair. "God?" he began in a weak and shaky voice, "I've been running and running and so far I've only gotten this far. And here You are, still with me. You and Your mother, your saints, You've been watching over me. God, my rebellious heart is tired. Please forgive me. I remember clearly your beautiful call for me to be your hands and feet. To save souls with you. But here's a new problem. If I join you at the Altar, in the trenches, helping people, to fight with You against the forces of evil, then what happens to this little baby?

"Trish is right, You conceived this child before You called me. You knew he would need a home before you called my name. What do I do? Please God, help me to know what to do." He hugged the child and laid him in his crib.

Exhausted, he lay on his own bed in the same room. Attended by angels he fell into a deep sleep. After almost a year of insomnia, he enjoyed profound rest that was a long time in coming.

~*~*~*~

In early September, requests for proposals were advertised for building the hotel, and adding Main Street landscaping, plus the first four tourism shops in Mountain, strip-mall style. A gift shop, an ice cream parlor, a café and a shoe shop, because Mountain had once had a shoe shop.

Brady and Drew worked together to develop the plans and specifications. Once bids arrived and were sorted, Alan reviewed the results, glancing through information about the construction firms. "Marcoux Construction," he read aloud. "That's Dara's dad's company?"

Drew added, "And her uncle."

"Costs are high on these three," he pointed, narrowing down the competition. "Looks like Brad Byron builds the hotel and Marcoux Construction will do the strip-mall." Alan took one more look at the hotel design. "This is going to be great. OK, send out the news, let's get this started. This fall, let's build a shed just west of town, past the Legion ground, to house the supplies for the hotel and strip-mall. Grady, please get everything ordered."

He handed the floor plans back to Drew and asked, "What do we hear from the Diocese?"

"About the new church?" Grady asked while tugging at another file. To Alan's nod, he replied, "Now's it's up to someone in Colorado."

"The Archbishop? Probably a Cardinal," he deduced. To the men at Drew's dining room table, Alan said, "Next, start drafting the dinner theater. Hmmm," he scratched his head in deep thought, reaching for his phone. As he headed out the door, Grady heard him say, "Ila? Please plan me a trip to Denver."

9 STORM'S A BREWIN'

Alan's laughter was honest and sincere, "Bea, the barfly?"

A former Byron's Bar barmaid, older than some, smarter than most, Bea Berglund was taking a new stand. "Not anymore, that's what I mean!" she chuckled along with Alan. "When Anna hired me last month to help in the grocery store office, it's like a new light flickered on that hadn't been shining for a whole lot of years. Now I feel like a real person again and I can't wait to discover my new me!"

"What does Doug think about this, this new you?"

"That old fart? He'll adjust, eventually."

~*~*~*~

Anna's mom, Candy Hannesson, dropped her woeful head onto Anna's shoulder. Her son, Jason Hillman, escorted by two guards, was brought forward from the jail into the district courtroom to be charged with rape. At no point did Jason look at his mom or sister, but only pleaded not guilty. A trial date was set. He didn't deserve their care and certainly didn't deserve the bail money. But somehow, he was released into his mother's care.

In those first few days, it was the whispers at the grocery store in Mountain, in and out of various shops in Cavalier, it was the whispers that kept dragging Candy down. That, and seeing Jason when she returned. Jason and his ankle monitor. No remorse, no guilt, just a face of boredom and an ankle monitor. Nothing her counselor, Roberta Simpson, could say would console Candy. She had months to cope with Jason before his trial. Another anxiety attack was starting. Fingers folded in prayer, she hid her face into the kitchen's cabinets praying, *Agony! Lord God, please guard me from this agony!*

Holly had been taught that Managing by Walking Around was good. What seemed to work even better was to get her hands dirty, to get in with her workers and demonstrate in person how work is done. The end cap that still needed signage and boxes of cereal was the chore at hand. Her new workers, Brody and Kyle, who had been asked by phone to help her set up furniture, now had their excuses in person. Brody explained, "Well, I'm just not an assembly sorta guy."

She had to agree, "Yes, that's clear from your attempt in aisle four."

"That was harsh," Kyle complained.

"You don't know harsh yet," she said, recalling her years as a single mom. "Someday, you'll learn harsh and you'll look back and wonder about the world. Hey, I told you when I hired you both, I don't sugar coat things. I wasn't expecting the help that you were asked to provide. I didn't ask for it, it wasn't assumed. But when Bea gets an idea, it happens. So, the next time she asks you for something on your personal time, just say no from the start. None of this 'OK', then the no-show. Don't be that guy." The pricing sign was secure above the shelving and the young men went on with their chore.

Holly had a call to return and headed for the office. Doug Berglund stood outside the grocery store office door, his ball cap in his hand, nervously fidgeting it from one hand into the other. Of average size and stature, Doug was always the life of the party at Byron's Bar. Ready with jokes and delightful stories, he was always the easy-going part of their twosome. Bea would flutter from one task to another when the chores at home needed doing. But that was changing. No one would accuse Doug of being easy-going with such a face. "Holly, good. Can you send Bea out? I have a question."

Bea rounded the door and looked at her spouse of forty-five years. He started, "I have been reading the boxes. Yes, I will try cooking tonight, but those boxes bring up way too many questions. Do you have a break or something?" The pair disappeared down the grocery aisles, but both Neil and Holly were too busy with their sundry re-orders, reports, and training more new workers to let Doug's sorrowful mood stop them.

Later that day, Holly parked her car and gathered her son. There was turbulence in the warm August air causing rumbles of thunder to bring many faces skyward with concern, including those of Holly and Cole. As Cole's face bent heavenward, he showed more childlike curiosity about the sky above and the atmosphere outside. Inside the bank, there was a whole different sort of drama on that Thursday night.

A line had formed in the bank. Generally, Holly liked to avoid crowds, but she'd received a sign-on bonus that day at Providence Foods, and it needed to get deposited so she could get groceries and supplies. Holly stood behind a young man who had a baby's car seat in tow. The line moved forward, and the young man did, too, but Holly tugged on the back of his shirt, "Don't forget your baby."

He looked up from the deposit form in his hand and blushed his embarrassment. As he moved to get the car seat, lightly covered to shade the child, Holly's boss, Neil, came from the teller's counter. "Holly! Good to see you here. Oh, I should introduce. Holly Christianson, this is one of our veterinarians, Will Sturlaugson. Holly used to work for me at Byerly's in the Twin Cities, mostly Burnsville. When Larissa gave her notice, yeah, Doc, you met Larissa. Well, she gave her notice and moved back to Salt Lake. I tagged Holly to come and be my right hand like she was before." Neil played with Cole, giving him a high five, "Wow, this little guy is sure growing fast! Give me five, Cole!"

Holly was embarrassed at how much of her personal information Neil was capable of sharing. *Verbal diarrhea, Neil. Could you please stop?*

she wondered. But aloud she quietly nodded to Will, "Nice to meet you."

Neil continued, but Holly's attention was split between the conversation before her and a familiar example of masculinity who had just walked in the door. Rene came from the door to Holly's side, pausing to shake Elijah's hand, who had come from the teller's counter. Surrounded by testosterone, Holly only smiled quietly when Neil suddenly asked, "Hey, Holly, is Troy here yet?"

"Troy?"

"Yes," he laughed aloud, adding, "Cole's daddy. Girl? Are you not getting sleep again?"

"Yes, Troy, I know who he is," she blushed, "but I'm not sure what the plan is yet." Both of the potential beaus quietly backed up and individually joined separate conversations closer to the large window and the stormy weather outside.

Neil's banking done, he waved and simply said, "Good night!"

She muttered in her mind, *Sure, Neil, drop verbal bombs and mortar rounds of gossip, then disappear. Good man. Thanks so much!*

~*~*~*~

The Saturday evening meal had been a secret all day at the Berglund house. When the time finally came, and the food had been blessed, the tick tock of the clock was the only sound they heard as they both took a taste of Doug's potato salad. Bea was gracious, "It was a very ambitious idea, potato salad."

Doug was more direct, "This tastes like crap!" He set his fork down, his shoulders instantly sinking, his face quickly turning morose. He asked, "What did I do wrong?"

"I don't know. Read the recipe and think about how the portions were followed." She reached for his hand, "This isn't a failure. This is training." With a quiet sigh, his eyes made hers melt with love. "Let's take a drive for a burger."

The Pit Stop was hopping on that Indian summer day. Bea and Doug got settled at a table surrounded by familiar faces. Dara kept Elijah at bay while he did his best to woo her. At another table Rene was chatting with fellow French Canadians who were traveling through. Cole seemed intrigued by their foreign sounds and kept staring. Holly was trying to teach him manners, but was failing that night. Though she was distracted by Cole's chatter, and his stubborn need to dip his fries in their vinegar, a tug at Holly's heart was surprising her. A jealousy was clearly developing when it came to Elijah.

Dara helped Holly to come back to reality. The two ladies worked together on marketing products for Providence Foods. The duties were split with Dara on the label designs, and Holly to get those products advertised online and in person. They both reveled in the friendship that was building. "Save me, girl!" Dara laughed and sat by Cole. Both women watched Elijah head towards the burger joint's front counter. "He's after ice cream." Dara whispered, "Seriously, I'm not interested."

"Wait," Holly whispered back, "in him or ice cream. 'Cause everyone loves ice cream, especially on a day like today!"

Dara pointed with one hand and sheltered it from Elijah's view with the other, "Him. I've already got a guy on the hook. Some women can handle a whole list of guys, but not this gal. Anything you can do to shake this guy loose, I'll owe you one!"

Elijah saw where Dara had moved to and came from the cashier with ice cream for all at Holly's table, including himself. Holly called out, "Bea and Doug, please join us! It's a party! Eli is buying a round for the house! Go ahead, Eli, bring us some more."

He wasn't impressed. "My name's not Eli, it's Elijah. Doug, do you want ice cream?"

"Naw, I've got food coming, but we'll sit here, if that's OK. My name's Doug Berglund," he said to Dara, extending his hand. He loved a good party.

"Dara Marcoux," she politely replied, then nestled in next to Bea.

He added, "This is my bride, Bea."

The two ladies were exchanging pleasantries when all were distracted by Holly. "Elijah, don't be rude," Holly reminded, "you forgot to offer ice cream to Bea. How can a guy with a Bible name be so rude? Did you know this, Dara? Rude," she repeated with a judging tone. As soon as the words had left Holly's mouth, she regretted being so hard on him.

Being outside of Dara and Holly's game, Bea was aghast at being stuck in the middle of what many would claim was much ado about nothing, but Dara could see Holly's logic. Playing along, Dara's eyes were suddenly sad, but determined as she looked up from her sundae to Elijah. "It's surprising, but yes, I suppose. Holly, can you give me a ride home?" None of the melting ice cream tasted all that good after Elijah felt that gut punch. Doug had many funny stories and jokes to tell, so to anyone looking in, the group was having great fun. Elijah's dish of melting ice cream was the only clue.

Sunday morning Saint Bridget's church in Cavalier drew a familiar crowd. Rusty and Ila, Brandon and Erin, Jim and James, and Rene. Alan and Anna were set to lead the music from the choir loft. As Anna prayed at the balcony kneelers, she surveyed the gathering congregation, noticing Will coming in carrying a baby's car seat. Other heads were familiar from her viewpoint but for one man who knelt, threading a Rosary between his fingers. He was a newcomer whom she promised herself she would meet.

Young Chris slept through the entire Mass as Will soaked up every word. It was good food for his hungry soul. The first reading was from Job: a daunting reminder of how small man is, how our own attempts at satisfying the ego can get us deep into our own pit of despair.

The second reading was from Second Corinthians. One sentence stood out, "So whoever is 'in Christ' is a new creation: the old things have passed away; behold, new things have come." This one sentence exploded as fireworks of hope in Will's heart. The Gospel reading told the story of Jesus calming the stormy seas. He watched as young Chris slept so peacefully. Indeed, after Will had given in to God, he too slept peacefully. When Will awoke refreshed, then the baby stirred, but not until.

Will was amazed by the personal way God was leading him, caring about him and caring for him. Will was humbled as he realized that the personal retreat he was experiencing was also being attended by so many friends, neighbors and co-workers that he had both annoyed and confused.

The final song still hung in the air. None of the friends or co-workers stopped to greet Will at this his first return to St. Bridget's since becoming a father. One man stopped as Will gathered his diaper bag. At a glance he recognized Fr. Christopher O'Donnell. The old priest grinned, watching young Chris sleeping. "Do ya s'pose he's dreamin'?" he asked.

"Padre," Will called, reaching toward his grandfather for a much needed hug.

Fr. O'Donnell whispered into Will's ear. "We priests, we call each other by our first names. So you can call me Christopher. That is…"

Will nodded, "I've just recently come back around to that idea."

"It's a notion I've been prayin' for. A Rosary every night."

"That explains a lot." Will motioned to the statue of Mary holding the Christ Child on her lap. "She's been trying to get me down off a steep mountainside, a mountain I kept falling off, every night."

Christopher smiled, "It's good to know prayers are heard."

Anna and Alan stood in the center aisle. "Hi, I'm Anna. You look like you might be new in town."

"Oh, I'm visitin'. I came to see my grandson."

"Oh, you're…"

"Father Christopher O'Donnell, miss."

Will leaned in, "This is my grandfather from Ireland. It was Anna's family who took in your son Chris when Grandma Victoria came back home without you."

"Your family did that?"

"Yes, cousins of mine."

"Oh, well, I'm very grateful. Soon after she left, I felt God's call to the priesthood and I didn't know about Chris until years later. Your family was entertaining angels all these years. You're Anna?"

"Yes, and this is my husband, Alan," she introduced.

"Father O'Donnell," Alan said, shaking his hand.

Will explained, "He's a missionary in Peru."

Alan nodded, "Oh, this is the one you've been bent on going to help," he said to the younger, then turned to the elder, "He's had grand plans."

Will conceded, "Well, plans that keep shifting. Alan's my boss who has been very patient."

Alan nodded, "Well, enjoy your visit." He gently nudged the small of Anna's back in the direction of the door.

Anna added as they left, "Will, if you need a sitter, I love babies!"

As the Zimmermanns moved off, Christopher commented, "I did some askin' last night when I got to town."

"Asking?"

"At the pub. Folks here don't know you very well. You're a vet. You sing and dance, but no one knew about your call."

"You asked?"

"No, I let them talk. They knew about some scandals. Not one woman, but two."

"No, like I said to God yesterday, I've been running but I'm tired of running. I'm a new creation and the old has passed away."

"Yesterday? Huh. Where does an old man get a bite to eat around here?"

Anna packed her music books into their car. "Alan? Why did you rush me away from Will and his Grandpa? We could've visited. We could've invited them for brunch. It would certainly be more positive than spending time with Mom and Buddy. Jason is such a wet blanket."

"Yes, he is, but Will and his Grandpa, those two need to talk," was all he said. Since Trish had shared Will's secret, Alan had been praying for God's will to be done. Now he could see God at work. Alan praised God for his care, but Anna's heart was mourning Jason's poor decisions all the way home.

James woke up swinging his arms, sweat glistening, shouting towards Trish as she came to find the source of the noise. Once James came to, he was embarrassed and humbled to have a witness to his pain. The brother and sister had a heart to heart talk about James' years away from home. Most of what haunted him was classified and couldn't be shared. "But I'm looking forward," James declared. "I'm pretty sure I've got a lady lined up, time will tell."

"Really? I've missed out on the details, all my time wasted on the vet clinic, when here under my nose is a budding romance? Please, do tell, who is it?"

"Laura," he said with a point of pride. "Laura Zimmermann."

Trish had been working since dawn with critters of all sizes and was increasingly irritated as one thought kept rolling through her mind. Laura had also been up early, due to a nightmare where she saw Jack driving her to Kraft Foods in Minneapolis and leaving her there. All the logical images that followed made even less sense when she awoke with a start and tried to sort it all out.

Both ladies were exhausted for their own reasons. Trish came to return some tools she'd borrowed from the Providence Farms' main dairy barn next to the cheese factory. The pair met in the parking lot. "Hey, Trish," Laura offered, then yawned.

Trish shot with both barrels, "What on earth do you think you're doing?"

"I'm getting in my car. Why?"

"No, this thing with James. My brother already has PTSD. He has enough troubles without you adding your own style of insanity. Leave him alone." Trish had wanted to say that all day, since talking to James that morning.

Laura swayed, holding the car door's handle. "What? Leave him alone. He, he's just one of my employees."

"Not according to him. No, Laura. Just stop it. You know there's more to it. No, woman, YOU are too crazy to be good for him. He's my brother and I know him better."

"Crazy? You want crazy?" All the chatter Trish had bored Laura with over the months was all running through her mind with increasing insanity-style volume. "Oh, just go hug a puppy. Do you realize how crazy you sound to any given person on the street about your, your God blessed," she stressed, not wanting to swear, "zoo that you take care of??? No one wants to know all there is to know about every animal you've ever seen, touched, heard, or cleaned up after. Just shut your face!" Laura finished, slammed her car door, and drove away.

10 THE TRUTH SETS US FREE

Dara's desk was in the main Providence Farms office in Anna and Alan's yard. She was just up the hill from Elijah's machine shop. Easily distracted that morning, but during the course of her work, she had to make a note and grabbed paper and pen. Since the uncomfortable dish of ice cream, Dara had been ruminating. The same thought kept gnawing at her. The pen rested on the pad of paper, still and quiet as she stared into space. Finally, she set down her paper and nervously twisting the pen, she headed down the hill.

The shop door was open but he wasn't at the work bench. After hearing his name called, Elijah slowly rolled out from under Alan's pickup. His coveralls were oily, his hands just as much. He stood and reached for a rag, but kept quiet.

She looked about, wondering how to start. "It wasn't her fault. It wasn't you. It wasn't me. I blame Joe."

A quizzical look covered his face. "First off, who's her?"

"Holly. I asked her to help me. I knew a relationship with me, right now, it just won't work. I asked Holly to help me to get you to back off. You're very clever, your jokes, your interests. You're fun to talk to. I like to laugh with you, you know, as a friend. But I blame Joe. I promised him I'd wait."

"Joe. Where is he now?"

"Arizona," she explained. "He works for my dad's construction company. They're heading here as soon as their work in Maricopa is done."

None of it made sense and shaking his head didn't clear it any better. "Holly just made it all up?" He tossed his rag and headed back to the pickup, muttering, "Women are weird."

~*~*~*~

Jim was behind the wheel as Trish's car pulled away from their house. James looked into the back seat. "I like the idea of fishing away the Autumnal Equinox, but wait, don't we need fishing poles and tackle?"

"It's all on the pontoon. Toni has it."

"Toni. I hear Toni is a she."

"She, yeah she is."

"And she's special to you."

"She is that. She's the nurse Trish hired to keep an eye on me when she was on her trip."

"I've seen pictures from that trip. She got her own souvenirs in the form of pets and such for Nick. But you? Looks like while the cat was away..."

"Teehee, yeah, I sure did!"

They drove on in silence then discussed the crops and people from Belle Fourche. "Hey, James, your first grade teacher, Miss Carney, she finally got married."

"Really?"

"Yeah, this business of waitin' and findin' love in your middle years is sorta catchy."

"Love. So this thing with Toni, is that love?"

"It's headin' in that direction."

James stared off into the soybean fields. "I'm not over Mom yet. Can you give a soldier a chance to visit his mother's grave before you bring home a new wife?"

"Is that why you don't want to ranch? 'Cause you're mad about Toni?"

"I don't want to ranch because I have no interest in ranching. It's not personal against you. What I object to are the animals themselves. Trish, she got my share of the animal loving genes, OK? I'd rather make cheese or maybe wine."

"They have a butcher shop, too."

"Na, I've seen enough blood. Just please be happy that I'm home and I'm living nearby. And, God knows, maybe I'm heading in that love direction, too?"

"Who's that?"

"Laura Zimmermann."

"Yer boss?"

"She is for now. I've got some ideas." The men shared James' brainstorm and soon the lake shore lay before them. James stretched, rising from the car seat, and headed for the dock. Toni and her pontoon were ready for a good afternoon on the lake. At Jim's quick nod, James held the pontoon's frame and asked, "Permission to come aboard?"

"Permission granted," she smiled.

"Toni, this is my son, James. James, ain't she pretty."

"Good to meet you, and yes, Dad, she is."

"Well, Captain? What are our odds?"

"The water's choppy but the low pressure is gone. I say we stay close to shore. There are rods and bait over there," she pointed, "take your pick."

As James studied the fishing rods, he heard kissing sounds behind him. He rolled his eyes and sighed, then called out, "Is it safe to turn around?"

Jim chuckled, "For now."

As expected, it was a good, crisp fall day out on the water. James recalled stories from North Dakota soldiers who had been fishing on Devils Lake. "When the white settlers heard the natives' name of this lake, it was translated as Devil's Lake, but it should be called Spirit Lake. The guys said there were problems with flooding."

"Yes, you can't troll with your anchor down or you could snag a chimney. There is no natural outlet for this lake so now during this wet cycle, the lake just gets bigger. The walleye are loving it, though."

Conversation was limited, for the sake of the fish, but Jim felt his cell phone buzz inside his jacket. Jim had a natural, normal phone conversation with Marty. James could tell that Jim had a quiet respect for Marty, even though the two South Dakota brothers together seemed to irritate their dad. Then there was a sudden change. *Ah, now Dad is talking, ever so quietly, almost a whisper, to Austin.* The wind had slowed down to change direction, and the sound of lazy waves hitting the pontoon barrels was only countered by squabbles of random migrating ducks. The peace that James listened to was soothing to his combat-weary mind. Suddenly Jim's voice came to full force, "Your brother deserves a welcome home party," James clearly heard his dad say.

James studied the shoreline thinking, *And Austin hasn't changed one iota.*

Layne and Danielle met in a Bemidji café for lunch. Other than catching up, as sisters do, Layne wanted a rundown on the charges and lawsuit they were bringing against Jason Hillman. Danielle broke the news, "Jason skipped town." Danielle listened to her younger sister vent her disgust, and tried to soothe her nerves. "I know it doesn't seem fair—the family had the money for bail, but that's the way the system works. It clearly has an advantage for the wealthy." Saying this out loud didn't make it sit any more squarely in Danielle's gut, but facts were facts.

Later that night, the topic had been eating up too much of Danielle's energy, so she found the business card she'd received from Spencer and called. Once he was on the line, she asked, "What are you doing about your lame brother?"

"There's a state-wide search going, plus my brother-in-law, Alan Zimmermann, has four private detectives on the search, too. Jason doesn't like to travel, so I can't imagine that this will take long. He's going to slip up, then we'll find him," Spencer promised. Once he was off the telephone, he wished he still felt as confident.

It was clear that he'd had a personal interest in Danielle from the get-go. But she was all business, and determined to see justice for her sister. *That's what lawyers do, I'd suppose. Jason, that's another way you make me mad. Instead of talking about you and your trial, there's no way that this gal will see past you and find me.*

Candy's stress level wasn't getting any lower in the days since Jason was released to her care, awaiting his trial. Her summer vacation from her job at the Cavalier school would've been the best time for her to be in such a situation, but autumn had officially arrived and classes were in full swing.

All the time that Candy was gone to work, she relied on the ankle monitor to handle the huge responsibility that had been dropped on her shoulders. Then a call to see if he needed anything before she left Cavalier and she'd be home to make supper for herself, Buddy, and Jason. On occasion, Alan and sometimes Anna would stop in to see Jason, but today wasn't one of those days.

Truth be told, Jason's boredom level was all a show for the benefit of his mom, hoping her stress level and anxiety attacks would reduce. He had been into her jewelry box and found the carabiner where the extra key for his monitor was kept. He fondled the key and wondered. Jason looked through the kitchen junk drawer and found similar old keys that looked close enough.

After work the day before, Candy had used the usual key. Nothing was out of order. But that morning, soon after she'd left for work, he reached into his sock and pulled out the extra key. He'd planned it all through the night before, where he'd find cash, clothes, a vehicle. He was gone. The landline phone rang on the wall as she waited on her end of the line, wondering why he wasn't picking up.

Christine rounded the corner into the coffee aisle at Providence Foods. There she found the man she'd met at Alan's house earlier that summer. "It's Rene, right? I'm Christine, we met…"

"Yes, at Alan's birthday party, hello, Christine. How are you?"

"Oh, today's a little crazy. I'm multi-tasking and I've never really been good at that. You? How are you?"

"Right as rain," Rene grinned, "once I decide on which coffee to buy. Too many choices here at this store."

Christine was sure, "Better too many than too few." The pair kept shopping and met each other again in front of the butcher's scale. Christine was on her phone, flustered. But when she turned and saw Rene, she hatched a plan. The phone was quickly pocketed as she asked, "Could you please do me a favor?"

"Madame, your wish is my command!"

There was a fresh glow in her cheeks at the thought, so much so that she almost forgot her request. "Oh, oh, yes. Could you please drop my groceries off at my house? I've just been squeezed in with my hairdresser for a trim and then a manicure. Oh, dear, I do need both, in the worst way! Could you? I don't want this meat to spoil," she explained.

"Yes, just give me the address. Yes, I can do that."

"The girls will be there today, it's Saturday," she said, checking her list.

"Girls? Or women?" He'd heard about the nest of granddaughters and great-nieces that she'd been boarding in a large house on the edge of town.

She had to laugh, "Oh! Well, in my head they're all still 13, but no, women, in their own right." She scratched her temple as she began, "Are you…" her voice fell off, inwardly pondering his marital status.

"Christine?" he had a warning tone in his masculine voice, but she loved the way he rolled her 'r'. "I've heard you're some sort of matchmaker. Don't try your magical spells on me. I'll find the right one at my own pace." He checked his list. "I have one more stop, then I'll meet you up at the checkout."

She watched him walk off. He'd drawn his line in the sand for her, but Christine's mischievous grin was telling her tale.

The tall Victorian house towered over the collection of cars surrounding the old house. It had been in Christine's sister-in-law Evonne's family, but as family either moved on or preferred a more modern feel, it was finally left to the only surviving brother-in-law, Christine's brother, Earl. Early Pearly, as he was known to the locals. Tales were told of his raucous behavior in his youth. But during that summer, Earl wasn't sowing many wild oats.

Years of ignoring his health and drinking an excess of alcohol quickly piled up on Earl. Among a string of medical problems, it was finally a stroke that put him in the nursing home. Earl had been wed to Evonne's sister, Irene, who had passed five years before. Evonne noted that Earl's drinking increased after Irene's passing, and Evonne stood up for his place in her family. Then Evonne passed suddenly with a heart attack. Those who remained soon all agreed that Christine should make use of the house until other plans surfaced.

As Rene drove into the yard, he passed a building that had been the old garage, and before that, the carriage house. But no one was parking indoors on that sunny, late-summer day. He gathered Christine's grocery bags and headed for the back door.

As the door opened, he explained, "I'm delivering these for Christine. She didn't want the meat to spoil in her car. She's at the salon."

"Excellent!" Hailey said as she peeked into the bags in his hands, adding, "I'm starved!" She quickly pulled the first, then the second bag from his left hand and proclaimed "Good God, woman! These are only ingredients! There's no food here!" More ladies seemed to hear her wail and a small crowd soon gathered as Hailey shook her head, "Typical!"

Rene looked from one to the other ladies. "Christine said you ladies don't care to cook. Is that right?"

A myriad of excuses were shared, the most common being either too tired or too busy. And it was unanimous. Everyone hated doing dishes. All eyes watched as he pulled an onion out of a bag and started to cook. Within moments he had bacon bits in one pan and onion and garlic sautéing in olive oil in the other.

"That's a great start," Hailey praised.

Without saying much, he peeled a few potatoes, then diced them, adding water and chicken bouillon to the sautéed pan. The bacon was pulled out and spicy Italian sausage replaced it.

The meat sizzled as Rene worked, patiently waiting through the pauses when silence overtook them. Not one of those six ladies, all cousins from Christine's family, knew Rene from Adam. Dora offered, "You're the only Rene I know. Wasn't it Rene who helped deliver Erin's baby during the parade?"

Another, Sarah, added, "Yes, and Holly Christianson, she said that there were four guys who came to help assemble her new furniture. One was Rene, right?" she asked the woman at her elbow, Katie Hillman, Anna's sister.

Rene confessed, "Yes, I was there. Do you know Holly?" he asked, curious about the young woman.

"Yes, she's one of our cousins," came the reply.

Family. Hmmm, he quickly considered, then aloud asked, "Troy, you know Troy? Does he treat her well?"

Blank stares abounded until Dora bounced and said, "Oh! That's the daddy. Her boy, Cole. He's Cole's dad."

Rene explained as he checked the potatoes with a fork. "Someone asked her if Troy was coming here. Yes? It would be nice for the boy if he did."

The consensus was uncertainty. "Anyone here know more?" They all agreed that Christine would probably know, and the group silence returned as he dug through the grocery bags.

Sarah quietly asked, "Is it true that you're Alan's cousin?"

"Oui," he smiled, rinsing and chopping fresh kale.

Another slowly drawled as she critiqued, "But he's tall."

"Oui, he is. He got that from the other side of the family, like Brandon."

Confusion seemed rampant. "Oh, you're related to Brandon, too?"

"No," he replied calmly, "he's German. I'm French. French Canadian."

They stood back and studied Rene. His eyes looked similar to Alan's. All the women stared at Rene as he looked from one to the other. He gave a quiet 'humph', then poured heavy cream into the potatoes and bacon, pressed the fat from the hot Italian sausage and tossed it and the kale, into the creamy kettle. He looked up from stirring the tasty concoction.

A new face had joined the group carrying her embroidery hoop. Her focus was down at her needle, but she commented, "Something smells good!"

At one glance, Rene knew that he liked what he saw. He, too, studied her stitches. "What are you making? Hi," he said, offering a handshake. JoJo looked up, surprised. He added, "I'm Rene LaRoque."

"Hi, I'm JoJo." She smiled kindly. "It's an eagle," she explained, shaking his hand, then popped the frame off to show the design. They both eyed the stitches as she added, "It'll make more sense when the other colors are added. You said Rene?"

"Oui."

There was a natural joy to her smile when she heard his simple 'oui', but it was the glow in her eyes that set off fireworks in Rene's mind. She said, "I've only heard of one guy around here named Rene, and that's the guy who saved my grandma's life. Eunice Johanneson?" His shoulders shrugging, Rene nodded the affirmative. She was filled with emotion, but held her poise. "Sir? You are very appreciated! Thank you!"

TJ spoke over her food, "JoJo, and he just made this soup, it's delicious!"

The others were dishing up soup as Rene asked JoJo, "Do you mend?"

"Mend. I suppose."

"I've been looking for someone to help with a problem. I have winter gear, like coveralls and work jackets. They get pretty beat up when we work outside. I don't want to buy new since they'll just get beat up again."

Cammy shook her head. "You're Alan's cousin, Rene, you can just buy new every year."

He disagreed. "That's not my money. No. I make my own way." To JoJo he suggested, "The mending, I laundered it last week, but kept it in my car, trying to find someone who mends, other than Anna. She's got enough on her plate."

"OK," JoJo agreed, "bring it in, Rene, let's have a look. I'll check with Grandma Eunice if I get stumped. It's ironic, a bit. If you hadn't been there and saved her, then I could ask all day, but get no reply. Lordy! I

151

suddenly have so many questions for her!" JoJo said as Cammy handed her a bowl of soup. He headed out with a quiet grin, hearing her exclaim, "I just heard that Anna is expecting. How did I miss that? Oh, OH! This soup is amazing!"

Before anyone was ready, snow was in the forecast, meaning that Halloween was right around the corner. Nick had been chomping at the bit, ever since they first started their role playing trip to Colorado, Georgia, and Vermont. Some of the costumes they had worn to hide their identity from one visit to another were morose, even sad. But the Dolly Parton look-alike wig and subsequent padding were stuffed into Trish's closet, as was the Elvis-style fake sideburns and loud 70's polyester disco shirt.

Danielle still made phone calls to Spencer, wondering if Jason had been brought home in one piece. Spencer watched his phone ring, recognizing her number. He let it ring and roll to voicemail, once again. He had no news and the prospects of finding Jason were fading. What wasn't fading, though, was Spencer's interest in one certain attractive attorney. Her message was the same as the others, though this one added one interesting twist at the end, "Bring that boy home so we can lynch him proper. Well, you know what I mean. I know he's your brother and you probably feel protective of him. I know I do with Layne. OK, you get the drift."

Did Spencer feel like protecting, even sheltering Jason? He wondered about that and looked around himself. Others in the realtor offices he manned were heading home to celebrate Halloween. He dished out candy to the small children who went through his lake cabin neighborhood, but the question Danielle had broached still hung heavy in his mind.

The Teddy Bear pup, a Shihtzu/Bishon-Frise cross, nibbled on Trish's toes as she applied her final layer of makeup. She looked into the mirror, "Oh, my! Macy, this is way too much, it's perfect!" She stepped back and picked up the puppy, looking into the mirror. This was the same get up she'd been secret shopping in the summer before. The body suit Anna had sewn for Trish hid her slight figure. What looked back at her was a Dolly Parton look-alike, a full figured woman wearing a high-necked, ruffled sleeveless top, emphasizing her huge breasts. The blue blouse was long and was also trimmed with ruffles at her rounded hips. In between she could feel her own waist as she cinched the black leather belt tighter. She wore tight white Capri pants and tall white sandals that made her feet hurt. The red wig on her head was curly and long, reminding Trish of old pictures of Reba McIntyre in the 1980's. The false eye lashes blinked back at Trish and she started to giggle. She cuddled the puppy and kissed into the mirror, "Oh, God help us! Halloween party, here we come!"

Nick wore tight black jeans with a knit printed retro shirt with most of the buttons left open. He wore a black soul patch of whiskers on his chin, a thin mustache and thick dark side burns on his cheeks. His hair was now black and combed back away from his face under a black baseball cap with the brim curved to frame his face. He wore sunglasses and a wide grin.

Nick knocked on the back door of Trish's house, eagerly looking inside, "Oh, Mamma!" he smiled. Macy, the puppy, barked a welcome. "Happy Halloween, Babe!" He pulled off his sunglasses and stared at her breasts, "Now that's what I'm talkin' about!"

"Dad," Trish called to Jim, "what do you think?"

"If I hadn't seen your photo album, I'd never have recognized either one o' ya!"

She giggled and nodded, "Let's roll." Trish tucked Macy into her bag and went around to open his door.

Nick put on his sunglasses and smiled, "Pucker up!"

The memory of the first time she'd worn the costume flashed into her mind. That cool Halloween night, Trish relived the conversation with Nick in the time it took to get to their first party.

She recalled the smell of the summer flowers in Georgia. Trish had reached for the veterinarian clinic door and grasped its handle behind her. Nick pushed her and the door to its stopping point as they kissed as they had never kissed before, his hands on both oversized breasts.

Carolyn, the receptionist, was in her fifties and had the most common sense of the bunch. "Can we help you?"

Lisa, the vet tech, rolled her eyes and muttered to the other girls, "Like she needs help."

Carolyn asked, "Dr. Tappan or Dr. Krause?"

Trish rolled out from Nick's grasp and headed for the front counter. "Tappan, please."

"Your name?"

"Bridget Gabor."

"Animal's name?"

Trish proudly proclaimed, "Macy," and pulled the puppy from her pouch. While Trish was getting registered with Carolyn, Lisa and the other assistants stared as Nick wandered behind, feeling his way.

Lisa asked Trish, "What's with him?"

"Mylo? Oh, he's blind. Oh, and we lost his cane," Trish explained and continued to fill in her form with fictitious information.

Nick heard a dog barking at him and went towards the sound and the older lady holding her pet. Nick sat down and leaned in towards the woman, saying, "Oh, you smell good," his mouth smeared with red lipstick and his hands caressing her shoulders. "How's about a kiss?" he asked.

Another vet assistant, Pam, came to the older woman's rescue. "Mable, you and Bitzy can wait in the exam room. Dr. Krause will be right here," she promised, pushing a chair into the room, but always keeping an eye on Nick.

Nick could see his surroundings but tried to let his hearing direct him. As he followed Pam, he spotted the other veterinarian coming closer. Luckily he was distracted by the sound of a cat on another woman's lap. "A kitty cat," he quietly announced. This woman was in her twenties and beautiful. He sat next to her and listened to the cat's meow, covering his lipstick-covered mouth and waiting to pounce. Dr. Krause breezed past him without even a glance. The coast was clear.

Trish was getting an ear-load from Carolyn. Dr. Krause was the son of Old Man Krause, who had just retired and given the practice to his inexperienced, self-serving son. Trish watched him. Dr. Krause was the man Trish had seen Lisa arguing with. *What a nightmare for her*, Trish thought sympathetically. Dr. Tappan, the vet who had applied for her job, was clearly the better of these two. He was the senior vet and he was being pushed out. But could he stand her test?

Nick tipped his head like a curious puppy as the cat meowed, "What's your kitty's name?" His mouth was still red with lipstick.

"This is Francesca. I call her Franny."

"Can I pet your kitty?"

The woman eyed the red lipstick and said, "Sure," then pointed to her cheek, "you got some…"

He stroked the cat's head, leaning in, "What?"

"Your lips, you've got…"

"You said you want my lips?" he asked, leaning in to kiss her.

She pushed him off and hollered, "No, don't you dare!"

Lisa looked up from her charts and scowled. "Carolyn, we need to do something! Where's Tappan?"

Trish had run to Nick's side, "What are you doing?!" she shouted, "Comin' on to my boyfriend like that??!!"

Dr. Tappan appeared out of nowhere. He'd had a quick review of the situation from Carolyn, who followed closely. "Let's not lose our heads. Stacey, are you alright?" The woman cuddled her cat and nodding, moved to Carolyn's counter. "Do you mind if I see these folks first and send them on their way?"

Pam whispered behind Stacey, "He's blind."

Stacey agreed, "Go! Get them out of here. Blind or not, you're a crude and a dirty old man!"

Trish defended, "Mylo didn't mean any harm. He's blind."

Dr. Tappan shook his head, "Ma'am, most blind people behave properly in public, just like seeing people. Sir, you need to apologize to my client."

Nick's face squirreled up in confusion, "The cat?"

"No, the cat is my patient, the cat's owner is my client. I value both my clients and my patients, and I won't stand for any chaos in my clinic, in animal or human form. Now, apologize."

"Uh, sorry, but you smelled too good."

Dr. Tappan muttered, "That was a pathetic apology."

Stacey turned away, "Dr. Tappan, please, just get them out of here."

Lisa pointed, the exam room was ready. Dr. Tappan ushered them, "Come in there, where's your animal?" Mylo followed Bridget pulling on her belt, feeling her real hips. Dr. Tappan slapped his fingers. "No, behave yourself in public," he reminded with a scowl.

Trish's face beamed, "My puppy's name is Macy?" Her voice bubbled, reminding Nick of Shirley Temple, "She's in here. I need her certified."

"What for?"

Trish carefully set the sleeping puppy onto the exam table. Lisa closed the door and stood ready to help or take orders. Trish cooed, "Isn't she cute?"

"A Teddy Bear from the pet store here in town?"

"Uh, huh!" she nodded enthusiastically.

"OK, I'll repeat, certified for what?"

Trish's voice was uncharacteristically perky, "Oh! She's gonna be a seeing eye dog for Mylo!"

One brow curved high above Dr. Tappan's left eye, and his right eye twitched. He paused and stood with this expression for a time then shook his head. "No, Ma'am, that won't work. Did the folks at the pet store say it would?"

"Well, no, I didn't tell them my plan. I've seen their dogs and I think they make such cute little pets." As Trish continued with her flawed thinking, Nick cornered Lisa and wore his intentions on his smile like a badge.

Stacey, Carolyn, and Pam all gawked as they saw Dr. Tappan haul Mylo out by his collar.

Dara had convinced Laura to go out for Halloween and shake off her depression. It was almost working, but then James arrived and was hanging out with his Cavalier American Legion friends. Seeing him just reminded Laura how lonely she was. Trish's opinion was pushing a wedge between James and Laura. The natural process of meeting and getting to know a person, a potential mate, was being skewed by Trish's overprotective nature.

Regardless of all that, the bar was hopping that Halloween night, with dancing and darts being the favorites among the hardy crowd. Laura headed for the ladies room and missed Elvis and Dolly Parton's entrance. Dolly headed for the restroom to check herself—padding kept shifting into odd proportions. As Laura came out of the stall, she caught quite an eyeful. All she could say was, "And you think I'm crazy," and headed out to her car, then home. That was as close as the two former roommates had been since their blowup.

Trish wished that there wasn't a new distance between herself and James. He was told in no uncertain terms that Laura was off limits. He was respecting his sister's opinion, for the time being.

And though Trish didn't know it, Laura was trying her darnedest through therapy to get past the guilt and obtuse sense of duty she felt when remembering her love, and then her hatred for Jack, to get past it, and move on. She was making progress, but in the background there always seemed to be a familiar load of anguish that lingered, like a load of old laundry that needed to be dealt with.

She got to the apartment building where she still had the two bedroom apartment she had shared with Erin, checking her mail. A slow walk down the hall was complete with the familiar cluster of neighbors chatting about the trick or treaters, their pranks and hijinks, it was all innocent enough. Inside her apartment, the news and weather were on, with warnings of the cold and mixed bag of snow and rain that was coming.

Now to be hemmed in by Ol' Man Winter, when what I really need is a serious spring cleaning, physically, emotionally, and spiritually. It had been quite some time since Laura had given her spirit any thought. She hugged her arms and asked, *Suppose we can have an easy winter?* The walls and belongings around her were stock still. She shrugged and added, *Suppose You're more into people's hearts and souls, and weather is just an afterthought for You.* She looked from the commercial on the television to the walls around her. Tears tumbled as her chin quivered. *God? Please help me and Roberta with the therapy sessions, that they work and I can heal from the pain that Jack dumped on me. I want to be whole again. And when I am, I don't want to be alone.*

11 SWEET & SOUR

The creamery/cheese factory was getting to be James' home away from home. He walked through, drawing a curious Laura to linger nearby. James looked from room to room. "Part of this building could definitely be used for a winery."

Laura looked at the warehouse space. "Why do you say that?"

"It's a similar process."

"Mmm. No, it's got to be very different. I mean I don't know how to make wine, but it has to be different. Tell me how is done."

The creamery process was only using two thirds of the building so far. James stared into the vacant corner. Finally he shook his head and said, "There's gotta be a way we can do this." Then he walked away and reached for his mop. The idea nagged Laura throughout the morning.

She didn't have time to ponder. "Augh! I don't have time to think about wine either! This guy is gonna drive me nuts." Laura was scraping out a vat of feta cheese as James walked by with a cart of clean tools. "James, help me please. I want to go to Alan about the winery thing, but I don't know enough about it. Please tell me how to make wine."

He stopped what he was doing, reached for a clean apron and gloves and went to her aid. Quietly they cleaned out the feta and he started to disassemble the tank for cleaning as he asked, "Is my work acceptable?"

"Well, yes."

"Am I a hard worker, dedicated and conscientious?"

"Yes, you are."

"Am I mindful of the rules you've set?'

She looked at the hairnet on his head, "Yes, James."

"So you feel like you can count on me?"

"Yes, I think so."

James was frank, "OK, can I have a promotion? I need more challenge."

"You're the last one hired and cleaning goes to the last one hired. That's the way it is."

"So what you're saying is, it would be easier to ask you out than to get a promotion? OK, you've got Joyce making cream cheese and butter and I'd love to get my hands on that, come on, it's just butter, and Joyce says she'd rather be cleaning. Can we swap?"

Laura was still stuck on the thought of him asking her out. "Uh," she uttered.

"Can we swap?" he repeated.

"You and Joyce?"

"Right."

"Before I let you do that, I want you to tell me how to make wine."

"Before I tell you that, I want to hear your story."

"My story?"

"Your history. I want to know what makes you tick, and I want to know how you got into making cheese."

"Why should I tell you my story if you don't have to do the same?"

"I was born in a hospital in Belle Fourche, South Dakota. By sixteen I'd had enough of that podunk town. To me it was the worst place in the world. So I turned seventeen and I ran away."

"Where?"

"East. I went through Nebraska and ended up working in a winery in southern Missouri. That got me through the winter, and I kept moving east. I worked at vineyards in Pennsylvania and then Virginia and finally ended up using the French I'd learned at home and in school, and I waited tables for a French restaurant in New York City. That's where I studied for my GED. The restaurant's owner, his father, he helped me study, and I helped him get his citizenship. His English improved and so did my French. Plus, the family next door paid me for English lessons so I started to learn Arabic from them. Once I had graduated, then that's when I enlisted in the army. I wrote to Mom and Dad that I graduated, that I was OK, and that I was through basic training, but I guess that letter got lost. When I called them from Baghdad they were pretty upset."

"Oh, my!"

"I wondered why I wasn't getting any mail. Well, that's it."

"What did you do over there?"

"At first I was translating Arab to English, then they sent me undercover."

"Anything you want to talk about?"

"No, it's classified. Suffice it to say that Belle Fourche isn't the worst place in the world after all. No, I found the worst place in Afghanistan. What's your story?"

"Are you gonna tell me how to make wine?"

"Yes, we'll do that simultaneously."

"What?"

"That means at the same time."

"I know that. Wow, that's a big word for a podunk boy from South Dakota. OK, I was born in a cheese factory in Vermont."

"In?"

"Yes, in the break room."

"Wow."

"Yes, by the age of three I was helping to break up curds, and if the press wouldn't close all the way they'd put me on top while they got their tools to make it shut. But the age of eleven I was making my own recipes. Yes, I, like many of my peers, was a curd nerd. After high school I also went to New York City. Stevens, Vermont, was my version of podunk and I was convinced the big city would save me. Wrong. My identity was stolen, I was evicted from the tiny apartment I had finally landed. Oh, I was devastated, so I went back to make cheese for my uncle and his boys outside of Burlington, Vermont, and when Alan moved west, I decided to follow him."

"I've heard your boyfriend is in a treatment center."

"He's not my boyfriend. That was just another mistake. I suppose you've left a string of broken hearts in your past."

"With wine you start with fresh fruit."

"With cheese you start with fresh milk or cream or both."

"Then cull, wash, and crush."

"Then pasteurize."

"Warm the fruit."

"Warm the milk or cream or both."

"Add yeast."

"Add culture."

"Yeast is a culture. Anyway, depending on the yeast and ingredients, you can get a different wine."

"Depending upon the culture and the process and the temperatures, you get different cheeses."

"Let the fruit ferment."

"Let the milk or cream curdle."

"Test the tannin and add nutrients."

"Add rennet."

"Let the wine ferment."

"Let the curd solidify."

"Rack the wine to remove the sediment."

"Strain the whey out."

"Rack the wine again."

"Salt and press the curds."

"Rack the wine again."

"Press the curds again."

"Clarify the wine."

"Soak the cheese in brine."

"Bottle the wine."

"Wax the cheese wheel."

"Age it in a cool moist dark place"

"Age it in a cool moist dark place."

James noted, "From what I see around here there are similar humidity and temperature requirements." James' arms crossed as he pondered, "So, what you're doing with cheese is taking a liquid and making it solid."

"And you're taking fruit, a solid, and making it a liquid."

"We really need to do this. I'll get the gear and we can start."

Laura looked around, "Don't we need a big building?"

"No, we'll start with five and ten gallon batches. I think Anna said she has a supply of frozen plums."

"Rhubarb, too. I helped her freeze it."

"So, will you let Joyce and me swap jobs?"

"Yes."

"Whoo!" he quickly squeezed her arms and gave her a quick kiss on the cheek, "Thanks, you won't regret this." Laura was stunned as James ran down the hall and talked to Joyce, "Hey, we're switching jobs."

"Good!" Joyce sounded as though she'd been relieved of a heavy load. "OK, now you have a job you like, now we have to find you a sweetheart."

Laura blinked as she overheard him say, "Naw, I'm OK. I have my eye on one certain little blonde."

~*~*~*~

Dara was invited for lunch at Anna and Alan's house. This wasn't the only time she'd been in the charming and expansive home, but she was looking at pictures Anna had been framing, adding family ties throughout, and it felt like she was seeing it all for the first time.

"OK, who are these people? I love this one—it looks like it's a boat, no, a ferry? Cars on a ferry?"

In the picture, Alan had been feeding a seagull, and his sisters were there helping. He went through the names, "Oldest is Bruno, then Carly, then me, then Nikki, then Dillon, he's taking the picture. This was before Christmas when I was a senior in high school. Good memory. But I miss Dillon. That's why I asked Anna to frame these pictures. Several of them have my brother, Dillon."

"You miss him?"

"Yes, he's on a walk-about. He's purposely out of contact with Mom, and it's driving her crazy. But I'd rather have my mom's problem than to be in Candy's shoes, right now."

As others discussed the detectives in search of Jason, and his upcoming trial, Dara was stuck on one picture of a handsome young blonde playing basketball with Alan. The two faces are caught in mid-air as one blocked the other's layup.

She stared deep into the picture, wondering why it looked so familiar?

~*~*~*~

Tickets arrived for Dara's Christmas holiday in Hawaii. She'd known they were coming, but the reality of holding them in her hands had her awestruck. As soon as she was able, she disappeared to call Joe, her sweetheart carpenter.

Christine, too, was making plans for an old fashioned Christmas at her new old Victorian mansion. She sorted recipes and made long lists in giddy preparation for celebrating the Reason for the Season. Her church-going friends tried to remind her to first get past Thanksgiving, and through Advent, before becoming lost in the build-up to Christmas.

~*~*~*~

Dara was finishing up the last minute work before leaving for her holiday vacation to Hawaii. Anna asked her to join her for a quiet lunch in the big house.

Since starting with Providence, Dara had enjoyed every excuse to stroll through Anna and Alan's home, now being set up with Christmas decoration. "I miss those little family pictures of you two with your siblings. They were some wonderful snapshots!

Anna had been un-decorating as she went, then redecorating to add enough holly, plus red, white and green to make the house feel like it was a bowl about to brim. "They're still here, in the formal living room," Anna pointed. They rounded the corner and saw the plastic tub Anna used to gather the treasures that she'd bring back out after Epiphany Sunday.

Dara reached into the tub and drew one particular picture. "This one," she said, holding Dillon's high school graduation picture. He was sitting on a log, his arms wrapped around his knee. "Someonthing about this one. What's his name?"

"Dillon. He's the one who's…"

Dara finished the thought, "…on a walk-about. That's what Alan said. Something in his eyes. I swear I've met him before." She instinctively snapped a photo with her phone. The two ladies shrugged and the rest of their visit consisted of exchanging Christmas gifts over a tasty lunch.

Afterwards, Anna wished her a Merry Christmas from the door, as Dara loaded her car, happily heading for the airport. Anna absentmindedly rubbed circles onto her very pregnant belly and watched the car disappear into the distance. She prayed for Dara's safety, but also for Dillon's Christmas. None in the Zimmermann family had any clue about his whereabouts. *Maybe we need someone new to find you, Dillon, maybe?*

12 THE HARE & THE HOUND

Alan prayed in the waiting room as the treatment center staff asked Jack if he wanted company. "Alan? Sure, send him in."

Jack was shooting pool when Alan walked in. "Jack, I heard the judge and you had a visit."

"Well, yes, we did."

"But that was after you got through your DTs. Delirium Tremens, right?"

"That's what it stands for."

"I don't understand how you can poison yourself."

"Oh, you're missing out. The choir boys are next door havin' a 'session'. I'm sure they'll explain." He confidently swaggered around the pool table and made a difficult shot.

Alan shook his head, "So much talent, Jack. You're a brilliant man, but this alcohol has got you by the balls. Don't you see it?"

"I see the little rich boy has to rebuild a house."

"You work their system, don't you? You have no remorse. You have no intention to make those twelve steps work. No, no, you don't because that would take courage and wisdom. OK, well, as I see it you are unemployed. You are unemployable."

"Yeah, it's a good thing you got your precious windmills up and running."

"Oh, it's not done until there's power to all those houses. But you didn't have the courage to jump on that crew."

"Go to hell."

"You did some tremendous things since I met you, Jack, but after getting out of jail, you'd be smart to not offer me as a reference, because I'd tell them the truth."

Jack ignored Alan, instead dropping his last ball into its pocket. He quietly set down the cue and walked away, leaving Alan to wonder.

The treatment center staff were supportive of Jack as he showed that he had remorse and sincere guilt for his actions. He was the epitome of what Alcoholics Anonymous strives to attain for all their card-carrying members. He'd made it through his steps, and his parents were so confident that he was on the straight and narrow. So it was no stress or surprise when Jack checked himself out of the treatment center. He had no use for it anymore since he was reaping the healing peace of his Higher Power.

~*~*~*~

Jason had changed his appearance, shaving his head, covering it with a light blue cotton scarf. Facial hair was growing in, though no man would call it a beard. He was bound for Mexico, but figured he'd bone up on his Spanish in New Mexico first. Downtown Albuquerque stood before him, but it had been a battle to get that far south.

When Jason walked out of his mother's house, away from his ankle monitor, he jogged to an old friend's grandparents' house. Those folks were gone to Texas for the winter months, lovingly called snowbirds by the locals. Trusting to the hilt, they even left the keys in their pickup parked in the garage. Jason backed the rig out and loaded it with treasures from the house and garage, including the title to the truck and items Jason would pawn for gas money.

He got two states away and met a couple in a truck stop. Back when sitting in Candy and Buddy's living room, he knew that if his plan was to work, that he'd need to find some dimwitted marks. *These two!* Jason judged, *their elevators are not running all the way to the top floor! Ha!*

Jason would have been reported as missing, but it would take some time to realize that his friend's grandparents' home had been broken into. Still, Jason knew that he needed to assume that the police and Alan's collection of private investigators were onto him.

So assuming that the vehicles' ID number, the VIN, had been broadcast to banks, he couldn't trust to just sell the truck outright. It took some talking, but Jason convinced the dimwits to use the car that they owned, the one that needed a new transmission, for collateral at the bank. Then he waited while they got the loan, then paid Jason the fifteen thousand dollars, in cash. It was a bargain for them, and *Good money for Mexico,* Jason thought.

Jason took a bus from Omaha to Denver. That was where he stole a pretty, blue Honda CRV. He drove to Las Vegas and switched the Honda for a Toyota.

His new talent and skill in car thievery was awakening a whole new level of boldness in Jason. Then he headed to Albuquerque. His plan was to take a bus into El Paso, then walk into Mexico and not look back. So by the time he got to downtown Albuquerque, he was feeling bulletproof.

Jason's look was still haphazard, but he saw his reflection in a store window and convinced himself that his shaved head and sketchy beard looked natural with his new hiking boots and cargo pants from Denver. The new blue ombre bag hung off his shoulder, harboring his stash of cash within.

Staring up, appreciating the southwestern architecture, Jason felt himself being bumped into, and looked into the warm brown eyes of a giggling, beautiful woman, "Sorry, oh!" She leaned on him, swaying, and laughed loudly. "I'm so drunk," she said and teetered again. Jason helped her stand upright, as he gazed at her curves, her skin, her obvious vulnerability.

In this quick encounter he stood wondering if he should bed her, staring at her sexy walk as she disappeared into the crowd, then realized, "She has my bag!"

Anna held her head. It was bad enough that she and her mom stressed over her brother, Jason. Now she also had hard news for Laura. "Jack disappeared," she started, on the phone with Laura.

Her phone call caught Laura shopping for groceries at Providence Foods in the cereal aisle. Will was there, too, innocently eyeing the choices for granola. He heard her moan and caught her as her knees buckled and they both knelt, wondering what to do next.

"Breathe," he coached. She began to weep in his arms, so Will spoke into the phone. "This is Will Sturlaugson, who's on the line?"

"Anna. Will, we just found out, Jack checked himself out of the treatment center. They let him go."

~*~*~*~

Jason's pace was good. He'd always been a fair runner. But the Latino woman with his bag was faster. It didn't help that she kept screaming, claiming to the crowd that he was trying to kill her. To which he would shout, "She's a thief!"

Finally, she ducked into a gate and Jason followed. She kept moving, but Jason stopped, dead in his tracks. Was it the pair of growly pit bulls or the one-eyed Rottweiler? Or was it the crowd of tough guys, muscle bound and skull-head-tattooed, whom she scrambled behind?

"Here!" she shouted, "This is what he wants," holding up Jason's blue ombre money bag.

The obvious boss of this den of thieves had judging eyes, greying hair on his temples and speckling his Fu Manchu beard, proving his age. "Loria, you bring us a gift?" He turned back to the young woman, "Don't bring your marks back here with you, girl. How many times do we need to train you?" he scolded as he opened the bag and pulled out another cloth like the one on Jason's head. Inside the man found Jason's stash of fourteen uninterrupted bundles of Benjamin Franklins, of $1,000 each, and what was left after Jason's Denver shopping trip, and bus fare.

"Loria! You are forgiven! Ha, Roxy, look in here," he directed to the mature beauty at his side. He quietly directed Roxy, "Now go check him out."

With a quiet wave of her hand, two huge men flanked Jason's sides and dragged him towards the table where the elder sat, Jason's feet often leaving the ground. Held tight before those at the front table, the two men were joined by one more man, tall, strong, with a sinister glare over flaring nostrils. He pulled Jason's scarf off and inspected, "Nothin' to scalp here, Clark. Roxy? What do you think?"

Roxy, who stood in a clear place of honor by her father, came forward to Jason. Her eyes pierced Jason's soul as he was judged. "No, he looks like one of those churchy types, but he's got a darkness to his future. No."

The taller man introduced, "Name's Patrick, a good Irish name. No, Roxy here said no."

"No? What was the question?" Jason innocently wondered.

The crowd laughed with the dogs adding their own vote. Patrick explained, "I can tell that Clark doesn't like ya, and with no future? Then Roxy says no—but let me explain, you not getting your money back? That's the least of your troubles. The last guy that Loria brought back? He didn't last long. No, it don't look good for you."

Panic welled up from Jason's belly, and the usually tough guy façade was quickly reduced to a young man vomiting his lunch at his own feet, with true fear of losing his life clearly written on his face.

An hour into the manhunt that spanned two counties, a call came in from Juliette Kasprowicz, Jack's mom. As she waited on hold, two words kept rolling though her head, "Tough love, tough love, tough love." The deputy finally came to the phone. "I'm Jack Kasprowicz's mother. Jack was just here. He didn't come in the house; he was just in the shed. He pulled a four-wheeler out of the shed. He had a back pack and he just left heading west. And, uh, I saw him take a drink from a booze bottle."

Once the deputy got to her house they searched the shed and found several other bottles of rum stashed. Also hidden was the missing supply of Providence payroll checks, except for the two he had used, and a supply of dynamite.

A deputy was assigned to stay with Laura and Anna. The air and land traffic was a buzz, broadcasting over the deputy's radio. Laura was a pool of tears. "Anna, what do we do?"

Anna asked the stoic deputy, "Are you allowed, I mean if you go with us, can we go someplace? This house is a target, her creamery is a target. We can't stay here."

Erin burst into the room, "Anna, did you hear?"

"Yes, Erin. You and Glory can come with us, too."

It was a relatively short drive to the Park River Bible Camp. Camp was in session and alive with fifth and sixth graders from the region's churches. Anna whispered as they got out of her car. "Sergeant, leave your pretty hat and gun in the car. Don't scare the kids. You're just a guy, you're not a sergeant right now."

"I'm keepin' my radio." It was wired to his ear. He followed the women as they walked along the Park River, sat down on its bank, and quietly prayed a series of prayers, beginning with, "Our Father, Who art in Heaven, Hallowed be Thy Name..."

The cold early-November wind was relentless, pushing man, beast and whatever vegetation still clung to the ground into survival mode. The helicopter ruffled the ditch grass around Alan's pickup. It was stopped near the four-wheeler, abandoned in its position near a ditch, and out of gas. An empty rum bottle lay nearby.

The Sheriff said to the group of men who volunteered to search, "His mother said that bottle was full half an hour ago. We have to assume his backpack contains dynamite, and with that much liquor that he's got a short fuse, and he's on foot." When others stood and awaited instruction, Rusty watched as James checked the ground around the four-wheeler and struck out across the soybean field, it's dry stubble still filling the space, covering the tracks of all who trod.

James' stride was long, his pace was brisk. He was matching his footprints into those he saw below him. About every other step was vaguely apparent. Through the bean field, over a gravel road. James stopped to catch his breath and saw "Jack's tracks" and a wet spot in the gravel, "Jack's urine, no doubt." The tracks led into a hayfield where alfalfa tufts were scattered among amber blades of once lush grass. *Trish would appreciate a crop like this,* he found himself thinking. James stopped for a breath and checked his bearings. He was headed up the escarpment, and purposeful or not, Jack had chosen one of the steeper faces that rose from a creek valley, four hundred feet up. James only advantage was that that close to the escarpment, he was in its shelter from the biting wind. A dozen flashes of Laura's smile rolled through his mind. "Allah, God Almighty, be my guard, be my guide," he prayed, and set out.

~*~*~*~

Jack had passed out. When he came to, he heard a helicopter, men, and machines. He climbed up above and through branches, and saw people in the distance. Then his focus was pulled closer, much closer, to one man on the run. He took a tall drink of rum for courage and pulled himself up the hill. Tree roots sprouted through the steep hillside. Tree trunks were a secure hold for his fingers and feet, then when he didn't expect it, brittle shale rocks crumbled in his hands. He was half way up and could see his assailant drawing closer.

Jack took another drink, more for thirst than courage. He swayed, his vision blurring in and out of focus. Adrenaline pushed him upwards. James was effective in his route and efficient in his movements. From the valley floor below, the sheriff could clearly see the two men climbing through his binoculars. From his windy perch he dispatched men to head up the Beaudeleau road and defend the property above.

As James pulled himself up onto the hilltop, he found Jack, motionless, passed out, the rum bottle next to him. Upon closer inspection, James concluded the sad reality. He pulled the radio from his back pocket, "Sheriff? I found him." He said slowly, "There's no pulse."

"No pulse?" the sheriff radioed.

"Copy that. No pulse."

Cold wind whirled around the two men as James caught his breath and pondered the life lost before him. Alcohol poisoning had taken Jack's life. The life of a genius who couldn't muster the courage to change. Who couldn't accept those things that would not change. A genius who's scientific understanding wouldn't translate to wisdom.

James knelt next to Jack and prayed for his soul. He looked up and realized Jack's probable destination for his bag of dynamite. The last of Jack's windmills, surrounded by county deputies, was turning steadily in the constant North Dakota breeze, a strong symbol of hope that wouldn't be brought down by its frail creator.

~*~*~*~

Early-November found Jason stuck in a world of hurt. With his arms raised in defense, he wailed and begged, "No, you shouldn't kill me, I can help you! That money? That's from a car I stole. I've stolen several between Canada and here. No, sir, ma'am?" he said to Patrick and Roxy, and then turned to their leader. "Clark? Please. I can help you. I'm an engineer, well, not graduated yet, but I can help with a great many things." Jason certainly never expected to make such offers, but first things first, he needed to stay alive.

"Like I need one more to feed for Christmas?"

Jason bargained, "You have all my money now. That should pay my way, more than before. You can train me to do anything, sir, anything," he suggested, his mind reassured as he recalled having hidden two stolen credit cards in the desert.

Clark, Roxy and Patric,k all huddled, then Clark came back to the group. "Roxy changed her no to a yes, for now. Not a yes, forever. A yes, for now."

Patrick patted Jason's back and shared a story of the Christmas before when they decided to help a woman out in Kansas City, a woman named Erin. "I remember that, good Irish name!" he proclaimed. Patrick described how Erin's husband was abusing her and how the gang had cornered Paul. Then how Patrick had beaten the life out of him. He finished by saying, "Those low-life asses who harm women like that one who maimed my mother? Well, they just do that for some sick pleasure. So, that's why I get such a pleasure outta killin' em."

Jason was being moved along by Patrick's arm deeper and deeper into the space where they all took shelter from the unpredictable Albuquerque weather. Jason was on the run from sure imprisonment for rape, and his stomach wasn't any better from when he'd lost his lunch. Now, he had jumped from the frying pan, straight into the fire.

13 THANKS FOR WHAT?

Laura vacillated between a stoic survival mode and mourning Jack's death. Among the consolations, Roberta also reminded her, "But before he died, you were making progress with disconnecting from Jack. I know that he had your heart twisted and confused, but what if we were to face the truth and reconsider that angle?"

"The truth," Laura repeated.

"Yes."

"No, wait. Someone died, don't we have to mourn the loss?"

Roberta nodded, "The family can feel an obligation, but are you family?" Laura's arms wrapped around Laura's head again, as her chest sunk back to her lap. "We're back to turtle mode? OK, that's fine. But just keep listening. He did you no favors, he abused your body and your trust on more than several occasions. As a human, and as a woman, you deserve better. He can no longer reach you. Your mind and heart are going to disconnect from him because his style of love was and is not healthy for you. Do you remember that we agreed on that last month?" Laura nodded her covered head so Roberta went on. "What has changed?" She answered her own question, "He died. It was wrong of him to drink so much alcohol. Would you agree with that?"

A muffled "Yes," was heard. Slowly, Laura rose from her lap. "Even in death, Jack is such an ass."

Roberta said, as she made notes, "Now you sound more like the Laura I know."

"OK, but I feel bad for Juliette, his mom. She didn't ask for this, either."

"All right. Then feel something for his mother. I understand that she's reaching out to her minister, but Jack hasn't earned your love, alive or in his death."

Laura broached, "Yeah, so about God. Is that something that you counsel on?"

"It's best if you reach out to a minister, priest, deacon or such. Who would you reach out to?"

Laura described, "He's not a priest yet, but he's going to the seminary in January. He was the one who helped me in the grocery store when I got the news about Jack checking himself out of the treatment center. I still can't believe they let him go. Anyway, Will, he's really easy to talk to."

"Will, yes, we've met." Roberta recalled their encounter and how, all professionalism aside, she was almost swept off her own stable and rational feet. She summed, "He's very handsome with a natural charm. But, Laura, you can't get your heart tangled up in another relationship right now. You need time to heal the current wound." Roberta was all too aware of Laura's weakness for romance.

Rene waited for lunch to dial his phone, then retreated to the basement of their client's new home before pushing 'send.' "LaDonna," he said to his mother's sister as she answered, "How are you?"

"Uh, you know." LaDonna's replies on any given phone call were brief at best.

"Arthritis still a problem?" She grunted her reply, so he continued, "Sorry to hear. Hey, I was going to ask, have you received anything from Dee?"

"Her again? Oh, Rene, no. Don't settle for someone who was so hard on you." To Rene's sigh, she added, "That tiger already showed her stripes."

"Yes, you're right, she had more than a few indiscretions, and I wasn't impressed then, nor am I now. OK?" LaDonna grunted her agreement, so he continued, "I don't want her to be that loose string that hangs out there when I attempt to pull together a plan here in North Dakota."

"Loose string? More like a loose cannon." Both listened to the silence between them until she added, "I miss you. I know you had to go, but I miss you."

"What's my stupid uncle up to these days?" Rene asked, inspecting the cut on his hand.

She laughed and said, tongue in cheek and a light brightening her eyes, "He's having to close down. The health inspectors were in and condemned the whole place. No, he never appreciated you when you were there, and he'll never voice it out loud, but it was you and your attention to basics, pure basics, that kept him afloat this long. No, when you left, his world fell apart."

"LaDonna, you know me, I don't wish ill on anyone, but in this case, it serves him right, the old grump. But I don't want to wallow in his misery, he can do that on his own. I want to know, how was your Canadian Thanksgiving? I missed calling you. Here, there's no talk of that holiday in October. Anyway, how was it?"

She wasn't good with small talk. "You talk about plans there in North Dakota, tying up plans. Is that why you forgot to call? What's her name?"

"Oh, LaDonna," he moaned, "she is so wonderful! Her name is JoJo Carter. She's beautiful, funny, compassionate, and a pretty fair cook. She mended my coveralls."

"What does it take to be a pretty fair cook in your head?"

Rene shrugged, gazing out the window, "She knows how to make Hollandaise sauce." His reply was met with another judging grunt. "And other cream sauces," he added. Another quiet grunt. "Aunt LaDonna, I wish I could talk to you in person. Your facial expressions give me many more clues about your thoughts. Please love her as much as I do, please?"

"How long have you two been dating?" LaDonna quietly asked.

"Oh, no, we haven't, not yet." Rene felt his confidence waning.

She firmly, slowly, and softly coached, "Get up the nerve to take her to a nice dinner somewhere to thank her for mending your work clothes. I've seen how tough you are on your coveralls and such. Did you pay her?"

"No, she wouldn't let me."

"Well, any woman worth her emery dust will certainly appreciate being thanked."

"What's emery dust?"

"Don't worry about that, just ask her. It's the little ball of dust used for sharpening sewing needles. Remember my tomato pin cushion? And how you always tugged on the little strawberry?"

"Yes?"

"The strawberry, it's filled with emery dust. Now, thank her properly, and then name your first daughter after me." LaDonna really didn't care for phone calls, but once she got going, she was on a roll.

~*~*~*~

During Laura's working hours, a tune crept into her mind and soon overtook her heart. It sang softly, patiently in the inner creases of her brain and pounded rhythmically through her being. On her way home to her small apartment, Laura finally allowed herself to recognize the melody.

A prayer, an unuttered thought had wafted heavenward the night before as Laura tried to fall asleep. She had no adult understanding of how to restart with her faith in God, but there was that one quiet thought.

Now it sprung like a torrent, a spring of water welling up inside her. With serious emotion rare to Laura Zimmermann, she reached for paper and pen to scrawl the words that came to mind. *Psalms, chapter 51.* The Bible that had been stored away for safe keeping was now hard to find. But before tears threatened, it was there in her grasp.

She looked up the book and chapter like she'd been taught in the private Catholic grade school she'd attended. After a quick skim of the words, lyrics to the music came to mind, bringing it all together as one, Laura quietly singing, "Create in me a clean heart, O God. And renew a right spirit within me. Cast me not away from Thy Presence, and take not Thy Holy Spirit from me. Restore onto me the joy of Thy salvation, and uphold me with Thy free spirit."

Laura hugged herself, as though embracing God, Himself. "Holy Lord, God Almighty! That was amazing!" From there she fell into two verses of *Amazing Grace.* "How do I remember any of that!?" She squeezed herself again and spun in a circle.

The rest of her night was a private one-on-one with Jesus, who listened to Laura's heartache, and spoke to her through random Bible verses.

The next day, Laura tracked down Dr. Will Sturlaugson between barn visits in eastern Cavalier County. Near Vang, North Dakota, in the Pembina River Gorge, Laura sat waiting for him to squeeze her in, in-between his appointments.

The veterinarian/would-be priest was glad for a break. He poured hot coffee from his thermos and offered Laura one, too. The fog and resulting hoarfrost from the night before left a flocked wonderland in the already breathtaking valley, all to serve as a quiet backdrop for Laura's question. But first, Will asked, "You called and had a question?"

"Yes. You probably heard about how Jack Kasprowicz died of alcohol poisoning, and he was my boyfriend. Well, that is, he called me his girlfriend, but I was not in love with him, not one bit. I looked for ways to get away from him. He didn't hold me captive in physical bonds, but verbally, I felt threatened. I've lived through him holding a knife to my neck and him bashing my head into a barn stall. OK. So, I'm going through counseling for abuse from Jack."

"That's good. That's very good. Roberta?"

"Simpson, yes. She is helping me understand me. Now, I need someone to help me understand God. So I thought I'd ask you."

Will was stunned. "Me?" He looked about, the sun was reflecting off the frost, providing a quiet glow. And above, a soft breeze was gently blowing the hoarfrost off the trees that rimmed the gorge, developing a series of rainbows.

Laura didn't sense the images that Will was seeing, but simply sipped her coffee and let him think. Finally, she quietly declared, "You're more than just a cute vet. I know you're much more than that. Will, will you help me? Because for starters, He gave me a Psalm to study, Psalm 51. You know it?"

Will had been studying it, too. "The Miserere, the Prayer of Repentance."

That same night, before it got too late, Eastern time, Laura called her mother. "Hey, Mom, how's it going?" After a brief summary of life in Stevens, Vermont, Laura announced, "I've got some news."

"Exciting!" Mae Zimmermann said, then tried to guess, "A new ice cream flavor?"

"Well, yeah, Pumpkin Cheesecake, but no. Jack died."

"What? No, he's in a treatment center," Mae maintained.

"No, he checked himself out, downed a couple few bottles of rum, and died of alcohol poisoning. Boom. He's gone."

"Oh! Honey, I'm so sorry, you must be devastated!" Mae cooed.

"No, Mom. Not even an iota. At first I felt guilty about not feeling sad. No, I've been trying to get away from him."

"Away? You were here last summer with those Al-Anon friends. Did they know you wanted to get away from Jack?"

Laura admitted, "Maybe a little. Bottom line, I wasn't in love with him anymore. Mom?" She needed to stress, "He was not ever wanting to have kids, and he was never going to let me come home to Vermont for visits. Never."

"That's ridiculous. Laura, I had no idea!"

"It was so crazy. He was mean. No, and I'm not family, so I'm not supposed to feel obligated, like I should be mourning him. Even though, I'm confused, because I did love him at first. Maybe? I don't know, but maybe I'm mourning the loss of the good relationship that we started out with?"

"He was mean?" A sure doubt hung in Mae's words.

"I think it's stupid," Laura judged, "There are some that call it date rape, just because I knew him. That date rape is somehow not as bad as being raped by a stranger, but Mom? Rape is rape, and I got sick and tired of being a damn sex slave." She heard the words and recalled to whom she was speaking. She reeled it back, "I mean." The truth had to be released, no matter how shocking it would be. "He held a knife to my throat at one point. I suppose. Most girls don't talk to their mothers like that, but…" She audibly sighed and closed her eyes, listening for a response.

Her mother's tears streamed, but a strength welled up to serve her as she quietly sang the same Psalm 51, *Create in Me a Clean Heart*. After the short melody, Mae quietly asked, "Do you remember when I was teaching you your prayers, how we'd sing that song, like a lullaby, before you went to sleep. You were eight."

The peace in her mother's voice held Laura in a quiet embrace, giving her strength. "That's where it's from?! I used to call that the 'Thy' song. I've been singing that song for the last couple days, and others, too! Mom! I've been praying the rosary, sort of in the background at work, and at home. I mess up sometimes, but just start again. Oh, and there's this guy who's starting at the seminary in January. We're doing a Bible study, sort of." Laura listed, "And I've got a counselor who is helping me with sorting out the blaming. I am not to blame! I'm not! And she's always reminding me to let my heart heal before I jump headfirst into another relationship."

Mae's heart was full, "All good things, counseling, prayer, Bible readings. These are all so very good for your soul, Laura. I'm proud of you, I'm happy for you, for the woman you're becoming. But now, wait, the part about jumping headfirst. You wouldn't be my little Laura if you didn't already have another guy picked out, waiting in the wings. Remember Cyrus Jefferies?"

Laura's laughter came from her toes, "Ahhhh! Yes, that little snot. Tyler Barry was so much more fun!"

"So, what's his name? I'll pray for him."

Laura tried to whisper, "But, Mom, you'll jinx it. Come on."

"One name." She was firm.

"James. He's a vet, veteran. He's fresh back from Iraq and Afghanistan. He's my friend Trish's brother, and he's got PTSD. Most guys come back with that, if they come back. I guess we should be grateful that he's still in one piece. He works for me at the creamery and slowly, slowly, we're getting to know each other. The problem with me and Jack was that I just jumped in off the high dive with Jack. What is it that Dad says? 'Look where you leap'? No, with James I'm trying to be rational. Oh, and the PTSD, my counselor says that I've got a form of that, too.

The nightmares, the flashbacks, night sweats. No fun, but it's weird. James and I have that in common."

Mae's heart was pounding with compassion, "Then I'll pray for both of you, that you have fewer nightmares and more good days than bad. I don't know what else I can do?"

Laura was honest. "Well, his sister, Trish, is pretty protective of him. She claims I'm too crazy and flighty. That he needs someone more stable in his life."

"That's sort of judgmental. You're creative. You've always been a free spirit."

Laura suggested, "Maybe you could add Trish to your prayers? See if God could help her to lighten up."

Mae took a deep breath, "OK, now one more question. What do I tell your dad?"

Laura proclaimed, "Tell him everything. The rapes, and knife to my throat, the threats of no children and isolation, the alcohol poisoning, Psalm 51, the Rosary and Amazing Grace, the counseling and Bible study. Tell him that his baby girl is growing up and there's a veteran who looks at her with love and steamy brown eyes, and his name is James. And that we both need Dad's prayers. God willing, James and I are both coming out on top."

Thanksgiving morning finally dawned. The refrigerator shelves and pantry cupboards told their tale: Christine was set for a feast, but the traditional contemplation of what one was thankful for was seriously lacking at her house

Several were expected at their parents' homes, but both Hailey and JoJo had no plans. JoJo's parents were invited to take a cruise with friends, and Hailey's folks didn't have extra money for such extravagant meals. Plus, both had to work on Black Friday. "That's the real holiday this weekend," Hailey voiced, "and I'm stuck schlepping turkey delights at Thompson's."

She received a sharp glare from Christine. "Well, woe is you, that café keeps you employed and their food is good. Don't sass-talk them."

Hailey volleyed her reply, "Grandma, they can't even hear me!"

"You could be more thankful than you are. It's Thanksgiving." The back door bell chimed. Christine rose to answer it, but Hailey was still in her nightgown, burping her sleepy one-month-old baby. The elder's steady glare followed the younger as she disappeared down into the basement. Christine brushed toast crumbs off her apron and opened the door. "Rene, and…friends." She reached out her hand.

Rene introduced. "Christine Gislason, these are Mac and Bob Whitney. Mac, I've never known your last name."

"McIntyre, pleased to meet you, ma'am," Mac smiled his most charming grin.

"Happy Thanksgiving, gentlemen, won't you come in?" She had never voiced her own plans for the holiday with her grand-nieces and granddaughters, because she didn't have any. This early morning chat over coffee was an opportunity for socializing and she gratefully served everyone, whiskers, tousled hair, and all.

"Me? Thankful? Thanks for what!?" Hailey whispered above her downy-haired daughter as they descended the stair. Usually sassy and flirtatious, Hailey was none of that as she heard the telltale ding on her phone. She had a message. The babe suckled on her pacifier and slept quietly in the old bassinette as Hailey read it, then set down her phone, her eyes blurred with salty tears. The dreaded reply had finally come. Sasha's daddy wasn't capable of fathering anyone or anything. He didn't even "dare to buy real houseplants," he had said. Now Hailey was remembering all the houseplants on the main level that her Great-Aunt Christine fussed over. *How am I gonna manage?* she wondered, *With*

two kids, and by myself? Oh, God, help me!

~*~*~*~

Bob Whitney's Magnum PI-styled moustache kept drawing Christine's attention. He was handsome in a simple, clean manner, with a few grey hairs dusting his temples. "Plumbing, is that right?" she had asked, gleaning all she could about the friendly bachelor. Christine deemed him a few years her junior, but she'd never been opposed to those they'd call Cougars.

Rene tried to finish explaining the reason for their visit. "So since there are so many bachelors in the construction trades here in town, far from family and not able to celebrate a decent holiday meal, we came up with a plan for Thanksgiving. We are allowed to borrow the First United Free Church, both their kitchen and dining room, to share a Thanksgiving Day feast. But this plan came together after the grocery stores had closed. Christine, can we buy some food from you? I've seen your freezer. You're stocked."

She considered it a compliment and before anyone could blink, she had a full menu planned, serving 36 lonely souls, including herself. JoJo and Hailey were pulled in to help, along with Myron Haldorson's sweetheart, Jody. All met at the First United Free church and got to it.

Apples were chopped, pumpkin was mixed and flour flew as Christine made seven pies, including her specialty, coconut cream. Rene set two turkeys and two pork roasts to cooking, garnished with aromatic herbs, while JoJo handled the sage stuffing. Jody rounded up fall-themed centerpieces and the tables were set. When not sleeping in her carseat, Sasha was passed about and many pitched in, men included.

Since Hailey's morning cry, she'd made a plan to hire a lawyer and seek child support, garnishing wages if need be. Her former sweethearts, sweet as they were, were one payday away from feeling her wrath. She was peeling carrots for a veggie tray when a man came through the swinging kitchen door, holding her daughter and playing a game of hide-and-seek with her son.

"I found you!" Matty called out, through giggles.

"Darn!" the man replied, then added, "I'm too tall, huh?"

Matty explained the game, "You're supposed to hide, like this!" The young boy crouched behind the kitchen island countertop, then sprung up, "See?"

He shrugged and asked, "So, Matty, is this your mom?" To the boy's nod, he extended his hand, "Mac McIntyre."

Christine finished the introductions from behind, while peeling potatoes. "Yes, and this is one of my lovely grand-nieces, Hailey Eskelson. She's a college student and works at Thompson's café."

Mac shook Hailey's wet hand, rubbing his then wet hand on his leg, then continued their game, "Where are you?" Matty, who was hiding his very best, was soon found. What gave him away was his unruly cowlick at the back of his head, bobbing back and forth like a blonde feather.

A few of the men set up a TV with a long coax cable that stretched to the neighbor's house. He had been paid handsomely by Bob Whitney for the use of his cable box. So the pre-game show was being enjoyed up until Christine banged her spoon against a kettle to gain their attention. Grace was prayed, and as the tables were filled with grateful souls too far from home, Christine soaked in the compliments, gratitude, and accolades. She was in her glory, especially compared to the way the day had begun. Now sitting between Bob Whitney, her new plumber friend, and Rene, all was bliss. On Rene's other side sat JoJo, so he was content, too.

Suddenly there was a skirmish in the kitchen. Bob and Rene both accompanied Christine to the buffet line to discover the source. There Myron Haldorson was being cornered between the wall oven and the fridge by his older sister, Gretchen. She was home for Thanksgiving, mostly since she'd caught wind of Myron's little deal, renting out her own bedroom to a complete stranger. She threw pot holders and extra dinner rolls at him, then reached, grasping the potato kettle handle, and took aim.

Bob was spry and caught her before damage was done, but the bottom-line was that Rene was evicted, that very night.

Hailey certainly didn't give any heed to Myron's or Rene's troubles. She was feeling sassy again, flirting with a rocker, sheetrock, that is. When the eviction collided with the ball game, she seized the moment and took her leave, with the excuse that she had to get her kiddos to bed. And as planned, he followed her to the parking lot, then to her basement.

14 A FULL HOUSE AT CHRISTMAS

Trish was so excited to be decorating her little house for Christmas. Years prior, she had patched together a holiday theme at the last minute and wasn't prepared for company by any stretch of the imagination. So much had happened since that spring day when she had come to Mountain to interview for her vet tech job! Meeting Nick the Easter before, helping her dad get his kidney transplant, and falling in love with Nick. Then traveling with Nick to shop for veterinarians, setting up Alan's new vet clinic and working one-on-one with such professionals. Memories tumbled through her mind and filled her heart to its brim.

Now that Thanksgiving had passed and Advent was beginning, she hauled her meager collection of Christmas decorations out of storage and tried to make a plan. There was a knock on the door.

"Anna! How are you feeling?" Trish asked as Anna waddled in.

"I know! I'm getting so huge! The end of January cannot come soon enough!" Anna's focus shifted to Trish's ornaments, "These are wonderful!"

"Yes, they were Mom's when she was young. Early 60's."

"OK, well, I came to recruit a helper. Are you interested in helping a big pregnant lady decorate a big house?"

Elijah was at work in Alan's machine shed when he got a surprise visit from an old neighbor from Concrete, his great-uncle. "Uncle William! Great to see you out making the rounds!"

William had a thick stand of snow white hair above gentle, pale eyes. He had been convalescing from hip surgery since the week before. The elder watched Elijah reach into the shop fridge and find bottled water for them both, then they relaxed in the nearby chairs set up for that purpose. "I had to give you a warning, Elijah."

"Warning. You have me intrigued!"

William had never been one to mince words. "I noticed you last Sunday at church. It seems that you've been flirting with several ladies in our parish and others from this area, too. The ladies, they're talking about how much you flirt. That you wouldn't make a good husband with such an appetite for, as one girl put it, 'All the ladies, all the time.' And this was at church, mind you."

Elijah innocently asked, "What would you do, Uncle William?"

"Don't spread yourself, your love, too thin. Your true love is bound to be watching, wishing you had the capacity for faithfulness. For goodness sake, Elijah, one of them called you Easy Eli. Easy to please, she said."

"But Uncle William, I thought that being easy to please would be an asset. No?"

Old Uncle William rubbed his chin whiskers, "Not when it looks like you're chasing every skirt in sight. Do you want a woman who's open to just any guy who comes along?"

Something about Christmas always made Spencer moody. The thought at the source of that emotion had been stuffed deep, way back, in the recesses of his mind, but always seemed to surface at Christmas.

He was getting dressed to be ready to help a friend pick out a Christmas tree at a tree farm outside of the Minneapolis suburbs. Snow had quietly blanketed the area the night before. Knowing that, he reached for his hunting boots, but when tying them, one of the laces broke. With dread, he closed his eyes and uttered a quiet prayer, "God help me!" Spencer's sad memory was bound up in his old boots. When he had pulled them from the back of the closet, he had frozen. Jason had borrowed those old hunting boots, and the memory of seeing them on his kid brother's feet was one that burned into Spencer's mind.

Before their dad had died, when Jason was fourteen, Johnny Hillman had warned the two brothers as they packed their blaze orange and gear for their hunting trip. "Don't ever go with the wrong guys for a hunting trip," he had told them, "the wrong guys will get you shot." Those words tied together into the laces of his old boots.

The following summer, Johnny died when a tractor rolled over him. That fall when deer hunting time came, it was Johnny's old high school friends who took his sons hunting. Spencer didn't know it at the time, but guys like those old friends were exactly the sorts that Johnny's warning had spawned from.

They drank liquor before, during, and after their hunt. The supper meal was of the liquid form, that is, more liquor. Spencer had never been one to skip a meal, but Jason was game to keep up with the gang. Two young ladies had wandered into the bar. After a couple drinks the most charming of their bunch swept the one girl off her feet and into his pickup truck. The other girl just kept drinking and flirting with the older men. One, Cordell, convinced Jason that "'No' only means no until you've fed 'er enough liquor!" So that's what Jason did, at the age of 15, while Cordell watched at the door of the men's room. Then Cordell gladly took what he called, "sloppy seconds."

Spencer could've done something. His dad would have expected that Spencer would have done something. But he hadn't. No one's hero. Certainly not Shyla's. That was the girl's name. Shyla. He prayed for her every Christmas. He gave gifts to charity with her in mind. Spencer never knew if Shyla remembered anything from that night. He pulled an old tennis shoe out of his closet and scavenged that lace instead. All while handling such a basic task, his emotions were gathering strength against him. Spencer knew, all too well, that he was sickened whenever this memory came back to mind. It haunted him through Christmas, through New Year's and past Valentine's Day. The memory of watching his kid brother take Shyla into the men's room would haunt him again this year. After all, it was his hunting boots that he saw last before the door closed.

Soon Spencer was ready to help his friend find the best Christmas tree, but no one ever saw those old boots. They weren't useable in Spencer's mind and not of enough value to give to charity. No, they got stuffed far, deep into the back of his closet.

Nine chairs sat at the old dining room table as seven young 20-something women mingled nearby. All had moved into the old Victorian house the fall before, with their grandma/great-aunt. It was a three story house, with its full basement, and it was full. Christine Gislason had made a comfortable suite for herself on the main level. Up two separate stairways there were four above her: TJ, Cammy, Sarah, and Katie, Anna's sister. Two women, Dora and JoJo, were up in the attic. Hailey had bedrooms in the newly finished basement for herself, her son, Matty, and a nursey for her baby, Sasha. Ten bedrooms in all were tucked here and there. The house was old and rickety, but the electrical and plumbing had also received upgrades, making it a safe nest.

Christine saw images in her mind, like photos to flip through, from when they had made the move. The leaves had been green, and the weather had been too warm and dry, though now as she glanced up out the window, winter surrounded them all. Christine's mind flashed back and heard TJ wonder aloud, "Amma," she had said, Icelandic for grandmother, "With all of us under one roof, what's to stop this from becoming just another reality TV show with back biting and…"

Dora added, "Voting people off our floor?"

Cammy chimed in, "And terrifying plot twists! No snails or worms.

Ugh! No!!"

Christine's worn hands rose to calm their waters. "At no point, ladies, will you find a camera in your closet, a microphone boom man hovering over you, or a type-A producer-type feeding you liquor to make the next scene even more of a blow-out than before. No. Now listen. This house is too huge to sell to just any family." Her brother, Earl, had inherited it from his sister-in-law but was soon bound for assisted living himself, so Christine had gotten the keys. "By giving up your various apartments and moving here, you ladies have helped families and young couples to have a warm place to be. Now I miss my little house on Cow Street in Mountain, but the little family who bought it are so happy to get settled in. Plus, the lovely art studio next to my bedroom here in this house, is so much more creative than any old ranch-style home. I'm sure you agree. Now, I admit, your old apartments gave you freedoms, which ladies your age are used to. I understand. I was young once. Well? There will be rules to keep this all in perspective."

TJ muttered, "Yup, here we go!"

Christine's tongue was quick, "OK, TJ, you guess. What is my first rule?"

"No boys," the attractive and sometimes brash granddaughter said, folding her arms.

"That's only partly correct. No boys in your bedrooms."

Hailey gave clear signals, both physically and verbally. "Grandma? I will certainly have a man in my bedroom if I want. You can't protect my virtues, Grandma. That ship has long since sailed!"

Christine was steady, "No, your parents are trusting me to…"

Cammy tried to finish the sentence, "Rule with an iron hand?"

The elder was losing her patience, "No! No, listen! Ladies." She cleared her throat and blew her nose. Silence was getting more and more of a challenge for the six cousins in the room. Finally, a quiet sigh escaped, leading to more tissues and a tear-filled rant. "Do you really want my new neighbors' assumptions about this house to become true? There's Christine," she waved to imaginary people, "in her 1905 Victorian brothel!" Eyes widened, and some rolled, as she made her point. "Yes, brothel! I am not anyone's Madame. But there's talk that this Victorian version of seven brides looking for seven or more available, sexy men, well, that's what I'm trying to avoid! I want to prove them all wrong and hold my head high when I attend church or any other event in this town. And, so, clearly, my beautiful granddaughters and grand nieces, I need your help."

Cammy raised her hand, "Amma, can I ask a question?"

"Yes, darling."

"Does Gwenny Hamilton next door have anything to do with that story? 'Cause that's bullshit."

Christine reminded, "Language. Ladies, that's the next rule. Yes, Gwenny is someone who assumes she is a moral compass for the masses and, yes. My good reputation in this, my home town of Cavalier, is on the line." Glimmers of high school days back in the early fifties flitted through her mind. She knew Gwenny, all too well. "She's snoopy and judgmental. But when she's here, I want you all on your best behavior, and assume at all times that's she's watching."

TJ summed, "So if we meet someone, we can spend time with them, somewhere, anywhere, other than here."

"You should use your best judgment, but yes. And just because you meet someone doesn't mean you have to jump into bed with him. If he was any sort of a gentleman, he wouldn't assume such a thing."

Hailey nodded "Like you say, you were young once, but these days, sex is different."

"Different?" Christine had to laugh, but suddenly curbed her enthusiasm, lest she pee. "Noooo. The hormones, the lust and lack of control? No. Your generation did certainly not invent that. But since the '60s there has been a sincere lack of common sense." Many in the room collectively rolled their eyes. "OK, well," she continued, "you get the rules. No boys in the bedrooms, no foul language. Oh, and there will be a schedule for you to sous chef with me, once a week."

Katie shook her head, "I heard that we only had to worry about cleaning." Katie had never embraced cookbooks like her sister, Anna.

Aunty Christine clarified, "You'll all be expected to clean, handle your own laundry, uh, we'll hire out the outside chores and you'll take turns at KP. I'll set up a schedule, and," she stressed, "only verifiable excuses will be allowed for. Now, I'm not just talking to Katie, this counts for everyone. Don't give me 'I'm not in the mood', no. Your rent is only your labor on a set amount of chores and this set up saves you a whole lot of money. Don't give me 'I'm not in the mood'." Eyebrows pitched to their collective peaks. She eyed the women, "Am I clear?" A smattering of yeses and quiet Oks returned to her.

Coming back to the present, Christine readjusted the centerpiece on the dining room table. Since giving the young ladies their house rules, little Sasha had been born and added her own voice and drama to the already raucous crowd. Regardless of what her dear granddaughters and grand-nieces sometimes said in sassy jest, Christine did sincerely love them. To their chagrin, Christine's version of loving them sometimes seemed more like discipline.

She adjusted the chairs. At her call, the ladies took their seats before the formally-called house meeting. Something didn't seem right to Dora, who counted people, then chairs. "There's an extra chair, Grandma. There are eight of us."

Christine patted the wood on the extra chair. "We have a guest, a new neighbor." Her grandfather clock chimed a steady rhythm, four o'clock on that Sunday afternoon. Her head nodded as warm eyes smiled out the window, "He's here."

"He?" they all asked in mumbled unison, following her to the dining room window.

As with any matriarch of a given family, Christine took the lead. She met him at the front door of the grand old home and shook his hand. "Rene, yes, so good to see you again." Many in the group had met Rene before when JoJo had mended his winter work clothes. The younger ladies bustled back to their seats as their grandmother held his hand and the pair stood, side by side, her arm in his as she announced, "Ladies, dear granddaughters and great-nieces of mine, this is Rene LaRoque. He has agreed to rent the carriage house," she stately clearly, slowly, as though she knew it had to sink in.

Rene's kind eyes looked around the table, gathering confidence as he smiled. "Hello, ladies."

Cammy piped up. "Grandma. Sir," looking at Rene, "it's not you. We need a decent place to have AA."

Everyone else stalled. Christine quietly asked, "What?"

"Attitude Adjustment!" Cammy proclaimed. Her humor, though tongue in cheek, was engaging the rest of her cousins and motivating the always unpredictable Cammy Helgeson. "Uh, Grandma, what the hell? The carriage house was supposed to be our party house! We were going to fix it up this spring." She looked at others for support, raising her hands like she was a school mascot, trying to rouse the crowd.

TJ's eyes had her seductive nature on high. "This house is already full, but you can share my room!" she offered, selflessly.

Christine waved her hand and directed Rene to his chair. "Oh, pffft. Listen up. He will have the carriage house."

Cammy was livid. "This came out of nowhere! That is our party house, Grandma!"

"No, I never agreed to that. Now, Rene. Please be patient with these ladies. Girls, he has already met many of you. No, that building is not your party house. It's set up like a studio apartment, with a small kitchen. I'm sure it will be comfortable. Now, ladies. This meeting is a chance for you to meet Rene and we'll set the ground rules. Hailey? Are your kids sleeping?"

"Soon, I just made a bottle for Anna."

Katie offered as explanation, "Anna, she's my sister." Since her kid
sister's fame was spreading, it grated at Katie to tag onto her younger
sister's coattails, but Katie knew, in the long run, the connection would
help her.

Rene smiled at Katie, then cleared his throat and grinned. "Thank you,
Christine. Let's break the ice with this." He handed his new neighbor a
menu. "This is from the last restaurant where I cooked. Bon Appetit, an
upscale French restaurant in southern Montreal. Christine suggested
that, once in a while, that I'd come here and do some cooking. When
that happens you can have any of these dishes, and/or 5,000+ other
recipes. I work full-time as an electrician's apprentice. My goal is to be
a licensed electrician by this time next year. The home where I've been
renting? That rental fell through."

"What?" Katie wondered for the group.

"The room I was renting belonged to a woman. Do you know her?
Gretchen Haldorson? She didn't know that her brother was renting it
out. She came home for Thanksgiving, and so, I've been evicted." The
menu kept changing hands as he spoke.

Cammy recalled, "TJ, this was the guy who made that soup last fall.
Remember?" All action stopped as all seemed to have the same thought.
"Right, this is Alan's cousin."

"Yes. We share a grandmother. She wed first, and had three children
including my father. My grandfather was killed in a hunting accident
and she wed again, Alan's mother is my aunt. Uh, step-aunt, I think.
He's a good man, Alan. I enjoy his company, but they're newlyweds and
I'm wearing out my welcome there these last few weeks. When
Christine and Anna came up with this plan, well, I'd hoped you'll all
agree that this could work out."

Dora quietly asked, pointing at the menu, "What's in this one? I never learned French, but I know some Spanish." The group talked about ingredients, failed attempts to travel to Europe, and Cammy's aversion to snails.

The conversation had returned to menu options, but when JoJo's hands held the menu, Rene looked up. He noted that his heart, once again, skipped a beat. His mind was recalling the few times before when he'd had an excuse to come to this old Victorian home. Whether for letting JoJo measure him for her alterations and mending, or for him to pick up the completed project, Rene saw every opportunity as a blessing.

Conversation surrounded them, and Rene engaged from time to time, but his focus was only on her. The light caressed her features, highlighting the glow in her face and the shine in her green eyes. Or was it his masculine hormones taking hold?

JoJo smiled wide, "But be honest, you don't only ever eat this rich French food, do you?"

He shrugged, "When I cooked for my uncle in Montreal? Half the time. Then, yes, you're right."

"Ah, Montreal," she grinned, "that's a very French town. Welcome to Cavalier, which only sounds French."

They both shook heads, simultaneously agreeing that Cavalier was nothing like a French town. But the light banter was soon cut short as Christine worked to gain everyone's attention. As she did so, Rene quietly pondered the beautiful blonde near him. Since arriving in the States, she was the only person to verbally welcome him, outside of Alan's greetings. *But he's family*, he justified.

Grandma Christine explained, "Rene, each of these ladies will be helping me with meals here. You're welcome to join us for meals if you want. Your kitchen? Well, it's small."

Cammy voiced the common thought, "When are we cooking? If it's my turn to cook, then you know what you'll eat, right?"

They replied in unison, "Frozen pizza," leaving Cammy with a pleasant grin.

Rene offered, "If I'm here, then I could coach, maybe teach if anyone wants to learn cooking techniques? I'm open to that. Maybe in return for lessons. Uh, I'll admit, I'm grossly inept at computers. When I start my electrical business, I'll need to have computer skills. I learned some in school, but…"

His words hung in the air until Dora spoke up, "Yes, Rene, I'd be happy to help you."

Christine grabbed the reins while she could. "Alright. Now. So that we start this off right, let's go around the table and tell the group your name, your favorite dish, your job and your current status. Cammy, you start."

"Cammy Helgeson. Uh, taco pizza, I'm a pharmacy assistant at Ye Ole Medicine Shoppe and status…you mean from Facebook?" she looked at her grandmother, "LOL?"

"Are you single, dating, engaged? Rene?" Christine shared, "I don't know how they all feel about this, but these days my sole purpose in life is to see that all these ladies get married off." She eyed Cammy again, "Before I die."

Cammy rolled her eyes. "No more blind dates, Grandma. I'm single. Grandma? How about you?"

"Christine Gislason, coconut cream pie, retired and widowed. Let's go this way," she said, pointing to Hailey.

Rene had sipped from his coffee cup and carefully set it down as he asked, "Now, wait. Do you say 'tit for tat' here? Is that a thing?" To a room of curious eyes who agreed and nodded, Rene asked, "Christine, what if these ladies decided, tit for tat, that they might marry you off, too? Widowed equals single, right? Would you let them do this? Little Miss Coconut Cream Pie?"

Now those same curious eyes shifted toward Christine. She slowly replied and pointed, "Uhh? Maybe. Hailey? Your turn." Her voice was sure, but there was now a blush in her cheeks.

"Ooooh, Aunty Christine, you are so getting hitched! Good one, Rene. OK, I'm Hailey Eskelson. I was born during a hailstorm, so that's where I got my name. I like a good Greek gyro, I waitress at Thompson's Café while I take online classes and, obviously, I've had relations since, yes, the little guy downstairs and this little pumpkin," she flashed a new picture of Sasha from her cell phone, "are obviously mine. The dads of my two kiddos can tell you just how much of a severe emotional thunderstorm I am capable of," she claimed with a bit of pride, shaking her hair to the side. Then suddenly serious, Hailey announced, "We'll see. I'm still waiting on a reply from her daddy, Brad Pitt, to see if he'll give her his last name. But you all know, it's not really Pitt, ha!" Laughing with her cousins, she added, "But otherwise, yeah, I'm single. Sarah?"

Sarah was nowhere near the flirt that her cousin Hailey was. But her answers held a new confidence that hadn't been there until the summer before. "I'm Sarah Gislason, I like anything Italian. I helped Grandma with the stuffed manicotti that's in the oven. Garlic toast is my specialty. I'm taking classes at UND in nursing and I'm dating Mac McGee, every weekend!" She laughed, "We can't get enough of each other! You won't see me much, but when you do, I'll have Mac with me." She giggled and turned to her neighbor, "Katie?"

Rene rubbed his chin, "Sarah, the first wedding cake? I will make picnic lunches for you and your sweetheart, but I want to meet him first." Her lips disappeared into her mouth as she instinctively covered her mouth and her body shook with joy.

Katie sighed at the younger cousin next to her. The eldest of the cousins in the house, Katie wasn't happy about her age compared to those like Sarah, who so clearly showed their love. She began, focusing on her reply, trying her best to ignore the jealousy, "I'm Katie Hillman, and chicken chili is my specialty. I work at the Cavalier school, Special Ed. And I was engaged, single, engaged again, and now single again. Yes, all with the same guy. Dora?"

"Well," Dora patted Katie's hand, "you tried." The younger cousins were oblivious to Katie's true emotion, but Rene gazed into the air, wondering, as the lineup of cousins continued. "I'm Dora Johanneson. Actually, it's Haldora, but please, call me Dora. I like all the varied regions of Chinese food. Yum. But not too spicy. My tongue loves what my stomach hates!" They all agreed as it was a familiar problem. She continued, "I work at the Chronicle, do their advertising and everything else. JoJo sort of spilled the beans this morning." Dora smiled at her neighbor, "Yes, sweet cousin, I have a new guy. That's all you get to know for now. JoJo?"

"A cliff hanger! OK, I'm JoJo Carter."

Rene asked, "Carter or Cartier?"

She looked at Dora and laughter burst forth. "No, uh, sorry. Private joke. No, just plain, ol' Hogan's Heroes-style Carter. My lovely mother is Dora's and Katie's mothers' other sister."

Rene cut in again, "JoJo, what is that short for?"

"Yes, good question, but I have no answer except that Mom's best friends in high school were Jolene and Jonina. She always insisted that if she had a girl, I would be JoJo. I'm not partial to any certain cuisine, though last weekend, for my friend's brunch, I attempted Hollandaise sauce. It wasn't a total failure, but I would take a lesson or two. But for comfort food I love a good cream soup. Scratch, not canned. I gladly travel to Hallock, Minnesota, and back each day for my job at the clinic because I love it."

Rene questioned, "You're a nurse?"

"No, coding insurance, helping seniors and young families, office work. Yes, I can help you with computers, too." She brushed at the tablecloth before her. Others looked on in anticipation. "Oh, TJ?"

Cammy reminded, "Your status?"

"Oh! Hmmm, well?" she reached into her pocket. "Let me check my phone. Oh, yup, I'm dating." She mouthed her reply to the man, *Sounds great!*, as her thumbs quickly typed.

Rene's arms crossed as his eyes squinted, "With a man who asks you out by text?" To her nod and broad grin, Rene added, "This is an odd country."

JoJo held her phone to her chest so her neighbors wouldn't see. "TJ?"

Rene asked, "What does TJ stand for?"

"Theresa Joan Johanneson. Call me that to my face and suffer the consequences," she threatened with a toothy smile.

"TJ it is."

"I'm TJ, I love all cuisines and my weakness is ice cream. I have a hair salon here in Cavalier and I am dating someone. Ladies, you haven't met him yet. It's a delicate thing, the first part of a relationship." JoJo and Dora agreed. "OK, Rene? Your turn."

He thought aloud, "My turn," and muttered, "Mon Dieu, aidez-moi," in French, dear God, please help me. "Uh, I'm Rene LaRoque. I like the work I do, lighting up peoples' worlds, but I'm not so happy about my boss. The emotional thing, Hailey, don't let it make you bitter like him. Food. I'm more interested in the typical Canadian comfort foods since the French dishes remind me of another hateful boss I had to put up with, my uncle. Uh, romance? Well?

"I came here after I found out that my girlfriend was moving away. She was the only thing that made living there bearable. She had to move home, to the South Pacific. The thought was that if I didn't care for North Dakota, that I'd take a trip to French Polynesia and find her. Her name is Dee, short for Dehlia. I think it would be best if I finished my electrical certification first.

"And, you all have Christine to be your support. That's great. My version of Christine is LaDonna. She's an aunt, my mother's older sister, who, after my mom died, made sure that I was raised to be the son

Mom would've been proud of. The way LaDonna would say it, 'To be a man worth catching'." He turned back to Christine. "Thank you for inviting me to be your neighbor. I don't know what to expect from Dee, but for now I will gladly help wherever I can, whether moving snow, helping with cars, or with cooking. I'll gladly be the guy next door."

Danielle's planning skills had long since been her strength. In 4-H, Honor Society, Girls' State speeches, and other leadership opportunities in her youth, through college and law school, Danielle had always been great with follow-through. And for the sake of her kid sister, Layne, Jason's lawyered-up victim, she was determined to leave a mark.

Once again, she left him a voicemail, "I know you're there. You're dodging me. Your brother is due in court on March 11th. Today is December 15th. That makes it 85 days for you to find him and bring him to justice. Eventually you will return my call, I have confidence in that. After all, you're a businessman, and your reputation is banking on success on your part in these next 85 days." Her messages were a curse in Spencer's ears.

Gwenny Hamilton didn't have the time or the inclination to keep up with what or who was happening at Christine's on that given day. Earlier in the day, her husband Richard had doubled over in pain. Richard seemed to be the only one person in the world who understood Gwenny, and he was sick. She had always been hopeless when it came to helping others with their ills, and today was no different. As soon as Holly's Cole left for school that morning, Gwenny just pushed Richard into the backseat of her car and headed to the Cavalier hospital.

Once x-rays confirmed it, she loaded him into the backseat and headed for the hospital in Grand Forks. As Richard was both drugged up and moaning, Gwenny had enough with just driving straight down the interstate to Grand Forks. It was one of the nurses there at the Pembina County Memorial Hospital who had remembered that Gwenny did daycare. She contacted the principal who chatted with Alyssa, Elijah's mom, and had Cole get off the bus at Alyssa's house in Concrete.

Angie and Debi were happy to play with Cole on the bus and again at their house. When their mom, Alyssa, got home, the girls already had a rousing game of Monopoly going. Holly had been told where Cole was and both moms were having a little visit about Gwenny when Elijah got home. He didn't see Holly's car and didn't know to expect such a situation.

He called from the entryway, "Mom, I got that almond bark for you." Before Alyssa could explain about Cole, he added, "You won't believe this. It was old Uncle William who told me today that I'm flirting..." he rounded the corner into the kitchen, face to face with Holly, and finished, "...too much. Hi."

Holly confirmed, "Yes, I'd believe that, Alyssa. I was there when, what are they, old high school friends? They were so shocked that you were so flirtatious. But yet, when you talk to me, all you ever talk about is my car. And yes, it's working just fine. Cole? Let's go."

Cole whined, "We're having fun, Mom!" With Debi's help, he was winning the game.

Alyssa knew how very awkward her eldest was with romance. She stepped away, getting busy cooking, and left Elijah to handle this, his latest challenge.

Holly was watching the game. Elijah studied the board as Debi praised, "Elijah taught me, and now I'll teach you," she said to Cole. Holly watched Elijah's smile beaming at his sister, then he looked back to Holly and could have curled inside himself with nerves.

Gently, though, he stood next to Holly and quietly confessed. "It's because I already feel safe with those old friends from school. And you're too pretty. You make me nervous. I don't know what to say to you, so I stay with the practical."

Alyssa called from the kitchen, "Holly and Cole, would you like to stay for supper?"

"YES!" Cole begged his mom.

Holly's face gave a sliver of hope in the form of a quiet smile back towards Alyssa's direction. "This once, thank you." She had heard the other ladies at the church talk about how quiet Elijah usually was with the ladies. How they couldn't get him to take them out unless it was a double or triple date, seeming to find strength in numbers. Holly tossed a glance back towards Elijah. "You don't have to be nervous, just be yourself."

She set the table and moved back into the kitchen to see what Elijah was stirring. Alyssa had set up a double boiler and the almond bark was slowly melting. "For starters," he tried a smile. "We're making bacon and eggs. These straight pretzel sticks are the bacon, this almond bark will be the egg whites, and then the yellow and orange M&Ms are the yolks." He moved closer to whisper, "Cole's dad. Is he coming here?"

To her equally quiet, "No, he's not," Elijah's smile seemed to glow that much brighter.

Christmas decorating, inside and out, was certainly taking shape. Some joined contests to compete for bragging rights. Others just followed their tried and true designs for showing their holiday spirit. Rene hadn't been one to decorate, but once he got his few things moved in, he helped Christine whenever he could. But inside the house, the granddaughters and grand-nieces were scheming.

Cammy insisted, pointing to the envelope that had arrived that day, "It's his sweetie, the one from the South Pacific."

"Ridiculous!" Dora maintained, "The return address clearly says 'LaDonna.' She is his aunt, the one who raised him after his mom died. Don't you listen?"

Cammy disagreed, folding her arms firmly. JoJo followed TJ into the kitchen. "What's all this?"

Cammy defied any and all, "I'm sure I'm right, Dora! TJ, who is LaDonna? The island girl from Guam. I'm right!" she insisted, nodding her head.

TJ was sure. "No. It was French Polynesia, if anything, but no. LaDonna is to him as Christine is to us."

JoJo pointed over TJ's shoulder, "This is postmarked in Canada. Sorry, Cammy."

Malla and Drew were pulling together their first Christmas. Wedding plans were slowing down. It would be planned for when her parents came back in early August. Instead they focused on their new Christmas traditions, some from Malla, some from Drew and children, and some that were new to all. One basic tradition that Drew had fashioned ever since BJ had been very young was an ice rink in their backyard for both figure skating and hockey.

Malla watched the children skating and stood in awe of the positive shift in her life since having moved away from Milwaukee. The children and Drew together had blessed her with so many new ways of expressing her love for them, for herself, even ways to express her love for God. She was beyond ways to verbalize it all, but tried to in her journal at night. *This will be a lovely journal entry, describing their grace, their skills and fun-loving antics on ice!* Malla thought as the glow in her face reflected her enjoyment back to them.

Later, with paper and pen in hand, Malla sat poised on her bed to do just that when a completely different thought came to mind. Drew had tucked his brood in, and, as was his custom, he headed into Malla's room to tuck her in too. The difference was that he was now in the habit of staying the night.

She stood and crossed to her dresser. He lay on one elbow, draped across her bed. The pocket calendar in her top dresser drawer didn't make any sense. "Um, Drew?"

"Yes?" he asked, his voice flirting.

Her eyes not leaving the calendar, she repeated, "Um, Drew?"

"I'm right here!" he assured her.

"How is this possible? I'm infertile."

"Infer...what?"

She repeated, "I'm not fertile, but I have normal cycles like ladies have. But I haven't had one for a couple months." Malla held her calendar with one hand and her chin and jaw with the other. "How is this possible?"

Drew was more direct. "Are we pregnant?"

A slow but bright beam gradually took over her face. "It seems that way!"

~*~*~*~

Hailey Eskelson was as sassy as they get, but she couldn't see for the tears as she drove home from work. It had been an average-to-boring sort of shift at the café in Cavalier. She never looked forward to a low tip night, but the extra quiet gave Hailey a chance to contemplate her reality.

The thought of calling her friend Meghan was first to come to mind. But Hailey coached herself, "I'm already crazed. I'd better drive and make it there in one piece first. *Like I need a car accident, on top of EVERYthing else!* Hailey thought as she drove. She was shaken to her already rattled core, "Oh, God! Please help me," she pleaded aloud, then, just as quickly, complained, "I pray for help and all I hear is quiet! No, please, please, Lord!" she begged.

The driveway to Christine's big house came into view. Hailey tried but failed to compose herself. The problem was that she was late. The sort of late that motivates one to buy a pregnancy test kit. But this wasn't just any late. She'd given birth to Sasha seven weeks before. She tried to hire a lawyer to set up child support from both dead-beat-dads who had fathered her first two children, but couldn't afford the legal fees. Now, how to explain it all to one more man whom she hadn't seen since Thanksgiving? *Call Meghan*, she directed herself, *she'll know what I should do!*

The eighteenth of December finally dawned and Dara's flight into Hawaii was on time. She gathered her carry-on bag and stood near the baggage claim carrousel, looking for her luggage. Joe, also known as Dillon, reached his hands around her waist and quietly greeted his one true love. Their reunion showed those around that this pair was deeply in love, had missed the other, and that neither was nervous about the public knowing it.

Myron Haldorson's sister, Gretchen, still couldn't believe that her brother had been renting out her bedroom. Many of the collections of treasures she'd hoarded over the years had been moved to a couple storage sheds in the back yard. Gretchen wasn't one bit impressed by Myron's makeover from a mousy, smelly young man, into the lovable fiancé of Jody Bernhardt, the First United Free Church secretary. None of that mattered. He was renting out her room, and she obviously couldn't trust him with anything.

Myron didn't have the nerve to fight back, to take his stand. Instead, he was in serious trouble with both his sister and his fiancé. Myron scheduled overtime whenever he could. Myron's memory of seeing Rene hauling his few things out, into fresh snowfall, was enough to make him take a step back, back into being a lonely, sad man with bad hygiene.

Rene's hand grasped his snow shovel. He didn't mind the fresh snow. He was getting up the nerve to invite JoJo out for a thank-you dinner. As though LaDonna could read his mind, she had sent him a card to remind him to 'ask her out, already!'

He grunted his response to his aunt and laughed aloud at LaDonna's nature. Rene was shoveling, but Hailey called from the house. "Can you come here?"

Once inside, she reached for his hand and led him downstairs where both her children were napping. Suddenly, she burst into tears and slugged his arm. "Why!?"

"What did I do to you?"

"Nothing!" She shook the positive pregnancy testing wand through the air, repeating, "Why!?" She sobbed again, then finally seemed ready to talk. "You've delivered babies. Do you ever do home abortions?"

"What? No, I have not, I would not. No, I won't."

"Yeah," she seemed to stagger toward the kitchen table. "Meghan didn't think you would, either."

"Who's Meghan?"

"My best friend in the world. She's the voice of reason!" she laughed and cried all the more, adding through sobs, "She lives in Fargo."

Rene hugged Hailey, "Can Meghan come to see you?"

"No, she does shift work like I do."

"Have you told Christine?"

"NO! I can't. You should've heard the lecture I got when Sasha had come along. No." Hailey cuddled into Rene's hug.

Rene offered, "I will watch the kids if you want to go see Meghan. You need the voice of reason. You need to come back here with a sure, stable attitude about yourself, about your children, about life. Can Meghan do all that?"

~*~*~*~

Later that day, Christine asked Rene to bring in firewood. He was at his task, about three loads in, when he stopped at the kitchen and asked Cammy, "What is that aroma?"

"The bird lady's at it again! I kid you not, JoJo, she makes homemade suet for the birds all winter." Cammy watched Rene, then added, "She's nuts."

JoJo came around the corner with arms laden with ingredients. Rene was stirring the kettle that simmered on the stove. "What is this?" he asked.

"Lard and peanut butter, the chunky style." She further explained, "I add corn meal, quick oatmeal, flour, a little sugar, raisins, bird seed in a bowl, then stir in the melted lard and…"

Cammy finished the thought, "Yeah, peanut butter. Then in the summer she feeds the orioles grape jelly. PB&J, for birds. You're crazy, woman!" Cammy left, muttering all the way, then shouted from the doorway to the back staircase, "Crazy!"

Rene thought through the process. "Then you bake?"

"No, freeze. The jumbo muffin tins work best. I line the tins with sheets of plastic wrap. If I have trouble with getting the suet to release, then I use a blow dryer on the bottoms of the pans, just enough to release them. I keep them in the freezer until I put them outside. The lard stays fresher that way." JoJo went on to explain, "I think that the store-bought suet has some sort of preservative since their fat doesn't melt at normal outdoor temps. Suet isn't for the heat of summer, anyway. Birds have plenty of bugs then, but I set out suet for fall, winter and spring."

Rene was set to finish his chore, but first he reached in for a quick hug, explaining, "That's from the birds."

Since hearing JoJo explain her strategies for feeding birds, Rene was sure to check her bird feeding areas whenever he was outside. Even from inside, he would watch the avian pecking order that formed at each feeder. On those few days before Christmas, Rene was delighted to sense a clarity in his mind: he was more than just a little enamored with JoJo.

Hailey made her plans and after work one night, Rene soon found himself being summoned down to Hailey's basement, not realizing the confusion that that caused the ladies upstairs.

Cammy had witnessed Rene coming inside the back door and head down the steps. "Uh, what the..." The next two souls in the door were TJ and Dora, so she reported her suspicions. "Men go down there for one reason only," Cammy accused.

The rumors and speculations had their birth in that image. But they were nothing compared to the sound that JoJo had overheard: Hailey's end of a conversation with someone on the phone. Hailey had said, "Rene, it's his..." the thought was interrupted, giving him credit for the idea for her trip to Fargo, but was followed by, "I know, I can't believe I'm pregnant again!" There was a mantra that held firm in JoJo's heart, a phrase that resurfaced and repeated in her mind, *Rene! I don't understand you!* JoJo wasn't about to add more fuel to Cammy's flame, to rile up even more rumors, so she harbored Hailey' and Rene's perceived secret. Christmas was soon upon them and JoJo had more gifts to make.

"Hailey just left," Cammy pointed through the dining room window at Hailey's car, driving away. "No kids with her, nothing. She took my pink overnight bag, the one she borrowed and never gave back."

A couple days later, Hailey was back, in a brighter mood, and nothing was ever said. Rene was done babysitting and headed back to stay at his carriage house. It was hard for JoJo. She was bent on feeding the birds like usual, but Rene seemed to be watching her with more and more interest. *I can tell you've got a crush brewing*, she thought, *I'm not blind*. As was her custom early mornings, she headed out to check the bird feeders. One morning she was greeted by a flock of wild turkeys. She said, "Shooo!" They all gobbled back at her. "This bird food is for the little birds." They gobbled back, again. No matter what she said, they gobbled. Finally, she heard Rene's laughter from the door of his carriage house. The birds gobbled at his laughter, too.

If JoJo hadn't been so annoyed with him for fathering yet another baby for Hailey, and then allowing her to go to Fargo for an abortion, she could've almost been amused at his amusement. But respect was hard-earned with JoJo, especially when it came to the lives of helpless unborn babies.

Spencer had had enough of Jason's game. And certainly enough of avoiding Danielle's phone calls. He searched through Candy and Buddy's house, but his mom wasn't there. In quick order, he found her at the main Providence offices. Spencer insisted, "I'm going to find him, Mom. I started this whole thing, and it needs to have a conclusion Not just to help Jason be a man, but to give his victims closure. And besides all that, I'm the big brother. I should've talked to him before now. Back when Dad died, Jason was only 15. I was 19 and though that's still not considered mature, I had had some talks with Dad about women, about life, about facing one's responsibilities. I need to pass that on, but first I need to find him." Anyone could tell that Spencer was both sincere and determined.

Alan had been listening from his office doorway. "Where do you think he is? We've got the law and private investigators looking for him. They haven't found anything beyond the car that he stole and then sold to innocent victims in Omaha."

Candy reached for Spencer and held him in a tight hug, "One son is on the run and doomed to prison when he's finally found. Why would I want my other son to disappear into God knows where?!"

"He's in Mexico." A voice came from across the room. Spencer, Candy and Alan all looked. It was James. He explained, "Alan, I was just waiting for you. I guess I was summoned about something."

Alan moved closer, "Yes, we're short-handed here in the barn. We can talk about that later, but why do you think Jason's in Mexico?"

"Or he's on his way there. Mexico is a good place to lay low. The cost of living is low, the weather is mild. He sure as heck isn't in Canada. He sold a car?" To Candy's quick nod James continued, "Then he has cash. Does he speak Spanish?"

Candy sighed, "Yes, from high school. He was pretty good at it."

Spencer had his plan, "See? I'm going to Mexico and drag his sorry ass back home."

Alan and Candy countered Spencer's plans until James piped in again, "I'll go with him." Again, he had their attention. "Make sure this one's OK. Then bring them both back," James offered.

Laura came in and headed for Ila's desk, "Hey, the vet. Will? I lost his phone number. Do you have it here?"

Alan interrupted, "Now, Laura, what if I was to send James off on a mission. Would you be OK with that?"

She looked from Alan, to James and Spencer, and back, then simply said, "I've been to see my shrink, and at this point I'm still encircled in Kevlar. Do whatever you want."

Anna came forward. "I can pitch in when he's gone to help make cheese. Would that help you?"

"Help me? Anna, you're eight months pregnant. Have you ever made cheese before?"

"Well, not successfully," came her reply.

Laura pointed back to Alan, "You've worked in a creamery. Find your favorite hair net, big guy," she said to him, then turned to James. "Do what you have to." She turned back to Ila and got Will's cell number, then headed back to her office.

Spencer hugged his fretful mother, "I'll be fine. James and I will be fine. We leave tomorrow, OK?" he asked James.

There was confidence in James' voice, "0600. We'll leave from this office at 6am."

Alan held up his hand, "Tomorrow? There's a winter storm in the forecast, a big one. And Christmas." He voiced what the ladies were thinking, save Laura, who was in her own world.

James' eyes went steely, as he rebutted, "The trail's cold enough right now. We can't wait. Eight hours and we'll be in Omaha. Let's leave now."

A quick check of the weather and Alan agreed. Both James and Spencer would head out, 6am. Spencer and his mom left to get packed, leaving James there with Alan. "Tonight, am I able to see what your investigators have found?" The two men agreed, then James asked, "What did you need? Short-handed, where?"

"Here in the main barn, as a relief-milker. I've gone through a couple. I thought the money was good, but it takes a special person to handle it, I guess. I'm advertising already. Until then, there are chores that need doing, especially if I'm making cheese. Wait, you're leaving."

"I wouldn't do it anyway. I strongly dislike cattle, and I've never milked a cow. On the Morning Star Ranch the cows always kept their calves."

With a sigh, Alan pulled out his phone and dialed. "Rusty?"

It was Monday night before Christmas, December 21st. Spencer's sisters, Anna and Katie, both seemed resigned to his plan to disappear on a mission. James' sister Trish was less understanding. "For cryin' out loud! James! You just got home!"

"I got home last summer. You must be bored with me by now." None of her reactions that night made sense to him. The one who made even less sense was Laura. *Do what you have to*, she had said. He remembered the calm, almost tranquil look in her eyes. *Is she that ready to see me gone?*

Regardless, the two men were both there that Tuesday morning, 0600. That was when the difference in personalities and priorities became clear. "We'll use my car," Spencer explained, "for long distance we may as well ride in comfort." James opened the back end of Spencer's brand new Subaru Forester. There were already three suitcases on one side, then a cooler and two bags of, as Spencer explained, "dry food. Should be plenty."

"You know that they have restaurants between here and Mexico, right?" James asked, as he opened the back seat door where he found a hanging garment bag and what looked like a bag full of shoes on the floor behind the driver's seat. James tossed in one small duffle, a small tool kit, and two gun cases. "I'm driving first," he muttered, then opened the hood of the car, made a speedy safety inspection and was quickly seated by the steering wheel. "Keys?"

Spencer reluctantly handed off his keys and the two men were gone.

Spencer dozed as James kept the silver Subaru in constant motion. With winter weather headed their way, there was no time to waste. A plan had been developing since James got a report from Alan, then additional details from one of the investigators, a fellow vet named Josh Martin from Chicago, whom Anna and Alan had hired before. Spencer squinted his eyes, tried to focus on the GPS device and asked, "Where are we?"

James was maneuvering icy downtown streets, as he replied, "Omaha. We're staying here tonight. Pick out a hotel for us to stay at."

Spencer eyed the streets, "Is that wet or ice?"

"Both, I'd guess. It's snowing hard behind us. We're lucky to be here before the storm." James parked in front of the police station. "You take over driving, find a hotel and come back to pick me up in a couple hours."

His fellow traveler was already grating on Spencer's nerves. "No, I'm coming in here, now, too."

The Albuquerque police were onto the pick-pocket thieves in Clark's band. Clark wasn't happy about Loria's fumbles and missteps. She was the reason they had to move on, leaving money in tourists' pockets instead of his, and he made sure she knew it. Jason was relieved that Loria was the one catching guff from Clark, instead of Jason. He had been the butt of Clark's wry humor and blamed for every little problem that came up, until now. Jason was still dressed for the Mexican beach, but a couple men from the gypsy tribe tried to help him with layers as the group headed for Farmington, New Mexico.

As they headed north, a vivid memory of the flavors and aroma of the guacamole that Jason had for lunch that day, the day that Loria had stolen his money, filled his senses. He had found the bus station that morning and had had plans that afternoon to retrieve the stolen credit cards he'd buried in the desert. Stopping to admire architecture was a mistake. Taking a second look at Loria had been an even bigger mistake.

"We're on a mission," Spencer had heard James say to the police lieutenant. Spencer's usual style of mission usually either involved scouting out the perfect lake cabin for his clients, or a school of walleye or lake trout for himself. At twenty-eight years old, he knew from both fishing and real estate that if he was going to take a stand in this new style of mission, it had to come soon.

James introduced the pair and held most of the conversation with the Omaha investigation team. There was a detective, who had researched a young couple whose loan was uncovered as fraudulent. He was helpful to a point. "It was these kids," he explained, opening the file, "vandals, small town thieves. Multiple priors. They were shoplifting in a nearby town, got nailed, and when they were being processed, their vehicle popped up as having been stolen."

"When did they last see the seller?"

"Just before Halloween. The banker who manages the branch their loan came from, they want you two to nail down the guy who tricked these two vandals into offering them worthless collateral." The next offer surprised both Spencer and James. "The county sheriff, his wife runs that bank. Your brother's sly way of conniving cash out of their system, well, it's embarrassing and they have to answer to auditors. We are willing to help nail this guy, too. What do you need?"

Spencer asked, "Were there any other vehicles stolen in that time frame?"

"Only one, but we already solved that case."

James was sure, "Then can we look at security camera video for flights and busses?"

It took two days, but the men were finally at a crossroads. "Are you sure?" James asked.

Banking mostly on Spencer's memory of Jason's quirky habits, his gesture gained in confidence as he stared, pointed and nodded. "He hasn't spent one Halloween without some sort of pirate hat." Still, it was a Hail Mary at the best. Was the man in the pirate hat with a blurry silhouette really his brother?

James pulled a list from his back pocket. "Alan said that these two credit cards still haven't been used, but with that much cash, he wouldn't need to use plastic."

The detective made a call to the bank, "Do you have a list of the serial numbers of all those one hundred dollar bills? I remember you said that they were all new. The bills were ordered in special. The sheriff's wife's bank, they wouldn't keep records of the numbers, but the source would. We get the Feds to give us a hand? Then it's smooth sailing." Within an hour, they came back to James and Spencer with evidence. Jason was heading from Denver to Las Vegas.

Spencer's grin was ear to ear, "And people say that God doesn't answer prayers, they're dead wrong!"

The Christmas blizzard of 2009 stretched from Texas to Canada, and many in the region changed their holiday plans to celebrate at or near home.

Unaware of the gossip that was building steam around him, Rene kept clearing snowdrifts and roads in Christine's neighborhood. His Christmas holiday was like a picture postcard or Norman Rockwell painting. His new neighbors made sure he was included in parties they hosted, and on Christmas Eve, he was invited to a white elephant gift exchange party. All was cordial and festive, but then an ambulance call alarm sounded on his phone when the game had been set to start.

His truck rolled into the yard after many others were in bed. He saw Christine's light was on, so he let himself in. Hailey's two cats greeted him. Rene ignored them and made noises to make sure the ladies knew of his presence. Rattling a kettle in the sink drain board scared the cats off. "Christine?" he called, "are you decent?" He looked at the clock, "It's after ten, but it's Christmas, are you up?" He wasn't ready for what came next.

A woman's voice, speaking French, said, "Little Rene, be good on Christmas!" She rounded the corner from the hall, shaking her finger at him.

"LaDonna!" he exclaimed and reached in for hugs and kisses. "You are such a happy surprise! Ahh, let me introduce," he switched to English, "LaDonna, meet my neighbor Christine." He tried to scold, "You are too good at keeping secrets!"

Christine laughed aloud, "It wasn't just me," then stepped aside to expose both Dora and JoJo, standing behind. Dora shrugged her shoulders and smiled. JoJo's face looked tired.

Rene questioned, "But the storm, how did you get here?"

"I flew into Winnepeg, then came here from there. Not so stormy up north," LaDonna noted, and smiled again at her hostesses.

Rene reported, "Anna told me that her brother, Spencer, he's stalled in Omaha. But I think that was their first stop." Rene grinned again at both Dora and JoJo, "Aunty LaDonna, of all of the cousins who live here, yes, it would be these two."

Christine wondered, "The ambulance call, what happened?"

Rene's grin beamed, "Twins were born, on Christmas Eve. Two boys. They came too fast for the couple to get to the hospital."

The group sat around a late night kettle of hot chocolate pondering babies and Christmases past. Rene realized that it wasn't just fatigue with JoJo. There was a nervousness to her face that night, no eye contact. Something was not right.

But it was Christmas and Christine was so happy to have a special guest. It was already set up. LaDonna was set up in Sarah's room since she was gone with her sweetheart, Mac, to visit his family.

JoJo gathered the cups and took them to the kitchen sink, where Rene asked her, "Are you OK? Something seems wrong."

Her quiet shrug and reassurance didn't convince Rene. He headed for his bachelor apartment questioning all the possibilities. He even asked the wild turkeys, "Did she tell you what's wrong?" Their gobbled reply didn't amuse him anymore.

Getting to Farmington, New Mexico, and then to Clark's acreage outside of town, meant Christmas break for everyone else. For Jason and Loria, it only meant slavery. "Cleaning the house, top to bottom," Roxy had said. That was where she lost Jason's attention, until she cuffed the back of his head. "You! I never should've let them convince me to try you out. You are more trouble than you're worth!"

"OK," Jason agreed, feeling badgered, "I'll clean." Using his opportunity to clean house, he also various treasures aside and stashed them into a dark blue duffle that he had found in a trash can. In between cleaning one room or another, he was given broken tools and inadequate cleaning supplies, but was expected to make due.

Remembering his mother's house, Jason pulled vinegar from the kitchen cupboard and made more progress. Little things, like using the few working tools he found, along with the meager shop supplies in the garage, to put a new connection on a garden hose, then bringing the water to the succulent collection outside and setting up a soaker hose. It was little things that he succeeded at, and he kept quietly adding treasures to the dark blue duffle.

Day by day they started to trust him with chores that involved actual soap and less-rusted tools. Weather was snowy and cold. He opted to put up with the games she played, but Roxy kept glaring his way.

New Year's Eve day in Farmington, New Mexico, was the end of the salmon season in the nearby rivers. All the men headed out to try their hand, but Jason was kept behind. "You can try it next year, Jason" Pat promised, then kissed his sweetheart, Roxy, and headed out.

"Listen to you whimper!" she accused.

Jason defended, "I didn't say anything!" but thought, *I'll be long gone to Mexico by then!*

"I can hear you think!" she huffed, putting a sudden chill up his spine. She passed him, heading for the kitchen, then stopped dead. The bottom edge of his short-sleeved shirt was twisted up to expose his skin. "What'cha do here?" The skin was purple. "Looks like you've been bitten."

"Bitten? What do you mean?"

"Brown Recluse spider. Too bad for you," she judged, then added, "Just as well, I don't like havin' ya here anyway," walking away to watch TV.

When in the garage the day before, he'd accidently rubbed his shoulder against a nail. That was what he blamed for the pain he'd noted the night before. A wash of chills flowed through him, then joint pain, excruciating joint pain.

He complained to Loria of his pain, but she had already received a fifty dollar bill to play along with Roxy, so she said, "It won't be long. Just accept it." Both women knew that many people confuse the lore of the Brown Recluse, but that though they may have a deadly reputation, few people ever died from their spider bites. Instead, some could get sick, especially if the victim is not medically treated. Jason was in the latter category.

Sounding as heartless as she could, Roxy groaned, "Oh, please, just start the seizures and get it over with!"

The fear in Jason's eyes grew as another wave of chills hit him, followed by sweats, nausea, and a spiking fever that took hold.

15 DOLDRUMS

The excitement of Christmas, and the thrill of New Year's Eve, then the inevitable let-down of New Year's Day slowly led into the dreaded Doldrums of Winter. This was a phenomenon that Christine had been long since guarding against, but it seemed to sneak into her house every year.

LaDonna had headed back to Winnipeg to catch her flight. The silver bells, and cheery red and green had all been packed away with care. The extra recipe cards were filed in boxes and special cookbooks were relegated to top shelves of her bookcases, until the next year.

The sense and order that Christine craved was quickly tossed about by Hailey, dashing across the room, heading for the toilet.

JoJo was back in from her bird feeder chores and witnessed the same. Both ladies hugged the half-bathroom door frame by the kitchen while Christine asked, "Dear me? You've got a flu bug?"

"Damn morning sickness," Hailey grumbled, holding her stomach.

JoJo and Christine blinked at each other. Christine asked quietly "Oh, you're pregnant again, so soon?"

"Again? No, still, for another seven and a half months as I figure it. Oh," she moaned, "these babies are way too close together!" She heaved again while Christine went to get the saltines.

JoJo saw Dora in the back stairway and pulled her aside, "She said, 'Again? No, still!'" To the blank look on Dora's face, JoJo began again, whispering in the stairway, and spelled it out. The pair descended, watching as Hailey came from the small bathroom on Christine's arm, then quietly joined the conversation.

Dora started, "Oh, Hailey, I hope you feel better soon. You'll get dehydrated," she said with compassion. "I'll stop and get you some Gatorade."

JoJo asked, "With Christmas and the stormy weather, I don't think I ever asked, Hailey, how was your trip to Fargo?" The group consensus had assumed that any pregnant woman who didn't want to stay pregnant, and suddenly heads to Fargo, must be seeking an abortion. JoJo's thoughts were laden, thick with that worry ever since Hailey left on her trip, but never dared to confront her. Now with obvious first trimester symptoms in full view, JoJo was hopeful that all their worries had been a stupid assumption.

"Meghan is always fun, but I was such a downer. I wasn't really ready for this baby, but Meghan…"

Dora cut in, "Meghan Nelson?"

"Yes, she is my rock. I told Rene that she's my go-to when it comes to the voice of reason. And I needed that voice. I can't believe this, looking back, but I actually asked him to do a home abortion. 'Course he refused. Meghan told me he would."

JoJo repeated to Dora, a spark of life returning to her mind, "He refused. Yes, Meghan is so wise."

Hailey agreed, adding, "Yes, so it was his idea that I go see her, so he offered to babysit." Hailey's baby monitor was making noises in her robe pocket, so she headed back downstairs to get Sasha.

The ladies in the kitchen breathed a collective sigh of relief. Christine summarized, "It was his idea, not his baby. Thank God above!"

The whir of Christine's cell phone contrasted with the rhythmic chime of her old grandfather's clock. With a quick glance she had to laugh. "A text from Rene with a picture. 'Tell JoJo', Rene says, 'now she has deer joining her wild turkeys at her backyard buffet'!"

James sat down across from Spencer in the hotel dining room. A sample of the breakfast buffet was piled high on Spencer's plate. "Figured I'd find you here," muttered James, then added, "guess I'll grab a plate."

"Was that a slam?" Spencer asked, adding between bites, "Because I don't appreciate your tone."

"No tone was intended. Just that I've noticed you like a hearty breakfast. I do, too." James soon returned with a loaded plate and sat down at Spencer's table. "It's natural to get on edge with a long case like this."

"On edge?" Spencer waved his fork from side to side, adding, "You haven't seen on edge."

"Oh you'd know what I've seen."

Spencer was on edge, but deflected, "There's always this wall that you put up. This 'it's classified,' wall that shuts down any understanding of what makes you tick."

James refocused, "The waiting, the sitting and waiting can drive a guy crazy. It's part of the deal with missions like this. We don't need to be at each other's throats. Wouldn't Jason love that! Then we'd be spinning in circles here and he'd get off, scott-free." Spencer closed one eye and the other one twitched. "Crimes, investigations, cases, they're never solved as fast in real life as they are on TV." Spencer rolled his eyes, but James continued, encouraging, "You're curious about me? OK, there has to be things, topics that we can learn from each other."

"What really happened in Afghanistan or Iraq, whatever?"

"I can't tell you that."

Spencer redirected, "You brought two guns in my car. What are their names?" he lightly joked, "Smith and Wesson?"

"A Ruger and a Glock, both 9mm."

He held up his hand, "Wait a minute. What's to stop you from killing me in the night? I don't really know much about you."

James' wry sense of humor wasn't timely. "Don't be crazy," he drawled, "We have separate rooms."

"What?"

The belly laugh from James was infectious to all but Spencer, "What! It was a joke!" He reeled in his wit; it was currently lost on Spencer.

Finally, Spencer got to his base question, "Do you really plan to use them? I know my brother's an ass, but this isn't the Old West where they 'bring 'em back dead or alive.'"

"I knew we'd get bored at some point. I hope I don't have to use them for our protection, but I never know what I'll need. No, I don't plan to shoot your brother. But let's start there. Instead of focusing on the differences between us, let's learn something new from the other to make the time pass. Do you shoot?"

Spencer cut more ham, "I go bird-hunting."

"Not big game?"

"I lost my taste for deer hunting when my Dad died." Suddenly the food on his plate was losing its appeal, too.

James encouraged. "Let's try some target practice after breakfast."

"Did you bring ammo, too?"

"Some, but not enough for target practice. Still, this is Las Vegas. They've got ammo."

~*~*~*~

Trish and Laura were still on a non-speaking basis, but neither realized the other was shopping at Providence foods that Groundhog Day. Nor did either want a longer winter than that which had already hit the Red River Valley of the North that year, but both were helpless to change it.

Laura rounded the corner into another aisle and didn't see Trish coming her way. Both were too focused on their shopping to pay any heed. It was Laura who first said, "Hi, Trish, Happy Groundhog Day."

If she could've turned invisible, all would've been well. As it was, Trish nearly turned inside out trying to shop faster and get away, without uttering an audible word. Laura could tell what Trish was thinking, though, and it wasn't pretty. She followed Trish down the aisle, "Please, Trish, let's end this silly quarrel. It's not good for either one of us."

Trish finally found her tongue. "Are you going to leave James alone?"

Laura was not about to be manhandled. "You realize that he's full-grown. That you're both full-grown and that he can make his own decisions. Right? You realize it is up to him, right?"

Trish wasn't about to be bulldozed. "Why is this even an issue? There are plenty of other men all around us who could make you just as happy. If Jack was an example of your sorta guy, well, you've proven a capacity for scraping the barrel. Find some guy without PTSD, who can handle your own version of chaos. Why add that onto James? He's got enough without that, too."

Laura was fuming inside, but held her ground. "Did you know that he calls me? I don't call him. He calls me."

Trish wasn't ready for this curve ball. James was in the habit of calling her once a week, on Sundays. They would discuss the current search update and the people who surrounded him, then she'd give an update of the happenings at home and they'd both sign off. Now news of James calling Laura, too, was tipping Trish's equilibrium. She insisted to Laura, "He doesn't call you, he doesn't have time."

Laura was done. She obviously wasn't going to make Trish happy, but added, "He makes time, every other night," and pushed her cart off in the opposite direction.

The two ladies tried not to but caught glances of each other as they shopped, although Trish was successful in not having to breath the same air.

Spencer's right eye twitched as he worked to close the left and shoot. The beer cans and tequila bottle James and Spencer had found in the desert had become their targets. James' side of the arid target range kept flying as he shot, beer cans meeting their doom. Spencer's side was fairly safe. James encouraged, "You're used to bird-shot. That old approach won't work. Whatever you're used to, change something."

Spencer remembered the pigeons he'd eradicated from his friend's farmyard. "Switch it up," he said under his breath. Finally, he closed his other eye, then squeezed the trigger. The glass bottle jumped and crashed into pieces as he let out a war whoop.

James chuckled, "OK, now you teach me something."

Spencer's wide smile was back. "After we check with the Feds about Jason's cash."

JoJo had assumed the worst about Rene and judged him harshly, though he was completely innocent. *Friends just don't do that to friends!* JoJo scolded herself when heading back outside. Under the guise of needing to get something out of her car, she walked past Rene, who faithfully swept new snow off Christine's sidewalk. "Good morning, Rene. That was a great picture of the deer and turkeys this morning."

"Thank you." He sensed a positive vibration, and finally popped the question. "Speaking of thanks, I've been needing to properly thank you for your work on these winter coveralls and this jacket." She could see that they were keeping him warm. "I'd like to take you out for a nice dinner somewhere, just a simple thank-you meal between friends."

JoJo suggested, "OK, yes, we'll work out a good day of the week, I'm guessing."

"Yes, perfect. Not a weekend night. To me those are date nights, and this isn't a date. Right?"

"West Virginia?" James asked, "The state?"

"Yes," Spencer explained, "it's W for watts, V for volts, and the A on Virginia represents amps. Now, mind you, if you're talking about Virginia, the woman, and not the state, then sparks will fly if you start converting her watts, so stick to electricity. Are you serious about learning about converting amps to watts, or volts to amps? You said you wanted to learn more about weird stuff like electricity and solar power. Well, when I was trying to sell a lake house that was off the grid, and my clients had to know how much their lifestyle would be changing, well, I learned about weird stuff. Or were you just playing with me? You multiply amps times volts to get watts."

James stretched. Their boredom from awaiting action on Jason had just about driven the two men stir crazy. "Yes, but first tell me more about Virginia, the woman."

February 1st was Anna's due date, and that had come and gone. Alan and Anna had been quietly surviving the doldrums. Food-wise, Anna was stable and happy. There were compromises she made for flavor, like adding Velveeta to the cheddar in mac and cheese, and then baking it. Alan was none the wiser and this way she could stomach it.

But the latest topic that surrounded them was parenthood. Regardless of Anna's daily encouragement, Alan doubted his ability to father, live up to the expectations that his prior visions had proposed. "When it comes to our ability to physically become parents, that's a slam dunk. But there's no instruction book that comes with a baby. You've witnessed my appreciation for a good installation guide that comes with equipment, or the owner's manual that comes with a machine."

Anna wasn't surprised by his mood; she'd seen and heard it since she started to show. The aches and pains that her body experienced were personified in his growing concern for her, for her body, for her life, and for the future success of his child. But she was surprised at his current timing. "Like I've said before, dear, we'll study the book of Proverbs every night. We'll read all the little stories, and play, you love to play, and we'll give our comfort. You've got this. I'm sure." As before, he hugged her tenderly and kissed her with love and compassion. That compassion, thankfully, was never a surprise either. But what was increasingly evident was the irony of his timing.

She held him gently, but then both her hands grasped a handful of his shirt sleeve fabric and held on tight. She breathed the way she was instructed by the hospital's nursing staff, then relaxed as her body released its grip.

"What was that?" Alan asked.

"What I thought was indigestion issues, you know, stomach cramps before having loose stools? Well, I now believe that was the beginning of labor contractions, like distant rumbles of thunder. I'll start timing them now." The shock and amazement in his face was precious, causing her to beam with a wide, open smile, adding, "Because that was the first actual contraction, like a spectacular flash of lightning!

The Las Vegas hotel elevator door opened and James entered. The two small-town investigators had been following up with their law enforcement contacts, but there still was nothing new happening. James stood, sharing the elevator with an older woman. There was a distinct aroma to her perfume that took James back. It was both sweet and spicy, but James didn't have to analyze anything. It was clear to him.

The scent in his mind put him back into his grandmother's garden, weeding around the tall, pale, purple irises. His Grandma had noticed James' interest in plants from an early age, so she was sure to take him on a camping trip to the International Peace Garden. The tall, pale, purple iris was by far her favorite. When weeding earlier that day, the flower's pollen had dusted his clothes and followed him into the night. That was the night he had decided to run away from home. The sudden onslaught of both memories, and sensory overload, had James stopped, physically, stalled, on a floor of the hotel that he neither recognized nor had business on.

Dora heard the JoJo's bedroom door slam. She waited a moment or two, then dared to knock on the door. "What's with you?" she inquired.

With JoJo's fists clenched and a stomp of her foot, it was clear, she was miffed. "Can you believe it? We finally get to setting up the Valentine's Day date and what does Darren do? A group party of friends, have you ever heard of having a group party for Valentine's Day? Yes, maybe the 4th of July or even Halloween, but NOT Valentine's, no."

Dora dared to ask the obvious question, "Overall, do you really think your relationship is going anywhere?" JoJo stopped to think, and Dora added, "What's the last romantic thing he did or said?"

JoJo quipped, "He was a lot more romantic before we started dating," and they soon both changed the topic.

Mac McIntyre had been dining at Thompson's Café ever since Thanksgiving when Mac got to know, at least a little, Hailey Eskelson. At first she seemed to think he was just another of the annoying men who tried to woo her through one shift into another. But something seemed to change before Christmas. She had taken a few days off and something turned a switch when she got back. Hailey wasn't only listening to Mac's version of sweet talk, but she was flirting back, which he loved. But then both he and Bob Whitney heard a rumor that was rumbling through the job sites, a rumor that Rene was the father of Hailey's latest baby.

James made plans and stopped at Spencer's hotel room. "Hey, I've got connections in LA. So, I'm going to go, you know, boots on the ground, check it out in person. If anything comes up, then you have my contact info. OK?"

Spencer didn't know what to say, but "OK," was his kneejerk reaction. He watched as James walked away, with the look of being in clear 'mission mode.' Spencer had seen that look before and was learning to roll with it.

What Spencer didn't sense was the doldrums that still plagued James, holding him back, since that fateful night when the spicy, sweet aroma from his grandmother's garden was the only good thing that he knew. Instead, he was on the run again.

Rene & JoJo dined at the Caribou steakhouse in Hallock, Minnesota. Conversation was light, then JoJo mentioned her boyfriend, Darren. As the waiter set down their food, Rene casually waved his knife in her direction, judging, "You don't see it from your perspective, JoJo, but this Darren, he is but a twig of a man."

"A twig. A twig compared to what?"

He laughed quietly, "Oh, you'll have to excuse me. These are theories from my teen years. I was always taught to be kind to the girls, but the guys, I could and would judge them harshly. Yes, a twig, in the vast forest of life, he is a twig, that is all."

"A twig. So what does that make you? A branch?"

His laughter was louder, more nervous. "Oh? Well!" he smiled and took a sip of his water. "Mind you, this is from my teens. In the vast forest of life I was a waterfall. Free. Spectacular! Glorious!" He watched for her response.

"Pretty full of yourself, weren't you?"

Rene stared at nearby artwork. "Ahh, these days I'm more of a reflective pool."

"And Dee? What or who is Dee in the vast forest of life?"

"More of an eddy, swirling. I was not the only man who she had spinning in circles, all at the same time. No, she wasn't faithful."

"But you're still going to French Polynesia?"

"No, LaDonna brought Dee's letter at Christmas that finally cut it off between us."

"Because waterfalls should be faithful? What did you say? Spectacular?"

His quiet smile belied his memories of those days, "Oui, free but faithful, and glorious, too."

"But I've never sensed that pompous attitude from you lately. What would take you from all that ego and calm it down?"

"My father committed suicide last year."

"Oh! I'm sorry, I didn't know!"

"It was a surprise. Total shock. Yes, it blew the wind out of this French Canadian blowhard's sails. But I still think that whatever his name is— he's a twig."

They were seated in a booth where Rene was facing the door and could see people come and go, but JoJo's view was towards the back of the dining room. She saw him walk past her. Darren. He had his hand in the small of her back as he and a beautiful woman walked back to their table. "Surprise, indeed," she quietly uttered, her eyes transfixed on the woman's back, and how his hand slowly dropped lower, onto the woman's derriere. Obviously, this was no work relationship. JoJo had

233

coordinated her thank-you meal with Rene to be on an evening when Darren was already busy with a business appointment. "Indeed!" JoJo's voice was controlled, but her volume was building up to steam. "Did you see him?"

"Who?"

"The twig! The melon-colored dress. See the woman in the melon-colored dress?"

Rene twisted around to see. "That's a nice dress," he casually said.

"What?" JoJo also saw a middle-aged woman in royal blue. "Are you looking at the right woman?"

He took another glance, "The melons? Yes, I see her."

"Melons? Wha… What are you looking at!? You're disgusting!"

Rene loaded his fork. "You say what you see, I'll say what I see. I'm sorry, I'm a man," he reasoned and took a bite of steak.

The woman in the melon-colored dress rose and innocently headed to the restroom, giving JoJo an opportunity to, as she said, "Give that twig a piece of my mind!"

~*~*~*~

"Hey, Mom," Spencer began, his cell phone held tight to one ear as his index finger plugged the other, "Thought I'd call with an update."

"Where on earth are you!? It's noisy."

"I'm still in Las Vegas. This dining room is packed. I'm here at the buffet."

"Any news?"

This was her constant question whenever he had called, to Spencer's chagrin. He didn't have any more news for this update than he did in the days before. He was in the doldrums, with nothing to muster him onward, stuck in neutral. "News? James left for LA today. He's got some contacts there. The federal agents, they have the serial numbers from the cash that Jason received for the first car he'd stolen. So, I'm checking with them daily. I'm sure they're tired of my face. I know I'm tired of theirs."

Candy moaned, "Well, that's crazy! You can't tell me that's all there is for us to do! Dear God! I pray for answers five, ten, sometimes twenty times a day, and we get nowhere!"

"I'm frustrated, too," Spencer assured.

"Frustrated!?" Candy lamented, "Yes, I suppose you are. I've got my only two sons out on a mission against each other in some journey of good versus evil, between here and Mexico. I've prayed all I can with our pastor." She shook her head and studied the floor, then added, seemingly resigned to a new plan, "It's time to bring in the big guns."

"Big guns?"

"I'm starting with the priest in Cavalier. What's his name?" Spencer muttered, but neither of them came up with anything. "It doesn't matter," Candy finally said. "They all answer to Father."

Mac McIntyre had been simmering, near boiling, for most of the day since learning that Hailey and Rene were going to be parents. Mac wasn't sure which one of them made him more upset, but he knew that his relationship with Hailey was still in the delicate stages and he didn't want to loosen those bonds. "Man to man," he muttered, with his blood pressure rising. The work day finally done, he quietly stowed his tools and watched for Rene's car. There were projects that the two men had looked into. If he didn't see Rene at one of the job sites, where they both worked, then he'd find him at the lumberyard.

And there Rene was, between the project idea books and the paint. Mac approached him, no holds barred, feeling strong and intimidating. In an angry growl and a sneer unnatural to the easy-going carpenter, Mac made his point, "If you think that I'm going to help you with your petty little projects after what you've done to Hailey, you are sadly mistaken. And don't call me your friend anymore, either. No friend of mine would do such a thing."

"What is this thing that I've done? Seriously, I don't know!"

Of all the nerve, Mac felt sure that he should *deck 'im now!* But instead he confronted, "Why would you not know when the whole town's talkin' 'bout it?"

"About what? Truly, what am I to be blamed for?"

"You and Hailey," Mac shouted. "She's pregnant again, and the baby's yours. Don't play games with me!" If others in the lumberyard hadn't already heard those rumors, the mistruths were certainly now exposed for all to hear and see.

"You're shaming her by not facing up to it, man!" Mac had hit his emotional zenith, where pinching the top of his nose between his eyes seemed to keep the tears at bay.

Rene tried to comfort and coach in whispers, "Mac McIntyre, you are a true friend, and I would never do such a thing to you. I've known that you are interested in her since before Sasha was born. But remember? This child was conceived on Thanksgiving night when you and I sat up and watched European soccer all night." Rene motioned for them to head outside and with the soccer revelation, Mac quietly conceded.

Mac was losing patience. "How do you know so much, and who is the father, then?" he asked, punching his own fist on the way out.

Once outside, Rene's whispers continued. "It was just before Christmas when she called me aside. She reminded me that I've helped women with birthing, you know, with the ambulance crew? Well, she wondered if I could also do a home abortion, which I rejected. That was when she said that her friend in Fargo, Meghan, that Meghan was the voice of reason for her and that she needed Meghan to talk sense into her again."

The bulging veins in Mac's neck were starting to reduce, and his nostrils no longer flared. Rene continued, "That was when I watched her kids for a few days, a long weekend, and she's been happy since, still pregnant and, young man, you are the best possible thing that's ever happened to her. She's happy because of you." Lumber delivery trucks were coming home to roost that late afternoon. Their dull roar squelched the two friends' conversation and gave Mac a chance to think. Curious souls with snoopy eyes came out of the lumberyard sales room peering to see if the two men were fighting, fisticuffs, but they weren't. Rene peered back at them. "I loathe gossip," Rene finally said, "it's such a twisting of truths and half-truths."

"All right," Mac finally replied. "I'm going to talk to Hailey. She did tell me that she's expecting, and I didn't want to judge her. I just wanted to love her as she was. She seemed to accept me with all my quirks. I wanted to give her the same blessing, I guess. Yeah, that's what I'd call it. At the time it didn't matter who it was, just that she was moving on without him. When I thought that that someone was you, I was more disappointed than anything, that you'd stoop so low. A deadbeat dad. Statistic-wise, over the years, such a huge disappointment for our whole society."

Rene patted his shoulder, "He's getting philosophical. That sounds more like my Mac, my friend." The pair watched more traffic and discussed women, life, and soccer.

James was back in Las Vegas and the small-town investigators still didn't know anything new. Spencer recalled, "Jason and I, we used to rumble, more wrestling than boxing. We still do, sometimes. Do you box?"

"You want to go see a boxing match? Is that it? Join a boxing club and train correctly?"

Spencer nodded, "Something like that. I want to know more about self-defense."

Alan was exhausted from the thrill and excitement, but Anna's exhaustion was gritty and real. After seventeen hours of labor, Braden John Zimmerman was welcomed into the world into his mother's loving arms. Her face still beaded with sweat, her breathing finally stabilized, Anna's heart was full as she quietly gazed into his curious face. "Hello, little one! Oh my, you are handsome!" she cooed. Alan watched on in amazement. "Come closer, Daddy, meet your little man."

The baby stretched as Alan moved closer to study every little detail. "God is so amazing to create such a miracle!"

Anna reminded, "Your folks will want to come visit. I'll call Mom, oh, and Braden, do you have a message for me from my daddy in Heaven? I'm sure you've been bouncing on his knee for a while. His name is Johnny Hillman, and that's where you got your middle name. What's that?" she asked, and tipped the boy closer to her ear, "He loves me?" Quiet tears rolled as the pair bonded and Alan took it all into his heart.

Gradually, it seemed to be a growing list of complaints that Roxy and her dad, Clark, had fielded from their band of thieves. Little things were missing. One man's Gerber pocket tool. A small mending kit. Food from the pantry. Random clothes and other small objects. Gone.

Roxy had sent Jason to fetch something from her car. She opened the back door from the kitchen and looked into the garage with a dropped jaw. Her car was gone, and so was Jason and his dark blue duffle bag.

16 PUSHING HIS LUCK

His car pulled around the corner and parked there in downtown Winkler, Manitoba. Rene was hungry for some good Canadian soul food, so started with a bowl of chili and a platter of back bacon and perogies and a mounding pile of mac and cheese. The waitress was alone that night, too. She flirted between his orders as he filled up on baked chicken, poutine potatoes and gravy, and cheese curds. Then both rhubarb pie and juneberry pie, or as they would call it in Canada, Saskatoon pie. By the time he tried to leave, she wouldn't let him go without first making a pass.

Rene explained, "I'm alone this night, but you assume I don't already have a sweetheart. It's complicated, but I think she needed space, so I'm here to eat. That's all." In his waterfall days, he would have been the one to make the first pass. That fact kept flashing through his mind, reminding him that he was certainly capable of a white water encounter with this lonely, very female soul.

Since JoJo had told Darren to never see her again, she now faced the first Valentine's day since she was 15 without a date. Most of the other ladies in the old Victorian house had plans that night, even Christine was busy with Bob Whitney. JoJo and Cammy decided to make microwave popcorn, drink wine and watch movies. By ten they both fizzled out. JoJo climbed the back stairs up to her attic bedroom wondering what Rene was doing for Valentine's.

~*~*~*~

Elijah asked Holly out for a Valentine's Day meal, but instead she invited him for a meal, story-time, then getting Cole settled for bed. When she finally sat down on her sofa, Elijah's nerves put him on his feet. Quietly, he described, "I feel like a puppy who's been chasing a kitten, one direction, then another. Now, I caught the kitten, but I don't know what to do."

Holly's arms reached up and rested on Elijah's shoulders. She playfully whispered, "Meow," and kissed him.

The smile on his face when she pulled back to study his reaction was classic. But in his mind, he knew that slow and steady would win the race, so he shouldn't try to push his luck. "OK, I'd better get going."

"Why?" she asked, then innocently purred.

Laura was more confident facing Valentine's Day alone than many in the Valley, propped up by coaching from both Roberta Simpson and Will Sturlaugson. Earlier in the day she had already greeted her mom and checked in with her grandmother, Adelle. As was promised, she would be expecting a phone call from James. Laura awaited his call and sat in her apartment in the quiet.

Will's emotional help for Laura came long distance. He would call from the seminary where he studied, and she would take notes as they talked. Then they would sometimes watch videos or hear other's podcasts or study blogs that related to her many questions. She was getting used to the idea of praying with him over the phone. But seldom did Laura pray on her own.

On that Valentine's Day night, when all lovers were lost in the eyes of their mate, Laura first sang *Amazing Grace* to set the mood, then offered up quiet praises. "Dear Lord God! Will said I should praise you, and then let you know about my questions or problems." She had to laugh, lightly so. She used to use the same tactic on her parents. "I praise you for my parents. Both Mae and Lonnie Zimmermann. They're such loving people, and deeply in love with each other. Help them to come closer to you.

Being closer to you, that's what I really want to be. Your wisdom is without end, you are merciful and loving with all who call on you. I am so very grateful for the path you've helped me to take these past months. I pray for safety for James, please watch over him. I pray for Trish and their family. I really need to understand Trish. She doesn't make it easy, at all. But I want her to be happy. Because if she ain't happy, ain't nobody happy. Well, you get the idea. Please help me as I struggle with that.

"I also pray for Will in his studies and for his son, young Chris. For the best possible situation for him, and though it's not yet decided, for young Chris' future parents. Bless them now and make this decision process happen more quickly than it is."

She went on asking for wisdom, patience and other facets that reminded her of the Al-Anon ladies she'd bonded with. She prayed for them, too, realizing that her version of PTSD was quieting some. There was still the occasional restless night, or sudden flashback at random times, but she was getting better, stronger within her own skin.

As her thoughts began to wander, the phone rang. She saw the phone number and knew, "Hi, James. Happy Valentine's Day!"

~*~*~*~

Since Trish's mother had started the tradition when they were young, Jim reached out to his children in her name. First, he visited with his son, Marty. They chatted about this and that, casual, natural.

But when he talked to his oldest, Austin, Jim's nerves got stressed. "I don't understand you. Why couldn't you come? I want to throw a party for James. He should be home soon. It's February, calving hasn't started yet," Jim reasoned.

"I got a load of hay coming," Austin barked.

Jim tried to coax his son, "Oh, you know the hay can wait."

"No, I won't be there, not if Trish is coming."

"Coming? It's her house." Jim was flabbergasted.

"No, count me out."

Jim had barely caught his breath from Austin's phone call when Trish walked in. "Trish, ah honey, it's good to see a friendly face. I just talked to Austin and Marty, and augh! I just get so infuriated." She had a quiet grin on her face and bent down, folding her hands on his knee. He must have read her mind since he smiled back and patted her hands. With the same loving attitude, he suggested "Hey, Trish I have an idea. When James gets home, we ought to pull together a welcome home party for 'im. It should've happened last summer, now that I look back."

Trish's peace filled glow was fading. Instead she absent-mindedly played with her car keys, "With all the brothers? Here?"

"Yeah, heck, yeah. I wanted Austin and Marty to come to the party but Austin, he's got something' against you. Trish, why would he be so cold to you? You're such a sweetheart."

She wasn't about to give any clues but only judged, "Dad, Austin's sorta weird. Who can figure some people?"

Hailey and Mac had innocently dozed off the night before during their Valentine's date. Mac came to, sorting dream from reality, then noted the time. He knew there were rules that Christine enforced about men in her granddaughters' bedrooms. Quietly he ascended the stairs into the kitchen. There she stood, one hand on a hip, the other was drumming her fingers on the counter. Mac noted the steady rhythm of her foot, tapping, adding to the tension in the room. "Hi," he smiled, then complimented, "the coffee smells good."

Christine reminded, "There are rules for a reason!" Then she pulled Mac by the ear, "You do right by that woman!" She released him and pushed her index finger into his chest, warning, "Don't push your luck, because this woman is watching!"

"OK, Grandma, you're right. I'm sorry. I will, that is, if she lets me, I mean, do the right thing." The thoughts in his mind tumbled over each other. Part of the problem was Mac wanted to maintain eye contact with Christine but kept knocking into furniture and things. Mac straightened the items around him and took off his hat, wringing it through his hands, as he slowly approached her. "Grandma? Can I call you Grandma?"

"Yes, you can."

"Good. Uh, Grandma, can I keep coming here to spend time with Hailey? The reason I ask is, well, I don't know for sure what her thoughts are, but I'm fairly sure that I love her. And. Um. Well, I don't think that the men who gave her children could ever have said that. Please give me a chance," Mac whispered, then hung his head.

She gently patted his arm. "Yes, you may. I'm sorry if I hurt your ear, but rules, especially when it comes to Hailstorm Hailey, she has to know that I'm serious. It's all for her own good."

"I believe you're right. I respect rules, for the most part. And I believe that you definitely have her future successes in mind."

Christine smiled her cheerful grin. "Thank you for understanding. Would you like some coffee?"

He looked at her grandfather clock as it chimed six bells. "Yes, but to go? I wish I could stay and visit, but this workin' man has to get crosstown to get his work clothes on."

She sacrificed one of her new travel mugs, snapping the cover on, then handing it off. She quietly kissed his cheek and added, "May God bless you richly, Mac McIntyre. This was a good talk."

"Thanks, Grandma."

~*~*~*~

Later that day, as another Valentine's Day was in the books, stories and memories were being shared amongst friends. Christine and Bob Whitney were playing two-handed whist when the rest of Christine's great-nieces and granddaughters came around with more gossip. Neither JoJo nor Hailey were there to hear the latest. "Someone said that they saw our Rene north of the border, that he went to Winkler and met someone there!"

Once Jason was out in the open, away from Clark's hacienda, the snow storm that had been predicted was becoming real before his eyes. The winter of 2009-2010 was a tough one for the hardy souls in northwestern New Mexico. But Jason didn't place any concern on the weather. He had handled colder winds with more snow in the upper Midwest. Nothing was going to stop Jason from finding the stolen credit cards he'd stashed, so he could get to El Paso, Texas, and stroll into Mexico.

Roxy's car was a great ride, but he knew that he'd be pushing his luck to hang onto it. Instead, he pulled into a busy truck stop. He had hotwired vehicles since he was eight, trying to get his dad's attention. Now that old skill would prove useful. There was no wasting time. Careful to dodge the security cameras, Jason stashed his dark blue duffle, climbed behind the wheel, and was back on the highway in no time.

He would've thought he was getting away with it all, maybe even feeling confident, except the couple whose car he had stolen was having their meal first, then they had planned to gas up. The car slowed to a crawl on the side of the road. Snow was getting thicker. Wind was growing stronger.

Young Chris was oblivious to the drama that his presence drew. Will's mom, north and west of Williston, had been caring for the boy since Will entered the seminary in the autumn before. When she became sick with what she thought was just the flu before Christmas, it turned out to be stomach cancer. That was when Anna arranged and paid for daytime daycare for the boy, and many in the Red River Valley started taking turns with overnight babysitting until a permanent home could be found.

Long before Candy's heart and mind were tangled up, worried about both Jason and Spencer, she had signed up for her turn with young Chris. *Where are those two boys?* was a constant mantra in the back of Candy's mind. Candy waffled between that and the reality of the brood before her. Besides her second husband Buddy's children, Logan in college, Alex a senior, heavily involved in sports, and Anne, there were the foster children, Katlyn, and Dustin. And for a short stint of four days and nights, they also took in young Chris, Will's baby boy who was in limbo until a permanent adopting family was found. Candy had more than an average load on her hands.

The baby was sitting on Logan's lap after their supper meal. Young Chris was eight months old and starting to sit and wiggle as he looked about. Logan seemed curious about the babe and asked his dad questions about what Logan was like when he had been a child.

The generations chatted about life, then Logan's next question seemed to start Candy's world spinning. "Why is Spencer pressing charges against his brother? We were talking about that in Biology today. The topic we're learning about is heredity. That and the whole nature vs. nurture theory."

While cleaning in the kitchen, Candy and Buddy stood still wondering what to say. Finally, Buddy asked, "What were your friends saying?"

"Bayley Norris said that since two brothers turned out to be so opposite, that nature had nothing to do with it. That instead, she figured it was something about the way that Candy and Johnny raised their sons, that somehow nurture had to be the reason for the difference."

His sister, Anne, jabbed her brother's side and pointed out the way their step-mom, Candy, was quietly crying by the stove. Alex's shoulders sank as he put his comments together with Candy's reaction. Alex rose and carried young Chris with him to Candy's side. Quietly they experienced a quick group hug, proving a newfound maturity in the young man.

"Candy?" he began. "I'm sorry, but I have another question." She nodded and leaned on the stove while Anne took over the dish chore. Alex asked, "Can anyone be a witness against someone?"

"What do you mean?" Buddy asked.

"Why do you ask?" Candy asked.

"I want to testify against Jason, too."

Candy quietly coached, "Explain."

Alex's story was stirring. "When I was only eleven, I was on a hunting trip with Cordell and his buddies. Dad, remember? You couldn't go since you got the flu all o'sudden. Remember?"

"I missed a hunting trip, yeah? Why? What happened?"

"That was when I heard Cordell say that, with the ladies, that 'No doesn't mean no, it means I'm not drunk enough.' Jason was on that trip. He copied everything that Cordell had to say. They were both so drunk themselves. They even offered me some beer. I tasted it, but I think it's gross. Anyway, that was after Johnny had died and his sons didn't go on their usual trip. So, it's nurture, pure and simple, but Candy and Johnny had nothing to do with it. Spencer was the same good example on that trip that he has been this winter. For standing up for good. For feeding Logan and me when everyone else was drinking. For explaining that hunting shouldn't be the way that Cordell and his friends were making it. That hunting with the wrong guys can get a guy shot."

Candy gasped as she recalled Johnny's voice saying that very thing. Buddy asked Alex, "You want to testify?"

"Yes, I want to testify. Passive bystanders, we talked about that in Biology today, too. Passive bystanders take in an experience like that hunting trip and do nothing with it. That was me up until now. Active bystanders report the bad guys. Besides that trip, there were also a few football games when Jason, Beau, and Nick Patterson were also pulling that same trick. They'd get the older middle school girls drunk in their cars, then, you know. All during the football game. Remember? I wasn't varsity yet, and I was out with that knee injury, so I wasn't on the field. From the bench I could see their car windows, all steamed up. Others could see it, too."

Buddy was concise, "And what, exactly, do you think 'No' means, Alex?"

"It means, don't pressure me, I'm not ready. Or don't be ridiculous, I don't even know you. Or. Maybe that I'm not ready today, but maybe when we're both older."

Buddy reached for Alex and hugged the teen's shoulder and kissed his hair. "Good answer, Man, good answer." Buddy had always wondered why his sons, Logan and Alex, had lost their taste for deer hunting.

Candy's tears were numerous as she held onto young Chris and cuddled him close. But her emotions were no longer ridden with guilt and shame over other's people's actions that she had no control over. She just missed Johnny.

Jason used his high school cross-country training and, with duffle over his shoulders, he jogged to a nearby farm. When handling the winter storms up north, he had the benefit of proper clothing. Now the shed where he hid, riding out the storm, was an odd collection of boxes, tanks of fuel, and a large crate filled with fabric. Jason climbed inside and pulled the crate cover to almost closed.

The next morning was sunshiny and fair. That was common up north when storms had passed over through the night. But there in New Mexico, this was something new. The snow was already melting.

Clark won't report his daughter's car missing. He wouldn't want to draw any attention. Suddenly, Jason wondered, *Did I leave any tracks? Will they find that stupid car and then find me?* Sudden panic sent his mind racing. Truly, Jason had more to fear from Clark finding him than the police. A quiet prison cell was suddenly sounding like a sweet deal.

After a youth full of watching old MacGyver reruns, and years of engineering classes, Jason took stock of his assets. The sunlight streamed in to make sense of the objects he'd been confused by the night before. He checked the house. It was locked and the owners were gone.

Back inside the shed, one discovery led to another, and before he knew it, Jason opened the wide shed doors and rolled out a treasure. The fuel was ignited and hot air soon had the balloon billowing.

Once inside the basket and building elevation, Jason used his training to make his escape. As he arose, it was clear that his tracks were still exposing him, and the abandoned car was swarming with Clark, Patrick, and their friends.

Jason felt too confident, but that was soon adjusted when Patrick started shooting at him. Patrick is certainly a good Irish name, but he was a lousy shot. The balloon was peppered with a few holes, so Jason wasn't able to achieve full elevation. It drifted, limping, over a canyon, stopping Clark's crew from following. The navigation controls were worthless and the balloon seemed to have a mind of its own. It continued to drift into the desert.

Clark and Roxy were livid! "I told you from the start!" Roxy reeled, "That kid is not worth the trouble!" She steamed, "The cash that he had. Where is it?! It's cursed! Let's spend it, and pronto!" The band of thieves headed back to Albuquerque and spent every bill.

Mac McIntyre had heard the rumor that accused his good friend, Rene, but of what? "It depends upon which version you listen to," Mac explained. "In one scenario, you've been living in Winkler since you were evicted, and that you were evicted since you lost your US citizenship. In another version, it's some waitress who you have twisted around your little finger. And in yet another version, you have a wife and family in Winkler." Mac shrugged. "Any of that true?"

"No. None of it. Oh, how I hate gossip. No one would believe such ridiculous words. No one."

The federal agents finally moved off dead center with new clues for Spencer's and James' case. "An extreme percentage of the serial number strings were all spent in Albuquerque, and the towns in that region."

Spencer studied the map, "Albuquerque? Then he doubled back?" A flashback of their youth, learning hunting strategies from their dad. Spencer was grasping straws out of a whole new box. His eyes moved down the highway, straight south towards Mexico, and fell upon a famous Texas town, *El Paso*.

The vivid joy Jason felt upon ascending into the sky, high above Clark and the rest of the thieves, was contrasted by the agonizingly slow decent back to the ground. Neither Patrick nor Clark nor any of the skull-tattooed-thugs were anywhere near his wicker basket or its pale yellow balloon. The bullet holes fluttered a constant drip, drip, drip, and left Jason with the painful reality: gravity was reclaiming his sorry soul.

But the closer he came to ground level, the more he was noticing the ground moving. Rattlesnakes were warming themselves in the sunshine, directly in line with his estimates for landing. The impact made the basket bounce, hitting the ground and kicking two rattlesnakes into the wicker basket. Three vultures had already been circling his balloon. They landed nearby and watched Jason brace for impact.

The trio was like a constant shadow that followed him across the desert. Desperate for speed, Jason took one last look through his dark blue duffle bag, pulled one critical item out, and tossed the bag, lightening his load. He looked into the palm of his hand. It was a compass.

Hour upon hour he walked to the specific spot outside Albuquerque where the stolen credit cards were buried. But there was a catch. Along with having buried his own treasures, Jason inadvertently loosened the sand enough to entice a new critter to join Jason's merry party.

Jason found the pile of five rocks that marked his treasure and started to take it all apart. A scorpion protected his home, which Jason was ripping to pieces. Once he saw the creature, he pulled his hand back, but not fast enough.

The pain of the scorpion sting was bone chilling, but after his experience with the brown Recluse spider, Jason had studied up to know which desert creatures would be harmful, and which he could live through. Though he could get sick, Jason knew he wouldn't die. If nothing else, this event made him even more determined than ever to get his bus ticket and make it across the Rio Grande.

With the stolen cards finally in hand, Jason kept walking, made it to the bus station, and bought his ride to El Paso, Texas.

Dora and JoJo were talking in JoJo's window seat late at night. It was getting to be a common sight, those two on the bench seat, trying to sort out people's actions and inactions. On that particular night, they were painting their toenails. The window looked over JoJo bird feeders, but also gave a flawless view of the carriage house. For JoJo, Rene's inaction was starting to wear on her. It was already the end of February, and he was still giving her space. "I thought he was interested. But then this Winkler thing comes up. I don't get him. He is so strange." She looked again at Rene's bachelor apartment. It was dark and quiet.

Dora noted, stretching her neck to see his place, "He's still gone, and it's after 11. No doubt he's gone to Winkler again." She repeated what they'd heard about Rene's new sweetheart, then wondered at what time the border crossing would close for the night.

Schedule or no schedule, silently, Rene's car rolled in, but not without JoJo's eyes catching the flash of his lights. She stared down at him and wished. *Those rumors can't be true. They just can't!* JoJo thought, blowing on her big toe.

Rene's eyes noticed her, too.

~*~*~*~

The swelling in Jason's hand and arm was still noticeable. Another bus passenger pointed and in broken English, asked him, "Scorpion? You kill?"

Jason nodded, "Si." At the news, his neighbor nodded and smiled. Jason wasn't sure if it was good or bad karma to put to death something that caused so much harm, but he sure wasn't going to be bitten twice. The billboards and road signs were gathering closer and closer together. His destination was soon at hand.

Having learned a certain amount from Clark's pickpocket band. Jason had planned on rounding up some extra cash from the pockets of as many unsuspecting tourists as possible in Albuquerque before heading into Mexico, but his swollen dominant hand put an end to that.

Instead, he only spoke Spanish and begged at the entrance to the shopping malls. That wasn't so successful either, since he was infringing on others' territories.

With the meager belongings he'd gathered by using the credit cards he'd stolen in North Dakota, Jason's mind teamed with anticipation as the bus made its twists and turns towards the bus station. The sky was bright and the late-February sun felt warm on the side of his face.

Finally, the men and women on the bus gathered their things and children and made a line, walking slowly towards the door. When Jason finally descended the short stairway, there was a familiar voice to his side, saying, "Hey, Bro."

At the sight of Spencer, Jason turned and stepped right into James. The force and speed of James' fist against Jason's face knocked him out cold. Vaguely, Jason recalled hearing James say, "That's what they call a sucker punch," before all went black.

17 TIME'S UP

The steady rhythm of Christine's old grandfather clock was the only sound inside the house. Her painting easel stood next to the clock, as though it was patiently listening to the old gears quietly rocking between the ticking and the tocking. One of Hailey's cats had been napping since the quarter hour, but stretched and yawned when the half hour noises chimed. The cat groomed herself and then lazily sat, ignoring the decorative hour and minute hands, but closely studying the smaller second hand that gradually made quiet progress.

The silence in Christine's old home was only broken by the sound of the wind blowing through the trees. Cammy's culinary prowess had grown beyond frozen pizzas to loading anything and everything into a series of crockpots. This was Cammy's self-proclaimed 'crockpot phase.' Now in the quiet, they each bubbled and occasionally hissed, the steam rising to mist the face of the old kitchen clock.

News of Jason Hillman's upcoming trial was quietly spreading. Anna's family was sad, angry and disappointed, all at once. Even with sharing the news of more abused souls coming forward to also testify against Jason, no one fully understood—there was no logical reasoning as to why some men could think such behavior was justifiable. The action was both as shocking and senseless as anything they or their friends or neighbors could ever have predicted. And as senseless as it was, there was even less that any of them could do about it, but support Candy and

252

her daughters, and thank Spencer for his bravery to take the roll of bystander to a whole new level.

As the days before Jason's arrest had slowly, steadily passed for both Spencer and James in the American southwest, Christine's old grandfather clock kept a steady rhythm, too. Passing time, the family waited and prayed.

James could see that the long-distance therapy work that Laura and Will had kept at was steadily building steam within Laura's heart and soul. She was relieved to see James back in one piece, but Trish was still insisting that Laura wasn't good enough, not sensing Laura's growth. Hearing Trish's opinion, James focused on work, knowing that the walls of the creamery held much more than just food.

Whether it was to fill an actual need or just to spend more time with James, Laura scheduled him for brush-up training, along with initial training for a new recruit, Kim.

James' and Laura's eyes felt an understanding that, although Trish was still opposed, that Laura was not, and time would see them both succeed. James watched on as Laura described the science of cream cheese to Kim. James remembered when he'd first started working by Laura's side, and noticed how much more peace-filled she was now, no longer allowing Jack or his sadness to envelope her. One thing was constant, "You warm the cream and add culture."

Laura had been sad for Jack, sad for his bad choices, sad that their relationship couldn't have worked. She was relieved, too, and felt guilty for that. The emotions that had pulled at Laura's heart had been heavily laced with guilt. After all, Laura had spent so much time in the last two years being angry with Jack. Now all that anger morphed into a huge kettle of guilt, warmed by other's mournful moods.

James was proud to see the fruit of her success as answered prayers, as Laura turned to work, but maintained a more active prayer life. Prayer would be that culture that would work on that guilt, breaking it down, bit by bit, and waiting for the right moment when love, the rennet, could be added.

James stood by and watched Laura. Kim carefully held the pitcher of rennet for the new batch of cream cheese, and at Laura's calm nod, the pitcher was drained, mixing it into the cultured mass. The trio stood watching in awe as the curd separated from the whey.

Laura stared at the whey, praying, wanting God to as easily sort whatever pain was being harbored in Trish's heart. She wanted Trish to know the peace that passes all understanding, and to get past whatever was holding that back.

As their instruction continued, Joyce watched on, happily cleaning after them. James watched Laura, wondering if his own kettle of PTSD could be so easily sorted and separated from his life. Something in her eyes gave him to know that Laura would stand ready with the analogical rennet, adding the love he needed, when the time was right. Time would heal, he had heard, and prayer to Jesus was his constant friend.

Friendship was blossoming at Sophie's house. Theo and Sophie were pouring over seed catalogs for expanding her flower beds. Carpenters had already reconfigured her home to its original state and official paperwork to establish her bed and breakfast was sent off in the mail. Meanwhile they drew out sketches, planning where mounds of day lilies and hostas would go, but all this was secondary to the important work of building their relationship. As with the prior summer, fall, and winter, the coming spring would find them together. As the garden would consume their time, love would consume them both.

Malla remembered how full her life seemed after reconnecting with her parents, becoming engaged to the love of her life, and was now expecting his child. Her life had changed in such a positive way once she opened her heart to the man at her side. She knew more joy than she'd ever hoped or prayed for during her years with TEK. After years of doubting her prayers for her own baby would ever be answered, she was absorbed into the hopes and dreams of a family, so alive and vibrant, that Malla could even feel it in the dark. Wedding plans would have to wait until the annulment process was through. In the meantime, their family would grow by one more, and she would ask her many questions, wanting to know him well when she finally said "I do."

Toni's time had been filled so unexpectedly. Her vast collection of DVD love stories was still packed away. Her life was as interesting a love story as she ever expected from Hollywood. When Rusty had announced his plans to move, she was devastated. Now, looking back, Toni found herself feeling younger and more alive than ever in her life. In the little room on Sonya's third floor, Toni picked up her crochet hook and quietly worked on a colorful afghan for the back of Jim's new couch. He had colored her life, and she had seasoned his. Now as she crocheted, she worried and prayed for Jim's continued healing from kidney surgery, and for his continued good health.

The doctor's office waiting room was again a destination for Erin as she waited with Brandon for her monthly check up. The new baby was active and Erin couldn't wait to meet him. Brandon held Erin's hand, wondering about her blood pressure, this time around. She studied her fingers, recalling her swelling with Glory Bea. He kissed them, and the two seemed to read each other's mind. At five months along, Erin's baby boy gently pushed against her ribs, and brought her back to the present.

Once Jason came to, he knew his time was up. His trial went faster than Danielle expected. She was prepared with evidence and expert witnesses, and their voices were heard. But the sucker punch that Spencer delivered in his testimony, along with the medical evidence, was all the judge seemed to need.

Spencer's step-brother, Alex, had also been brought in. Due to his accounting, and research that Danielle had done to bring more victims forward, Cordell was also arrested and awaited trial.

Danielle was pleased with the progress she was making in her personal war against those who make sexual abuse their hobby. But she was also curious about the source of her success. *What really makes Spencer Hillman tick?* she wondered. *Why would a man send his kid brother to jail?*

~*~*~*~

JoJo was frustrated. She had only seen Rene come and go late at night and early in the morning for the last couple weeks. *Where is he? Why is Rene never home?* She wondered. *The Winkler deal, that has to be wrong. They're all crazy, they have to be wrong!*

JoJo's cousin, Hailey, was in a much more positive place with Mac McIntyre, coming to spend time with her and to play with Matty and Sasha. Christine was Mac's biggest fan, pushing him to eat well and inviting him even more than Hailey did, or so Christine thought. No, Hailey was happily surprised at how her heart was spinning as the reality of Mac's dream of true love finally was coming true. "It's been years, waiting for the right one to come along," Hailey whispered to Christine with a knowing wink.

Alan's old diesel mechanic friend, Larry, was back in the Red River Valley after spending the last year in western North Dakota in the Bakken oil patch. Larry left a certain amount of mystery behind him in Williston and was close-lipped about the goings on out west, or why he ended up coming back when he did. Alan was relieved to see his old friend, but he almost didn't recognize the old mechanic. Larry had acquired a new style, with a new confidence with women that hadn't been there before. Alan's only clue to the mystery from Larry was that "It was time to move on."

Danielle knew that Spencer was back to work, so she called and made an appointment under a different name. Time was up; he was no longer her client's perpetrator's brother, and she had been too curious for too long.

The Bloomington, Minnesota, real estate office, with its well-manicured landscaping outside, was furnished to impress inside. Danielle saw Spencer through glass walls, working in a distant office, and politely took a seat to wait. Once he came to the lobby to meet his next client, her gig was up. He looked at the card in his hand, "Mrs..." then focused on Danielle's face, "...Hello."

She rose and shook his hand, "Good afternoon."

"Would you rather meet here, or should we take a drive?"

Danielle nodded, "A drive would be nice."

"Are you buying or selling property?" He asked the common realtors' question, pulling the main door open.

She walked past and replied, "Property? Neither. Although coffee would be nice, my treat. I know there's a Perkins nearby. We'll drive separately."

Once settled in the ubiquitous Perkins booth, Spencer watched the waitress take their simple order and turned his gaze on Danielle. "OK, what's up?"

"What is it that makes a backwoods pilchard like yourself turn in your brother, and when he escapes, you track him down and bring him to justice?"

Spencer's eyes rose to the ceiling as he considered his reply. "The backwoods barb, I'll accept. When it comes to backwoods properties, my understanding of backwoods, as you say, makes me a comfortable living." His eyes studied hers as he continued, "But, pilchard. Did you know that those are fish? From the herring family. You called me a fish?"

She adjusted her angle. "You were quite well-dressed at the trial. Now, too when you're back to work. What makes a backwoods pilchard be such a dandy?"

"More name calling. Am I supposed to just..."

She cut in, "A dandy is a man who wears colorful or coordinated clothing. Knowing how much time you spend fishing, it's just surprising." She stared at and motioned towards his salmon-colored sweater over a white, collared shirt, both above pale yellow slacks. "You can't deny it." The sleeves of his sweater were drawn up, casually, and she was embarrassed to realize that she couldn't keep her eyes off the hairs on his forearm.

Spencer was glad to have her attention, even though she used degrading names. "You've probably been taught that old phrase, 'dress for success'?" she nodded and he continued, "My success, early on, was purely due to my gift for gab. The 'dress for success' deal didn't catch on, and anyone at my office would tell you that I was in a perpetual casual-Friday mode until after Anna's wedding." The waitress brought their coffee as he recalled.

"Anna had offered everyone in our family a free education. I know, it was a surprise to everyone," he said to the shock in Danielle's eyes, then continued, "Plus for me, she gave me a trip to Florida to go deep sea fishing, because I had always been nice to her. Sword fish, marlin, whatever I was in the mood for. Any fisherman's dream. I got out on the water and noticed this pod of dolphins following our boat. They would not just follow, but would also gain speed to tease us and do tricks along the way.

"Then suddenly I recall, with surprising clarity, the conversation I overheard in the airport. The two old ladies were complaining about someone, and how 'the sole basis for his life was fishing. Pity he died young before he could learn the beauty of life, instead of being hid away in some mosquito-infested...'" His voice trailed off as the waitress walked by and Spencer stopped her to ask, "Could I have a piece of chocolate cake?"

Danielle summarized, "Anna's wedding, swordfish, dolphins, and now someone died young. Where is this all leading?"

"When Dad died, he was young. It wasn't a life well lived. He was still learning things. Well, when he died, I tried to remember all that he'd taught me to that point. The most fun was fishing, so when I would go fishing, it was like we were fishing together. But I know now that I wasn't allowing myself any balance. It was all the fishing, all the time, and it didn't make me miss him any less. The hole was still there. So fast forward and here's this backwoods prairie boy out on the ocean, but Dad wasn't there. The sound of those dolphins laughing, they still bounce through my mind."

The cake was delivered and he continued, "No, I didn't fish for swordfish or anything. I called off the deal with the fishing guide. I paid him for half the day, which was more than was needed, and I was wandering along the beach, thinking about my life, when a beautiful woman comes along. I follow and end up in a men's clothing store. She was going to work. Well, we were talking about sales in general and she defined the 'dress for success' theory in a realistic, down to earth manner and something clicked. I would've bought more from her, she was that good.

"So I got home with my new luggage full of new clothes and learned to read care instruction tags. I had to dry clean some. Well, lo and behold, I end up finding clients at the drycleaners. I wear my fancy pants shopping for vegetables and I find more clients. I know I over-packed for the Mexico trip with James, but I ended up spending some of my down time networking, finding properties and connecting my boss with sellers in the Vegas area. Maybe I'm a dandy, if that's what you call it, but it's part of my uniform to be a better realtor. With the extra I've earned since Anna got married and announced about education scholarships, I paid off my own school loans and paid her back for the swordfish guide and the new wardrobe."

"I understand. Thank you. But there was something else that I'm curious about. Before you came back with Jason, I was researching your family. I didn't find anything odd, except that there was mystery around your father's death. You were 19 at the time."

He dug into the chocolate cake while he explained, "Yes, and now we know that it was a suicide. Dad had left a suicide note for Anna, but she only recently opened it."

"No note to his wife?"

"My mother? No, she was tangled up in an affair with my current step-dad at the time. So, understandably, she blamed herself, but didn't drag her children into that guilt. In other words, we were clueless. But that was when I perfected my positive spin. No matter what was happening in our dysfunctional little mixed family, I put a positive spin on it, and then Mom could cope. That's what sales is really all about, spin."

"Someone said that you were engaged to someone."

"Yes, Amy. She was, no, she is," he corrected himself, "a wonderful lady. She is, wonderful." He absentmindedly played with the frosting on his fork.

The frown lines on Danielle's forehead creased, "She called it off? Why?"

"She got tired of me going fishing and her being alone. She said that I wasn't fully committed to the relationship, and that I had some growing up to do."

"Ouch."

"Maybe, with the whole dolphin incident, maybe I am growing up. Maybe. Now I only fish with friends and we make it an excursion, it's fun. Before I would fish by myself, make it all about filling my limit, and my freezer, but really I was just sulking, missing Dad. Now when I talk lake life with my clients, it's not all about fishing. It's real, it's families and..." His voice trailed off.

Danielle watched him staring towards the nearby window. "And. And were you finished with that thought?"

"I guess." Spencer adjusted himself in his seat. "Hey, why am I doing all the talking and you just ask more questions?" He watched her quietly shrug and offered, "This cake is good, do you want some?" He pushed the half eaten treat, and his fork, in her direction.

She ignored the cake and noted, "Earlier you said something about how Anna treated you with that deep sea fishing trip since you had been kind to her. Do I have that right?"

He sipped his coffee. "Yes, that's what she told me."

"So, now I'm back to my original question, which you never answered. What makes a guy turn in his kid brother, taking the term 'active bystander' to a new level, along with being uncommonly kind to his sisters? Why?"

Spencer took a moment to stare at the distant window, then replied, "With Jason, it was for Shyla's sake."

Danielle asked, "Shyla?" seeming to note it mentally.

Spencer went on. "She was the first victim that I know about with Jason. I wasn't an active bystander that night, by any means. I sat by and let it happen. I have no idea where Shyla is, but through-out the year I pray for her and at Christmas I give donations to charity with her in mind."

He played again with the cake crumbs, sighed quietly and continued, "With Anna, she makes it easy. We've always connected. But early on, Dad told me that there's nothing better than a good woman. He used my grandmothers, Mom and aunts as examples. He'd quietly point out when any one of 'em would be caring for their children or cooking their husbands' favorite dish, how some would show their love publicly, but then sometimes just laugh at some silly joke and hold hands. When I started dating, he reminded me that my date was a good-woman-in-training. To take care and have fun, but always treat her like a lady. I'd point out a crabby, witchy woman and he'd just shake his head and shrug. He'd say 'She didn't get treated right. It's not the horse's fault that you got bucked. Who mistreated the horse before you came along?'

He set down the fork and continued, "It broke my heart when Anna explained that she had been raped." He finally looked up to see a glistening of tears in her eyes. "I miss him. He taught me a lot." He stretched his legs and leaned back. "I'm done talking. Your turn."

Danielle looked at her watch. "Oh, look at the time. I'm due crosstown in half an hour. I'd better go." She flagged down the waitress and handled the bill, then hurried off.

Spencer sipped his coffee in silence. *Lord God? Looks like Shyla's not the only one I should pray for.*

18 CHAIN REACTIONS

Though a common workday, JoJo's whole day had been spent wondering about Rene. Throughout the day it was a constant lament of questions: *Why would he just suddenly shift from his crush on me to someone in Winkler? Who is she? Why would he be so irrational? Is it love? He's a passionate Frenchman, it's plausible, I suppose. Why wouldn't he at least say something to me?*

Trish was still dining out with Nick, and Toni had headed to her small apartment, leaving Jim in the quiet. There was an innocence and simplicity to Jim's next task. He needed to find an envelope to mail in a Menards rebate receipt. That was all.

Trish's roll-top desk was closed, but he'd seen where she stored the ornate gold key. Jim worked the key and rolled open the top. The right-sized envelope would be in one of the many small holes that lined the top of the desk. As Jim retrieved what he needed and fingered the gold key, he noticed an envelope marked with Austin's name, written in Trish's hand.

Jim had always wondered what stood between his eldest son and his only daughter. With a curiosity that billowed above reason, Jim opened the letter and read.

It was a handwritten version of the confrontation letter that had been typed and sent to her brother. Of course, Trish's father couldn't have known that, or that the letter had been sent years before, and only recently been pulled from the bottom drawer and reread after Trish was awoken from a vivid dream that recounted the same molestation that had happened in her youth.

Now Jim saw it and felt its sting for the first time. He was both dizzied and sickened at the thought. With a father's love, it was a horrid sight in his teary eyes. Slowly he refolded the letter and refilled the envelope, gently rolling the desk closed and replacing the key. A steam developed behind his eyes as he thought it all through. The Menards receipt was crumpled in his hand and tossed to the trash as he quietly wandered out into the garden. The setting sun was totally lost on Jim that night.

Gwenny was having a fit. The classic 'lipstick on his collar' scenario had only ever been a distant issue in fiction, not a part of Gwenny McTavish Hamilton's reality. As the red, greasy spot against his yellow striped cotton shirt glared back at her in her brightly painted laundry room, the darkening sky outside was quickly mirroring the world around her.

Coming from Minnesota and driving into the brilliant sky in the west, JoJo's mind was still on Rene. The wisps of clouds were spread like feathers or fingers against the sky as the setting sun made brilliant shifting hues of light playing against the distant fog. JoJo slowly pulled into Christine's yard and parked her car, sitting there, staring at the trees and the sky behind them. Then suddenly she noticed someone moving among the trees.

~*~*~*~

Gwenny held the shirt and its stained collar in her fist, showing him the evidence. His eyes slowly rose from the newspaper he was reading in the well-worn leather chair. Richard had no reply to her loud rant. He slowly turned the newspaper page and kept reading, in affect daring her to act or to be the doormat that he'd known too well for too many years.

The sky was on fire above as the shadows below Christine's many trees shifted from side to side in the light breeze. Rene was strapped into his harness with rope and rigging above. He was hanging birdhouses amid the tree's branches. His strong arms pulled him up or dropped him lower as the need required. Slowly, he was moving from branch to branch. JoJo exclaimed in surprise as she drew closer. "What on earth are you doing!?"

"Oh, you're home, good. I thought I'd better get these up so your feathered friends could move in. The snow is melting. The birds will be here soon. You like?" he asked with his usual French accent.

"Yes! They're wonderful! Where did you find these?" JoJo wondered aloud.

"I made them." Rene explained, "The first ones I made before Valentine's day. They are way up high," he pointed, then added, "Mac helped me with the machinery and hardware. We had a shop set up in an apartment garage. It was all very borrowed and temporary, but not heated, so I was so glad to have those warm coveralls that you mended. There are carpentry tricks that Mac taught to me. It was a fun pastime to fill the winter evenings."

JoJo's heart was awaking to his meaning as he moved above, adding a new brightness to her eyes under the brilliant sunset. Rene pointed, "Those first three will hold a nest and function OK, but they're not so pretty as these bottom ones. Mac said it best,' he quoted, "'Nice from afar, but far from nice.'" His handsome wink was lost in the shadows and the distance, but she recognized his playful mood in the tone of his voice.

"Valentine's Day," she finally broached the topic, "I heard you went to Canada that night."

It finally dawned on him that people like Gwenny Hamilton weren't the only ones bitten by the gossip bug, but that JoJo was also drawn into the story. "Yes, but just for food. And way too much food. I was sick for two days after that." Rene steadied his footing, and then quietly, genuinely said, "Please don't listen to the crazy stories. I promise you, it was only for comfort food." JoJo's mood was quickly improving as they spoke. He saw the gleam of her smile and asked, "If I lower this netting down, will you send up the second bag?"

The delight in her eyes was contagious as she scrambled to the back seat of his car and found a white netting laundry bag full of colorful bird houses.

Jim came into the creamery. "Where's Alan?" he asked a new worker who shrugged, and turned to James who stood, leaning on a mop.

"He's givin' a tour, what's wrong?" James wondered.

"Ah, nothin' you need to concern yourself about. No. Ah, it'll wait. Yeah, I'll wait at his house. Tell Alan I need to talk to him at his house. Ah, it's about cattle."

Jim O'Malley sat on a lawn chair next to the blue playhouse. It was surrounded by flowers and plants and Jim looked out of place as Alan eyed him. "Jim? Are we ready to talk cattle? How many head can you spare?"

"We talked about half, didn't we?"

"Yeah, what does that amount to?"

"Are your fences ready? I mean, in North Dakota you need fences, right?"

"Yes, but how many?"

"Alan, I've got a terrible, terrible story to tell ya. I," he paused, "can't even say it out loud." His anguish was pure.

Alan's soul reached out with compassion to the broken spirit before him. "OK, take your time, I've got all day. But let's go inside." Alan led him into his house and walked him into the living room and pulled the pocket doors closed behind them. "No one can hear but you and me and God."

Jim still looked as stunned as he had felt the day before. "I learned this yesterday, and it still baffles me. I thought it wouldn't cut so deep after sleepin' on it, but who slept?"

"OK, where were you when you heard this news?"

"I made the mistake of looking for an envelope in Trish's desk. It's a roll-top…I just needed an envelope to send in a Menards rebate form." As Alan expected, Jim broke down and started to sob as Alan also heard Anna's voice calling him.

"Alan, where are you?"

He pulled the doors open and closed them behind his back, "Anna, I'm here. Please get me a box of Kleenex."

She came from the kitchen, handing it off, "Here, what's wrong?"

"It's Jim."

"O'Malley?"

"He's telling me a sad story right now."

"OK, well, we need to discuss adopting young Chris."

"I can only deal with one thing at a time right now, and a grown man needs this box, so."

"Well, we have room."

"Anna? I love you," he reminded.

"Well, invite him for lunch."

"That's gracious. I'll ask, but honey, look at me, I have no idea how long this is gonna take, so please. OK?" He turned and went inside, closing the doors behind them.

Anna quietly pouted, "I like babies."

Alan handed off the box to an embarrassed old cowboy. "What was that?" Jim asked, wiping his eyes and face.

"My wife, you're invited for lunch. Please tell me, Jim, what brings an old cowboy like yourself to tears?"

Jim stared into the corner. "My wife and I, we had three boys. I loved havin' boys, but she wasn't satisfied, so we tried one more time and the doctor said twins, twin girls. Oh, Valerie, she was so excited. Then one day she started to spot and I didn't think anything of it, but she knew to get herself to the hospital at Belle Fourche. That hospital, babies and broken bones, that's all it's good for.

"She'd lost the one twin, but Patricia, my Trish, she was OK. So I had these big boys and my pretty little girl. She was tough, always trying to keep up with the boys. Her and Marty and James all got along pretty good. Well, as time went on these boys became young men."

"Jim, don't torment yourself. She already told me. She was in tears, too."

"My oldest boy molested my little girl. She's so sweet." He took a moment to clear his throat and looked at Alan with clear resolve. "And so, we're not talkin' about half the herd anymore. You get 'em all."

"All?"

"There was as much as 1,500, but there's less now. I think about 850 plus this years' spring calves. I wanna do this, now."

"Is this legal?"

"I own the Morning Star herd. That lazy SOB, when I was layin' there dyin' he didn't even get tested. When I felt hopeless he tricked me into deedin' him the land, but yes, I still own the cows, calves, the bulls, every one. Are your fences ready?"

"Ha! Uh, OK, yes, they are. OK, we need to pull together some trucks, some men, some vets. Can we make it there and back in one day?"

"It's a seven hour drive, one way."

"Fourteen hours? That's stretching the DOT regs," Alan thought aloud, combing his hand through his hair.

Jim reminded, "Plus loading up."

"OK," Alan said, studying his hands, "Jim?"

"Yes sir."

"Why do you want to do this?"

"He's standin' on the lion's share of my inheritance right now and he doesn't deserve a penny."

"This is revenge?"

"No, this is makin' a strong statement. This is discipline. Trish verses Austin, that's a classic case of Good vs. Evil and in the West, young man, the Good Guy always wins."

"Does James know?"

"No, I don't think so. Trish can tell him. It's not my place, but no, he stays home. All money and cattle sales aside, it's to restore my daughter's honor. She's a good woman worth fightin' for."

"Fighting? Does Austin know we're comin'?"

"Hopefully no, not 'til he sees the whites of my eyes."

Contrary to Jim's emotions, Alan's mind buzzed with unspoken questions. The logistics of such an event had his imagination teeming.

Alan and Ila spent the rest of the day secretly lining up an armada of cattle trucks, then called a meeting of his men for the next morning.

Gwenny's world was spinning. Richard's yellow striped shirt was in the laundry trash can, and she had been packing the rest of his clothes and other belongings into garbage bags all through the night. There was a growing pile of black bags cinched and tied in tight knots, then tossed as hard as she could into the garage where he kept his shop. The noises she'd made in the night were lost on her husband of forty-four years as he slept in relative comfort on the family room couch.

By dawn, Gwenny's box of trash bags was empty and so was her heart. She dozed at the kitchen table, waiting for him to come to her. Waiting for him to be contrite, and to grovel for her forgiveness. That never came. He slipped out as she dozed. What awoke her was the usual knock on the door from Holly. She was heading to work and dropping off Cole. As was usual, he ignored Gwenny and headed for her kitchen table for breakfast. "Oh! No, Holly, Cole. No, I can't do daycare today."

"This is three times now that you've left me without help, with no warning." Holly wasn't aware of Gwenny's troubles, only seeing her own.

Gwenny rose and stood in front of Holly. "Here's your warning. Holly? I'm sick today. That's all I have for you. I'm sorry, but in the vast scheme of things, I'm sure you'll be able to cope. You're young." She held a tissue to her mouth and quietly shuffled off to the nearby half-bathroom. "He can have breakfast here," she threw over her shoulder, then slowly claimed with a monotone voice, "I don't care," before she shut the door.

~*~*~*~

James saw an inordinate number of pickups in the Providence parking lot as he got to work. He filtered through, asking one man, "What's up?"

"Alan called a meeting. Did he call you?"

"No, he didn't."

"Ah, you're a lucky man."

Yes, James thought, *I am. I am a lucky man.* With confidence in his stride, James walked into the creamery and stepped into Laura's office. "Can I ask you a question?'

She set down her pen. "Hi, sure." James watched as Laura's cheeks blushed, "Your question?"

"In the vast configuration of things here at Providence Farm, is there any plan for setting up a winery?"

"I don't think, a brewery, yes, but a winery? Naw, I haven't heard about it."

"Well, and you're in the inside circle, so you would know."

"There is no circle. Just go ask Alan," she suggested.

A tendril of Laura's hair had escaped the hairnet on her head. James stood quietly, studying Laura's eyes as he slowly tucked the errant strand back in. "Is my sister still cold to you?" he asked softly.

"Yes, some prayers are slow to answer."

He held his fingers to her cheek and jaw, leaving her with a wash of passion as he promised, "I'll talk to her." She quietly watched James walk away, then tried to focus on work.

~*~*~*~

Alan's message before the group of men who agreed to haul Jim's cattle was simple. "Jim offered to sell me his herd of Angus cattle, a mix of red and black. First off, Jim has a doctor appointment scheduled at Fargo. A check up for his kidneys. He and I are going to meet you in Aberdeen the first day. We'll get to Belle Fourche by nightfall and stay at a motel there. We'll load the following morning and get back through Aberdeen, then home. This is three full days and two nights, if all goes well. Who has questions?"

One man reminded, "You can't just haul cattle here to North Dakota. The…"

Alan cut him off, "The bovine TB. Yes, it's a real issue. But we have veterinarians going with us to help assure the North Dakota state vet that all is well. I've been working with their office since before I moved here, and with moving in all the Jersey dairy cows. Plus, Jim has impeccable records. Next? That was a good question."

Another man asked, "Jim's been here since last summer. Who's been taking care of the cattle?"

Jim piped up. "My sons. Listen, my sons have been selling off that herd, but I own it, free and clear."

The same man asked, "Well, do they know you're selling?"

"No." There was a buzz of whispers and more questions than Jim had answers to.

Gabe, one of Alan's farmhands, said aloud, "Then I'm bringin' my pistol."

Alan was firm. "No, no one's bringing any guns. No."

Gabe ranted, "You can be as liberal as you want on your own farm, Alan, but don't ask me to go somewhere where I could get killed and then expect me to go unarmed."

~*~*~*~

272

It was the end of the day. Rusty was one of the many men who packed for the quick trip to South Dakota. "I guess it's a hotel at Belle Fourche the first night, then back to the same hotel the second night, and then home the third day" he told Ila on the phone. "Maybe several similar trips in my future to collect them all. We'll see on that. I'll miss you, Ila."

The couple had been growing closer together and were already talking about wedding plans. After a heart rending 'good night', Rusty set down his phone and stared into his overnight bag. He was good with packing light, he always had been. The convenience of being single had long since been an advantage for him, but of late, it was a growing irritation. Ila would certainly be a loving spouse. Of that he was sure. But something else was plaguing his heart. Wherever he went, to church, the grocery store, or driving past the local grade school, the sound of children talking to each other and playing was a growing fascination.

It had started with Ila's grandchildren. He built doll houses, then tried his hand at a garage for storing vehicles of all shapes and colors. It was awakening his playful spirit, but something else was tugging at his heart. None of the children he was getting to know could ever be his own flesh and blood. *Lord, God Almighty? These children tug at my heart. Is it at all conceivable that Ila,"* he paused and doubted, *"I know that she's older. But could she conceive? What am I sayin'? For starters, can you get us past this cattle round up and bring us all back alive?*

The sun had long set and Alan's promised conversation with Anna about young Chris had been looming on his mind. Finally, Alan could put her off no longer. "Anna?" He found her in their master bathroom. Braden was sleeping in the bassinette beyond their bedroom, in the nursery. "Anna."

"Yes, my love." She held the pregnancy testing wand in her hand. "I thought that nursing mothers were not fertile."

"You peed?"

"Indeed. We are pregnant again." Anna set down the device and walked into his open arms.

"Don't hate me for saying this, but young Chris needs to live someplace else."

"Why? We have the room, lots of love, and money isn't an issue. We can do this."

"Yes, and if no one else comes forward we would, but look at us. You and I, we have every opportunity to have a large family. We have time on our side. We're both young, and apparently very fertile," he said holding her close. "But think about this. There are people who are older who would make excellent parents, but they just don't have time on their side. People like Ila and Rusty. Rusty's never gonna know what it's like to be somebody's father unless we step aside."

"Ila's a grandmother."

"Yes, it's unlikely that she'd be able to bear Rusty's children."

"So, this is an opportunity for them?"

"Yes, and Braden John will appreciate you even more, and so will this next one. How are you feeling today?"

"Actually pretty good. Oh, and I got a sauerkraut recipe from James that he wants me to try."

"Saurekraut and pork roast? Yum."

"No, starting with the cabbage and fermenting it, that sort of recipe. You like sauerkraut?"

"Hey, I AM half German."

She tickled, "Hmm, which half? I know you're French from the waist down," she flirted. He chuckled and kissed her all the more.

~*~*~*~

It had been a fitful day for Gwenny. She heard all the juicy gossip that rolled about town, but was more concerned with not becoming the center of attention once her own story got out. Instead, she was uncharacteristically quiet. Gwenny's aggravation was real. It manifested itself in a trembling in her stomach, and a twitch that was developing in the corner of her right eye.

Flitting in and out of her current rage with Richard's poor behavior, she also found herself reliving the uncertainty of having been laid off from her librarian job at the school four years before. No, daycare had never been her idea of a career. She only just tolerated children.

Just like in 2005, she told herself, *it narrows down to feeling the sting of not being valued.* The school superintendent had appreciated neither her love for books, nor her vast understanding and dedication to the Dewey Decimal system. But it was her inability to adjust to the computer age of scanned files and data storage that had sealed her fate.

Now it was another faceless foe who was larger than life. He still hadn't confessed whose lipstick was smeared on his new Easter shirt, or had the decency to apologize. Gwenny still didn't know who to be mad at, besides him. It was a stale mate.

She had never been good with computer skills, just as social skills had always eluded Gwenny, too. Now the added layer of doubting every woman in her path was challenging Gwenny's substandard knack for small talk. Over time, she slipped into a habit of chatting with folks about anything that involved gossip, or sometimes the weather. But to discuss her feelings? Truly, she didn't have friends who she could trust with her troubles, and so wasn't able to vent. *I need answers, and tomorrow morning, darn it, I'm getting them!* To the random neighbor on the street, she was just crabby. But inside, Gwenny vacillated between an emotional hot mess to being loaded for bear.

~*~*~*~

Young Chris had slept well, and was on his first bottle of the day. Ever since Ila found out that Will's mother was sick and that young Chris was needing a home, Ila had given it serious thought but hadn't discussed it with Rusty yet. Of all the women in that region, Ila was the one who headed to the chart in the Catholic church the most often to sign up for the duty. Or as she thought, *for the privilege.*

Her turn had come around again the evening before, after her chat with Rusty. Life had been planned around her chance to cuddle both Rusty and young Chris close. Now she held the latter, quietly humming a lullaby in her rocker. *Adopting you,* she wondered, *young Chris Sturlaugson, what would that be like?* She gazed off into her house plants and imagined it all until she heard him having finished his bottle. Instinctively, Ila stood and patted his back and bottom, then softly whispered as she bounced and burped the growing baby, "Once again, could it be one of the Hillman cousins who would be raising an Englishman?"

The babe supplied a burp, stretched and spit the last sip of formula onto his chin. Ila sat on the edge of a chair and laid him onto her lap. She wiped his mouth and sat studying him. "What would Rusty think about adopting you?" she quietly asked. There was no reply from young Chris. He was fast asleep.

But Rusty had heard from the doorway. He had been standing there, adoring the pair, wishing. At the sound of such a question, Rusty wondered if he'd been dreaming. "Maybe we should," he quietly suggested.

Her head bounced to see and hear. "Did I hear you right?"

Rusty moved to the chair and bent down on his knees. Whispering, he explained, "I was just at Alan and Anna's. They want to suggest to Will that we get a chance to adopt. What do you think?"

"Let me set this boy in his crib and hug you proper!" she quietly giggled.

He walked her through the task and they settled by the kitchen sink, sharing a quiet glass of cold water. "Life doesn't get better than this!" Rusty said, smacking his lips.

"I will gladly help you raise that boy into a fine young man, just like you," Ila cooed, adding, "I love you both! But now, look at the time. I thought you left early this morning."

Rusty caressed his hand over her shoulder and arm. "I needed one more hug before I go." The pair embraced as young lovers do. With a tender gaze and three more kisses, Rusty promised, "We'll get the paperwork pulled together after Will and I get back."

The sun shone over the convoy of trucks, heading south. Anna was shredding cabbage to try Auntie Betty's sauerkraut recipe. Instructions had been vague but it kept her busy while she prayed and wondered about the men.

Will was in his pickup loaded with veterinarian supplies, hauling a horse trailer with eight horses and saddles, while Brandon, Grady, Rusty, Cody, Larry, Gabe, Elijah, and thirteen others pulled empty cattle trucks. Anyone with a CDL, Commercial Driver's License. Even Mick and Cameron Carlyle each took a seat behind steering wheels. All in rented cattle semi-trucks heading for Aberdeen, South Dakota. Alan and Jim would meet them in Aberdeen after Jim's appointment, and they'd roll on west to Belle Fourche from there.

Only Jim, Alan, and Trish's other boss, Will Sturlaugson, knew the full purpose of that cattle round up. And yes, so did Erin and Brandon, since Trish had shared. But for all the rest of the friends and neighbors in that corner of the Red River Valley, all were blissfully unaware of Trish's secret or of Austin's guilt. James and the crew at the creamery, Drew and Malla, Theo and Sophie, Holly and her friend Karen in Akra, or her neighbor Magnus. Not Kathy from the Red Owl or Terah from the post office, not even Jody from the First United Free church. Neither were Will's neighbors or the folks at the C-store. All were oblivious to the whole story. But Laura was catching on. There was an odd email that had appeared on Laura's computer.

It was sent from Halee. Not Christine's Hailey, who was named after a thunderstorm. No, it was Will's Halee, the nurse who had intende to marry the would-be priest and go with him to Peru and would be young Chris' mom. She had been too far into a bottle of red wine when she decided to tell Trish exactly what she thought. It was Trish, after all, who had sent the letter that made her doubt Will and his love, effectively putting the kibosh on Halee ever being a mom. She was still unable to bear children, and Trish was the cause of her marriage to Will not working out.

Laura couldn't understand how on earth Halee had gotten Laura involved, except that the email addresses for major players in Providence Farms was on the new website. The email was only directed to Trish, but copied to Laura.

She read the note again, *Trish, you heart-less witch; Will were never going to love you! WHY did you have to make mee doubt him!? He told me about U and your petty problem, you think you're such a victim with being molested by your jurkk of a brother. Well………little missssy/ real people have REEL problems. I had to have a abortion when I was the same age, 17, and now I cann't have children!! Now they are adopting young Chriss to strangers when I want two love him!!! Well you should be fired and so I'm telling your boss, L Zimmerman, what a lazy/dumb fool you are!*

It was all there waiting in Trish's e-mail account. Trish and Nick were on a four-day mini vacation to Winnipeg, and would wait until after they were back into the States to turn their phones off of airplane mode. It waited, and the old grandfather clock slowly made its measured rounds.

19 MOVE 'EM OUT!

The clinic doors burst open before Alan and Jim. Their extra early trek to Fargo that morning had paid off. Now Jim's good report was a minor bump in the day. Jim had bigger fish to fry. The need to be there, to confront Austin, was consuming Jim. The fields and side roads flew past them as Alan drove his pickup to Aberdeen. In the passenger seat, Jim was finally in control. What had been a life of chaos, where even his kidneys didn't work like they should, Jim had plenty of other areas that were just as dysfunctional.

The years of blood, sweat, and tears, of building up a respectable herd from nothing, all that time had gone into his herd. If there was a windfall for whatever reason Jim reinvested in his herd. The medical problems, Val's death, and more medical bills had brought chaos front and center . Now. Now he was finally in control.

His health, his finances, and his love life were all looking up. But relationships within his own family were spinning out of control, all due to Austin's bullying ways.

Before Jim could have expected, Aberdeen was before him. Grown from a western watering hole to a sprawling and modern prairie paradise, it was currently heavy on veterinarians and cattle trucks.

Alan and Jim stopped long enough to hook his pickup to his horse trailer. Twenty-five trucks lined the parking lot on the edge of town, ready to follow Alan and the four pickups of vets, including Dr. Tappen, Dr. Spencer, another from Casselton, North Dakota, and bringing up the rear was Dr. Will Sturlaugson, on break from seminary classes. The fleet was off and moving west, heading cross country to Belle Fourche.

Trish and Nick had enjoyed a quiet morning in their hi-rise Winnipeg hotel. Pondering their happy life, she logged onto the hotel's WiFi connection and drilled down to her email account to show Nick the online receipt for her latest E-bay victory. Her contented grin faded.

"Nick! Nick! Look at this!" Trish held up the Ipad for him to read. "That Halee, she was Will's short-term fiancé —I didn't know how snarky she can get! Augh!!"

Nick read through the email and simply asked, "Why is Laura copied here?"

"WHAT?? Why would she do that??" The acid in her stomach started to burn and her head pounded. They cut their mini-vacation short and Trish fell into a funk wrought with worry and disappointment.

Gwenny met the moving crew at the garage door. "Yes, I'd like all this stuff put into storage. The lady who answered your phone number said that you could pack the boxes and the whole works. Right?"

Jon and his United Van Lines crew had Richard's belongings boxed and loaded into a storage garage by the end of the day. Jon mentioned that his moving truck had brought Alan and Anna's things to the region a couple years before. Gwenny smiled politely, but the novelty was lost on her.

Trish's turmoil had her imagining every different scenario all the way back from Winnipeg. Once she was back to Cavalier, she promised that she'd be fine, and would get some much needed sleep. But as soon as Nick drove off, Trish was in her car and heading to the creamery to find Laura.

By nightfall the rigs were parked again at the truck stop and motel just out of town. As the men headed inside to get a hot meal, Jim opted to lay low and asked Alan for a sandwich-to-go. He was conscious of the locals and knew several inside the café.

While Brandon and several others, all wearing their favorite dirty baseball caps, headed inside, a cowboy rose from his booth and adjusted his cowboy hat.

"What the hell is this?" his friend asked nodding at the newcomers. "East River?"

The first cowboy glanced their way. A rancher from a neighboring booth pointed at their trucks, "North Dakota plates."

His friends chuckled, "Worse yet."

The first cowboy shrugged, smiling, "Maybe they all heard 'bout Rosy's chicken wings." He grinned and headed for the till, more focused on his chances with the waitress than starting trouble with travelers. "Good night, Ella, see ya tomorrow," he said, tipping his hat. Outside, the wind pushed at the brim. With a tender touch Marty O'Malley headed into the wind and mounted his trusty, rusty pickup. Heading back to the ranch didn't appeal to him, but what options did he have?

Austin kept chasing Marty's sweethearts off. Marty would protest, "I ain't meant to be a bachelor!" Confrontation from Marty was only fuel for violence, and Marty never landed on the top side of any of Austin's beatings. Marty figured Austin's logic kept Marty focused on managing the cattle. This was a job he took seriously, a job at which he excelled. If it wasn't for Marty's attention to the herd, their health, their reproduction, their safety, Austin wouldn't have the truckloads of cattle to sell at market. Austin took the financial end of their empire very seriously, a world Marty ignored.

Baptized Martin Xavier O'Malley, unlike Trish, Martin preferred his given name, Martin, now that he had grown. He still accepted Marty from his schoolboy friends, but more and more he was suggesting people call him Martin. Austin taunted him, calling him 'Smarty Marty Dumbass', consistently, since he was nine.

As a direct contrast to Austin, Martin esteemed St. Martin, his namesake, and everything the saint stood for. The patron saint of soldiers, Martin often stood humbled by his own cowardice. Most days he believed the condescending garbage that spewed from Austin's mouth. But at night, Martin fought clear of those demeaning thoughts and prayed, studying the lives of the saints like St. Martin and St. Francis Xavier, the patron saint of animals.

When no one was listening, Martin shared those harrowing stories with his dogs, horses, and cattle. Yes, Martin Xavier O'Malley was more of a man than Austin gave him credit for. He pulled into the yard and took a deep breath. "Lord Almighty," Martin whispered. The remainder of his prayer was silent, but understood.

The race cars on TV roared as Austin snored in his recliner. "Praise God," Martin thought, "no beating tonight."

Aggravation piled on top of exhaustion for Trish, but she finally found Laura. She was at her apartment. Trish saw her through the first floor window. Laura was alone, writing at her kitchen table. Trish stood outside of the window, wondering what to do.

Do I confront her now? It had to be her counselor, Roberta Simpson. I only saw her once, but Laura's always talking to her. Who else did I tell? Alan, Will, and Brandon. Wait, Erin? No, she wouldn't. Did Will tell stupid Halee? How does Halee know Laura? This is too bizzare!

Trish was so far into her own thoughts that she didn't notice that Laura had seen her and was looking out the window at her. Trish turned and headed back to her car, but Laura dashed out to catch her. Laura touched Trish's fender, but she was gone, leaving Laura to watch the taillights that turned out of the parking lot and down through the street.

20 A NEW DAWN

Morning came, but Trish's sleepless night had offered no relief from her aggravation and worry. And it was about to get worse.

Since having been gone to Winnipeg, Trish had to make a quick stop at the post office on her way to the clinic. It was a morning routine, and Trish count on routine when she was tired.

Terah Anders was at the counter, along with both Magnus and Kathy from the Red Owl. They were more than curious, and in walked the perfect person to help answer their questions. "Hey, Trish," Terah started, "What gives, why is your dad selling all his cattle to Alan? That sounds weird. Don't you have some brothers back in South Dakota?"

"All the Morning Star Ranch cattle? Are you sure?"

"Dang right," Magnus drawled, "but I hear that your brothers don't know what's comin', so some of the guys that's truckin', well, they took guns with 'em..." Trish disappeared without her mail. It was going to be a long day! She tried to think of how she could contact Jim and the only thing that made sense was to call Anna and pass on a message.

Earlier that morning, one by one, the trucks headed out, pulling out of town. Not in a long dramatic line, but staggered, single. Farther down the road they began to cluster into a group They were led by Jim who took them around back to the back door of his spread of land. He knew where the hills and draws were that would conceal the fleet of trucks. As they waited for the sheriff, Jim noted no improvements in the land, but he studied the shine on the coats of the cow/calf pairs that dotted the countryside. His herd was healthy and growing well. The brand he had designed clearly identified both cows and steers. A proud red Angus bull drew to the ridge above Jim, looking down on the growing crowd of pickups and semi-trucks. The bull was a beautiful specimen, a sure winner at any fair or rodeo. Jim wondered about his age, his pedigree.

A strong voice called from the hill behind them; simultaneously they heard the man's rifle cocked to attention. "Back those trucks off this land!"

The man came out from behind a bush, his gun aimed at the back of a very startled Brandon Zimmermann, who held his hands up, though his unbelted pants threatened to drop. "Who's in charge of this band of rustlers?" the man demanded, "Now!! WHO!!??"

Alan was even more nervous, knowing how many of his crew could also be drawing on the demanding man. Alan stepped forward, "We're not rustlers. I have a legal bill of sale."

The cowboy focused through the glaring sun. "Dad?"

Jim grinned, "Hey, Marty."

His shoulders dropped, lowering his gun. "What the hell?!"

Jim calmed him, "Marty, just relax and let me explain."

"A bill of sale? You could'a called me."

Alan moved up the hill and stretched to hand him the paper. Confusion spread across his face. "This is extreme, Dad. This is…"

"The whole herd, every hoof. It's my herd. It's my inheritance and I'm movin' it to North Dakota."

"Dad," he paused, rubbing the back of his neck, "you own it, so you have every right. But this herd, these animals, they've been my whole life! You can't take them unless you take me, too."

"I don't know, Marty."

"Call me Martin, please, like Mom used to."

"Martin, I doubt I can trust you. Both you and Austin, you've…"

"I will NOT share the blame for anything Austin does. He's a horrible man, a bully who's been beating me into submission for years. No, please don't lump me into that same category. I would hate him but hate is wrong."

Jim explained, "Austin tricked me into deeding him the land, then he left me in that dirty nursing home to die."

"Dad, when Trish called, I got tested. I did, but I just wasn't a match to help you."

"You did that?"

"Yes," he said firmly, emotion in his voice.

Jim moved closer, scratched his chin and quieted his voice, "Did you know about what he did to Trish?"

"What are you talkin' 'bout?"

"Trish, after high school," Jim started, but couldn't say it out loud.

Alan had followed when Jim moved up the hill. He moved forward and whispered into Martin's ear. Martin rejected it in disgust, "NO!" Alan continued, repeating the sad sick story and Martin shuttered, "How sub-human IS that?!"

Alan patted Martin's shoulder and gently removed Martin's gun from his hand. Alan turned and looked around Martin to the truckers. "Now I want all of you to put down your guns, too." There was a pregnant pause, but then thuds of metal hit the dry ground before them.

Martin eyed the burly crew before him with a wrinkled brow and a pungent stink-eye, "Where do you think we are," he asked them, "in Wyoming?"

Alan shrugged and motioned, "Excuse me, you two were talking."

Martin and Jim both met half way. Jim's eyes were hopeful, and his voice had returned to its normal level, "You got tested?" The men around them listened in.

"Yes," he repeated.

"And you never knew about Trish?"

"No, Dad. Not any more than you knew about the beatings."

"Beatings?"

"Austin, that's how he kept me working for him all these years. Do you know how many girls he has chased away? Women I cared about? No, Dad. I'd be married and givin' you grandchildren by now, but Austin's got me stuck."

Jim nodded and pointed to the proud bull. "What's his name?"

"That's Vincent Ferrer. All the bulls are named for saints."

"Is that Austin's idea?"

"No, mine. I name them 'cause I'm the one there, calvin' with 'em at all times of the day and night. They're named for saints 'cause that's how Mom named us. I study the saints at night—it keeps me sane. He's Vincent Ferrer, the Builder ."

Silence hung over the draw where the men stood in a circle around Jim and Martin. The hush was finally broken when one man offered, "Well, if you're movin' up north, I got a sister you could meet."

"Megan?" another man asked, continuing, "Yeah, and Chuck, what about Cassie? She dumped the dentist, didn't she?"

The first man nodded, "Sure did, but now what about Chrissie?" he teased.

Larry proclaimed, "She is not available. We're datin', thank you very much," nodding a warning to Martin.

Martin held both hands up, "Whoa, I never touched her."

"Sir, my name is Larry and I'm from Vermont."

"Vermont?" Martin stopped him. "Liberal politics. Good ice cream."

"Some 're more liberal than some. Excuse me, I'm tryin' to tell you about my experience. May I continue?"

Martin waved him onward. Larry grinned, remembering, "The folks I've met since moving' there to the Mountain, North Dakota area, they have been friendly and warm. We all have good jobs workin' for a fair and generous boss, that's Alan," he pointed. Alan gave a little wave as Larry continued. "And once housing gets finished, it'll be near on perfect. The women are pretty, they know how to cook, the wage is high and the huntin' and fishin' is pretty decent. Now, I wanna know one thing. Do you got a bull named St. Lawrence, named after me?"

"Not yet, there are a lot of saints." Martin started sensing a friend in Larry.

"What did St. Lawrence do?" Larry asked, obviously curious. Their bonding would have to wait, the sheriff's SUV pulled up. Once Jim and Alan explained their position and Martin gave his take on what was happening, the sheriff called in additional deputies, and Jim's revised plan was put into action.

Alan headed to Spearfish and got a moving trailer with a supply of boxes, blankets and tape while the men moved their trucks into position. Jim's excitement grew as he began to realize the true value of his long ignored son, Martin.

~*~*~*~

Trish's morning had started just as early, but not because she was expected at the new vet clinic. *I still can't believe that, of all people, it's Laura that knows my secret! What's she gonna do with such info. What was she writing?* Trish's list of questions was as long as her time on her pillow was short. But it was the sound of Magnus' voice describing the guns that men had hauled with them to the Morning Star Ranch that kept rising to the top of her mind.

Trish drove up to Alan and Anna's house, reliving a flashback of when she had first come to the farmyard and office area of the barn for her first interview. She had saved a cow from dying and was hired on the spot.

There's so much I would've done differently, if I could have. I wouldn't have told Will or Alan about stupid Austin, and then I could still breathe right now. I, I...

Anna was at the side door by the back patio, "Trish, come in," she beckoned. The side door where Anna stood led to the sidewalk that also led to the barn and office. How well Trish knew the path between the friendly house and her love, the barn full of her many friends.

Trish was ready for a good heart to heart with Anna, but didn't realize that Laura and Dara were also at the kitchen table.

As the moving boxes and supplies arrived, they were formed and taped in the quiet of the lilac bushes, then handed down the old outdoor cellar stairway that led into the house's basement. That was where all Martin's belongings were. Many of the boxes were loaded with his clothes and his collection of books and movies about angels, saints, and raising cattle. Many other boxes were loaded with family heirlooms that his mother had cherished, but Austin wouldn't allow Trish to have.

It wasn't that Austin had any attachment to the antique lanterns, crocks, cabinets, rocking chairs, and treadle sewing machine. Martin had gladly moved these and others out of Austin's way when he had brought home new electronic toys, all charged on credit. Martin cherished the antiques because his mother had held them dear. Now they were being padded, boxed and quickly labeled by a small army who worked in whispers.

Upstairs Austin was captivated by a video game. Martin walked in the front door in clear view of Austin, followed by Larry. Martin had given his new friend an old cowboy hat so he would look the part. Larry and Martin picked up and discussed the few items of Martin's that had made it to the ground floor. Martin didn't introduce Larry to Austin and Austin didn't ask. He was captivated within his own world.

As the two walked out the back door, Martin grabbed the calendar off the kitchen wall, "This has friends' birthdays and phone numbers for when my cell phone crashes again," Martin said and nodded to the sheriff and deputy.

Sheriff Mack asked, "Are the boys done downstairs?"

Alan turned to Brandon, "Calving records?"

He nodded, "On the computer, yes, we got everything but the dining room set."

"OK," Alan scratched his head, "Jim? The Bill of Sale? Are you sure you want to do this?"

"As agreed. I should have taught that boy a lesson a long time ago."

~*~*~*~

"Anna," Trish began, "I have dreadful news. The men who drove down to my family's ranch, they have guns."

"Yes, I know," Anna said as Trish walked past her through the music room door. "Alan couldn't convince them to leave them home. I thought you went to Winnipeg," Anna finished, standing in the library.

"I was, we were, but then I decided to come home. Seriously? Dad's selling the whole herd?"

Anna confirmed, "He said every hoof. Like 850 plus calves."

Dara's voice called from around the corner. "Come and join us here at the kitchen table." Dara had become a close friend of Trish's in the time that Trish had snubbed Laura.

Before moving, Trish reached to grasp Anna's hands and whispered her question, "Why, why the whole herd? Do you have any idea on that?"

Anna shrugged, "I asked Jim and it made no sense. 'To protect Trish's honor.'" Anna shook her head, "I have no idea what that means."

Like she'd been hit by a knock-out punch, Trish rounded the corner past the kitchen and saw Laura sitting in one of the chairs. "OK, I'm leaving," Trish said.

She turned into Anna behind her. "Why? You just got here."

"Then I'll leave," Laura offered, explaining, "Trish doesn't like my company."

Anna wouldn't have it. "That's ridiculous. The four of us are friends, aren't we?" She motioned and said, "Sit," towards Laura's chair, and the same to Trish. The two foes were seated diagonally, with supportive friends in either direction.

Dara started, "How did this riff get started? You've both been cold and dodging the other for at least two months."

Trish looked away. Laura confessed, "She thinks I'm too flighty for her brother, James. She said that he needs someone stable to deal with his PTSD, not someone who would make it worse. I'm too crazed."

"Hmm, and flighty?" Dara repeated.

"Thing is, I have been growing up a lot, a whole lot. Doc Sturlaugson, Will, he's been very encouraging with finding supportive Bible passages. My mom and dad and I have been sharing those passages by email with Mom and well, Dad only communicated with old fashioned paper and pen. But we've been discussing the meanings, the background of the culture of Biblical times, all that. That's who I was returning a letter to last night when you saw me."

Trish had been wading in the slurry of confusion, now realizing that her dad had somehow found out about Austin. *Why else would he punish Austin so? For my honor? God have mercy!* She looked up at Laura and laid it on thick, judging, blaming, "So you told them all about it, sitting here in your little cozy Bible study. Soon all of Vermont will know and sure, why not, tell these two ladies and step back, my deepest secrets will be rolled through Mountain on parade! Now you just need a marching band!"

Laura shook her head gently as she said, "I didn't say anything to them about you, only sharing my dad's latest meditation on Romans 8."

Anna confirmed, "No, Trish, Laura has been moody, and I was trying to figure out why, but no, she is only discussing herself, her parents, and the Apostle Paul." Anna looked into Trish's eyes, "Would you like to tell us what's bothering you? Because, Lady, you are not yourself."

Instead of telling Anna or Dara, she only addressed Laura, "Why were you on that email?"

"I don't know," Laura started, "I haven't figured that out, yet. Do you have any theories? Who was the drunk who wrote that email?"

"Drunk?"

"The spelling, the grammar. I'm guessing wine, and a lot of it."

Anna and Dara listened in, asking, "Who was drunk?"

Laura explained, "The woman who wrote the email. I'm not about to explain anymore. I don't know enough to have an opinion."

All eyes were on Trish. "It was the woman who Will was engaged to in Williston. She was going to be a mom to young Chris and a wife to Will. OK, back up the bus. I heard through a friend that Will was up to this. I was at the hospital in Fargo, doctoring with Nick and Dad. There was a chaplain at the hospital who I went to confession to, and explained that I knew about a guy who was called to the priesthood, but that he was avoiding it, and was about to marry some nurse and run off to Peru.

Well, last summer the Chaplain helped me send a letter to this Halee, the woman who sent an email yesterday to both Laura and me. Back when I sent that letter, I knew it would sabotage Will's plan to marry. I wasn't jealous, as she implies, I was helping him do the right thing.

"Well, now, fast forward to this weekend and the woman I used to call a friend is copied on this raunchy email from a sad, lonely woman who wants me to hurt as much as she does. So, she sends this email. She said that I should be fired. I don't know, maybe Will had suggested it, back when they were together. If that's the case, and she was drunk, like you say, then maybe instead of Laura, she was looking for Alan. She labeled L. Zimmerman in the email. Maybe when Will talked about Alan, it sounded like 'L', but there was no 'Al'. So she looked it up, drunk, in that goofy email list and got Laura. Why does that email list have to be on the new website? We didn't vote on that. I don't think I like that at all," Trish vented.

"Al," Anna noted, "no, he'll never let anyone call him that."

Dara defended, "The new website has its value."

Laura noticed the conversation heading south, so she said, "Well, Trish, I don't know enough to have an opinion, but I for one am very sorry for whatever it was that happened to you back then."

Anna snapped to, "What happened?"

Trish was a sudden ball of knots, "Augh, please, don't sound just like Terah at the post office, please! And why do we have to call her Terah? Augh! I'm in a mood!"

Laura added, "Talking about something like that is the first stage in healing from it. You're in a safe space here. We are all friends who love you, even if you don't love me back."

Anna had had enough counseling to add, "We don't need details, and you don't have to say anything, if you don't want to. We will accept you at whatever stage you're at. But please know, discussing whatever it is, in a safe space, is a healthy thing." Anna pushed her chair back and added,

"Laura and Dara, go to the restroom or something. Let's give her a chance to breathe, and we will be back to this table with coffee and chocolate cake in five or ten minutes. Nothing heals like chocolate cake."

~*~*~*~

James was busy working on another batch of Emmentaler cheese. Confidence grew with every batch. At break time he was given a message to call Trish on her cell, not knowing where he was finding her. Trish's phone rang as Anna was busy in the kitchen and the others had disappeared. "Sista, there's that Happy Iddy Biddy Girl," he teased, using a name he'd tagged her with when she was three and he was five.

"James, oh, I'm not a Happy Iddy Biddy Girl today."

"Why? You're always a iddy biddy happy, aren't ya?"

"Not today."

"What's wrong? You're where, Winnipeg?"

"No, I'm home, now packed full of worry. Well, aren't you worried?"

"No, what for? Hey, I got another batch of Emmentaler cheese made this morning and it's beautiful. But it won't be ready for a while. Hey, how 'bout some cheesecake since you're back?"

"Do you know where Dad is?"

"He said him and Toni were goin' fishin'."

"Oh, he lied to you, too. Yes, that's what he said before I left for Winnipeg."

"Say what?"

"He lied, James. Him and I don't know how many others, but they took I don't know how many trucks and four veterinarians to Morning Star ranch. He's selling the entire herd to Alan."

"The... That's extreme. Are you sure that's right?"

"Yes. Anna confirmed it, but when I asked Dad about his plans, he lied, point blank."

"This seems ridiculous. At my birthday two years ago Dad said they were well over 1,200 head. Maybe 1,500 by now."

"No, it's closer to 850 now, plus calves. Austin must be selling 'em off."

"OK, to pay off medical bills. That makes sense."

"No, Alan paid the bill, James."

"Well, regardless, you say he's moving the entire herd to Providence Farm? Why? That leaves Austin and Marty with nothin'. In effect that takes 'em out of business. That doesn't make sense. Yeah, Austin'll never win any congeniality contests, but damn, I don't get it."

Trish sighed and salty tears rolled as she explained, "The only thing I can figure is that Dad is punishing Austin for what he did."

"You mean selling the cattle? Yeah? They weren't his to sell."

"No, for what he did to me," Trish moaned. Anna looked at Trish, set down the coffee cups and covered her ears.

"No," James said with a horror stricken tone, "Oh, God no," staring off into the corner of an inspirational poster.

"He," Trish started, then more tears caught her. Trish pulled Anna's hands from her ears, and watched as eyes welled with tears. "When you were gone, he would come into my room during the night when I was sleeping and..."

"No, Trish! He didn't rape you, did he?" James asked, afraid of her reply.

Anna's hand caressed Trish's back. "No, but like I told Nick, a girl should be able to sleep at night without her brother's hand in her crotch. Don't you think?"

"That son of a…" began the torrent of James' vulgar string of words. They colored the air and defined his mood.

"Mom would be after you with Ivory soap. Listen to you," she scolded, then smiled into Anna's face.

"Ah, shit, you sound just like her, Trish. Austin makes me so angry! Augh, God!! Trish, we're supposed to love our enemies but this is too much to bear. How? I've been trained to use my hands as lethal weapons and right now I just wanna…"

Dara was at the edge of the kitchen peninsula, and Trish waved her into Anna's side as she warned, "James, don't. Don't think that way. Maybe that's why Dad lied to ya, to protect you from yourself. Can't you just see it? You beatin' on Austin, Dad in the middle, getting hurt, the sheriff hauling you off to prison, and we bury Austin, without ever having taught him anything. What good is that?"

"Where is Marty in all this? Did he hurt you?"

"Marty? No, never. Oh, we always got along. He was proud of me going to be a vet tech. But since Dad got sick and Marty was the one who found Mom when she died, ever since he's been standin' in Austin's shadow, seemingly without a thought of his own. I don't understand him. Maybe he's depressed. I don't know."

"Shell shocked. Maybe Dad lied to you so you wouldn't worry."

"Oh, pfft, it's my nature. I got that from Mom."

"Trish, I heard him describe to one of these neighbors that his first wife worried herself into the grave. If that's your nature, wouldn't he have every right to be concerned about your reaction?"

"He lied because he loves me?"

"Yeah, and he loves me, too. So we're here on the outside and they're at the ranch doin' God knows what."

"God knows."

"Hey, Iddy?"

"Yeah?"

"Why didn't you tell Mom and Dad back when it happened?"

"Mom was iffy?"

"Her heart, yeah."

Trish continued, "And Dad was always workin' or crabby. I didn't want to add stress to his day."

"Well, how do you hold in a secret like that?"

"What kind of cheesecake do you want?"

"What?"

"I choose not to think about it. I told myself it didn't happen and I chose not to think about it. Cheesecake?"

"Yes, with strawberries. I can pick you some fresh strawberries, Joyce said that Eva still has some in her patch."

"That does sound good."

"Can you choose not to worry about Dad and the boys?"

"I can compartmentalize stuff that impacts me, but with other people, there are too many variables. Variables that can get so out of hand so fast. I don't know exactly how Dad found out about Austin. But he told Anna that it was all to protect my honor."

"Cheesecake," he whispered, "with strawberries."

"Yes, such a beggar. Yes, OK."

"OK, Trish," James broached a different topic, "Since you're in a giving mood, could you please back up and give Laura and me a chance? I think she's beautiful and my soul, well, she's got me reading the Bible.

Can you think of anyone else who could do that for me? No, not even you. Please. Just give us an iddy biddy chance."

Trish, Anna, and Dara stood in a group hug and shared a good cry. The release of the emotion and hormones did Trish wonders. She wiped the tears and asked the others, "Where is Laura?" Anna pointed out towards the blue playhouse garden. The early spring was bringing perennials to life, a few blades of green at a time, but sassy red tulips were already strutting their stuff.

Trish was worried, wondering what to say, "Laura?" Trish quietly began and was quickly done. "I've been very mean and judgy, and I'm sorry." She chided herself aloud, "That didn't come out right."

Laura's usual cheerful smile was a bit crooked, as tears quickly overtook her. "You silly! That was just fine. Hey, I'm sorry, too. I was just really going through a lot, and well, I know not to disrespect your animals because I don't expect anyone to disrespect my cheese."

"I love your chocolate marshmallow pecan fudge frozen yogurt. But as much as I like that, I think I love you more. You are a great friend. I just lost sight of that. Yes, you were going through crap, Laura, piles and piles of crap and I wasn't there for you. I'm sorry." The two friends hugged and made up. Finally, Trish offered, "Well, hey, don't waste all your time with me. Go find my cute brother and tell him that I took his advice. I backed up and got out of his way."

Jim led the way around the house and up the steps, in through the front door. He was followed by Alan, the sheriff, and two of his deputies. Austin held the video game's joystick controls and nimbly turned and spun this way and that. So caught up in his fictional battle, he wasn't aware of the new challenge facing him.

Jim called his attention, "Austin," he said firmly.

"Dad!? Uh, Sheriff?" He recognized the deputies. They had partied with Austin before. Now they stood ready for battle, no fun and games here. "Boys? What's goin' on?"

Sheriff Davis took control. "Austin, we have been asked to come here and witness your agreement or disagreement to this legal document. This Bill of Sale describes a purchase of cattle from Morning Star Ranch, legally owned by Jim O'Malley and sold to Alan Zimmermann. Austin? Do you agree that the cattle on this ranch are wholly and solely owned by Jim O'Malley?"

Noises from the video game were squelched by Martin who pulled the plug. Austin looked from Martin to the sheriff and replied, "Yes, he owns the cattle. I own the land."

"So, he has every right to sell what he owns?"

"Yes. Dad, what's goin' on?"

Jim's eyes cut deep into Austin's soul. "I'm movin' my inheritance north."

Sheriff Davis continued, "Austin? Look over this agreement, study it so it's clear to everyone here that you understand." Austin walked to the dining room table and took a seat, reading the Bill of Sale.

As he read, his world began to spin. Larry and Brandon quietly picked up dining room chairs and carried them outside. Carefully Martin removed the model race cars that lined the inside of the china hutch. Once empty, he waved and two others carried the cabinet out to be padded and packed onto Martin's trailer.

Unaware of the action around him, Austin rose from his seat to turn to Jim. The men moved the table and its leaves and the remaining chair as Austin moved toward his father. He had finally caught on, "Dad—this is crazy. You can't do this! These are Morning Star cattle. You can't sell the whole herd!!"

"You just told these deputies and this here sheriff that, it being my property, I can do with it as I want. Did you not understand what you were sayin'? Or maybe when you tricked me into deedin' you the land when I thought I was dyin', maybe you just didn't know what you were sayin'. Or maybe when you ignored your sister's pleas to get tested to see if you could donate a kidney to save your dad's life, maybe then, you just didn't know what you were sayin'.

"Is that it? Son, you have been pilin' up one transgression after another and I've been ignoring your bad behavior and at the same time, I've been ignoring your brother Martin's good behavior. You know full well that the shine on their coats out there," he said pointing, "is due to Martin's good care. All his efforts have amounted to what? Cash for you to buy toys?" Jim kicked a model race car across the floor.

"No, Austin, you've built up one problem on top of another and I've just recently learned the last two straws that broke this camel's back. You beat your brother to keep him under your greedy thumb all these years, and years ago, when Trish was out of high school my oldest boy, the one I trusted with my inheritance, you molested my little girl while she slept? You don't deserve anything, but your brother, a man who is a hundred times the man you will EVER be, he has asked me to be merciful and leave you one bull and three heifers. That's all you get, but hey, that's what I started with," Jim reminded. It was a story that had long since bored Austin, but Martin heard the same story and was inspired. As Austin rolled his eyes, Jim's anger was refueled, "I'm registering my brand in North Dakota. You have to come up with your own."

Sheriff Davis cut in, "Austin, there are 25 cattle trucks and we will be guarding the loading docks as they get loaded. He's sellin' more 'en 25 loads, so we'll be guarding you in between loads and there will be no smuggling or rustling of these animals. Do you understand what I'm saying? These trucks…"

"But you don't understand!! I've got an agreement—I've got sales for 25 of those steers on Saturday!"

The sheriff was cool, "Is that right? How is that possible, Austin?"

"Rex over at the Sturgis auction barn, he's handlin' it for me."

Jim was getting riled, but Sheriff Davis held up one finger, "So, Austin, a few minutes ago you agreed that those cattle are owned by Jim, wholly and solely. Now Jim, do you have an agreement with Rex?"

"No, I do not."

"Austin, are you selling cattle you don't own? In my little sheriff dictionary we call that fraud, with a certain degree of extortion tossed in, considering how you've been treating Marty. Fraud and extortion…and you did what to your sister?"

"She lied, she made it up."

"Marty?" Sheriff Davis called. "You look like you might have some insight."

"Uh, two things. I've been livin' here in the basement and Austin and Renee had the upstairs. I wasn't the only one he beat."

"Yeah? Renee, she left in a huff, I understand."

Marty recounted, "It was after Austin got a letter from Trish."

"Did she tell you what the letter was about?"

"No, sir, but that night I heard them fightin'. It was terrible awful. After the noises stopped I went up and checked on Renee. She was bleedin' and half dead in the corner. I took her to the hospital. She had three cracked ribs, a busted nose and she miscarried. Yeah, Renee left in a huff."

The sheriff nodded to his deputy, "Carl, start a list. We got fraud, extortion, spousal abuse…"

"And," Martin added, "I was livin' here when Trish was done with school. She was the baby of the family and Mom made a big deal about her graduation. That was when what I thought were nightmares started. It was the reoccurring type. In these dreams I'd hear Trish holler, 'No, get out. I'm your sister, leave me alone!' I'd wake up with a start 'cause I just couldn't imagine that she'd ever say somethin' like that to me—I thought I was dreaming, but after this mornin' when he told me what she said Austin did, it all started to click."

"Carl, add sexual abuse and incest. We'll let the suits sort out the legalese. We'll need to talk to Trish and Renee and get their sides of this. And Marty? Hypnosis could help pull a nightmare into a verifiable set of evidence. Anything else?"

"No."

"Jim, have you had your say?" Jim nodded. Sheriff Davis turned to Austin, "For now let's deal with fraud and extortion. Austin, can you estimate for me the dollar amounts of your cattle sales since Jim got sick and had to leave the ranch?"

"What?"

"A dollar amount, ball park, I'm just trying to get an idea of how many years you'll be serving before we tack on spousal and sexual abuse, and 'course, there'll be restitution."

"No, I don't have a dollar amount."

"Carl, we'll have to subpoena his tax records and as in most fraud cases, the IRS will want an audit." This thought stirred more pain in Austin's mind.

Jim asked the sheriff, "The Bill of Sale, can we start loadin' now?"

"Yes. Austin? Just so you know, I've got guards at their four loading docks. They have four vets verifying the health of the cattle and horses."

"Four loadin' docks?"

"They brought one and we're borrowin' from the Baxters and Craguns."

"The neighbors?"

Jim added, "They may be interested in buying land. I'm not sure you'll get a good price."

"Money," Austin muttered, "What good is that if I'm in prison?"

Jim quietly began. "Austin, your mom gave you that name. It's for her sake that I'm havin' mercy. I'm not pressing charges. Now, Renee and Trish, that's up to them. No, no prison on account of me, but no inheritance either. Your offenses—they bite me hard and for the sake of your sister and your brother, I had to bite back. God, he's the sort who, if you're truly sorry for your mistakes, well, He might forgive you. But me? I don't know, Austin, you gotta earn my respect first."

"Trish said she forgave me."

Jim noted, "I read that letter that Martin talked about. It was the handwritten one. There were notes there about typing and when she mailed it, certified. Yeah, in that letter, though she confronted you, she forgave you, too. And you repaid her forgiveness by ignoring her pleas to help me, and then beating your wife and losing her baby. God created that child and you murdered it." Jim walked away, then turned to say, "I'm not shunning you like you did Trish, but earning my trust and respect is gonna take some time. The mercy's not my idea. It's your Mom and God." Jim turned to leave.

As they loaded truck after truck of cattle, Jim sat back in the shade of the truck. Brandon pointed a man towards Alan. "I'm Steve Baxter. I talked to Craguns. We're both willing to hire out to truck the rest of the cattle. He's got four trucks, I've got five and we can get a few more." They agreed upon a timetable and a price, and then Alan turned to Jim, handing off his phone. "Anna texted me. Trish found out we're here and she's very worried."

"How do these damn things work?" Jim asked, fumbling the phone.

With a few clicks Alan dialed Trish's phone. "Hello?"

"Trish, honey, Alan said you were worried."

In her swing in the backyard garden, Trish cuddled with Nick. She asked, "Oh, Daddy, are you OK?"

"Yes, I'm fine, no need to fret."

"Well, guess who came home from Winnipeg early? Dad, you're not at home, are you? And you're not fishing either, are you?" Her tone had turned from a relieved fretful daughter to that of a woman scorned.

"Uh, no, I'm not."

She looked around and loudly whispered, "No, you're at the ranch and you lied to both me and James. What the hell are you thinkin', making me worry so?!?"

"Ah, calm down. Austin's been humbled, but he's not fightin' us. Martin is packed up and ready to move up north with the cattle and I'll be leavin' with the first four trucks. I'll be home by nightfall."

"Marty's moving to Mountain?"

"Yes, but her prefers Martin. He's a grown man now and a damn good rancher. We'll have to do some rearrangin'. My ol' knees aren't happy with those stairs, so I want to move into your bedroom and Martin can have mine upstairs. I want to remodel the basement to make you a nice space down there. We'll paint it up pretty. Remember when you were always pickin out paint for your bedroom? You can give that some thought and help me come up with a plan. It's all temporary until I get my house built, but what do ya think?"

"OK, we can do that, but Daddy, you lied to me. You know I don't like that."

"Yes, and you're right. I was thinkin' you'd be mad, but I was hopin' to protect you, honey. I'm sorry. I'm plannin' a party for when we all get home."

"A party?"

"A welcome home party. It was gonna be for James from Iraq, and then now it's for Martin, too. We've got a second chance to be a real family, Trish. Won't that be good?"

"It's a prayer answered, Dad, a monumental prayer answered!"

Laura knew where to find James. The hillside that rose up above the fertile valley floor was called an escarpment by the geology folks. On one particular edge, a precipice jutted out, allowing for James to step out and either stand or sit, and then quietly soak in nature and the beauty of the valley below him as he pondered life, worked out one problem or another, or most lately, sat in the quiet and adored Laura from afar since holding her close wasn't an option yet.

He was sitting on a boulder when she came near. She quietly claimed, "You spoke to your sister."

James looked up into her eyes as she filtered his hair through her fingers. "Yes," he simply said, pulling her gently onto his lap.

"God has truly blessed us!" she whispered into his ear.

She gazed off into the beauty that surrounded them as he gently held her close. For a man who knew far too much about war, James let out a breath that he had seemed to be holding for years. *Finally, peace.* Holding Laura in his arms was a satisfaction he hadn't known since Afghanistan. With his past so tightly woven into military secrets, how could James ever really be totally honest with Laura? He pondered these thoughts and remembered the women he'd held, still pushing back memories of why he had run away at the age of seventeen, and instead wishing all mankind could know the peace he was finally feeling.

Laura stared off to the distant bank of clouds. Like a puppy chasing a butterfly, she had finally caught James just where she wanted him. But would she drift back into her old flighty ways? She knew not to promise since Laura heard her mother's voice asking, "Is it too soon?"

Anna received a phone call from Alan and was relieved to know all was calm, or at least legal, in South Dakota. After hanging up her phone, she pulled Braden into her arms for a snuggle before his next feeding. A ring of the doorbell surprised her. It was Dara.

"Did you forget something?" Anna asked.

Much like Trish finally confessing a long held secret, Dara spilt all her growing suspicion and confirmation of the truth with Joe at Christmas, but then held the secret for him until that night. "It's Joe, or, I guess you know him as Dillon. Dillon and Joe are the same person. I'm sorry for keeping this from you, from Alan and his family, especially their mother, Claudette. I met her last fall, but since Christmas I've been feeling so sad for Claudette since. I guess I've been protecting him. He asked me to. He's coming, he and my dad and the crew. They're coming to build the Mountain strip mall."

Anna asked, "When did you find out?"

Dara was truthful, "At Christmas he confirmed it. I had suspicions before. When does Alan get back? I should tell him in person."

The pubic still didn't know, neither about Richard and Gwenny Hamilton's split nor the identity of Richard's new sweetheart. But when it came to the public's first thought of Richard, some would describe his knack for finding scholarships for their Cavalier, North Dakota students. Others would tout his reputation as an award winning Math teacher. Still others would wonder why or how he ever got stuck with Gwenny. She was the odd duck whose reputation for snooping and talking about others private business behind their backs just didn't jive with his goodness and professionalism.

Along with his clothes, Richard also owned a fair amount of tools. Something about figuring the angles for all different reasons, angles had him intrigued. He started making picture frames for his and Gwenny's college diplomas, then started making puzzles to confuse and confound his students. As time marched on, Richard got more and more complex in his workshop challenges, from layering different woods together, then using the lathe to shape meticulous matching candlesticks, to making his own roll top desk.

So whether hardware or tools, or his collection of Cavalier Tornado sportswear and the variety of sweaters and buttoned shirts, his belongings had been delivered for storage, according to their family lawyer. After receiving that phone call, Richard headed to Grafton towards the end of business hours to get his key and pay his storage bill. He checked through the storage garage in Grafton to see what might be missing. He stared at the inventory list comparing it to the labeled boxes before him, and wandered through his memories of the total amount of tools he had owned. "Hmm, no man in his right mind wants to make a return trip to that house," he told the nearby router jigs, "but I have no choice." The small plastic crate of antique tools from his grandfather was well hidden from could-be thieves, up above next to the garage door opener. Anyone else would've thought it was part of the motor and gears of the opener.

Richard called ahead to the home number, but there was no answer. He made the trip to his and Gwenny's house, nestled on a cozy lot between "Christine's Victorian brothel" on one side, to use Gwenny's description, and the Icelandic baker, Malla and her wild brood, on the other side.

He left the storage garage in Grafton and remembered the first time that Gwenny had met Malla. She was far too European for Gwenny's taste. He laughed aloud at the memory of such a stinkeye on his wife's face. He'd heard it all and grew more and more tired of it all from day to day. First they lost great neighbors to too many run-ins with Gwenny, then Malla moved in. Gwenny still wasn't coping with Malla when Christine had knocked on his door. He welcomed them both to the neighborhood, but Gwenny had her own set of standards. She couldn't and wouldn't be associating.

Richard approached the house and, as expected, his garage door opener still worked. He muttered, 'That'll take two years for her to get that changed." He was right. Gwenny didn't have a technical bone in her body. He stepped into the kitchen briefly but backed out. He'd made his choice. But in that slow descent to the garage floor, his marriage with Gwenny flew before his eyes. *How did we get to this point?*

It was the mid-70s. Raised in Walhalla, North Dakota, Gwenny was a high school cheerleader and Richard was on the basketball team. She was pretty, and giggled at his jokes. The pair were soon inseparable, from high school through the end of their college days when Richard landed his first real job as math teacher in the Cavalier school system. Gwenny was snapped up as the school librarian and everyone was happy. But Gwenny had a series of miscarriages and she finally gave up that dream.

That was when the stand-off began. They had both been pleasant and social to each other for many years. Richard was the only one who could understand how strong his wife could sound, but inside how vulnerable she actually was. She certainly didn't want to discuss her own problems, and repeating gossip was an easy form of communication. In their early fifties, this made up Gwenny's outer shell, having developed a judging tone over the years. Richard had long since told her that 'if you can point your fingers at others, then you will also need to accept that there will come a day when others' fingers will also be pointing back at you.' Whatever Richard knew about Gwenny's persona, he was the only one who had ever witnessed her tender side.

He stood below the garage door opener and stared up at the camouflaged box he was after. The tall ladder he had usually used had been lent to a neighbor down the street. He used a shorter one and stretched to reach for the plastic box. As he did, the ladder started leaning the wrong way. It kicked out from under his feet and there he landed on the cement, breaking his ankle in five places.

Dara had left the message for Alan to talk to her as soon as he got back. He called when he drove through Park River and met Dara on the sidewalk by his house. "My boyfriend asked me to tell you. I've been calling him Joe. You would call him Dillon. He's on my dad's carpenter crew, coming to work in Mountain."

Alan sighed and leaned on one leg, thinking. Wasting no time, he pointed to the phone in Dara's hand, asking, "Dial him up for me, please?"

They both heard the phone ring and she tentatively handed the cell phone off. A familiar voice said, "Hey, Dara."

"Nope," he countered, "this is Alan." The two brothers seemed to share a collective moment of silence. Finally Alan asked, "Should I call Mom and have her come to visit?"

Alan appreciated the reply. "Yes."

Though she didn't know it yet, God had already answered Claudette's continuous prayers and was still quietly working on the hopes and dreams of so many around them:

Spencer Hillman's curiosity about Danielle Morrison was piqued. She had done plenty of research on him. Now it was his turn to try his hand at finding out what the pretty lawyer was hiding...

Jason was behind bars and Candy's heart was broken, but she was a mother to more than one. She still prayed for love and goodness for her children, especially her daughters Katie and Brooke. Katie seemed to repel men and Brooke only seemed to attract trouble. Could they both be lured into true love, love that was based on a mutual love for God? Candy had already made significant mistakes, errors that she would never want her daughters to relive...

Martin O'Malley was as down to earth as they come, but the new guy in town was finally out from under his brother's thumb, out into social situations that studies on the saints had never prepared him for....

Then there was the argument over mercy. Was Austin O'Malley redeemable? This was the constant question Trish mulled over...

We are a curious lot. The time and worry we spend on ourselves, our family, our friends, these are all minimal compared to the tender care that God has had for us each, each day. Can we face the hard truth? Truth does hurt, but too often it's the exact answer we're looking for.

ABOUT THE AUTHOR

Marilyn Gregoire has been working on this project since 2007. ***The Sisters in Silence Collection*** is near and dear to her heart, but she's not done yet! Two trilogies, six books, are accomplished, but three more books are planned for the ***To Forgive is Divine Series***, then the collection will be complete, the saga will be finished.

Are you wondering about the outcome to storylines of characters on the prior page? So is Marilyn! She started writing back when she was learning to spell and found the wonder and awe of chapter books.

Now reading takes a back seat to writing since there are so many exciting possibilities when you are telling the story. Plus it expands your vocabulary!

To anyone who is interested in preserving their memoires or family history stories, Marilyn will be happy to share information on self-publishing. In this digital world, the prospect of 'vanity presses' have lost the stigma they once held. Self-publishing has its rightful place in today's world.

Marilyn and her husband, Jon, have adult children who have their own children. Both Jon and Marilyn find grandparenthood so much more fun! They live in rural Thompson, ND, and have downsized to a smaller garden. Both are looking forward to someday retiring. But until then, a full time job shares reality with this time-intensive hobby called writing. It's a matter of writing 'during lunches, at night and on the weekends.' Really, whenever an opportunity presents itself.

With all that in mind, be sure to thank Jon Gregoire for his patience if you see him!

www.ingramcontent.com/pod-product-compliance
Lightning Source LLC
Chambersburg PA
CBHW051517260626
47170CB00003B/661